ALSO BY MAGGIE MCPHEE

Autumn In The Desert Series

Death In Autumn, prequel novella

Renaissance, Book 1

Second Chances, Book 2

At Last, Book 4

NEVER TOO LATE

AUTUMN IN THE DESERT, BOOK 3

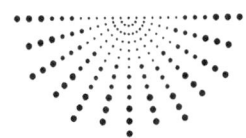

MAGGIE MCPHEE

This story is a work of fiction. Names, characters, places and incidents either are the product of the author's imagination or are used fictitiously, and any resemblance to any person or place is entirely coincidental.

Cover by: Zoran Petrovic, Fiverr.com name, visual arts

Map of Palm Lakes by: Maria Gandolfo, Fiverr.com name, Renflowergrapx

Copyright © 2017 Maggie & Nigel Percy

ISBN: 978-1-946014-18-4 (Ebook version)

ISBN: 978-1-946014-21-4 (Paperback version)

Sixth Sense Books

150 Buck Run E

Dahlonega, GA 30533

Email address: authormaggiemcphee@gmail.com

In memory of my parents,
with thanks for the lessons and inspirations

CONTENTS

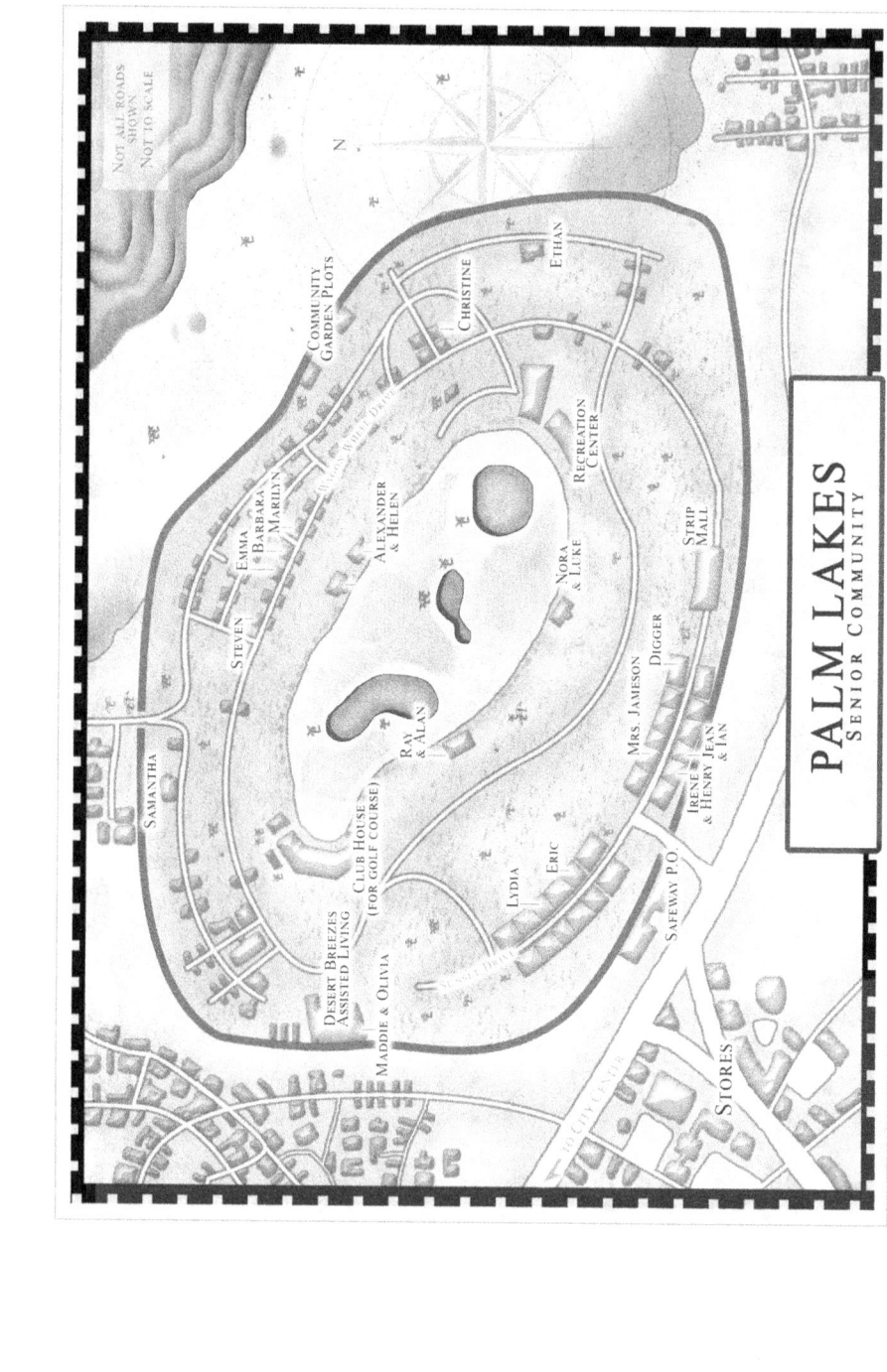

PALM LAKES
SENIOR COMMUNITY

NOT ALL ROADS
SHOWN
NOT TO SCALE

N

COMMUNITY
GARDEN PLOTS

CHRISTINE

ETHAN

EMMA
BARBARA
MARILYN

STEVEN

ALEXANDER
& HELEN

RECREATION
CENTER

NORA
& LUKE

STRIP
MALL

SAMANTHA

MRS. JAMESON

DIGGER

RAY
& ALAN

IRENE
& HENRY JEAN
& IAN

DESERT BREEZES
ASSISTED LIVING

CLUB HOUSE
(FOR GOLF COURSE)

ERIC

LYDIA

MADDIE & OLIVIA

SAFEWAY P.O.

STORES

CHARACTERS

Residents Of Palm Lakes
Maddie O'Neill
Samantha Taylor, the O'Neills' daughter, and her husband Arthur
Alexander & Helen Stirling
Mary Beth Costello, an illegal resident of Palm Lakes
Ethan Westerfield, widower and volunteer with The Helpers
Barbara Blackstone and her husband Ben and their dog, Jack
Eric Johnson, member of The Posse
Lydia Stern, divorcee
Bernie, a neighbor who is a widower
Christine & Jerome Sommers
Ray & Alan, a gay couple, and Ray's granddaughter Becky

Wagon Wheel Drive residents (single family homes)
Barbara and Ben Blackstone, & their dog Jack
Emma Lightman

Sunset Drive residents (condos)
Lydia Stern
Eric (Red) Johnson

Mrs. Catherine Jameson
Irene & Henry Dubois
Digger Jones
Jean & Ian Clarke

Living along the golf course
Alexander & Helen Stirling
Nora & Luke Fontaine
Ray & Alan

Living at Desert Breezes Assisted Living
Olivia Deschamps
Maddie O'Neill

Nonresidents
Julio, landscaping contractor
Jack Temple, landscaper

ACKNOWLEDGMENTS

Once again I must thank my husband Nigel for being my alpha reader and editing and proofreading my manuscript. His suggestions helped me to tell a better story, and having another pair of eyes on it averted many mistakes.

I wish to thank my mother-in-law Winnie for her constant support in my writing efforts. There's nothing more motivating to an author that having someone keep asking when the next book is coming out. Per her suggestion, I've added more of the 'naughty bits' to this installment of *Autumn In The Desert*.

A heartfelt thanks to Elizabeth, a wizard with scissors, for sharing my work with her other clients. Finding an audience is always one of the bigger challenges an author faces, and word of mouth is the best type of referral.

To members of my reader group who volunteered to be advance readers, and who left reviews for me on Amazon, thank you very much for helping get the word out about my writing.

I am grateful to readers who have written to say that it's refreshing to read a book set in a retirement community, where most of the characters are of their generation. The theme of my *Autumn In The Desert* series is that life isn't over when you retire; you can make a new beginning any day by making new choices. Seniors face more challenges than adults of other ages. Yet I have found my autumn years to be filled with the greatest adventures and fulfillment of my life. I believe it is never too late to find happiness, and I hope my stories encourage others to pursue their dreams.

TUESDAY, MARCH 19, 1996

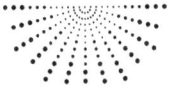

Eric, 2:30am

a t the first sight of blood, Eric felt a powerful, unseen force begin to suck him into the past. *Not again.* Cold sweat bloomed on his skin despite the warmth of the night. He clenched the steering wheel and stared fixedly ahead at the darkened parking lot to avoid seeing the tiny, nearly black rivulet inch along the back of his hand, but in spite of his efforts, he was transported back to the murder scene, where his neighbor Tanya was bleeding out.

Her life's blood pooled around her in an expanding scarlet lake on the white kitchen tiles, the coppery smell assailing his nostrils. Her red silk bathrobe was gruesomely two-toned and soaking wet. The panic in her blue eyes waned as her life poured out onto the floor. He applied pressure to the vicious knife wound on her throat, but he only succeeded in soaking his hands with warm, sticky blood. Her gagging mocked his powerlessness. So much blood...his heart pounded in response to the carnage, but also with the knowledge that he was about to be stabbed in the back by the man who had done this.

Then suddenly, he was back in present time. He let out the breath he'd been holding and raggedly sucked in air. It was over. For now. He took several more deep breaths, willing his heart to calm and prying his hands off the steering wheel one finger at a time, as if they belonged to someone else. He turned his hands this way and that, almost surprised that they weren't drenched in blood.

He reached into his pocket and pulled out a handkerchief, blotting the trickle of blood that had triggered the flashback. Then he examined the hand for the source of the blood. A minuscule crack had opened at the cuticle end of the nail of his index finger. It was so damn dry in the desert, he often developed these insidious cracks in his skin. They were tiny, but they hurt, and when they opened, they bled, which was not good for him right now. That was an understatement. Lydia was always going on about moisturizing. If only the solution were that simple.

His water bottle and the Tupperware container with homemade cookies sat untouched on the passenger seat. He'd pulled into the parking lot at Desert Breezes, the assisted living place in Palm Lakes Senior Community, and parked under a street light so he could have a snack halfway through his night shift with the Posse, the community's security force. He sucked another deep breath in, then let it out gustily. He was still shaking and felt a little weak. Not to mention foolish.

He hadn't told Lydia that the sight of blood made him return to the time of the murder, when he was stabbed by Owen Schmidt, Palm Lakes' own serial killer. With her help, he'd gotten to the point where he rarely had nightmares about the incident anymore, so she thought he was improving. But he hadn't told her about the flashbacks. He couldn't understand why he'd developed this pattern of freaking out when he saw blood. Prior to retiring, he'd seen plenty of blood as a homicide detective, and he'd never had an adverse reaction. Hell, his nickname 'Red' referred to a bloody incident with a perp. If he didn't overcome this problem...it didn't bear thinking about.

Leaving the cookies untouched, he guzzled the water, then, feeling better, he piloted his Posse cruiser through the deserted streets of Palm Lakes, windows down, letting the mild breeze flow over him, no music on to cover the night sounds, not that he expected much in the way of noise. Bedtime came early for most residents.

The new moon guaranteed a spectacular showing of stars in the cloudless sky. He paused when he reached the next stop sign, marveling at how many stars he could see and how bright they were. Anything to distract himself from what had just happened.

He'd been patrolling for hours, and the only vehicle he'd seen was the other Posse car when he'd met his partner to choose which portions to cruise at the beginning of the shift. But there was plenty of nonhuman nightlife, thanks to the undeveloped desert that bordered Palm Lakes on the east and north. Disturbingly large bats danced around street lights, no doubt feeding on the insects attracted there. A coyote had slunk across the road as he passed the golf course, and the occasional cottontail sprinted across the lane in front of him, testing his alertness.

It was easy to get lost in the winding streets of Palm Lakes if you weren't familiar with them, but after serving with the Posse for nearly two years, Eric could navigate them in his sleep. He was patrolling the half of Palm Lakes to the south and west of the central golf course, while his partner cruised the other half. This route would take him by his own condo several times, where Lydia slept, awaiting his return when the shift ended at 7am. The graveyard shift was a boring, routine task, but for now, it suited him to be up while everyone else slept. Sleep had become problematic after what had happened eight weeks ago.

He turned onto Sunset Drive, the road he lived on which ran parallel to the 6-ft block wall that formed the boundary of Palm Lakes. It was these homes with the outside world on the other side of the wall that had the highest level of property crimes. He crawled down the street, nodding his head as if to greet Lydia as he passed by his condo, looking into the back yards across the street which had the boundary wall. Recently, there had been some thefts from garages where homeowners had forgotten to put the garage door down, a frighteningly common occurrence in this community of seniors. He hadn't found any doors up so far tonight, so maybe it would stay quiet.

As he cruised down the road enjoying the silence, he mulled over his present situation. Lydia had expressed a hope that he'd get off night shift. It made sense, because their schedules currently had little overlap, but she hadn't pushed him. She knew he was struggling to get back to how things were before January 27th. She saw so much, and she didn't agree with his choices, but she didn't complain. He'd never had a relationship where he was given so much support, and it pained him to keep things from her, but she didn't need to know how much trouble he was still experiencing. He had to sort it out before he'd know if they had a future, and he wanted one. The problem was, he had no idea how to resolve the issue himself, but telling her about it didn't seem the way to go. He was already leaning on her far too much.

He crossed the main road that exited the gated community south of the intersection. On this side of the four-way stop were a strip mall and some other businesses, then it graded back into single family homes. He'd just gotten back into residential when he thought he spotted movement near a house up ahead on the right. The shadows were too tall to be coyotes, and it was unlikely a homeowner was creeping around at nearly 3am. He killed his lights and eased the car over to the curb at the house next door and peered into the darkness. Sure enough, the garage door was up. Maybe he should radio his partner for help. By the time he got here, though, it would all be over. Mostly, it was kids doing this kind of shit; nothing to be afraid of. In spite of that, he felt tension pluck his nerves and anxiety fog his mind like poison gas. Unsure whether he was overcompensating or merely being reasonable, he decided to handle it alone. He grabbed the flashlight that lay on the passenger seat, slipped out of the car as quietly as possible, clicked the door shut and put the flashlight in the loop of his belt. When they heard him, they would probably run off. Unless it was some drug-crazed loony. He paused and reconsidered calling for backup, then dismissed it.

This was an older section of town, and a mature olive tree dominated the front yard of the home, blocking his view of the garage next door. He ducked around the tree, crunching on the gravel as little as possible-- almost all of the homes in Palm Lakes had gravel instead of grass--and slipped closer to the open garage, which was on this end of the neighboring house. He hadn't seen anyone since the earlier shadows and wondered if they were gone. He hoped so. His heart was hammering in his ears, and his hands were sweaty. He'd been in much worse situations and kept his cool, but that was before January 27th. He pressed on anyway.

Just as he arrived at the corner of the house, two people raced out of the garage, nearly running into him. He grabbed the smaller one--it was only a kid. "Posse! Stop right there and put your hands up."

Neither one obeyed him, and he wondered if they understood English, as even in the dark he could see they were Hispanic. He had a grip on the younger one's shirt, and the boy wasn't struggling much. It was obvious he was in shock. The older one--he might have been late teens--pulled a knife and menaced Eric. "Let him go now or I'll cut you, viejo," he said with bravado. *Well, at least one of them speaks English.*

The drumbeat of Eric's heart turned into a roar as he looked at the knife. It was a wicked-looking military blade, and the kid held it like he knew how to use it. Eric put his hand on the butt of his gun, wondering if he could make himself shoot a boy, as darkness began to fill his peripheral vision, shrinking his field of view to only the knife and the hand wielding it. He felt faint. Glad he had the kid to lean on. He didn't have the strength to draw his gun, even if he could commit to shooting it.

The knife-wielder was a good ten feet away from him, backing up as if he intended to run into the back yard and jump the wall to get out of Palm Lakes. Not wanting to be abandoned with the lawman, his younger companion struggled to free himself from Eric's grip, but Eric tightened up, taking a handful of shoulder so the kid couldn't rip out of the shirt and escape.

Keeping his eyes on the older one and his hand on his holstered gun, Eric stood silently but shakily and let the other kid run away. Still leaning partially on the boy, he bent over to catch his breath, glad that his normal vision was slowly returning. The boy had stopped squirming and stood like a rock, probably terrified of what was going to happen next.

Eric dragged the boy to the front door of the house and rang the bell. After a few minutes, the door opened. A groggy elderly man with thinning white hair squinted at Eric. "What's wrong, Officer?"

"Sir, your garage is open, and I found some kids in it. I don't know if anything is missing, but we'll need you to check it out first thing tomorrow and file a report if you believe anything was stolen."

The old geezer stared at the boy next to Eric. "Is that pipsqueak a thief?" he asked incredulously.

"He was with an older kid, maybe 18 or so. I didn't see them take anything, but both were in the garage. Will you let us know first thing tomorrow?"

"Sure thing, Officer. Thanks for the help."

"And sir? Please put your garage door down before you go back to bed."

"Oh, right." The old man shut the door, and Eric waited for the garage door to go down before heading back to his car, young would-be thief in tow.

When they got to the vehicle, Eric stopped and looked hard at the kid for the first time. He didn't look very old. Dark hair hanging into his equally dark eyes, gangly body, a face that radiated innocence. "So, kid, what am I going to do with you? Last thing I need is a lot of paperwork in the middle of the night. But your friend was pretty scary, pulling a knife on a police officer."

The boy drew himself up to his full height. "He wasn't scared of you, and I ain't, either."

"Well, you ought to be. How old are you, anyway?"

The kid looked like he was unsure whether telling the truth was a good idea. "I'm almost 12."

"What would your parents think about you being out at night stealing?"

"I didn't steal nothing. I just came along for the fun. I never did this before." He looked down at his feet and shuffled them. "I don't think I'll ever do it again."

"That's the smartest thing you've said so far. I'm going to take you home. Where do you live?"

The kid's dark eyes filled with fear. "I can walk."

"Sure you can, but I want to talk to your folks."

"I don't have any folks. I have foster parents."

Eric felt bad for the boy, but it didn't change the plan. "I still have to take you home, talk to them and verify your name and age in case this man lodges a complaint. You better hope he doesn't." Eric opened the rear passenger door. "Get in nicely and I won't cuff you." As if his cuffs would be any restraint for such small wrists.

The boy looked at him as if gauging whether he meant it, then scrambled into the back seat. Eric shut the door, went round to the driver's side, got in and pushed the button to lock the back doors so the kid couldn't escape. Last thing he needed was the boy falling out and hurting himself.

Ten minutes later, following the child's halting directions, he pulled up in front of the boy's home in a modest, well-kept neighborhood not far from Palm Lakes. By now, the kid was deflated and scared, but he didn't attempt to run away. He got out and went with Eric to the door and waited stiffly after Eric rang the doorbell, as if in anticipation of trouble to come. The door opened on a sleepy-eyed woman of about 40. Her dark hair was in a single braid, and like the boy, she was Hispanic. "What?" she said when she saw the boy. "Miguel, what is this?" Eric could feel the boy shrinking, but the child remained silent.

"Ma'am, I found him in Palm Lakes with an older boy in the garage of a resident. I'm not sure what he was doing, but it wasn't good. At the very least, it's trespassing. Are you his mother?"

She shook her head as if still trying to process the information. "Foster mother. We have several children we foster, and Miguel is the oldest. He isn't supposed to be out at night. I thought he was in bed."

"If it turns out anything is missing, the homeowner will be filing a complaint tomorrow. I will be back tomorrow afternoon and let you know either way. Will you be home after lunch?"

"Yes, I can be here all afternoon."

"I'll see you then and let you know what is going to happen. Keep him inside at night from now on." Eric turned and walked to his car without looking back. He made a decision and reached for his radio. "Nick, you there?"

A burst of static preceded the answer. "Sure, Red. Whatcha need?"

"I had a little tussle on Sunset drive with two hoods in someone's open garage. One got away, and I just took the other one home. Do you think you can take the shift for the rest of the night? I'm feeling like I need to go home." He didn't have to say why. It was common knowledge what had happened on January 27th.

"Sure, Red. You go on home. Nothing else gonna happen tonight. I've got it."

"Thanks. Johnson out." He drove the two miles back home, reaching for the garage door opener as he turned into the driveway. Lydia would probably hear the garage door and wonder why he was home early. Not much chance of slipping in unnoticed. He sighed, resigning himself to having to explain to her.

As the garage door closed behind him, he breathed deeply a few times and let the tension slip away as much as he could. He shook himself, then got out of the car, taking his water bottle, the uneaten cookies and his flashlight with him. He got all the way into the kitchen before Lydia caught him.

"What's wrong? Or did you just stop to refill your water bottle?" She yawned and stretched as she stood in the doorway, her thick, curly hair a dark curtain around her face. She had on a thin cotton nightgown that wasn't meant to be sexy, but the way her curves filled it out, it was. He felt a stirring of arousal and was pleased. At least something was returning to normal.

He smiled at her, knowing that she was reading him and there was no point lying. Not that lying was his style; well at least, not outright lying. He just wasn't telling her everything.

"I had to deal with an incident--nothing terrible--and I asked Nick to take the rest of the shift on his own. I caught some kids messing in a guy's garage. He'd forgotten to put the door down. I only managed to hold on to the small one. Damn, but they start young these days. He wasn't even 12. But I don't think they stole anything. The man will let us know tomorrow morning...this morning."

She stared at him, and he knew what she was going to say. "What else happened?"

"The bigger kid pulled a knife on me, one of those fancy military ones, probably a KA-BAR." He drew in a deep breath, then sighed heavily. "I had a flashback. I didn't black out, but if the kid had wanted to take me, he could have. I didn't have the strength to pull my gun; I could barely stand. I'm lucky he ran." He shook his head and dropped into the chair by the kitchen table, setting his burdens down on the table as he did.

Lydia said nothing, but walked over to him and put her hands on his shoulders. She was good that way, no, great that way. She always seemed to know what to do or say. "I'm so grateful you're OK." She began to massage his shoulders, and it felt heavenly. "How about a hit of herbal remedy?"

"Yeah, I could use that for sure."

She stopped what she was doing and went to the cupboard and pulled out a quart-sized brown glass bottle. She squirted a couple droppersful of liquid into a drinking glass, then added some water and handed it to him. "Bottoms up!"

He smiled weakly. "Thanks." He drained the glass in one big swallow, then sputtered a little. "It would be nice if it tasted better."

She grinned at him. "Quit your bitchin'. It isn't even technically legal, but it works."

"Damn right it works. My woman is a genius with weed." He regarded the empty glass with distaste. "No one would suspect this is marijuana."

"Has it really been helping with the nightmares?"

It was hard to take her scrutiny. "Yes, I rarely have nightmares anymore, but apparently, when put in the position of being threatened with a knife, I get incapacitated." He looked down at the empty glass. "I was hoping it was getting better." He wasn't about to tell her about the flashbacks when he saw blood. This was bad enough.

She looked at him quizzically. "Of course, it's better. It just isn't cured. It takes time. Why are you so pessimistic?" She studied him with dark brown eyes as she stroked his shoulder.

"I know you're reading me."

She nodded. "And I know you're keeping something from me. It would be nice if you trusted me enough to tell me."

"It isn't a matter of trust." He frowned, because he hated her thinking that. "I'm frustrated at my lack of progress. Grateful for all you've done for me, because I know without all you've done, I would be far worse off. Thanks to you, I was able to get back on patrol. But after tonight, I have to admit I'm a liability to the Posse. Me, a guy who worked homicide in St. Paul for years can't handle a teenager trying to fake me out with a knife." He wasn't sure what he was going to do with his life now. And unless he recovered completely, he couldn't ask Lydia to marry him. He couldn't saddle her with a psych case. He knew she could tell he was holding out on her, and he hoped she didn't think it was anything to do with her. He balled his hands in frustration.

"At least until you feel you're back to normal, it might be a wise decision. But don't regard it as permanent. You've made more progress than you seem to realize. Why not take a leave of absence and focus on allowing yourself to heal?"

It made good sense, yet seemed a bleak future. "You're right."

She started kneading his shoulder muscles again. "Would you like a scotch before you go to bed?"

"You read my mind."

She kept massaging him for a couple minutes, then fetched him a double. "You had a rough night. But, it was just an opportunity to see where you are in your healing process. You aren't up to facing an armed subject yet. And if I were given a vote, you would never face one again, but I do believe that with time, you will get your old confidence back. Just be kind to yourself."

He gulped down the scotch instead of sipping it like he usually did. "You're right again. I'm lucky to have you be the voice of reason for me. I can't stand feeling broken."

"Don't talk like that. You aren't broken. Being stabbed is traumatic. Anyone would be affected. Most would still be trying to heal physically. Speaking of which, do you have any pain?"

"Occasionally, but not bad."

She sat down in the adjacent chair and reached over to stroke his cheek. "I'm grateful to have you home at a time when we can sleep together."

A spike of fear flashed through him. He wasn't up for sex, in spite of noticing how delectable she looked. He tried to hide his fear, but she'd seen it. "I can't hide anything from your X-ray vision."

She smirked at him. "Then don't try. I'm not trying to seduce you. I know you've had a shock and sex is the last thing on your mind. Come to bed and get some sleep. I meant it would be nice to wake up next to you in the morning."

He gave her a sheepish grin. "That sounds good."

2

WEDNESDAY, MARCH 20, 1996

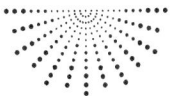

Mary Beth, 6:15am

*M*ary Beth pulled the brush through her thick, curly dark hair, tugging at the snarls while assessing herself in the bathroom mirror. She was looking better than when she'd first arrived here last year after a devastating divorce, but maybe it was all relative. At 45, she had to be one of the youngest people living in Palm Lakes. Not that she was legal. That's why she was being tossed around town like a ping pong ball; she wasn't supposed to be living here full time and had to move whenever she was reported to the Homeowners' Association.

Slipping a scrunchy around the mass of hair, she opened the bedroom door and headed for the kitchen. She didn't like breakfast, but if she skipped it, she found it hard to concentrate at work. At least she no longer constantly craved a cigarette.

Her elderly landlady Maddie was seated at the dining room table, her head bent over a jewelry project spotlit by a study lamp in the contrasting darkness of the living-dining area. Maddie kept the heavy curtain for the sliding glass door closed all the time, and the windows on the opposite side of the living and dining area had special screens that cut down on the light even when the drapes were open. Maddie said it was supposed to save on the electric bill during warm weather, but to Mary Beth, the constant darkness was oppressive. Not that she was going to complain. She felt lucky to have a place to live.

Maddie didn't even look up as Mary Beth stood beside her, examining progress on the necklace, which was made of leopardskin jasper and freshwater pearls. Mary Beth was proud that after working so often with Maddie, she now recognized most of the semi-precious stones used in jewelry. "That's a beautiful design! I hope you'll show me how you managed to alternate the single strand of jasper with double strands of pearls. It adds nice contrast."

Maddie paused and looked at her through her special magnifying glasses, pale blue eyes shining at the praise. "I think it turned out well. I'll be glad to show you anytime."

Mary Beth gently patted Maddie's shoulder, cautious of the pain her osteoporosis caused. "Thanks, that would be great. I'm grabbing some toast and coffee before I head to work. Would you like anything?"

Maddie was already back to threading beads. "No, I had coffee a while ago. I've been up since four. I'm not hungry yet."

Mary Beth went to the coffee pot and poured herself a cup. "How about I make spaghetti tonight?"

"I'd love that, thank you."

Mary Beth couldn't help laughing. "You'd eat spaghetti every day, wouldn't you?"

"Just about. I think I'm compensating for having to eat like Stanley most of my life. He wouldn't eat spaghetti, and I hate cooking two meals. I'm making up for lost time."

"Make two meals? Hell, I like to cook, but I won't make two meals." She shook her head sympathetically. "You must have some Italian in you to like the food so much." She rummaged in the refrigerator to find the bread and put two slices in the toaster oven.

"Not that I know of. But I could eat Italian food every day of the week." Maddie paused and regarded Mary Beth seriously. "What are you going to do when I move?"

Mary Beth shrugged. "I'm not sure. I'm getting used to feeling like a ping pong ball, I've lived so many places in the last year. Catherine offered me her couch--again--but her place is too small. I'm grateful for the offer, but I don't think it would work. Helen offered me her casita. She feels it's been long enough since I was thrown out of her old condo, and she and Alexander want me to housesit for them when they go to France this summer. That would even be legal."

Maddie frowned, the tip of her tongue captured by her teeth as she concentrated on her project. Mary Beth wondered if she knew she did that a lot. "You'll probably like that a lot better than being here," Maddie mumbled grumpily as she continued threading beads.

"I'm sorry you're giving up your house, Maddie, but in the long run, it's safer and will be less expensive to live at Desert Breezes, and Samantha tells me it's pretty nice. I promise to come visit. We're still going to do jewelry, right? I have a lot I need to learn from you. I want to get good enough to make a living selling my pieces."

Maddie harrumphed. "You're already good enough to do that."

Mary Beth glowed. "Thanks, Maddie. That means a lot, coming from you. I don't think I'll ever be as good as you are. I'm lucky you aren't competing with me."

"Nah, I don't want to sell stuff. It's too much like hard work."

"You got that right. But if I'm lucky, maybe, just maybe, I can substitute it for working at Palo Verde Landscaping."

"Those guys don't pay you enough. They're prejudiced against women."

Mary Beth had strayed into a mine field. Maddie was highly opinionated on some topics. "They have their reasons. I don't think they mean anything bad. But you're right that it isn't enough for me to live on. They pay the guys on the installation crews more than me. They said they're supporting families and need it more." Mary Beth stood at the counter buttering her toast.

Maddie huffed. "Who's going to support you if you can't? Speaking of which, when are you going to tell me what you and Ethan are up to?"

Mary Beth felt herself blush. She munched a piece of toast to buy some time. When she swallowed, Maddie was still staring pointedly at her, the magnifying glasses giving her a mad scientist vibe. "Well..." She wasn't sure what to say. It was her private life, but Maddie had provided a roof over her head when she needed it, so she hated to lie or be rude.

Maddie continued to stare. "I don't want all the details. I'm not interested in that sex stuff. But you didn't come home the other night, and since you went to dinner with him, I assume you were with him all night."

Suddenly, Mary Beth felt like she was 17 and on the carpet in front of her dear departed Mom, having to explain why she'd broken curfew. "We had a lot to discuss about where this relationship is going. I'm still not totally certain, so I can't tell you much. Ethan's concerned about the age difference."

Maddie grunted. "He ought to be. He has no business chasing a young girl like you."

Mary Beth almost choked on her toast. "I'm 45, Maddie. I'm divorced. I'm not young. Just younger than he is."

"That's what I meant. He should go after someone his own age. There are plenty in this town."

Mary Beth didn't know how to respond. She finished her last bite of toast, wondering how much to say. She'd learned that some topics were impossible to discuss with Maddie. Anything she could say would be like pouring gasoline on a flame. She rinsed her dishes and put them in the dishwasher. "Do you want me to run the dishwasher?"

"Quit changing the subject. What's up with you two?"

"I could tell you to mind your own business, but I know it won't do any good."

Maddie cackled, and Mary Beth felt herself relax. "I think I love him, but beyond that, I'm not sure. I haven't been divorced that long. Then there's the age difference. I'm still trying to figure out how to find a place to live and work. Losing my Mom really threw me." She hated to admit that was true. Her Mom had died three months ago, but the pain was still fresh.

"I feel for how you've been tossed from one place to another, and I'm getting ready to do it to you again on April 1st. But the time came for me to move on, even though I don't want to. I worry about you. What are you going to do? You can stay for a while at Helen's, but what next?"

Exactly. What next? Mary Beth had no idea. "I wish I knew. I'm going to have to take this one step at a time. Ethan seems to be serious--not that he's talked about marriage--but he doesn't want me living in his house for fear of what the neighbors or his kids will think, mostly about me. He's old-fashioned."

"At least he has *some* sense."

Mary Beth smiled. "Yes. He does. He also has a large extended family and kids who revere the memory of his late wife, and he probably doesn't want to get in their face about replacing her."

"Sounds like he may not be sure what he wants to do. Maybe he isn't ready to move on."

"The thought had occurred to me, but if that's so, it's subconscious. He's a stickler for doing things the right way, or what he sees as the right way. He's a good man."

"Yes, he is."

Mary Beth did a double take at the rare compliment. Maddie wasn't inclined to speak well of Ethan. As a volunteer with The Helpers, he spent time each Saturday doing things for her like taking out trash and walking Beau, and her resistance to accepting help made her stingy with praise or thanks for his efforts. "I better be going. They like me to get there no later than seven."

"Go on, then. Don't be late for work. And don't forget spaghetti tonight. Do we have all the ingredients?"

"Yes, we do. Do you want me to pick up a bottle of wine?"

"Does the Pope wear a funny hat?"

Mary Beth laughed obligingly at the worn Catholic humor. "I'll get some on my way home. I'm going to simmer the sauce for a couple hours, so it will be just the way you like it. In fact, maybe I'll make up a big batch and freeze portions. You have a kitchen in the new place, don't you?"

"Yes, it's tiny, but I can either eat at their dining room or cook. It would be nice to be able to thaw out some good spaghetti sauce." That was as close to a thank you as Maddie usually got.

"Should I start the dishwasher?"

"Yeah, go ahead."

Mary Beth started the dishwasher, got her bag from her room and came back through the dining room to say goodbye to Maddie. "I'll be back for lunch today. Usual time."

"See you then."

Mary Beth found herself feeling she should at least hug Maddie, so she did. A rare smile bloomed on Maddie's wrinkled face. "Go on, now. Don't be late." Mary Beth smiled back at her and headed for the front door, patting the big golden lab who was lounging on the tile of the entryway as she strolled out.

* * *

Lydia, 9:00am

LYDIA PARKED in front of the Sixth Sense Consulting office at the strip mall just down the road from her condo. As she got out of the car, she admired the sandwich board at the roadside that advertised Reiki and Tarot card readings. Then she shook her head, wondering if Palm Lakes was ready for such things.

She entered the office, smiling at how professional it looked with its Southwestern decor and comfortable seating in the reception area. Jean sat at the reception desk, poring over something. "Lyd! Good morning." Then her smile morphed into a frown. "What's up?" Her best friend might not have special vision like she did, but she sure could read Lydia.

"Eric had a bad night, and I wish I could help him more. Here we are trying to sell energy healing services, and my man is struggling with post traumatic stress. Makes me feel like a charlatan." She sank into the chair nearest the desk, suddenly too tired to move.

Jean stood up, brushing her short blonde hair back from her face, suddenly in take-charge mode. "What you need is a cup of coffee." She marched down the hallway where the coffee maker sat on a narrow table and came back a few minutes later with a mug. "Here, drink this."

Lydia sighed. "Thanks. I didn't realize how much it takes out of me, not being able to fix things for Eric."

Compassion poured from Jean's blue eyes. "It's hard when someone you love is hurting. But you've done so much for him. I'm sure he'd be worse off if he didn't have you."

Shrugging her shoulders, Lydia sipped the hot coffee, wishing she could tell Jean everything, but she'd promised Eric she wouldn't tell anyone she was giving him a herbal extract of marijuana. She'd been lucky he was willing to try it, and she couldn't afford to go against his wishes, even though Jean was her best friend. "He's doing better. Even he admits that. But last night was bad. He had to deal with a knife-wielding vandal, and he had a relapse. Plus, he's holding out on me. And the distance between us...it isn't changing. I'm beginning to worry if he's going to pull back permanently..." Lydia abruptly clamped her mouth shut, annoyed at herself for whining. Complaining wouldn't solve anything. "Where's Ian?"

Jean raised her eyebrows at the change of subject. "He's in the back office, working on our website." Then she pursed her lips, and Lydia could tell she was going into counseling mode. With that shift in focus, the multi-colored energy field that surrounded Jean suddenly became dominated by blue and silver.

No matter how hard she tried not to, Lydia saw colors around people that revealed all sorts of information she didn't really want to know, yet she'd committed to using this ability professionally in their new business. The way she was feeling now, she wondered if she'd made a mistake coming out about her so-called 'psychic' talent.

Jean put her hands on her hips. "I know you're reading me, but I'm going to say it anyway. You're not giving yourself enough credit, and maybe you aren't trusting this relationship enough. It takes time to heal the kind of trauma Eric has been through. Your ability to see his aura may give you a false sense of responsibility for his condition. It's the down side of a psychic ability, to know more than anyone else. But you still can't know everything, and it's up to him to heal. You know that."

Lydia couldn't argue. "You're right. I do feel I should be able to fix him, and it frustrates me that it's taking so long." Then grumpiness asserted itself. "I do wish you wouldn't call what I do a psychic ability. I just see things other people don't see." Lydia rebelled at being singled out as a freak, in spite of knowing Jean didn't intend that.

Jean put her hand lightly on Lydia's shoulder. "I'm sorry. I don't know what else to call what you do. You have to admit it's a rare talent, and how are we going to advertise it if we don't use the term 'psychic'? That's what everyone expects us to call it, even if you dislike the term."

Lydia felt chastised. "You're right again. I'm probably too sensitive about people's perception of me. I've spent my life hiding what I can do, because people make fun or accuse me of lying or call me a freak. Coming out of the closet is a big step for me. I wish things were more settled between me and Eric. Like I said, I can see he's holding out on me, and maybe that's making me fearful about our future together. What's worse is that somehow he's able to block me. I've never had anyone block me before. It's piling stress on top of the nervousness about letting the public know what I can do."

"The timing really does stink. I'm so sorry for you. If there's anything I can do to help, let me know. That reminds me. Ian wants to tell you about a technique he heard about. It might be useful for Eric."

Lydia perked up. "Really? That would be so wonderful! I appreciate you doing Reiki on him, and he loves the crystal healing I do, but to me, progress seems slow. The residue of trauma made him flashback so bad last night he's going to take a leave of absence from the Posse, and he's really depressed about it."

Jean frowned and motioned for Lydia to follow her as she headed down the short hallway flanked by two rooms on each side. They had tentatively reserved the largest of the four rooms (it was only marginally bigger) for events, one for Lydia's treatment room, one as a treatment room for Jean and Ian, and the third as shared office space that held the company computer and two workstations. "Let's have Ian tell you about this new therapy. He's more familiar with the details than I am."

They trooped into the last room on the right, which was less sumptuously furnished than the reception area, but still inviting and professional-looking. Ian pushed back from the desk on his side of the two-person workstation when they entered the office. "Ladies. Come into my sanctuary." He pointed to the two other chairs.

"Lydia wants to hear about this technique you think might be useful for Eric. He had a bad experience last night."

Ian scrunched his shaggy gray eyebrows together in sympathy. "I'm so sorry, Lydia. What happened?"

She paused briefly, still taken aback by his beautiful British accent. "He confronted a couple kids who were in someone's garage, and one pulled a knife on him. He had a meltdown, and now he's considering leaving the Posse." She heaved a sigh. "I wish I could do more for him."

Ian nodded in sympathy, hazel eyes solemn. "Well, I'm not sure, but there may be a way."

"I'll try anything. He doesn't want to be on psych meds. He's had friends on them, and they became zombies. But he needs to do something to deal with this. He also won't consider going to a shrink."

Jean leaned towards Ian, urging him to go on. He shrugged his shoulders. "I don't want to give you false hope. You know as well as I do that any method works, but no method works for everyone or on everything. But what I've found out about this technique is promising, because they claim it treats post traumatic stress and phobias almost magically. Of course, it isn't accepted by conventional types, but I was watching a video of a session. You're going to want to see it. It's of a guy who is positively phobic about water and couldn't even get into the shallow end of a swimming pool. By the end of the session, he's in the water, feeling fine, even ducks his head under. I think maybe we should look into it. It works on addictions, pain and myriad other situations."

Hope crept into Lydia's heart. "How does it work?"

"Well, it's pretty simple. You tap on a succession of acupuncture points while saying certain phrases, and it releases the emotions that have you stuck in the unwanted pattern. It helps you let go and move on."

Lydia's jaw dropped. "That's amazing! And it sounds easy to do."

"Oh, it is pretty easy." Ian scratched his jaw thoughtfully as the colors of his aura dimmed. "But it's very expensive to learn."

"That's no problem. I'm happy to pay for us to get trained. This could really help our business. Do you think it's worth investing in?"

Jean looked at Ian, and Lydia could see the colors shifting in their auras. "Come on, guys, don't be prejudiced against letting me spring for training. It's an investment in the business."

Still silent, but radiating resistance, Jean looked to Ian. He appeared to be pulling in on himself. Finally, he spoke. "Lydia, we've already allowed you to put up all the money for renting and furnishing this space. And we aren't making enough to break even. We don't feel right letting you spend more money. Getting certified in this technique would cost thousands of dollars. We don't want you to pay for us. Maybe you could take the training and then teach us?" His cultured voice and beautiful accent were so distracting, she almost couldn't decode his words. She replayed it in her mind until it became clear.

"But I don't want to go alone. Jean and I have always done classes together, and now it should be the three of us. I have more than enough money to do this. Plus, it could help Eric."

She could tell Jean was crumbling; she'd do anything to help Lydia keep Eric. Plus, they always had fun taking courses together. Ian looked at Jean, and Lydia saw wordless communication pass between them, and she knew they were on the verge of agreeing. "I'm even thinking maybe we should include Eric. I know he isn't part of the business, but if he quits the Posse, he'll need something to do, and this would be very empowering for him." She gave Jean and Ian her best smile, hoping they could see how sincere--and desperate--she was.

Ian broke the silence. "If we were to get certified, it seems to me it would make sense not only to offer treatments, but to teach others how to do it themselves. The biggest room here would be fine for holding classes, at least the size we'd be likely to have. I've been thinking we need to offer courses in addition to services. The market for services here is pathetic, but you've told me everyone likes to take courses." His look darkened. "Of course, the cost to become certified in the tapping therapy is very high. I doubt we'd sell enough courses to pay you back. But maybe we can do other courses as well."

Jean brightened up. "What a super idea! It would be great to offer a variety of trainings. Between the three of us, we're pretty much experts in a lot of subjects that people would like to know more about. Crystals. Dowsing. Reiki. And now tapping. Why didn't we think of that before? We love taking courses. Others will, too. There's a pretty good market for that."

Lydia relaxed. She could see they were going to agree. Then Ian's eyes pierced her, and her heightened intuition warned her his mind was set about something.

"Lydia, Jean and I don't want to take advantage of you as an angel investor. It's time we reviewed our progress and decided how long we are going to continue this way, and what we can do to improve the return on your investment." Ian's handsome face hardened with stubbornness. It was clear he wasn't happy letting her pay his way.

She didn't want to argue, but she needed to convince him. "Ian, Jean and I are best friends, and doing business together is like a dream come true. But it takes time to turn a profit. Weeks aren't going to do it. We need to be in it for the long haul." She paused, inspecting the energy that surrounded him. His resistance was diminishing. *Good.* "I promise I won't invest more than I can afford to lose. You're right that we need to evaluate our progress to avoid turning this venture into a black hole for money. What are your ideas?"

Ian's grimace disappeared, the mood shift confirmed by the change of colors surrounding him. "Like I said, offering classes should help our bottom line. We can offer to empower people to help themselves and save money. We might also offer the occasional free presentation to bring in people. Jean tells me the chiropractors around here do that, and it builds their practices. They offer valuable health advice for free and then give people a chance to invest in taking it further." He turned to smile at Jean, and she nodded in confirmation. "We'd need to brainstorm what to offer free and how to follow up. If we can't make this pay, we'll need to let go of this office space, but right now, it's a great opportunity for doing events and courses."

Jean reached over and put her hand on Ian's. "We probably ought to decide what a realistic period of time is for giving this a chance. If we give up this space, we'd have to work out of home, and that would be fine for sessions, but then we'd have to hire a space to do events." She turned her hand palm up and pointed at Lydia. "What do you think?"

Relief flowed through Lydia. "I appreciate you guys and your integrity. Let's hit the event aspect hard. Start with something free and once we get them here, share how we can help them further with services and courses. We just need to figure out what. I know you guys need to be making money to pay your bills. What time frame do you have?"

Jean frowned, and Ian's face went blank. Jean said, "I have some money from the settlement in my divorce, but we don't have much else. It will tide us over for a while, but then, we'd end up falling back on my only credit card. I have good credit, but I hate to accumulate debt."

"You mustn't do that!" said Lydia vehemently. "How long until you get down to about three months' living expenses?"

Jean scrunched up her face, calculating. "Thanks to Helen letting us rent-to-own her mostly furnished condo, and the fact that we aren't big spenders and I have a car that's paid for, we're probably good for a year."

Ian's mouth was tightly shut. You didn't need to be psychic to see the frustration pulsing in him. Lydia decided she needed to defuse things. "Look, you guys do whatever feels best to you, but I think we ought to give this a fair shot. I can go on like this for a year. I think we should give it the full time. If we give up too soon, we'll never forgive ourselves. I know success isn't guaranteed, but this is what we love doing. I am grateful for the chance to work with you two. If this venture fails, it will be as bad for me in some ways as it would be for you. I don't know what I'd do without this project.

"Ian, I know Jean is grateful that you were willing to leave your mother country behind, and all your friends and family, and start fresh here. It will take time to adjust. This is our home, and you need to accept that you gave up a lot to come here, and we want to support you while you get settled in to a very different lifestyle and culture. It's not like you're a kept man." She flashed him a smile, and his hard look melted.

"To be honest, that is what's bothering me. I want to contribute."

Jean looked at him in surprise. "You *are* contributing. Lydia and I know nothing about building websites and the world wide web. Without your suggestion, we'd still be focusing totally on local prospects. Your ideas could make all the difference. You're not giving yourself enough credit!"

Lydia was pleased to see how forceful Jean was. In the past, she'd been so shy and retiring. Ian was so much better for her than Richard had been. "I think we should measure success by how happy we are and how much of a contribution we feel we are making to our clients. I'd appreciate it if we could put the money more into perspective. It's a tool. It's also a way to measure progress. But it isn't our main reason for doing this."

Jean and Ian got quiet, both of them seeming to reflect on what she said. Ian spoke first. "You're right, Lydia. It was my pride talking. But I want you to know that I am committed to making this work, and that if it doesn't appear to be succeeding, I vote for dissolving the business before it costs you too much."

Lydia looked at both of them. "I'm glad we talked about this. We'll revisit it in the future. But what do you say we give the business our best for a year? We'll have weekly meetings and tweak what we do, but if you feel comfortable giving it a year, I know I do."

Jean's shoulders dropped with a sigh. "I'd love to be able to do that. I don't want to have to get a job at McDonald's." She poked Ian's shoulder. "Ian doesn't, either, do you?"

He grinned crookedly, the tension gone. "No, I don't want that. I'd hate that. We need to make this work. I can't imagine myself in commuter traffic, wearing a suit and tie and going to a job I hate. I suppose what makes me nervous is this seems such a gamble. But I'm committed to making it work."

Lydia felt relief wash over her. "Tell me the details for this training you found for us. I'm psyched."

* * *

Emma, 10:00am

EMMA STEPPED from the patio to the graveled yard, urn in hand. It was already warm, unseasonably so. The northern exposure gave her some shade closer to the house, but she could tell it was going to be a hot one. She had grown to love the clarity of sunshine and heat in the desert, so unlike the cloying grayness and moisture of the Pacific Northwest.

As she took measured paces toward the labyrinth, her mind fixed on her mission, a rabbit startled from under a bush and raced across her path, scattering gravel like ricocheting bullets. "Oh my God!" she shrieked, nearly dropping the urn. She paused, heart beating madly, and reflexively looked left and right as if to check if anyone had seen, but the block wall around the yard shielded her from prying eyes.

She drew a ragged breath and continued to approach the labyrinth, its pattern laid out in narrow lawn-edging material, gravel the same color, but a smaller size than that in the rest of the yard. She entered the labyrinth and followed the curving path as it folded back on itself time and again. When she reached the center, time stood still and peace wrapped around her like a warm cloak on a cold day.

23

She looked up to the clear blue sky as a slight breeze caressed her face. "Are you having the last laugh, Leo? You were right. I'm ready to move on now. I thought you'd like the labyrinth. It's the most peaceful place I know, and every time I walk it, I will be with you."

She set the urn down on the gravel, careful to keep it upright, then knelt down beside it. Her shoulder-length black hair swept across her crystal blue eyes, and she pushed it back, looking up again to the sky. "I know you're watching me, Leo. You've always taken such good care of me." She took the lid off the urn, then paused.

"You said at the end that you wanted me to move on, to find a man to love. I told you I never would, that I was happy with your memory. And I was for a time. But something unbelievable happened, and maybe I do have a chance to be loved the way you said I should be." She shook her head. "You'll always be with me, in my heart. But I probably won't be talking to you as much anymore. It doesn't mean I don't love you."

She sighed and then cleared her mind. Tears fell onto the gravel as she gently scattered the ashes around the center of her labyrinth, a place that represented safety and harmony to her. When the urn was empty, she replaced the top, got up and slowly retraced her path back to the house.

She slumped onto the couch after replacing the urn on the corner table where it had always sat. She was going to have to find a place to store it now that it was empty. She sighed, allowing herself to feel the sense of loss, the emotional milestone of scattering her late husband's ashes. Leo was such a good man, even if they had been married in name only, since he was gay. She'd thought he was crazy to suggest that someday, maybe she could heal from her uncle's sexual abuse of her, that she could learn to love and be loved physically. He had been right, but he would never have imagined the complications that came with it. She sighed again, got up and went to the kitchen to make a cup of chamomile tea. Her stomach was more settled these days, but she still found the herbal tea a relaxing habit.

Julio would come by after he finished work and they'd go to the community garden. To their garden plot. She'd begun to think of them as a couple. It felt strange thinking that way. Two instead of one. Even when she'd been married to Leo, she hadn't felt like his partner. They were best friends, but they'd had separate lives.

Now for the first time, a man professed to love her, even though she had yet to have sex with him. It seemed inconceivable that this would happen so late in her life. He stuck with her even when it cost him his place in the family business. And his family. Guilt washed over her. He obviously loved his family, and because of her they had turned against him. Why would he risk so much for someone a lot older than he was? He was so handsome, he could have any woman. She shook her head and wondered if it would ever make sense to her.

On rare occasions like this, she wished she had a girlfriend she could confide in. She needed someone to tell her what was normal and what wasn't. She had no point of reference, and it all seemed so fantastic to her. She reached for the romance novel she'd been reading, the third of three books she'd borrowed from the library. Never one for romance, she was finding it surprisingly interesting. But how real was it? She couldn't believe men could be like that. Yet, the story she was reading had a hero just like Julio, who was courtly, gentle, patient and so kind. He could easily be the dark lover in this romance, in spite of being a landscaper instead of a duke.

She pulled out the bookmark and started reading where she'd left off. An hour later, she put the book aside, her pulse racing. Do people really do *that*? She was so ignorant about sex, had avoided it like the plague her whole life. She'd never even attended an R-rated movie. Now she really wanted to know about it and had no one to ask. A 55-year-old widow shouldn't be this clueless. Maybe she ought to ask Julio. He'd tell her the truth. If she was going to ask him, she better finish this last book and make some mental notes. It was going to be embarrassing, but he wouldn't laugh at her.

* * *

Lydia, 2:30pm

LYDIA PAUSED before entering Eric's condo. During the past few weeks, her confidence in their relationship had eroded to almost nothing. She slept here most nights, cooked here often--had shifted the focus of her life into his space, but it didn't feel like 'home.' Every time she let herself in with the key he'd given her, she wondered whether their relationship was existing on borrowed time.

The euphoria she'd felt after talking with Ian and Jean about the tapping course had evaporated quickly, exposing the anxiety that was dogging her about Eric. She had no appointments scheduled, so she left work early to hide her morose feelings. A year ago, the business venture would have kept her on a constant high in spite of the risky nature of it. She hated to admit that compared to her relationship with Eric, the business meant little to her. She feared it would be only a hollow pastime if they broke up.

She stuck the key in the lock and let herself in. Classic rock was playing quietly in the living room, but Eric wasn't in sight. He had the same model condo as she did, just reversed in layout. But somehow his place seemed totally different from hers. Eric's condo was obsessively neat, had no clutter and a spartan decor. She missed the bright colors and softness of her place, the lived-in look and feel. But given the choice between comfortable surroundings and Eric, she chose Eric.

She walked past the empty kitchen into the bedroom and found him changing clothes. "I left this morning before I got a chance to talk to you. Do you have time now?"

A hooded look telegraphed his resistance. He stopped dressing, his uniform shirt dangling from one hand. She held her breath as he distractedly ran a hand through his short, graying blonde hair, his pale blue eyes unwilling to meet hers. "I have to go talk to the parents of that kid from last night. I have an appointment at four. I thought I'd go by the Posse office first and tell them I need a leave of absence."

The colors surrounding him were still muted compared to how they'd been before Schmidt had stabbed him. And the silver that had always been so prominent, showing his openness, was weak and pale. Even if she couldn't see everything his aura told her, she'd know by his body language that he didn't want to talk. But she had to try. "Please, Eric, don't shut me out. I want to know what's going on. Maybe I can help."

She saw anger spike through him as he straightened to his full six feet, his solid chest and muscular arms accentuating his implacability. "I don't like to talk about it." He shut his mouth tightly and folded his arms across his bare chest, rubbing a spot at the base of his index finger with his thumb. Before, just looking at him half naked would have her thinking about luring him to bed and getting the rest of his clothes off. But that hadn't been going so well since January 27th, either. Her stomach knotted.

"I was hoping you'd share with me. I have something to tell you about, something that might help. Can you take the time?"

He glanced downward, and she read guilt in his face. She wasn't seeing everything in his energy field; it was maddening to be shut out. Lately, theirs had become a push-pull relationship, and she was wondering when she was going to push or pull too hard. She'd even been thinking about giving him some real space. She wouldn't mind doing it if she were certain he'd come around eventually, but she was afraid that was unlikely. Still, her irritation was growing, and she often felt like threatening to leave him, even though she knew it would be counterproductive. She shook off her anger and reached for his hand. "Let's go sit down for a few minutes and talk."

He relented and followed her, but he dripped resistance as he sat on the couch a good foot away from her, still tightly wound. "What do you want me to tell you?"

"Could you please tell me why you are so upset, and what you are planning to do?"

He let out a gusty sigh. "When that kid pulled a knife on me, I lost it. I could barely stand on my own two feet; everything shrank to nothing, and if he'd come at me, he'd have gotten me easily. I'm lucky he ran. Like I said last night, I'm a liability to the Posse. I don't see how I can stay with it if I can't overcome this problem." His eyes softened and filled with tears. "Don't get me wrong. I appreciate all you've done for me. It's made a huge difference. I'm OK as long as I don't get put on the spot like last night. But I don't want to give up the Posse."

There was something he wasn't saying, but she wouldn't push. She reached over and touched his arm. "Why don't you take a leave of absence, and we can concentrate on getting you well? Ian has an idea that I think could work, and if it does, you can get back to the Posse if you wish."

He looked at her with such longing that she prayed she wasn't giving him false hope. "I can't promise anything; you know that. But I think it might work. It's a therapy based on tapping acupuncture points, and it has helped people with post traumatic stress and phobias."

"How does it work?"

"It releases blocked emotional energies, allowing you to adopt new behavior patterns. Jean and Ian and I are thinking about becoming certified in it, because it would be great for us to have a therapy in common to offer our clients, and I'm particularly excited because it holds promise for you. I was wondering if you'd like to attend class with us. I know you wouldn't be using it professionally, but it would allow us to spend some time together and give you a tool, so that it isn't always me doing things for you. I know you want to do for yourself."

A tentative smile dawned on his face. "I have no faith in psychiatrists and was worried my only other option was drugs. I knew guys that took them, and they said they always felt zoned out. Even though it tamped down the symptoms, they didn't feel alive. If you think this might work, I'm open to doing it. What does it involve, and what's the cost?"

"It's a week-long certification course in Denver next month. You'll get way more information than you want, but Jean and I have always enjoyed taking courses together, and it would give us a vacation of sorts. Jean and Ian and I plan to attend. It's pretty expensive, but I'm picking up the tab for all of us."

She divined his response from his shocked look, but still, her heart sank when he said, "You already do enough for me. I can pay my own way. How much is it?"

Anticipating a negative reaction, she blurted, "$2000 for the week."

"You're planning to fund that for four people? I know you told me you had enough money to start this business, but how loaded are you?" Then he put his hands up. "No, it's none of my business. I shouldn't ask."

"I don't mind telling you. I'm just a little embarrassed about how much money I have. It would not be a strain for me to pay for everyone's trip." The colors in his aura indicated dismay, and she didn't know how to interpret it. "You'll still have to learn to use the therapy, and there are no guarantees, but I think it's worth the investment. I'd do it for our business, but this is so much more important to me. *You* are so much more important to me." Instead of the warmth she expected, he exuded a chill, but said nothing to explain his reaction. "What's wrong? Why is my having money a bad thing?"

She winced as he shot to his feet and stood towering over her. Unwilling to give him the upper hand, she stood--she still had to crane upward to see his face--and put her palm on his bare chest, distracted by the hardness of his muscles in spite of the worry that was racing through her. He frowned as he looked down on her. "I need to get going. I can't give you an answer right now. I'll think about it. I don't have that kind of money, but I'm not comfortable with you paying my way, even if you say you have plenty. It's too much."

She opened her mouth to speak, but clamped down on the words. Nothing she said was going to move him while he felt this way. Suddenly, the anger she'd pushed down flared to the surface. "What is the matter with you? Why are you pushing me away? What have I done besides be supportive?" In spite of wanting to get control of herself, she couldn't help it. Her anger had taken on a life of its own. "What future do we have if you have to be so goddamn stubborn about traditional gender roles and money? You've been holding me at a distance for weeks now. I'm getting tired of it."

Then, without thinking, she marched out the front door, careful to close it quietly, despite wanting to slam it for emphasis. She stalked down the sidewalk, past the 'For Sale' sign at the empty condo that stood between hers and Eric's. Tangentially she wondered how long it would take to sell Tanya's old place, given a murder had been committed there. Once inside her condo, she collapsed on the sofa. "What have I done now?" she whispered. A sense of loss swept through her, but she was still mad, and what made her angrier was that now she felt she owed him an apology. As if she'd done wrong, when all she wanted was to help. "Serves him right," she muttered. But all she could think of was how she was punishing herself more than anyone else.

The phone interrupted her depressed musings. She wiped tears away, determined to sound happy. It was Jean.

"Lyd. I'm glad you're home. Ian had a great idea, and I didn't want to bother you if you were at Eric's. Well, I think it's a great idea, and I wanted to run it by you right away."

Lydia struggled to respond enthusiastically. "What is it?"

"Well, he suggested we do a psychic fair. I know you don't like that word, but people love to attend them. Even if they don't believe in it, they find it entertaining. We could make it free to enter or charge a small ticket price. People could get a mini-tarot reading from Ian or dowsing from me or an aura reading from you. We could even divide the day and have intuitive readings in the morning and healing services in the afternoon. Just do little sessions to give people a taste. What do you think?"

It was next to impossible for Lydia to think clearly with all the negative emotions swirling within her. She hesitated a fraction too long.

"What's wrong, Lydia? Is everything OK?"

She knew there was no point in lying. "I had a tiff with Eric and walked out on him, and I don't know what's going to happen. I got fed up with him not letting me do for him. And he's a snob about money." Hearing herself talk like that made her feel ashamed. "I'm acting like an idiot. I probably pushed too hard. I invited him to go to the class with us, and he doesn't have the money and won't take mine, and I snapped. I don't understand why people can't just be happy when opportunities present themselves. Why do they have to find ways to reject them?"

"Oh, gee, Lyd, I'm so sorry. But it doesn't sound like it has to be permanent. So you got mad. You're both really strong, stubborn people. He'll come around if you say you're sorry. Or is this about something bigger?"

"He hasn't been the same with me since the incident with Schmidt. I try not to push him too much. But he's keeping distance between us, and now he's using the money as an excuse to back off. For the first time in my life I don't trust what my eyes are showing me, and it's so much less than usual. I see some, but I can't see all of what's going on with him. Then I wonder if maybe I simply don't want to see that he's gone off our relationship and doesn't know how to let me down." Lydia felt the tears well up in her eyes and brushed them away. "I'm sorry to be whining to you. I had high hopes this was going to work out. Until Schmidt knifed him, it was going really well. I can't seem to get back to the way it was before."

There was a long silence on Jean's end, like she was thinking of what to say. Lydia wished she hadn't spilled her guts this way. She didn't like women who complained about their men. "I'm sorry I put this on you, Jean. I shouldn't have. I need to work through this myself. I want Eric in my life, but I'm not sure he still wants me. I'll figure it out." She tried to get back on a more positive track. "I like the idea about the psychic fair. I don't like calling what we do psychic, but you're right, as a marketing approach, it's a good idea. And it might be a fun way to introduce people to what we offer. We need to talk about details and set a date for it." Lydia found herself warming to the topic.

Jean sighed. "Lydia, don't do anything rash. Don't assume it's all over with Eric. Maybe you'll feel different in the morning. Or maybe he'll call and apologize."

Lydia didn't know what to say, so she said nothing.

"Do you mind if Ian and I close up early? There hasn't been any traffic, and there are no appointments, and Ian's burned out on working on the website."

"Sure. I'll see you tomorrow. I like the idea of having flexible hours. Don't forget to bring in the sandwich board and set the call forwarding. That is such a blessing, and thanks for manning the phone for us after hours."

"That's part of my job. See you tomorrow. You hang in there."

After they ended the call, Lydia obsessed about what was going to happen with Eric. Questions led to speculations, but no answers were forthcoming. So much for being 'psychic.' After twenty futile minutes, Lydia heard the seductive tones of a pint of Ben and Jerry's Chunky Monkey ice cream calling her from the freezer. Unable to resist the temptation to sweeten her life artificially, she trudged to the kitchen, grabbed a spoon and dug into the pint container while standing at the sink. She couldn't remember when she'd had a worse day.

* * *

Julio, 3:10pm

JULIO PULLED his white pickup truck into Emma's garage, pondering where things were headed between them. He didn't like to admit it, but he missed working with his brothers, and being ostracized by his family stung him. All that on the off chance that things would work out with Emma. He really loved her, but they were a long way from anything permanent, and he hated feeling so adrift. He shook off the depressing thoughts and went into the house to find her sitting on the couch with her nose buried in a library book.

Whenever she was reading, she was lost in another world. He paused at the edge of the room, drinking in her beauty as she sat, oblivious to his presence. Shoulder length straight black hair, crystal blue eyes, perfect milk-white skin, naturally red lips. You couldn't see her slim figure for the baggie clothes, but he knew how willowy she was. Her legs were curled up beside her, and the observation of her flexibility led inevitably to his imagining her bare legs wrapped tightly around his naked body, which awakened a sharp ache in his groin. Just then, she looked up at him, and her eyes sparkled with joy.

Jumping up, she ran over and threw herself into his arms, kissing him. It swept away the morose thoughts he'd been entertaining, but inflamed his desire more. If only she knew the power she held over him. She wordlessly pulled him over to the couch and made him sit next to her. It pleased him that she was finding it easy to touch him.

She looked at him as if he were the center of her universe. "How was your day?"

He'd never had this much attention before, and he could easily grow used to it. "It is a new routine for me. I am settling in. There is certainly a market for yard-watching and proper maintenance and design work, and if necessary, I can expand into the other retirement communities nearby."

She scrutinized him as she pushed her dark hair behind her ear. "But?"

"I did not say but." She was reading him better all the time. "I guess there is one. It is hard to do everything myself. I have come to rely on having the girls in the office answer the phone so I could focus on appointments. It is an adjustment, doing it all myself." He gave her his best smile to prevent her from thinking he was blaming her.

"I have a solution for that."

He was puzzled by her quick response. "What would that be?"

"Let me add another phone line here and use it for your business. I could be your receptionist. It's not like I'm so busy. And I'd like to help. I know you'd have to reprint your business cards, but they aren't that expensive." The pleading in her voice convinced him she was blaming herself for his problems.

"You do not have to do that."

Her chin jutted out stubbornly. "I have plenty of money, and I have plenty of time. And I am very organized and good at taking messages and answering questions. I could make appointments for you, too. You could give me a book and say what to do. I want to help your new business be successful. Will you let me be a part of it?"

He had to admit it would help a lot, even though he didn't want to make her work. "OK. I appreciate the offer."

Emma jumped up and clapped her hands. "Good! I'm so excited about being a part of your business."

Her enthusiasm was infectious, and he felt himself relax and smile. "So are we going to the garden today?"

"Not yet. I have something I want to talk with you about." She looked down shyly, as if uncertain how to proceed. He felt his stomach twist in anxiety. Was she going to dump him? No, it couldn't be that. "I spread Leo's ashes in the center of the labyrinth today. It felt like it was time. I've put the urn away. I wanted to let you know, because I'm ready to move on."

Relief washed through him. He knew it was too soon to ask her to marry him, and maybe it would never be appropriate. She had much more than he did, and he didn't want to look like he was taking advantage. Besides, she still seemed uncertain she'd ever get over her phobia about sex, and she wouldn't let him marry her unless she could overcome it. "You will always love Leo, and that is good."

"Yes, but he was only my best friend. We were not lovers, because he was gay, so our marriage worked for us both." She began to wring her hands. "It's embarrassing to me that I have no real knowledge of sex beyond what my uncle did to me when I was a child."

He clenched his fists, even though there was no outlet for his rage. He'd kill the bastard if he wasn't dead already. "What he did to you was child abuse. I want to make love with you."

"I know." She paused, looking unnerved by his anger. "I've been doing research of a sort." He constantly had to remind himself how sensitive she was. He deliberately unclenched his fists and smiled. Taking a deep breath, she pointed to a stack of library books on the table. "I've been reading romance novels. I have questions." She sat down next to him, apparently looking for answers.

He had no idea what she meant. "You know I am not much of a reader, and I do not read that type of story."

"I mean I want to know how realistic they are. I've read three of them now. The heroes all seem to be like you, and you're real." She paused as if lost for words, staring at him adoringly. "I've never met a man like you before. You're like a storybook hero." She got shy again and looked down. Her hair fell over her eyes, covering the small scar on her left cheek, a memento of her uncle. She sucked in some breath, seemed to draw courage from deep inside and looked straight at him. "They describe things in a lot of detail, and I want to know how much of it is true." Her face colored a pleasing shade of pink.

She was asking about sex. That was probably a good sign. "How can I know, since I have not read these books or any like them?"

"I know, that's a problem." She scrunched up her mouth and squinted her eyes. He gazed at her face while she puzzled out what to say. He loved that she didn't use much makeup, just the occasional bit of lipstick. Finally, she seemed to get her courage back. "They do more than kiss and more than normal sex. They use their mouths on each other, and they make it sound pleasurable, but I can't imagine. Do people really do that?"

Now it was his turn to blush. "It is real." He felt himself hardening at the thought of putting his mouth all over Emma, and he tried to draw attention away from his tightening jeans by shifting his weight.

She smiled a deliciously innocent smile. "I thought so. It was very interesting reading about it. It made me feel...I don't know how to describe it...I thought of you and me doing that, and it made me tingly all over."

It made him tingle all over, too. This was the first time since a disastrous attempt at sex some time back that she said she might want to do something with him other than kiss. And he was more than ready. He wasn't sure what the best response was, but he went with his gut. "I would be happy to show you...anytime."

Her eyes widened. She reached over and laid her hand on his bare arm. He took it as a signal and drew her into his arms, kissing her deeply, spurred on by her sighs. He'd never touched her below the neck, but it felt right to caress her face, kiss her neck and then slowly travel down to nuzzle her breast. She moaned in pleasure when he took her nipple in his mouth, gently suckling through her thin shirt. She shuddered as heat radiated off her.

He stopped and regarded her seriously. "Would you like to do more?"

She nodded silently, and they stood up and walked back to the bedroom. As he followed her, he prayed it wouldn't end up like the last time. He didn't feel he could hold back much longer.

When they reached the bed, she paused long enough to let him pull off his work boots, then they came together in a rush and fell onto the bed, clawing clumsily at each other's clothes. She hesitated only slightly when they were completely undressed, and he rushed past the awkwardness by kissing her and pressing his body against hers, reveling in the heady feeling of skin on skin. She flinched when she felt his erect penis against her, but didn't stop kissing him. As difficult as it was for him to hold back, he took his time, coaxing her ardor from tentative flashes to flaming heights, showing her that the stories she read were true, delighting in being the one to unleash the desire she had repressed for a lifetime. It turned out that once she got past her inhibitions, she was the most passionate woman he'd ever been with. When he finally sank into her, he felt he was coming home.

They never did get to the garden.

* * *

Eric, 4:00pm

ERIC SLIPPED into his car and removed the reflective shades from the windshield, oppressed by the heat that had accumulated during the brief time he was in the Posse office. Only March, and already the mercury had hit 90. He'd been hoping for a little more spring this year, but it looked like he was out of luck.

Out of luck. That described how he felt. He started the car and turned the air conditioner on full blast, windows down and door propped open. He felt he was suffocating. It seemed everything was being taken away from him. Lydia was pissed off big time, and he wasn't sure what to do. He couldn't promise her anything. No wonder she was so annoyed. He was surprised she'd stuck it out this long.

It pained him to think of not seeing her again, not holding her in his arms, not hearing her rich, sensuous laugh. When was the last time they'd laughed together? He wasn't sure their relationship could be repaired. He was a broken man, and he was taking steps to admit it. Admitting it by letting her walk out on him, even though it was the hardest thing he'd ever done. Admitting it by taking a leave of absence with the Posse, when that job gave him more satisfaction than anything else he did in this wasteland called retirement. He mentally shook himself. Enough self-pity.

The A/C was finally doing its job. He closed the car and headed out to meet Miguel's foster mother. At least there was some good news today. No charges had been filed, as the old guy--who was he calling an old guy?--hadn't found anything missing from his garage. Maybe there was some way to help the kid get turned around. If it wasn't too late.

His optimism, faint as it was, surprised him. What he'd seen as a cop hadn't convinced him it was a simple matter to put a kid on a good path once he'd started down the wild side. The parents, more often than not, were negligent or missing because they worked so many jobs, and the temptation to take short cuts and risks was simply too irresistible to kids.

As he strode up the sidewalk to Miguel's house, he reminded himself to tread carefully. Parents often didn't want to believe ill of their children, even when the kids are caught red-handed. He couldn't assume Miguel's mother would see things his way.

The front door opened before he pressed the doorbell. The frazzled woman he'd met last night had transformed. She was dressed for work in a skirt and blouse, her dark hair tamed in a bun, black eyes assessing him sternly from behind glasses with red frames. "Please come in, officer. I didn't think to ask your name last night. I'm Elizabeth Sanchez. My husband José is still at work and cannot be with us, but I took some time off for our meeting. A neighbor is watching our other children, so we can have some peace and quiet."

"I'm Eric Johnson from the Palm Lakes Senior Community Posse."

She shook his outstretched hand. Her handshake was firm, but her smile didn't touch her obsidian eyes. She waved him into the small foyer and shut the door. "Let's sit in the living room. Can I get you something cold to drink?"

"No, thanks, Mrs. Sanchez. I won't be long." He followed her and sat in the chair she pointed to. Miguel was perched on the edge of another chair, looking very small for almost 12 years old. He didn't even look up from the floor when Eric entered the room.

"So what is going to become of Miguel?" She cast a withering glance at the boy, who had glanced up at the sound of his name, but immediately shifted his gaze back to the carpet.

Eric sighed. "Well, it's a very lucky thing. The homeowner whose garage the boys were in says nothing is missing, and nothing was damaged, so he doesn't want to file any charges." Relief spread across Mrs. Sanchez' face so quickly, he felt himself relax, too. She blinked repeatedly as if fighting tears. "This is really good news, because that means Miguel has another chance. I'm here to report that no charges were filed, but I wanted to see if there is any advice I could offer that might be of assistance."

Mrs. Sanchez' look ossified. "He may have gone out without our permission, but we're good parents. He knew he was not allowed to go out. We have other children, and he's the oldest. We trusted him to behave." She shot daggers in Miguel's direction. "Obviously, we were mistaken. But José has spoken with Miguel about this. He is grounded for two weeks. It's our job to discipline our kids. Not yours."

No stranger to scathing comments from mothers of wayward teenagers, Eric didn't argue. "I didn't mean to imply you had done wrong. I was just wondering about his friends and after-school activities and if they were appropriate. You and your husband aren't able to be here all the time, since you work. Is he in sports or any programs for kids?"

Mrs. Sanchez shrugged. "Since we both work, my husband and I can't drive Miguel all over. He can only participate in things he can walk or ride a bike to." She turned and addressed Miguel for the first time. "Tell the officer about how you got involved with that older kid."

Miguel shrank even smaller. He looked like he'd told the story before and was anticipating judgment. "Raul lives nearby. That way." He gestured vaguely to his left. "I'm not ratting him out to you, no matter what you do to me," he said defensively.

"I wasn't planning on asking you to do that." Eric sort of admired the kid's nerve.

"Well, I won't." Miguel did his best to glare at Eric, but it fizzled out, and he looked down again in shame. "I didn't take nothing."

"Anything. You didn't take anything," his mother corrected. Eric almost grinned, but managed to suppress it.

Miguel plodded on without acknowledging. "I wasn't going to. Raul asked me to go with him. Me. Raul's 18, and he could have picked anyone, but he chose me. He said he thought I was brave and fast. He needed someone brave and fast." Miguel's lower lip quivered slightly. "He didn't tell me he had a knife. We were supposed to be having some fun."

"Fun!" shrieked his mother. "You call it fun breaking into someone's home? Fun waking your parents in the middle of the night when a cop brings you home like a criminal?"

Miguel stared harder at the floor. "I know. I didn't mean it that way. It wasn't fun. At least not the way it was supposed to be. And Raul left me to take the rap."

Eric took pity on the kid. "Well, you were brave, but you weren't fast. One out of two isn't bad."

The boy looked up questioningly, his dark hair hanging in his eyes, but said nothing.

Mrs. Sanchez looked at Eric sheepishly. "He won't tell us any more about this Raul. I suppose we could go asking everyone and someone would know, but we have better things to do. Miguel has promised he won't hang around with Raul anymore. We were unaware that was happening." She shot Miguel a measuring look. "I don't know what else we can do. Miguel is a good boy. He does well in school. He's never done anything like this before."

Miguel looked up, a hopeful gleam in his eyes.

"Do you play any sports, Miguel?" The words slipped from Eric's mouth before he even considered why.

"I like to shoot hoops, if I can find a place. I like to run. I am fast." A defiant glint filled his dark eyes. His mouth was a tough slit. "There isn't a lot to do around here."

"I run some, too. I don't how fast I am. I do it more to stay fit than to win any race. There's an indoor track at the Rec Center in Palm Lakes. Have you ever run on an indoor track? They're really nice, especially in hot weather."

The boy shot a suspicious look his way. "No, never been on one."

"Mrs. Sanchez, do you think it would be useful if Miguel had a chance to do something like that regularly?"

Now she looked suspicious. "Of course it would, but we can't afford a gym membership."

"I was just thinking...maybe, if it were all right with you, he could come run on the indoor track with me one afternoon after school. I could pick him up and bring him back."

"Why would you be doing something like that? Are you some kind of pervert?"

Great. No good deed goes unpunished. "I didn't mean to offend, and no, I'm not. I'm a retired cop from Minnesota. Today I turned in a request for a leave of absence from the Posse. The incident with Miguel proved...well, I got stabbed in January while subduing a murderer, and I need to sort some things out before I put myself or anyone else in a position where someone pulls a knife, which Raul did last night." He suddenly felt horribly embarrassed and pressed on in spite of Mrs. Sanchez's shocked expression. "I didn't think this through. It's just that I have a lot of time on my hands now, and you say Miguel is a good kid. Maybe if he had somewhere to go now and then, he would find it easier to avoid Raul and others like him who prey on younger boys. Maybe I could help him see how he likes running, so he can consider track in high school. We also have a basketball hoop--not a court, most of us old guys don't want to run up and down a basketball court, but plenty still like to practice their shooting skills. We have a weight circuit and a bunch of other stuff, too. I can get him in on a guest pass; it costs next to nothing."

Miguel obviously hadn't expected anything like this. His attention was riveted on Eric, and excitement had replaced the shame and defiance on his face. The boy turned to his mother. "Can I? I promised to stay away from Raul."

"Mrs. Sanchez, you can check me out through the Posse and the local police department. I don't mind."

She smiled, and for the first time it reached her eyes. "That's OK. I don't need to do that. But you'd have to let us know where he was at all times. I can give you our phone number, and you give us yours. If you let me know ahead of time, I'm OK with him practicing sports with you now and then."

"Thanks, Mom!" Miguel was now sitting up straight, his muscles tense, as if he were ready to launch. "When can I see the inside track?"

"Your Mom and I will exchange phone numbers and compare schedules. But I think I can do it within the next week." Eric looked at Mrs. Sanchez, who nodded and rose from her seat, apparently having forgotten that Miguel was grounded for two weeks. He wouldn't tell. He figured this would be better than punishment for helping turn the kid around.

She smiled. "Let's go to the kitchen. I'll check my calendar and write down the phone numbers." Then she stared at Miguel and pointed her index finger at him. "Your father grounded you for two weeks. We'll have to talk to him and see if he'll make an exception."

Busted. Miguel deflated visibly, but nodded.

She grinned at him. "I'll tell him I think it's a good idea."

Miguel broke into a smile and jumped up from the chair.

As Eric followed stolid Mrs. Sanchez and a child who was bouncing off the walls, he wondered what had prompted his suggestion. Lydia would wonder if he'd lost his mind. Lydia. Thinking of her gave him a sharp pain of loss. How was he going to get by, not having Lydia to talk to?

When he returned home, he changed his clothes and poured himself a scotch. Sinking into the couch, he stared at the blank TV screen glumly, musing about all the things that had been taken from him. His health, his sanity, his job on the Posse and Lydia. All gone. His stomach rumbled with hunger, and he added something else to the list. Cooking wasn't his thing, and he'd become addicted to Lydia's skill in the kitchen. Now he was going to have to go back to eating takeout pizza and frozen dinners like any retired single cop. And sleeping alone.

A second scotch failed to drive away the blues, so he got up and put on some music to go with his mood. "Don't Cry Now" by Linda Ronstadt, an album he'd picked up during his first midlife crisis. He hadn't listened to it in years--it wasn't really his kind of music--but the plaintive tunes gave voice to his despair, unleashing it from his core and splashing it around the room. Pouring a third scotch, he reconciled himself to ordering a pizza and eating alone.

* * *

Ethan, 5:00pm

ETHAN WESTERFIELD PULLED off his reading glasses and set them on the table by his recliner. He laid his book on the table, unable to sustain the concentration required to read. He rubbed his eyes and wondered yet again what he had gotten himself into. He hated men who chased younger women. It was pathetic. Was that what he was doing with Mary Beth? She was so much younger and so beautiful. He had no right to saddle her with someone who could become a burden all too soon.

He stood up and stretched his back to the disturbing sound of a few cracks, then headed into the kitchen for a beer. He didn't drink much, but lately he found himself turning to a drink or two in the evening. His life felt more empty than it had in years. The only time he felt alive was when he was with her. And he wasn't with her often enough.

He popped the top on an MGD and guzzled half the bottle in one swallow. Just what he needed, to add more weight from the empty calories. He scowled down at his slight paunch, which had never bothered him until he became interested in Mary Beth. Now he was painfully aware of his age, his gray hair, his extra weight and wrinkles, the little aches and pains. He was old. He only felt alive when he was around her and wanted to find a way to be with her more. Yet what did he have to offer her? It annoyed the hell out of him when she made dreamy comments about Helen's handsome husband Alexander. He couldn't compete in the looks category, and no one seemed that impressed with his high IQ, not that he ever flaunted it. At least he could put a roof over her head, but how romantic was that?

He stalked back to his recliner and dropped into it. He sipped the beer, lost in reverie. If Martha were still here, he wouldn't be in this mess. He glanced towards the framed photos of them, their kids and grandchildren which lined the mantel. Smiling at the warm memories, he shook his head. Maybe he was getting senile, panting after a young woman like Mary Beth. Why did she sleep with him the other night? He'd been fending off the advances of women in Palm Lakes ever since Martha died of cancer. He wasn't the least bit interested. But Mary Beth was different. He'd met her at Maddie's and they'd struck up a friendship before he knew it, and for him at least, it had blossomed into affection and then love.

He'd been so lovestruck, he'd taken her up on her offer to go to a motel. It seemed to him that maybe that would mean the start of a big shift in their relationship, yet she was still distant and distracted most of the time, and there hadn't been a repeat performance. He was afraid to suggest it. Maybe she hadn't enjoyed herself. God knew it had been a long time for him, and he didn't consider himself a Casanova. It was frightening how long it had taken for him to get going, but she didn't seem to mind all the foreplay. Who could tell with women? Maybe she was doing what Meg Ryan did in that movie a while back. What was it called? "When Harry Met Sally." That was it. Yeah, he couldn't get a clear feeling of what was going on with Mary Beth, and it bothered him. She hadn't said she loved him. Who knows what passes for love with young people these days? Maybe he was making a fool of himself. He'd never been very good at figuring people out.

Well, nothing ventured, nothing gained. He might as well test the water again. Even rejection would be better than this torture. He went over to the phone and dialed Maddie's number, hoping Mary Beth would answer. If she was there, she always answered to save Maddie the trouble.

"O'Neill residence." Her voice poured into him, filling empty places in his soul.

He chided himself for being so pathetic. "It's me, Ethan." He wasn't sure what else to say. An awkward pause hung in the air.

"Oh, hi, Ethan. I'm sorry I've been so busy. Maddie moves April 1st, and I've been trying to sort out where I'll live and help her get ready to go to Desert Breezes. It's been kind of crazy."

That was plausible, but he still wasn't sure if that was the whole reason he hadn't seen her. "How about I take you to dinner sometime? Friday? Saturday?" He held his breath, hoping she wasn't going to cut him loose.

"Sure, that sounds good. Let's do Friday. I'm making spaghetti for Maddie tonight, and I was thinking of lasagna tomorrow. I'm freezing the extra so she can have food she likes when she moves."

He felt guilty for thinking she'd been avoiding him. She was always so thoughtful of others. Maddie and Catherine Jameson, another widow Mary Beth had 'collected,' seemed to rely on her. And she had a full time job, plus her jewelry hobby. "Friday is great. Do you have a preference where we eat?"

"Anything but Italian. I love it, but I'm ready for a change."

"Leave it to me. I'm going to find somewhere special."

He could feel her hesitation. "You don't need to spend a lot of money on me. Any place is fine."

"We don't see each other that often. I feel like celebrating with something special."

"I know I haven't been around, and I didn't follow up like I should have after the other night, but I can't talk about that here." There was a defensive edge in her voice that made him suspect she felt guilty, but it wasn't guilt he wanted her to feel. He didn't want her apology. He wanted her love.

"We can talk on Friday. Don't worry about it. You have a lot on your plate."

"You got that right."

"OK, I'll let you go."

"Yeah, I have sauce simmering on the stove. What time on Friday?"

"Is five too early?"

"Hell, no."

"OK, see you then." He waited until she hung up and returned to his recliner. It didn't seem she was trying to break it off with him. She wasn't the type to lead a guy on. But she didn't seem to be a woman in love, and that hurt his feelings. He didn't want to be alone in this. Well, time would tell. He picked up the empty beer bottle and stared at it, turning it in his hand. Friday seemed a long way off. He decided to get another beer.

3

FRIDAY, MARCH 22, 1996

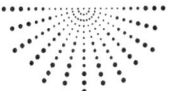

Lydia, 12:45pm

*H*elen, Jean, Barbara, Emma and Lydia sat at a table near the koi-filled faux stream that flowed through the Jade Dragon restaurant, enjoying their regular lunch outing. The round table was large enough and the din so loud that Lydia, sitting on the opposite side from Emma, had to strain to hear what her friend was saying. Either Emma was too shy to shout, or Lydia was losing her hearing. Or both. *God, it's a nuisance getting old.*

"I'm sorry, Emma, but I can't hear you. Maybe I need a hearing aid."

Emma paused and smiled shyly, then raised her voice a notch. "I'm sorry, Lydia. I wanted to share something with you all. But I don't want to have to shout." She looked down, as if gathering courage to speak. Her aura danced with clear, bright colors, the best Lydia had ever seen around her. Emma was getting healthier, happier and stronger every day, but she was still shy.

Lydia rushed to encourage her. "I don't want to miss out. I'm all ears, if only they worked." That got a chuckle from everyone, and Emma smiled. She brushed her shoulder-length raven hair back from her face, exposing the small scar on her left cheekbone.

"I haven't known how to bring this up, but you are my best--my only--friends in Palm Lakes, and I want you to share my happiness. I hope you'll be OK with what I tell you." Emma began to look nervous, her colors dimming as the muddy pink of fear shot through her aura.

Barbara was the first to speak. "Emma, you don't have to tell us anything unless you want to. And whatever it is, we're here for you." Murmurs of agreement came from Jean and Helen.

"I have a boyfriend...a man friend...I'm not sure what to call him," Emma declared with exasperation.

No one shrieked in excitement. Lydia had seen the colors weeks ago that announced Emma was falling in love. Barbara apparently had noticed something, living next door to Emma. Only Helen and Jean seemed surprised, though happy, but both of them had recently found the loves of their lives, so they knew how great it felt.

Before Lydia had a chance to say anything, Jean jumped in, "So tell us all about him. You guys got to hear about me and Ian, so now it's my turn for some good gossip."

Helen agreed. "I told you all about Alexander." Lydia noted a shift in Helen's colors that indicated that wasn't 100% true. *Interesting...*

Lydia couldn't resist teasing, "Not for a long time, you didn't, Helen." That brought snickers from the others and a blush from Helen.

"Well," began Emma, obviously struggling for the right words. "His name is Julio."

Helen gasped. "Julio the hottie from Palo Verde Landscaping?" Emma nodded affirmatively.

Helen blushed. "I'm sorry. I can't believe I said that. I've never even laid eyes on him."

Barbara smiled warmly. "I saw he'd been visiting a lot. I sort of guessed he was more than your gardener. He is a very attractive man."

"Attractive doesn't begin to describe him, or so I've been told by my friend Mary Beth, who works at Palo Verde and is the one who calls him a hottie. Is he gorgeous?" asked Helen.

Once again, Emma nodded, parsimonious with words. "Yes."

"Aren't you going to tell us more?" Jean prodded, as a thoughtful look crossed Helen's face. Lydia wondered what that was about. Had she heard something negative about Julio? She'd have to remember to ask her later.

"It's complicated. There are many impediments, but both of us seem to be able to ignore them, at least so far. His family threw him out of the business." Emma's voice, tinged with sadness, dropped again.

Shocked murmurs erupted from everyone. Helen volunteered, "Mary Beth, whom I don't see too often, mentioned he was no longer working there, and she thought it had to do with some woman, but the brothers aren't saying much. He must really love you."

"I think he does," acknowledged Emma. "I'm not sure why."

"For heaven's sake, Emma, you're a beautiful woman. Any man would be proud to be with you." Barbara's voice was filled with conviction.

"But he's so much younger than I am, and now his family has abandoned him and he has to start a new business. He's taking it really well, but I'm racked with guilt. He's already given up so much for me." Emma looked down again.

Lydia couldn't hold it back any longer. "You aren't looking at what he's getting out of the relationship. He obviously feels he's getting a good deal, or he wouldn't be involved with you. Unless you're saying you think he has some ulterior motive."

Emma was quick to reply. "No, it's not that. I worry that he's so much younger than I am, that he's given up his family and has to start a new business. He doesn't seem to mind, but I wonder what's in it for him?"

The silence swelled around the table. Looks of consternation were aimed at Emma. Finally, Lydia decided to take her in hand. "Emma, you don't realize how absolutely striking you are, how thoughtful and how kind. Any man would be grateful for your love." She paused before plunging ahead. "Has he asked you to marry him?"

All eyes were riveted on Emma. She shook her head 'yes' as she said, "No, he said he doesn't want to be accused of marrying me for my money. I think he's afraid it will cause even more talk."

Helen sent a sympathetic look Emma's way. Jean reached over and patted her hand in solidarity. Barbara expressed what they were probably all thinking. "No matter what you do, some people will judge and talk. You can't live your life for them. You have to live your life for yourself. For your happiness and his. If he makes you happy, that's what matters. Don't give a thought to what anyone else thinks."

Lydia was pleased to see Emma's colors brighten as she queried, "So you'd all still be my friends if I married Julio?"

"Of course."

"Yes."

"Why wouldn't we?"

"Definitely," added Lydia. "But I'm going to ask the question that's on everyone's mind right now. When do we get to meet this hunk of a man?"

Emma blushed. "Whenever you want to. I'm not that good at social stuff, so I'm not sure how to do it. And I'm also not sure how he'll feel about being under a microscope."

Barbara came to the rescue. "How about I host a small barbecue at my place next weekend? We could do it like a pot luck and have it be for us and our spouses or significant others. What do you think?"

Emma's shoulders dropped in relief. "That would be great. I think it would be a big step forward for me and Julio. And I believe he'd be OK with that."

"Great. I'll contact each of you so we can plan the menu." No one was better than Barbara at organizing an event. Lydia could see how this would really help Emma and Julio feel accepted in Palm Lakes, but she felt chagrined that she wouldn't be bringing Eric. Now wasn't the time to share that. She couldn't spoil Emma's moment.

Dessert followed, then coffee, while the conversation turned to lighter things. With the bombshell dropped and the dust settled, Lydia found herself more and more drawn to study Barbara's aura. Barbara was sitting next to her, so she only saw her head in profile most of the time. But whenever Barbara turned to address her, Lydia saw a strange discontinuity in the normally vibrant colors of Barbara's energy field. Above her left ear was a space the size of a kumquat that held no color at all.

Lydia struggled to quell a sinking feeling in her stomach. She hadn't often seen such a thing, but on the few occasions she had, it meant there was something damaged in that area of the aura. Maybe it was still purely energetic. But if it progressed to brown or gray or black, it could mean something physical like a tumor in that region of the body.

She couldn't finish the last of her creme brûlée, but no one noticed. With Emma's announcement and seeing the damage in Barbara's aura, she'd forgotten to mention about the Psychic Fair, and Jean hadn't, either. Well, that wasn't as important. Torn about how to proceed, she mumbled her goodbyes and drove home, debating her options. By the time she pulled into her garage, she had worked herself into quite a state.

She'd told Eric before they got involved that living so close to each other made having a relationship a mistake, in case things didn't work out, but in reality, it didn't matter whether he lived two condos down or two miles away. Living in Palm Lakes was weird that way. She hadn't seen him once since she'd walked out on him. She wasn't sure whether that was good or bad.

Now she was going to have to go to Barbara's pot luck without Eric. Every day since their breakup, it seemed she discovered something else she was going to miss. The worst thing was she really wanted to talk to Eric about what she'd seen at lunch. She tried not to talk about one of the girls to the others. It didn't seem right. Who could she consult about this? There was no one but Eric. But she couldn't bring herself to close the gap between them. It needed to be his decision to try again.

Pushing aside the Barbara issue for now, she decided to call Helen.

"It's me, Lydia."

"Oh, hi. What's up?"

"I had to ask. When Emma dropped her bomb, you seemed to be registering some concern, but you didn't say anything. Do you mind me asking what that was about?"

"I keep forgetting you see things other people don't."

"You don't have to tell me if you don't want to. I guess I could wait for the barbecue and see what Julio looks like, but I'm curious."

"Well, this is second hand, so I can't vouch for it. But Mary Beth doesn't make things up. Julio apparently has quite a reputation for sleeping with women in Palm Lakes. Mary Beth said he even bragged to her and Samantha once. I was a little concerned about how serious he is. Emma isn't the type to have a fling, and if it goes south, she'll get hurt."

Lydia sagged into the nearby chair. "Oh, shit. Emma's doing well, but

I can't imagine how she'd take it if he was just playing with her. She's so sensitive."

"Tell me about it. I hope he's turned over a new leaf."

"I'll be sure to watch him at the barbecue to see if he's serious about her."

"That's all we can do."

Lydia ended the call and strangely felt a little better about her own situation. She was strong, and she could handle whatever came next for her. Since the office was closed for the rest of the day, her plans would definitely include fortifying herself with a glass of chilled white wine and a bar of chocolate.

* * *

Christine, 1:45pm

CHRISTINE SOMMERS DROPPED her handbag and clipboard on the table so she could pick them up on her way back out. As she passed the kitchen, she saw the groceries hadn't been put away. Jerome could be counted on to put perishables in the refrigerator after a shopping trip, but beyond that, he was hopeless.

She ground her teeth and went in to tidy the place up, annoyed that the detour might make her late for the board meeting of the Homeowners' Association, of which she was currently secretary. She needed to feel she was in control of her life, and things like this derailed her carefully planned schedule. Why was he so dense? Couldn't he complete one task to help her?

As she put the flour and canned tomatoes into the pantry, Jerome stepped into the kitchen. "So you're back already."

"Yes, I'm back, but it would certainly help me if you could finish one task I've set you. I'm going to be late for my meeting. Can't you put all the groceries away instead of leaving it to me?" She shoved a couple cans of peaches onto the shelf with the other canned fruit.

"But, dear, you know where you like everything. I always put things in the wrong place. Then you yell at me when you can't find them."

God, his whine grated on her. Why couldn't he man up? "It isn't rocket science, Jerome. Everything has a place, and it's pretty easy to guess from looking at what's where. Why do you have to act so helpless? Is it to get me to do all the things you don't want to? Never mind, I'm almost finished." She slammed the aluminum foil into the drawer by the refrigerator and glared at him. "I need to prepare for my meeting."

"Seems to me you cut it close yourself. Why drive around before the meeting? What's the point?"

She heaved a sigh. How could a college-educated man be so clueless? "You know darn well I want to run for President next time they have an election. I drive around the community before each meeting and take notes of any obvious covenant transgressions. I'm the one who sends out the letters to residents, and I like to see what I'm writing about. Most of the idiots on the board don't take it seriously. If we don't enforce the covenants, our property values could plummet. They simply don't get it."

Jerome rolled his eyes, but said nothing. She glared at him. "Just today I noticed that someone has installed a screen door that is not an approved color. It was some God-awful purple. We can't have people going off half-cocked and painting their homes tacky colors. Before you know it, Palm Lakes would look like some third world Caribbean island."

Jerome's laughter seemed inappropriate to her. "I'm not sure that sounds bad. It might be nice to live in the islands."

She huffed. It wasn't worth arguing with him. "I'm going to go to the meeting now." She pushed past him and strode down the hall to the powder room to check her makeup. How had he ever made it in banking? He was a total incompetent in spite of his fancy-schmancy education. Without her, he couldn't make it in the real world.

* * *

Maddie, 2:30pm

MADDIE GRUMBLED to herself as the air conditioning kicked in yet again. An all-electric house was a selling point the year she and Stanley had moved to Palm Lakes long ago. Now it was a millstone around her neck.

She had to run the A/C all summer and the heat most of the winter. The house wasn't that big, but the electric bill was monstrous. Even with Mary Beth contributing 'rent' money, she couldn't keep up with all the costs of maintaining her home. But then, that was one reason she'd decided to sell out.

Mary Beth would be home before long, but tonight she was going out to dinner again with Ethan. Maddie wondered if she'd come home or not this time. Wasn't any of her say-so, but she didn't think staying out all night was appropriate.

At least Mary Beth had set aside some leftover lasagna that she could microwave. The girl had been a godsend in terms of cooking, cleaning and company. She was going to miss her.

Feelings like that were impossible for Maddie to verbalize; they got stuck in her throat if she attempted to speak them. That only made her feel more inadequate and undeserving, and she knew it made her appear unappreciative. It didn't matter; she still couldn't express certain things. People had to take her or leave her as she was, and mostly, they left her. She was used to it.

She wouldn't be alone this evening, but she didn't have a fun date planned like Mary Beth. Samantha would be over after dinnertime and mess around in the garage or closets, trying to find things to sell, give away or toss out. It grated Maddie that she was having to get rid of so much. It was impossible to explain to her daughter that simply having those things in her home made her feel better, safer, happier. It didn't matter that she hadn't seen this or that item in years. She knew it was in the house, and that gave her comfort. Getting rid of things she'd had for decades felt like tearing off an arm or a leg. But Samantha had no sympathy. It was impossible to convey to her the extent of the pain it caused.

Sighing, Maddie pushed herself up from the dining table, where she had been immersed in a jewelry project since early morning. Every joint in her body screamed with pain, but she did her best to ignore it. Suddenly, she realized she was thirsty, so she went to the refrigerator and got a cold beer and poured it into a glass. When Stanley was alive, she never drank before dinner. It was a treat to have a beer when she felt like it, knowing no one was going to scowl at her.

Shuffling back into the living room, she eased herself onto the couch, regretting her choice immediately, because getting up was going to be difficult. She'd have to stay there a while. Her latest novel was sitting on the end table, and she picked it up to find her place while sipping the beer. The library was stocked with many bestsellers, but most of them were trash in her opinion. Seemed next to impossible to find a book that didn't have sex in it. She couldn't understand what was wrong with people. But this one was a crime thriller, and so far, it was pretty interesting and unoffensive. At least, if you didn't mind murder.

Beau padded over, quiet for a large dog, and put his big yellow head in her lap. With sad, chocolate brown eyes, he implored her to give him a treat. "I don't have anything to give you, and I can't get up now. I'll share potato chips later tonight." He blinked at her as if he understood, blew out a sigh of disappointment and lay heavily at her feet. She didn't know what she was going to do without Beau. It seemed such a betrayal to give him away, but Samantha had promised he'd be OK. She was evasive about how she was rehoming him, but Maddie knew Samantha loved Beau, so she tried to put aside her worries.

The beer was gone all too soon, and because it was so painful to get up, Maddie decided to stay where she was until Mary Beth came home from work. A few minutes later, she drifted off and dreamed of flying over her favorite part of the desert in Moab.

* * *

Ray, 4:45pm

RAY CHECKED himself out in the bathroom mirror as he combed his hair. Longish gray hair, stylishly cut. Brown eyes. Intelligent, high forehead. Smooth skin for his 65 years, tanned perfectly. Lean, muscled six foot frame.

He'd never had to fight middle age spread, but he worked to stay in shape--more than his partner Alan, who shuddered every time he suggested they work out together or go for a run. Their shared love of gourmet cooking didn't show on Ray, but Alan had to be cautious; he liked to say he had the 'fat' gene. There was a softness to Alan, but it was the softness of a warm sense of humor and a laid-back attitude. Alan brought laughter and joy to Ray's life and an unconditional acceptance he'd never had.

For the hundredth time, he wondered what would happen to him if Alan split because of this fiasco. He wasn't sure Alan was made for the kind of challenge they faced. If it overwhelmed him--and Ray was pretty overwhelmed himself--he might leave. The thought of not having Alan in his life and having to face this problem alone wrenched his stomach. He couldn't picture himself on his own, and he would have no clue how to find someone new, if he even wanted to. Alan was the one with social skills. Ray had always been embarrassingly grateful that Alan cared so much for him. The AIDS epidemic was terrifying to read about, but until now it had merely been a tragedy for others. AIDS would be a real threat if he were single. Not that he'd have time for a social life anyway, with a child to raise.

He sighed and laid the comb on the counter. If this went wrong, his life might as well be over. "Alan, are you ready to go? We have to be there soon."

Alan's head popped around the bathroom doorway. "Don't you look divine tonight! I love that you've grown your hair out. You used to look like such a stuffed shirt."

"*Your* hair is short."

"Yes, but on me it's a fashion statement. Everyone knows *I'm* not a stuffed shirt." Alan disappeared back into their bedroom. At least he was sounding like his normal self. Did he dare bring up the subject? Surely Helen and Alexander were going to. They needed to get on the same page.

He reached deep for some courage. "Alan, we need to talk about what's going on before we head over to Helen and Alexander's place." No response. That was not a good sign.

Ray went into the bedroom. Alan sat on the bed putting on his shoes, acting as if he hadn't heard Ray. Maybe he hadn't. He pressed on. "So how much do we tell them? For that matter, how much do we tell anyone, and what are we going to do?" It wasn't like him to waffle or turn to Alan for advice. He'd always been the leader. But this development had knocked him flat. He had no clue what to do, and he was afraid of losing Alan.

The cheerfulness vanished from Alan's blue eyes. "It seems to me it's your decision what to do. What do I have to do with it?" He huffed out a petulant sigh and went back to tying his shoes.

"You and I are partners, and everything I do affects you, and vice versa. So of course you get a say. We need to figure this out before we start talking to others."

Alan looked dismayed. "I don't see how we can resolve this happily. Either we let your granddaughter go into the system, or we wreck our lives and raise her ourselves. I don't like either option, to be honest."

"Raising a kid certainly wasn't part of my retirement plan, either." Defensiveness swamped Ray. "Look, thanks to you I know who I am. I like who I am. But I can't change the fact that before I met you, I was married. It was a disaster, and now my daughter is gone, leaving behind a 10-yr-old child no one wants, whom I've never met. I'm lucky that cousin let us pay her to keep the kid this month while we sort things out. Can we at least be honest with each other about what we want and what we think our options are?"

Alan nodded stiffly, and Ray relaxed a little and continued. "I love living here. I love you. But I can't see letting my granddaughter be swallowed up by the foster care system. If they knew I was gay, I'd never stand a chance at getting her. She's living in the Deep South, and you know what that means. But for now, I have a shot. If I want her. But the covenants are pretty clear about not having resident children. If they find out, they could take our house away. Or at least drive us out. I'm as torn about this as you. I don't know what to do. There don't seem to be any good options." He sighed and fought tears.

Alan stood and put his arms around Ray. "I'm sorry I've been upset. I know there aren't any easy choices. I don't want this to come between us. I never wanted kids, but I wouldn't leave you if you decided to keep her."

Ray felt like he'd been given a reprieve from the gallows. "Thank you. You mean everything to me. I never wanted kids, either. But somehow I feel I can't let her become another unwanted child. We have the money.

We could move if we had to. Or we could fight the covenants. Maybe they'd make an exception."

Alan snorted. "For a couple of queers raising a child? You think for a minute they'd do that for us? Some of the people here are great, but lots of them would love to see us run out of Palm Lakes on a rail. But let's put that aside. If we keep her, how do we raise her?"

"That's easy," said Ray. "We tell her the truth about us. That we love each other. That we love her. And we do our best by her. What any parent would do."

Alan's blue eyes sparkled. "I like how you think. I'm not sure I'm up to the task, but I'm open to it."

Ray hugged his partner. "I'm not sure I'm up to it, either. But if you're with me, I think I can make it work."

"Everyone says that about me." Alan's banter was typical deflection, but at least things were almost back to normal. Ray felt he could face dinner now.

* * *

Mary Beth, 5:30pm

WHEN ETHAN TURNED into the parking lot of Casa Linda, Mary Beth almost squeaked with excitement. It was the most popular Mexican restaurant in the city, and she'd read that the menu and ambience made dining here a memorable experience. Plus it was expensive. Ethan was obviously trying to impress her. Well, he'd succeeded.

The ride over had been unusually silent, and the tension was palpable. She'd had too much on her mind lately to dwell a lot on where their relationship was going, but maybe he was stressing out about it.

His crooked smile was colored with concern as he parked close to the entrance. "I read this was really something. I've never eaten here before, so I can't promise."

She beamed at him. "Any meal I don't have to cook and clean up after is a good one for me. So I'm not going to complain, no matter what. But I've read about this place, too, and I've been dying to eat here. They say it's amazing."

Ethan grinned and got out and dashed around to her side of the car. She held back the impulse to open the door herself, although it went against her nature to be helpless. The first few times they'd gone out, they'd gotten into a tug of war every time a door needed opening because he was unable to let her open them herself, so she finally gave up and let him be chivalrous. It was unsettling to her because it underlined the age difference. On the other hand, her ex, Jason, asshole that he was, had never treated her with the kind of respect Ethan showed her. She had to admit she kind of liked it despite the concerns it spawned.

Her eyes hadn't had time to adjust to the trademark darkness of a fancy restaurant before their server arrived to lead them to their table. As best she could tell, the restaurant was laid out with a courtyard at the center, complete with a fountain and trees, surrounded by intimate indoor dining rooms. Their server finally stopped in a cozy room with four empty tables on the opposite side of the central courtyard.

As he pointed to their table in an alcove guarded by potted dwarf citrus trees, Mary Beth congratulated herself for being able to identify them, thanks to her job at Palo Verde Landscaping. On the table a single candle burned in an ornate copper candleholder. Next to it, a vase held a single red rose. It looked real. A small window, the only one in the room, gave a view of the area behind the restaurant. She'd read that they had their own garden, and they were using it as a nice backdrop. She could see plots with all kinds of plantings and greenhouses in the rear. It was as orderly and pleasing to the eye as an English garden. Soft Latin rhythms played in the background as they took their seats on opposite sides of the table.

Their server told them about the specials and took their drink orders, which consisted of a fine bottle of red wine Ethan picked from a list on the separate menu. Then they were alone.

"This is beautiful," she said, fingering the burgundy-colored cloth napkin that was wrapped around the silverware. "I really like how intimate the rooms are. Maybe we'll luck out and no one will be in here with us. We can pretend we're eating in our own mansion." She reached over to stroke the petal of the rose. It *was* real. How could they afford that? "This rose is real!"

He grinned at her animation. "This is an unfashionable time, so maybe we'll get the room to ourselves. Supposedly, the food is great here, too, though it's not traditional Mexican. It's Nuevo Mexican. Or something like that. I know you like tasty food."

"I love Mexican food."

After an awkward pause, Ethan asked rhetorically, "So Maddie's moving April 1st?"

"Yes, that's the plan. Her new apartment will be ready then. Samantha has been working out the details. She needs to get the house on the market as soon as possible after Maddie moves, because Maddie doesn't have much money other than what's in the house. So I'm planning on getting out at the same time. I offered to help Samantha with the cleanup. I can't imagine one person doing it alone."

Ethan nodded. "Maddie does seem to be a bit of a hoarder."

"Ya think?" Mary Beth laughed. "She's the queen of hoarding. But she's the kindest and most generous person I've ever met."

"So tell me about your next place."

"Helen and Alexander--you know Helen used to live across the street from Maddie? Did you ever meet her when you visited Maddie?"

"I saw various neighbors, and I know I must have seen her, but I never spoke to her that I recall. Was she the one with strawberry blonde hair?"

"You have a good eye for color. That would be her. You probably remember some details of her story, but maybe I never told them in order?"

"I never heard the whole story told in chronological order."

His grin didn't seem forced, but once again, Mary Beth marveled at how encouraging he always was. She still wasn't used to having a man willing to listen to her. "When Helen sold her house after she was widowed, she moved into a condo on Sunset Drive next door to my Mom. That's how we met and became friends. I was lonely and at loose ends. She introduced me to Maddie, because it came out in conversation that I was interested in learning to make jewelry. Which was where I met you, because we both went to Maddie's on Saturdays. Not too long after that, Helen married Alexander and moved to his house on the golf course, leaving her condo empty. But she was reluctant to sell it. There wasn't room at Alexander's place for much of her furniture, and she'd grown attached to the place. She'd spread her cat's ashes around the tree in back after having Samantha redesign and plant the yard. Then when Mom died and I had to sell her condo, since I'm not old enough to own a place in Palm Lakes, Helen offered to rent me her place for a ridiculous price. What a break that was! You know what I was going through then. But the HOA got wind of my living there, and they demanded I leave. That's when Maddie stepped up and offered me a bedroom at her place. She was lonely with Stanley gone, and we love doing jewelry together. As you know, it hasn't been quite what I planned on, but there's never a dull moment with Maddie. I'm going to miss her, but thank God Helen has offered me their casita for as long as I need it."

"It amazes me the twists and turns in your life this past year. That we met seems nothing short of a miracle."

Mary Beth nodded. It did seem incredible. "I've never been big on destiny or karma or whatever, but maybe I should start believing. If not for doing jewelry with Maddie, I'd never have met you." She sighed and reflected on how lucky she was. She hadn't felt lucky in a long time. It was a nice feeling.

"Speaking of Maddie, is she still as down on me as ever?"

"No, just this morning she paid you a compliment. I think she's grumpy because it's hard to let people do for her. I've been running into that a lot. She won't clean house. In fact some things she couldn't do even if she wanted to at this point. But she doesn't want me doing them. I push her anyway, cooking and cleaning at least the rooms I spend time in. She isn't grateful. I think she feels judged."

"I like working with The Helpers. To me, it's satisfying to help people have more comfortable lives. So many of the older folks here have no support system, no family nearby, but like Maddie, they don't want to leave their homes. I don't mind that she's ornery. I might be that way myself, if I were in her shoes."

Mary Beth took his measure. "I don't think so." A small smile graced his face and his silvery eyes lit up. It took so little to please him. "You remind me of my Dad," she blurted without thinking.

His frown embarrassed her, causing her to backpedal. "I didn't mean it the way it sounded. My Dad was the most wonderful man I ever knew. You remind me of him because of your good qualities."

"They don't seem to count for much."

Mary Beth's jaw dropped. "Of course they do. I loved and respected my Dad. He was perfect. But I went and married the exact opposite. Maybe I was being rebellious. Or who knows. Jason was a total asshole, pardon my french, and in the end he showed his true colors. Not that I want to revisit that drama. He was flashy, self-confident and handsome, and that's the kind I've always found attractive, in spite of knowing they aren't worth a damn. I often wondered if I could fall in love with someone nice. Someone like you. I thought maybe I was defective."

His gray eyes betrayed his confusion. How did she get started down this path of self-revelation? It was quicksand. "So have you fallen in love with me?"

She realized she'd never said the words to him. But she did love him. She wasn't sure it was enough, and she hated to hurt him until she was sure. "Yes, of course I do. You think I sleep around?"

Even in the dim light she could see him blush. "Of course not. I just didn't know what it meant to you."

"My life has been so chaotic these past months, my head is always spinning. I feel I have to constantly adapt to something new. What I feel for you is different from anything I've felt in the past. I've never felt safer or happier with anyone, except maybe my Dad. Don't get it into your head I'm looking for a sugar Daddy. That's probably one reason I'm reluctant to dive in. I don't want to make another mistake. Maybe I'm rebounding from asshole Jason to nice Ethan. It wouldn't be fair to use you as a transitional relationship. You deserve and want something more. And I guess, so do I. I'm sorry it's been so strange."

The arrival of their meal broke the tension. The fragrances were heavenly, and in spite of the uneasiness, Mary Beth felt her appetite awaken. When the dishes were all laid out, the server left. Ethan topped up their wine glasses. Mary Beth put a fork into her enchilada. "This smells terrific. I'm hungrier than I thought."

Ethan didn't let her change the subject. "So we have a relationship, but we aren't sure where it's going?"

"That's about it for me. I don't mean to sound commitment-phobic, but I really don't want to make a mistake. Is it going to be all right with you if we take it slowly and see what happens?"

She was surprised to see him relax, as if a burden had been lifted from him. "That works for me." He took a bite of his carne asada and sighed in pleasure."This is delicious. So tender and seasoned perfectly." He chewed some more, then changed the subject. "Tell me about the accommodations you'll have at Helen's place."

"They have a huge house on the golf course, but it also has a one-bedroom casita with kitchenette, bathroom and living room, which is where I'll be living. There's room for my car in their garage, so it's unlikely anyone will notice I'm staying there. At least that's the plan. I've already talked to her, and you're welcome to come over and spend the night anytime."

That put the twinkle back in his eyes. "I'd like that. I was thinking, maybe after dinner, I could show you my place. We could have a glass of wine, and then I'll take you home. I don't want to ruin your reputation by having you spend the night, but I'd like you to see it. See how you like it. What do you say?"

He was so earnest, she couldn't possibly say no, and she was curious. "That sounds lovely."

Later, as they sat on the couch in his place sipping a dessert wine, Mary Beth scanned the living room. The decor was not up to date, but it was pleasant. The house was clean, but maybe he'd tidied up in anticipation of her visit.

There were family pictures on every flat surface. Family was obviously important to him. Or maybe his wife had done that. Either way, it was a message. She'd noticed during the house tour that in the master bedroom a framed photo of his wife still occupied the bedside table. Martha had been blessed with an ageless beauty. Her ash blonde hair was done in a style still popular with ladies of that age in Palm Lakes. Very First Lady-ish.

The photos were actually rattling her. She felt she'd been dropped into a time machine and was somehow inside his old life, but she wasn't a part of it.

His voice pierced her musings. "So what do you think? Do you like it?"

Mary Beth didn't know what to say. What was he really asking? Did she dare tell the truth? "It's a nice house. I've gotten so used to small places, it seems very spacious to me. I like the laundry room. And the kitchen is big. That matters to me. I like to cook. So many of the homes here have small kitchens. I guess the trend is to eat out after you retire?"

"Martha liked to cook, too. This is one of the better models for that. I'm sure it's small compared to Alexander's house." His strained voice telegraphed some emotion. Was he jealous of Alexander? He didn't even know him.

"I'm lucky they have this trip to France. I get to watch the house and the dog and cat, so it's totally legal. And you can come over anytime. Their kitchen is the biggest one of all the models here, but yours is great. They wouldn't mind if I use the kitchen now and then. How about I cook you a nice meal in their fancy kitchen?"

That perked him up. "I'd like that a lot."

"Then that's what we will do."

"Finished your wine? I ought to take you home. I'm sure Maddie is restless and wants you back. How did she feel about you going missing the other night?"

"She grilled me about it, but I said as little as possible. It's not really her business. She doesn't like being alone at night, and so it was hard on her when I didn't come back, but she knew I was OK."

Ethan stood and took her wine glass. "I'll put these in the kitchen and get you home then."

She was disappointed that he gave her a platonic kiss when he dropped her off at Maddie's. Even that felt tentative. Fear flashed through her. If her being confused and cool drove him off, how would she feel? She knew she was giving him mixed signals, but she didn't know how she could behave any differently.

* * *

Samantha, 7:30pm

SAMANTHA LOOKED at the blank paper on her clipboard, then up at her mother, who sat rigidly on the couch, her features tense with resentment.

If only she could help make this easier for her, but Maddie O'Neill was not one to let things be easy. "Mom, I know this is hard. Your new place is a one-bedroom apartment, and you must let most of this stuff go. I realize how painful that is for you, but we need to come to grips with it soon. I can't put the house on the market unless it's empty, and you need the proceeds from the sale to pay your bills at Desert Breezes."

"I know that," snapped Mom. "I just don't know how to choose, and I hate giving all my things away."

As sympathetic as she was, Samantha thought that 75% of what her Mom had was junk. But she wasn't about to say that. Things were already too tense. Mom had never thrown anything away in her life. Dad had begged her to get rid of stuff when they'd moved West, even throwing out things he wanted to keep in order to give her good example. All to no avail. Now it was time to face the facts. Sometimes she wished she wasn't an only child.

Maybe a different approach would work. "What do you think of this? How about we think about the new place. Picture it in your head; you've seen it. And think about what you really want to have once you're living there. I'll put those items on the list. When you have everything you need on the list, you can begin to add things you want, space permitting."

Mom surprised her by relenting. "Let's do that." Her wrinkled face smoothed a bit, and she let out a sigh.

"Let's furnish the bedroom first. Which bed do you want to keep?"

"That's easy. The one in the guest room that I've been sleeping on. It's nice and comfortable and smaller than the one in the master bedroom, so it will make the room seem larger."

Samantha wrote "Bedroom" and noted the guest bed as her first entry. "Do you want the dresser from that room as well? It doesn't have a mirror like the one in the master suite."

Mom snorted. "The less I have to look at this wreck of a body, the better."

Samantha took that to mean the guest bedroom dresser was the one she wanted. She wrote it down. At last, progress was being made. "Now, the living room. It's large for an apartment, but I've been thinking, and you're going to want your jewelry table, some furniture for sitting on and watching TV, the TV, and possibly your computer desk. Do you think the computer desk would fit in the bedroom, since your bed is only a double?"

Mom appeared to be getting into the swing of things. "Yes, I do think it will fit. But it may be a tight fit. We forgot I need a nightstand and a lamp in there."

"Good thinking." Samantha added that to the bedroom list. "You want the office chair for your computer desk, right? It's more comfortable than a straight back chair."

"Yes. This dining room table won't fit anywhere," Mom noted with obvious dismay as she stroked the dark wood.

"We can take the breakfast nook furniture instead. That will fit in the dining alcove off your kitchen." She hoped to distract Mom from the loss of her beloved dining set. No way would that giant hutch be coming, either. "You'll want a table for jewelry. You don't want to have to clear the table every time you eat. I think Price Club has some cheap tables that might work. Would you like me to check?"

"How big are they? Bigger than card tables? I need something pretty large."

"Yes, they're rectangular, like the type you see at expos. I'm sure it will work OK, and we can put it up against a wall. You'll need a chair for the jewelry table, too. Which one should we take?"

"Your grandmother's oak chair will work."

Samantha scribbled frantically to keep up with the pace. Thirty minutes later, they had furnished the apartment without spending money, except for the jewelry table.

Now came the hard part. "There isn't much storage space in the apartment. You have a large closet in the bedroom, but it's nowhere near as big as the two closets you now have in the bedrooms here, and you won't have a garage, and a lot of your jewelry supplies are out there." She could see the resentment seeping back into Mom's face. "I could go to Ikea and get a shelving unit for your bedroom closet, and we could put a lot of the jewelry supplies there, but it will mean giving up some of your clothes and shoes." She knew Mom's bedroom closet was bulging with clothing she hadn't used in decades. Maybe this would help get rid of it, as nothing held higher priority to Mom than jewelry.

Mom's face lit up. "That's a good idea."

"You also have a smaller closet near your front door, and we could do the same there. I think it might accommodate all your supplies."

Now Mom was smiling at her. "I like that."

By 8:45, they were done, and Samantha was drained. "I think we should quit here. I'll come back again and work on the rest bit by bit. This was the hardest part, getting the apartment furnished."

Mom frowned, as if in contradiction. She was probably thinking about all the stuff she was going to have to sell or throw away.

Samantha didn't really want to bring up Beau, but she needed to make sure Mom was still on board with the plan. "My new boss Jack said he'd give Beau a good home, and he even said he'd bring him to work, so he wouldn't be left alone all the time."

Tears came to Mom's eyes. "I hate giving up Beau. He's such a great dog."

"I know. I wish they'd let you keep him, but they have a size limit on pets, and he's way over it. Plus, there's no way you could take him for a walk with your osteoporosis. I'm grateful Jack wants him. Arthur doesn't want a pet, and we have no fenced yard. I was worried how we'd resolve it. He'll be well cared for. I promise."

"How can you be sure?"

"I'll see Beau at work. I'll know if he's happy and well fed."

Mom nodded, but looked unconvinced.

Samantha stood up. "I need to head home." She was weary from trying to handle Mom. As she walked to the front door, she turned around and asked, "Where's Mary Beth tonight? I was so absorbed I didn't think to ask."

Mom sniffed. "She's out with Ethan. Supposedly she'll be back later. But she didn't come back the last time."

That got Samantha's attention. Mary Beth hadn't told her. She needed to make a point of having lunch with her soon to catch up on things. It wasn't a subject Mary Beth would want to discuss in the office at Palo Verde. Besides, this was a busy time of year in landscaping, so they rarely had a moment to chat at work. "OK. Tell her I said hi."

On the way home, Samantha detoured to the Rec Center. Ignoring the twinge of guilt, she stepped into the phone booth just off the lobby and dialed Jack's home number from memory.

"Jack, it's me. Samantha."

"Sam! It's good to hear from you. How are things going with your Mom's move?"

She rather liked the way he'd shortened her name. "On track for April 1st, but it's a real grind. I'll be glad when it's over. Are you still able to take Beau?"

"Of course. I love dogs, and he sounds wonderful. When do you want to bring him over?"

"I'd like to do it the day before the move, so Mom has him as long as possible."

"That's a Sunday, right? That would be perfect. Do you want my address now?"

"No, let it wait. I'll call you from home and set that up. I've given notice--again--at Palo Verde. So I'll be ready to start the day after her move, if that's OK with you."

"Of course, it is. I'm really glad this is working out."

"I hope it does work out. I still have reservations. But it's too good an offer to pass up. Palo Verde is nice, but since Julio left, it's not the same. The brothers are moody. They resent the woman he took up with, and they're being pissy with all us women. Mary Beth wishes she could leave. Maybe they'll improve later, but the timing sure is right for me. I'll call you to set up the handover of the dog next weekend."

"Sounds good."

The silence stretched out, and she reluctantly said goodbye.

Arthur was watching TV, a beer in hand, when she walked into their house. "Finally, you're home." The grimace on his face was reflected in his voice.

"I told you I was helping Mom sort out what to take. There are going to be a number of evenings like this before the move. It's like pulling teeth, getting her to let go of stuff." What was he complaining about? She was doing this all by herself. She bit back angry words. She was tired not only from the long day, but from swallowing what she wanted to say with everyone--except Jack. Maybe that was part of the attraction. She could speak freely with him.

"Hold your horses. I wasn't complaining. I wouldn't want to do what you're doing for any amount of money. I feel guilty about not helping. If

66

you want, I'll come with you. You know I'll help load and carry stuff on the day of the move. I didn't think I would be much help until then. Maddie would think we were ganging up on her."

"I'd like to gang up on her. But you're right. It's easier for me one-on-one. But not as easy as I'd like."

"So what happens with Beau? You haven't told her we'll take him, have you? We don't even have a fenced yard."

Samantha sighed in exasperation. "I arranged another home for him. Jack said he'd like to have a dog, and he'd even bring him to work. It seemed like a perfect solution."

Arthur raised his eyebrows but said nothing. Which was probably worse than if he'd challenged her. She was certain he was suspicious, even if he wasn't sure what to suspect.

"Aren't you glad I found a place for Beau? We would have had to take him otherwise. I won't have him killed because Mom is moving to assisted living. I thought you'd be glad not to have him. I like Beau and would have been happy to take him, but I didn't want to impose on you. And you're right. Without a fenced yard, it would require one of us to walk him a lot."

Arthur shrugged. "I'm glad you found him a good home. This Jack guy is shaping up to be a real knight in shining armor, isn't he?" His voice was laced with sarcasm.

She wasn't sure how to answer that. "I'm grateful I was able to get the job with him. If you recall, you're the one who insisted I apply, so I don't know what your problem is. And I'm very happy he wants Beau. It solves a big problem for us."

Arthur went back to watching his show without responding. Samantha stalked down the hall and into the bedroom, exhausted from the day's work, tense about her new job and the fact that Arthur was out of sorts and acting suspicious. It was only going to get worse when she started working with Jack. Maybe this hadn't been such a good idea after all.

4

SATURDAY, MARCH 30, 1996

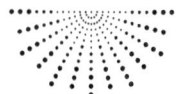

Samantha, 10:15am

he wildflowers splashed a rainbow of colors throughout the Botanical Gardens, thanks to abundant rainfall during the previous winter. As Samantha sauntered along the path with Arthur, Christine and Jerome, she soaked up the magic of her favorite season in the low desert. The brightly-colored, huge glass sculptures of the special art exhibit, placed strategically throughout the gardens, enhanced the beauty of what was already one of Samantha's best-loved places.

"Oh, look, a snake," shrieked Christine as she pointed at some penstemons and jumped to the far side of the path, her hands up as if warding off an attack. Biologist Arthur stepped forward in curiosity to get a closer look, as did Samantha, but Jerome stood stock still, reaching a hand towards Christine protectively. Or maybe he was as scared as she was.

"No problem, it's just a king snake, Christine," assured Arthur.

"I don't care what kind of snake it is. I hate snakes," she hissed dramatically. She moved down the path and put distance between herself and the offending creature.

Samantha lingered after everyone else had gone, watching the snake slowly wind its way through the undergrowth. She thought he--or she-- was magnificent. Christine's reaction bothered her, but then she chided herself for not being sympathetic. Of course, not everyone was expected to like snakes. That didn't make Christine a bad person.

As she came around a bend in the path and caught up with the others, Samantha halted and gazed open-mouthed at a huge display of flame-colored aloe blossoms that had captured the men's attention. Jerome stood shoulder to shoulder with Arthur, leaning forward, examining the brightly-colored flowers more closely. He and Arthur were about the same height, and both had gray hair, but Jerome dressed a little more formally than Arthur, who was wearing a Hawaiian print shirt and unfashionably short shorts that showed off his athletic legs. Jerome, on the other hand, was dressed for golfing in his polo shirt and chinos, walking shoes a contrast with Arthur's sandaled bare feet. They were about the same age, but Arthur's toned body made him look years younger than he was.

Arthur stayed active and had never put on weight around his middle the way most older men did. She had to admit he'd always had it in the looks department, but over the years they'd been married, she'd grown lonely because of his emotional detachment. At least that's how she rationalized her attraction to Jack Temple. Arthur's occasional flashes of empathy, which had once seemed adequate for her needs, no longer satisfied her. Maybe she was the problem after all. It wasn't him that was changing. It was her.

Shrugging off her unhappy musings, she walked over to stand next to Arthur. She was pleased he'd relented to go on this outing, because socializing wasn't his thing. It wasn't fair to judge him. She was living a great life and had so much to be thankful for, and he was behaving well today. No one was perfect, and it wasn't fair to compare Arthur to Jack. Jack had faults like anyone else. He must have. She just hadn't discovered them yet.

Christine was standing apart from the guys, gazing off to the right, her hand shading her squinting eyes. Perhaps she was looking at the sculpture in the open area beyond where they stood. It was a brilliant blue confection of curves and stood at least 12 feet high, maybe more.

Samantha was glad the men seemed to be getting along, though it was stilted. Maybe she was trying too hard. Now that she was leaving Palo Verde Landscaping, she wanted to have something to tie her to Palm Lakes, some friend, and Mary Beth wasn't sure she'd be living there much longer.

Samantha admired how together Christine was, how organized and focused. Her home and yard were always a showcase, and she'd been very kind to Samantha, who always felt out on the fringe of things in Palm Lakes, being so much younger than average. Samantha wandered over to Christine.

"Ah, Samantha. There you are. How could you stay so close to that terrible beast? You're very brave. And you're so knowledgable about all the desert plants and animals. You know, my club loved your presentation. I'm still hearing rave reviews about the tips you gave them for their plantings."

"Oh, it was nothing. I love teaching people about desert plants. I'm glad I could help. They were very nice."

Christine looked hard at Samantha. "I'm glad you feel that way. As I told you, CSL is a kind of sorority. We do wonderful work raising college scholarship money for women. I spoke with the girls, and they all agree that you'd make a nice addition to our chapter."

"I've never heard of CSL." Samantha immediately regretted the comment. Christine's frown said she had misstepped.

"There are CSL chapters all over the country. You have to be invited to join. Our chapter voted, and I'm giving you a formal invitation." Christine pressed her lips into a thin line, as if waiting for Samantha to redeem herself.

Anxiety gnawed Samantha. She felt backed into a corner. "I'm honored, but I'm not sure I have time for an outside activity, since I work full time and have to take care of my mother." What she didn't say was that she'd never been much of a joiner, and the only reason she would even consider being in CSL was to further her relationship with Christine, because it would be a way they could spend time together without the husbands. She hated sororities, had avoided being in one in college. It felt wrong to her, people sitting around passing judgment on others, deciding this person was a good fit, that person a reject.

Samantha hadn't fit in anywhere and couldn't overcome the feeling that Christine didn't really know or understand her that well.

Christine waved her hand dismissively at Samantha. "That's the point. You would fit in perfectly. Our members are very active, do a lot of volunteer work and love learning new things. That's why I think you should join us. Think about it and let me know next week some time." Finally, a warm smile blossomed on Christine's face.

Grateful for the reprieve, Samantha nodded and smiled, determined to enjoy the beauty of the Botanical Gardens today. Tomorrow posed its own problem: she had to pick up Beau and take him to Jack's. Arthur had declined to join her, which both surprised and worried her. Some part of her wanted Arthur to be jealous and suspicious, maybe even chaperone her, while the more rebellious part was grateful he had chosen to let her go alone.

Well, tomorrow would be soon enough to worry about all that. And next week, she'd decide whether to join CSL. She was sure that refusing would offend Christine and ruin any further chance at friendship. She already knew she'd probably give in, and she was having trouble ignoring the queasiness in her gut. She was tired of trying to get approval. It never seemed to work, and it made her feel dishonest. Why couldn't she just be herself?

* * *

Mary Beth, 11:20am

MARY BETH STOOD on the front step of Catherine Jameson's condo holding a casserole dish of homemade ravioli, waiting for her to answer the door, which often took a little while, since Catherine wasn't light on her feet these days. She waved to Irene Dubois, who was across the street emptying her mailbox, the mailbox that had once belonged to Mom. She was happy the Dubois' had bought Mom's condo. All the Canadians she'd met were so nice, and Irene and Henry were even friendlier than most. Coming back to the old neighborhood was such a pleasure; it was like coming to visit Mom. The front door swung open and Catherine's eyes lit up even though the visit was no surprise.

"Mary Beth! What did you bring me? I bet it's something yummy. Come in, come in."

Mary Beth followed Catherine's short, squat figure down the hall into the small kitchen. Catherine must have recently had her hair done; it was a brighter blue than usual. Her pale aquamarine eyes twinkled behind the thick lenses of her glasses as she reached to take the dish from Mary Beth. "Thank you so much, dear." She peeked under the foil and beamed. "Just what I love. And I bet it's homemade. You spoil me!"

Mary Beth sat at the small kitchen table and accepted the coffee Catherine offered her.

Catherine eased herself into the opposite chair, obviously suffering from her arthritis. "There, now. Tell me all the news."

Mary Beth still couldn't get over how she'd become best buddies with the widow she'd originally thought was ratting her out to the HOA. Catherine had become like a mother to her, even more so after her own Mom died. She warmed up to give Catherine some entertainment by sharing as much gossip as possible.

"Well, I'll be moving into Helen and Alexander's casita on April 1st. It's huge, really. They're going to France in May, and I'm their petsitter. Plus I get the run of the big house, not that I'll use it much. It's the first place I've been that is even halfway legit for me to live in, and I'm looking forward to it." She paused. That was true, but she had no clue what would happen after that, and it scared her.

Catherine appeared to pick up on her hesitation. "So why do you look worried?"

"I guess there's so much about the future that's undecided. I still haven't figured out what I want to be when I grow up."

Catherine sniggered at her lame attempt at humor.

"I don't make enough at Palo Verde to pay the bills if I live on my own, and it hasn't been as much fun there since Julio left. The brothers are really grouchy. I do have a nest egg, but it won't go far if I leave Palm Lakes. I have sold a few pieces of jewelry, but I'm becoming convinced that a jewelry business is going to take time to build, and I don't have time." She frowned as she reflected on her prospects for financial security.

"Do you want to stay in Palm Lakes?" Catherine peered at her intensely.

"I like it here. But I can't stay legally, and sooner or later, I'll be thrown out."

"What about your young man?"

Mary Beth had given up telling Catherine that Ethan was hardly a young man. "He seems to be thinking long term."

"That's an odd way to put it. Does he love you or not?"

"I believe he does."

"You told me you love him. Do you still feel that way?"

Mary Beth cringed. She didn't like to come across as indecisive. "Yes. I love him. But is it enough? And am I kidding myself so I'll have a place to live? Plus, when he had me over to his place the other night, it sort of freaked me out."

"What do you mean?"

"I don't know. There were pictures of his family all over. One of his wife on the bedside table. It was like she was still there. I felt out of place. He didn't do anything wrong, but it made me wonder what the hell I was thinking, even considering a long term relationship with him."

Catherine pulled off her glasses, wiped them and put them back on. "So you don't think he's ready?"

"I wonder. But he probably thinks the same of me. I haven't exactly been attentive, with all that's going on. He acts hurt, but never confronts me."

"How's the sex?"

Mary Beth's jaw dropped open. "Really, Catherine, you can't expect me to tell you everything."

"You told me you went to a hotel with him. You implied it was good. Where has it gone from there?"

"Nowhere. We haven't slept together since then."

"So that's what's wrong!"

Mary Beth couldn't help giggling. "It feels so wrong to have someone old enough to be my grandmother talking to me about my sex life."

"Sex is important. Have you had a frank talk with him? Does he even know whether you enjoyed yourself? Does he want more?"

Guilt flooded Mary Beth. "I probably haven't been as forthcoming as he might like." Catherine's questions caused all kinds of self-judgment to blossom within her. She put her head in her hands. "I asked him if we could go slow, and he said yes, but that's the extent, beyond finally admitting I love him. What do you think I should do? Do you think a man whose house is flooded with pictures like that is ready to move on? I can't see myself living there. I'd feel like I was being a bitch if I asked him to remove any of the photos, but damn, having his wife staring at me in the bedroom would be too much."

Catherine tried to reach over and pat her hand, but the distance was too far. "There, there, dear. Don't worry. These are reasonable questions. A second marriage must be a hard thing. I know you don't want to have another failure--not that I think your divorce was one, just that I know you see it that way--and you're trying to feel your way through a difficult time. I'm grateful I never had to deal with the kind of decisions you've had to make for the past year."

No one had ever been so kind to her. The tears began to flow, and Mary Beth blinked them back as best she could. "I don't know what I'd do without you, Catherine."

"Likewise, dear. You do so much for me. Most of all, you spend time with a lonely old woman, when you have so many other demands on you."

Mary Beth warmed to the compliment. "I love being with you." Her eyes strayed to the kitchen counter, where a pillbox sat, segmented into days of the week. "Are you on a lot of medications?"

"So many I can't remember what's what. That pillbox is useful. Once a week, I fill it up, then take my pills each day."

"How have you been feeling, aside from your arthritis?"

Catherine shot a sharp look at her from behind thick lenses. "I'm not getting any younger, child. My blood pressure is high, and I have sugar diabetes, plus the arthritis. And what do they call it, the eye problem?"

"Macular degeneration? Glaucoma? Cataracts?" Mary Beth couldn't think of the names of any other conditions.

"Glaucoma, that's what it is. They say the pressure is too high in my eyes. I use drops for that."

"Do you have any symptoms other than the pain from the arthritis?"

"What's all this quizzing about?"

"I told you my Mom's death was probably caused by that new med the doc put her on. Not that he meant to harm her, but it hadn't been out long, and people died from it. I'm concerned that doctors are so busy, they don't have time to educate themselves about the new drugs that are coming out all the time. They accept what the reps tell them, but what do the reps really know? They're just saying what they've been told to say to sell drugs. I don't want you to end up hurt."

Catherine seemed to retreat into herself, a vague look on her face.

"What is it? Have you had some symptoms?"

"I'm a very old woman, Mary Beth. Of course, I have symptoms. But how could we know what the cause is? If I open my mouth to the doctor, he wants to prescribe another pill. I'm sick of pills. I'm kind of sick of being old, to tell you the truth."

"Don't say that, Catherine." Panic swamped Mary Beth. She couldn't deal with the thought of losing Catherine.

"Well, my time will come, and probably sooner than I wish. But then, I'll be reunited with my Harold. Don't you worry about me."

Mary Beth dug in. "So what are the symptoms?"

"Sometimes I get faint or dizzy. Or I feel a bit weak. But that's normal for my age."

"We need to speak to your doctor and see if it could be a side effect of the meds."

"I don't like to be a bother."

Mary Beth had the impression that Catherine wasn't telling her everything. "I can be the bother, then. I'll go with you and we'll get it sorted."

Catherine beamed. "I can't remember the last time I had such help and kindness."

"Catherine, I wish I could get situated permanently so you could live with me. I don't like you being here alone. We get along great. I mean, if I can live with Maddie, I can live with anyone."

"I'm not sure that's high praise, given what you've told me about Maddie."

Mary Beth giggled. "Don't be silly. You and I get along famously, and I wish I could help out more, be with you more."

Catherine extended a wrinkled hand which was twisted with arthritis. "You already do so much for me."

Mary Beth closed the distance and held her misshapen hand. "I'm serious about going with you to the doctor. I can go any time you say."

"We'll see. I appreciate your concern."

"That means you aren't going to take me up on my offer." The fear of losing Catherine gripped her heart, but she knew she'd pushed hard enough for today.

"Maybe. Maybe not. I don't like to stir things up. If it gets bad, we'll go see him."

Mary Beth relented. "Good enough. So what shall we do now? Want to go shopping? Take in a movie?"

"A movie would be great."

Mary Beth went into the living room to get the paper, and they spread it out on the kitchen table to see what was showing.

* * *

Ethan, 1:15pm

ETHAN PARKED his car in front of Maddie's house and braced himself before going in. She wasn't happy about the move, and she'd never been that nice to him, but he didn't feel right letting her move without saying something. She didn't need any more things to throw away, so he'd brought a nice bottle of wine for her to enjoy later on.

Beau barked as he pressed the doorbell. A short while later, the door opened on Maddie's bent figure.

"Oh, it's you, Ethan. Come on in."

Beau nuzzled his hand as he came into the foyer. Ethan squatted down on his heels and gave Beau a good petting. "How's my buddy doing?" Beau's thick tail thwopped on the tiles. Wincing at the hitch in his knees as he stood up, Ethan held the bottle of wine out to Maddie. It wasn't in one of those gift bags. He was pretty sure the less he made of it, the happier she'd be.

Maddie's pale blue eyes widened, and a rare smile showed coffee-stained teeth. "Is this for me?"

"It's not for Beau. He isn't of drinking age."

She rolled her eyes, took the bottle and looked at it. "I hope you didn't spend a lot of money. I'm not a connoisseur."

"Neither am I. I know you're busy with the move. I just wanted to say I hope that your new place works out well for you."

Maddie frowned, adding to the wrinkles on her face. "I have to give up Beau."

"I know. That's hard. Didn't Samantha find a good home for him?"

"So she says, but still, it will be hard on him. She says she'll see him a lot, since he'll be living with her new boss. I guess it's all right. But I'll miss him." The dog in question was staring at her intently, as if he understood. His perpetually sad face made it appear he was agreeing with her.

"Is there anything I can do? Take out the trash? Walk Beau? Move something heavy?"

Maddie waved her hand. "No. Samantha will be by later on. She's at the Botanical Gardens with a friend. She's got it pretty organized. We know what's moving and what isn't."

"Well, that's a big help." Ethan didn't know what else to say. "You take care of yourself, Maddie. It's been a pleasure helping out each Saturday."

Maddie snorted. "I'm not sure it was a pleasure for you. I'm not always easy to be with."

It looked like that was as close as he'd get to a thank you. That was good enough for him. "Can I give you a hug?"

A genuine smile from Maddie said 'yes' before she spoke. "Sure."

Ethan gently encircled her with his arms. She was so short. Seemed like she'd shrunk since he first met her. "Give my best to Samantha," he said as he released her. "I imagine Mary Beth is coming over today to do jewelry?"

"No, with the move, we aren't. She said she was going to visit her friend Catherine and maybe take her to a movie."

"Well, give Samantha my best and good luck with the move." He petted Beau one last time as he made his way out the front door. It shut behind him as he stepped from the dimness of Maddie's house into the brilliant sunshine and heat. He meandered down the sidewalk to his car, lost in thought. It was sad seeing people forced to give up their cherished homes. In the old days, families lived together and took care of each other. He wasn't so sure this was progress. Shrugging, he slipped into his car and turned it on, cranking the air conditioning.

He couldn't blow off the depressive atmosphere. Maddie was really hurting about this move. He wondered how many old folks up and died, unable to make the transition.

Where to next? He'd been obsessing for a couple days about getting a ring for Mary Beth and proposing to her. She liked jewelry, but he was no expert on rings. She wasn't wearing any rings from her previous marriage. In fact, she didn't wear rings often. He couldn't make up his mind what to do.

It had been so long since he had romanced a woman and proposed, he'd forgotten how. Not that he'd ever had much experience with women. And the age difference shook him up so bad, it made him even more clumsy than his normal nerdy self.

Perhaps instead of buying a ring, he should talk to his kids, ease them into the idea that he was seeing someone. That way, he wouldn't have to shock them with an announcement that he was remarrying. That felt right. Galvanized, he set off home.

He settled in his favorite chair with a beer to fortify himself. Never very good on his feet, he practiced what he would say a few times to build up confidence. He needed to keep it light and say as little as possible, just enough to give them the news that he was dating. What a horrid word.

He reached for the phone and pressed the speed dial number for Winnie, sweating in spite of the cool of the room.

"Dad, it's so good to hear from you!"

"How are you doing?" He winced at the lame opening.

"Same old stuff. This isn't when you usually call. What's up?"

"I can't get anything by you." A voice in his head was saying, 'abort, abort.' Maybe he could postpone his announcement.

"So spit it out." Her chuckling encouraged him to open up.

"I wanted to let you know I've started seeing someone." Saying it lifted a weight off his shoulders.

The chuckling stopped, but Winnie quickly recovered. "That's great, Dad. Good for you. Tell me about her."

He heaved a sigh and plunged in. "Her name is Mary Beth. I met her at the home of one of the people I visit each week for The Helpers. She and this lady, Maddie, would be making jewelry each Saturday when I came by to do my thing. We got to talking and struck up a friendship. We've been out to dinner a couple times lately."

"That's wonderful, Dad. But you sound worried. Is there a 'but' to this? She isn't married, is she?"

"Oh, for heaven's sake, of course not. I don't mess with married women."

"But...?"

"She's a good deal younger than I am."

"Ah...," Winnie didn't sound judgmental, which was good. Just surprised. "You're a dark horse, Dad. But you're a real catch. You're smart, supportive and have oodles of integrity. Plus, you're handsome."

"Yeah, don't forget handsome," he said sardonically. "She's in her 40s. She's beautiful and full of life. She makes gorgeous jewelry and sells it. She had a bad divorce a while back and came here to live with her mother, who died a few months ago, and she's been from pillar to post because she's too young to own a place here."

"You don't think that security might be part of the reason she's attracted to you?"

Offended, he countered, "No, she's very independent. She's not looking for a sugar daddy. She's not that type."

"OK, OK, I didn't mean to imply she's a bimbo. You don't go for bimbos."

"No, I don't. She's a very nice girl. She took care of her mother, and she's living with Maddie now, cooking and cleaning for her and putting up with Maddie's eccentricities."

A silence stretched between them. That was all he was prepared to say today. "Look, I just wanted to give you a heads up. We're only going out now and then. It isn't anything more at the moment, and maybe it won't be. But I really like her, and I felt I should tell you about her. I haven't dated since your Mom. This is a big step for me." He flinched again at his use of the word 'date.'

"I appreciate that, Dad, and I'm glad you felt you could tell me. I trust your judgment. She must be a nice person, or you wouldn't want to spend time with her."

"That's my girl. I'm glad you feel that way."

"I want you to be happy. That's the most important thing in the world to me."

"Thanks, Button." He reverted to her baby name, for cute-as-a-button.

After catching up on the latest family news, Winnie ended the conversation. "Let me know how it goes, Dad. I love you."

"I love you, too."

She hung up, and he put the phone down. One down, one to go. The hard one. William was going to be a problem. He was sure of it. They'd never seen eye to eye, and this would inflame him. Best to get it out of the way.

Pressing the speed dial for William, he held his breath. William's wife answered, as usual. "Marie, it's me, Dad."

"Oh, hi, Dad. Did you want to speak with William? Is everything OK out there in the desert?"

"Yes, it's fine, and I do wish to speak with William for a minute, if he's there."

"I'll get him." He heard her put the phone down. "William, it's your Dad." He could hear William's muffled reply, and a short while later, his son picked up the phone.

"Hi, Dad."

"Hi, William. How are things going?"

"Great. No big news since last we spoke. What's up with you?"

"I just talked to Winnie, and I wanted to let you know, too." He squared his shoulders and prepared for a strong reaction. "I've started seeing a woman."

"Really? Are you sure that's what you want to do?"

"Why wouldn't I be? Your mother's been gone a good while now, and I found someone I get along with. I wasn't looking. I haven't been on a date since your mother, and it's awkward, but she's nice."

"Who is this paragon of virtue?" he asked sarcastically.

"Her name is Mary Beth Costello, and I met her at the home of one of the people I help through the club I'm in. We got to talking each

Saturday, and it became a friendship, and then I took her out to dinner a few times. I really enjoy being with her."

"So she lives in Palm Lakes?" In typical fashion, he'd nailed the weakness right away.

"Yes, in a manner of speaking. She was staying at her Mom's house until her Mom died some months ago. Now she's living with Maddie, a widow I help out each week."

"How old is she?"

"Forty-something."

"You're kidding me, right? She's young enough to be your daughter!"

"Well, almost."

"She's looking for a husband so she'll have security. Why else would she go after you?"

"Thanks for the vote of confidence. Maybe she actually likes me."

"Dad, you're so gullible. You're a financially secure widower. That makes you a target for gold diggers. Especially in a place like that. And if she's in her 40s, she might even be able to pull the old 'I'm pregnant' routine and force you to marry her. You better watch out."

He knew Mary Beth wouldn't do that. She'd insisted he use condoms the night they'd spent together; it had necessitated a trip to the drugstore. But he could hardly volunteer that as evidence. He didn't want to admit they'd had sex. That would only give William more to speculate about. "Look, give your old man some credit. I admit the age difference concerns me, but not for the reasons it concerns you. I know Mary Beth. She's a good person. I'm not a doddering old fool yet. I only told you so you wouldn't be caught unprepared if it turned into something more. We're dating. That's it. I'll let you know if it grows."

"What happens to us and our kids if you remarry?"

So it was finally out in the open. He'd known it would come to this. "Obviously, if I die first, which would probably be the case, she inherits everything. What am I supposed to do, put her out on the street so you and Winnie can inherit?"

"That's totally unfair." William's voice simmered with anger.

"Look, we aren't talking marriage yet. If it gets that far, I'll see what she says. I don't think she has any family. She has no kids from her first marriage."

"Oh, great, so she's divorced? Just what you need is someone who couldn't make it work the first time."

"This is getting out of hand. I'm not going to argue with you. I've told you what's going on, and you need to accept it. I don't know for sure what will happen, if anything. Quit borrowing trouble."

William sighed heavily. "All right. I need to get back to what I was doing."

"Fine."

William hung up the phone, and Ethan reached for his beer. It hadn't been worse than he'd pictured, but it hadn't been good, either. How could he consider bringing Mary Beth into a situation like this? Winnie would be OK, which was weird, considering she was the single parent struggling financially, not William. She was the one who would be impacted the most if his marrying a young woman put off her inheritance. Maybe he was being selfish, wanting to have someone to love at his age. Maybe he should put his kids first. Or not. He sipped his beer distractedly.

* * *

Lydia, 4:45pm

LYDIA BALANCED the homemade chocolate silk pie in her left hand, a plastic grocery bag with a container of whipped topping looped over that wrist, as she hitched her purse higher up on her right shoulder. Someday she was going to have to give in and switch to a smaller purse...but not today. There was something comforting about knowing she had everything she could possibly need in that purse, even though Jean liked to kid her about having purses the size of overnight bags.

She knocked on Barbara's screen door, then let herself in. "Barbara, it's me, Lydia."

Barbara's voice welcomed her from around the corner. "Lydia, come in. We're setting things up."

She was the last of their yoga troop to arrive. Helen and Alexander stood on the opposite side of the long counter from Barbara and her husband Ben, laying out what looked to be fancy homemade hors d'oeuvres. She couldn't wait to taste them. Helen and Alexander were known for gastronomic creativity. "Hi, Lydia," Helen waved. She was wearing slacks and a sleeveless top in a turquoise pattern that complemented her strawberry blonde hair. Alexander flashed her his movie star smile. His emerald eyes, wavy silver hair, perfect tan and tall, hunky body made him a classic heartthrob. And he was such a nice guy. Helen was lucky, but she deserved it after the life she'd had with her previous jerk of a husband.

Barbara was dressed elegantly in black slacks and a white silk top. A pendant with a large, round black onyx hung from her neck. Ben wore his usual golfing attire, casual tan slacks and a short-sleeved pink shirt with a designer's logo. Both of them beamed at her in welcome.

Jean scrambled around the end of the counter and came for a hug. She wore a long colorful skirt, loose sleeveless green blouse and simple leather sandals. Ian hung back, grinning, looking relaxed in jeans and a black polo shirt, his gray hair hanging loose to his shoulders instead of tied in his usual ponytail. "Everything looks absolutely delicious." His British accent made the bland statement worth hearing.

Emma and Julio stood a slight distance from the counter. At least, that had to be who the handsome younger man was. Dressed in jeans and snug-fitting knit shirt, he stood close to Emma, who wore loose clothing that didn't show off her trim figure. She managed to look stunning and self-conscious simultaneously. Julio was a shade shorter than Ian, maybe five foot ten, with shiny dark hair that hung loose to his shoulders, so thick and naturally curly it was obscene. Women would kill for hair like that. It was usually wasted on a man, but not on him. His hair's body and shine showed he took care of it. He must be pretty confident to wear it like that. It even looked better than hers, and she was proud of her hair. The tight jeans and shirt showed off his impressive physique. Maybe working in landscaping kept the muscles toned. But what really stood out for Lydia was that his overall energy field was vibrant and dominated by green and orange every time he looked at Emma. He was in love. *Thank God.*

Emma tugged on Julio's hand and led him over to Lydia. "Julio, this is my friend Lydia."

A smile split Julio's coffee-colored face, showing perfect white teeth.

Lydia took his hand and shook it. He had a nice, firm handshake. "So pleased to meet you, Julio. I hope you're not intimidated by the scrutiny."

He laughed pleasantly. "I am grateful that you are so supportive of Emma and me." She decided then that this was going to be a fun party. It turned out she was premature.

There was a knock on the door, and Barbara yelled, "Come in."

Lydia couldn't imagine who it would be. Everyone was already here. She turned to see who it was, and suddenly the party wasn't fun anymore. Eric was standing in the foyer, holding a large paper bag and looking nervous. Finally, he strode into the kitchen area and handed Barbara the grocery bag. She began to unpack it and put containers on the counter. He'd gone to Trader Joe's and gotten an assortment of different salads, a good idea for a barbecue. But what was he doing here?

Eric nodded at Lydia, looking sheepish and tongue-tied.

"Why didn't you two come together?" Barbara queried. As she looked back and forth between them, it was clear she guessed the truth. Lydia hadn't told anyone yet. She'd hoped Eric would make up with her, but he hadn't. This was going to be awkward. Barbara attempted to mend things by grabbing Eric's hand and pulling him over to the bar. "I'm drafting you to be the bartender, Eric, because Ben is in charge of the grill. Can you do that for me?"

Eric grinned at her in relief. "As long as I can still drink."

Barbara chuckled and waved her hand at him dismissively. People drifted to the bar and started ordering drinks, and Ben went out to the grill, which was smoking. Lydia held back, and Barbara came over to her. "Did I do something wrong?" Barbara whispered. "I called him to say he didn't have to cook for the barbecue, but that some salads from Trader Joe's would be nice. Are you two still together?"

"I don't think so," sighed Lydia. "I'll tell you more after the party is over. It's OK. I can handle it. We didn't have a big fight. I walked out on him because of how he's been acting."

Barbara patted Lydia's arm. "We'll talk later if you like. Can I get you a glass of wine?"

"That would be nice. I'm going to have to work up to talking to him."

Barbara sped off in the direction of the bar, leaving Lydia standing alone, wondering what to do next. So she went out to the grill to say hi to

Ben. Barbara came out minutes later with a glass of white wine. "Thanks, Barbara. It's going to be fine."

Ben looked up from the burgers he was flipping. "What's wrong, Lydia?" His inquisitive blue eyes demanded an answer.

"Oh, Eric and I aren't together anymore."

Ben reacted with alarm. "So why's he here?" He put down the spatula, pushed his fashionably long gray hair off his forehead and straightened to his full height, which was perhaps all of five-ten. He looked ready to do battle for her. What a dear.

"That's my fault," offered Barbara. "I called him to assure him he didn't need to cook. But why didn't he tell me? Maybe he wants to get back with you, Lydia, and that's why he came. If he were upset, he'd have stayed away." Barbara's aura said her composure was slipping. She fingered her short, auburn hair on the left side of her head. Right where the empty spot in her aura was. Lydia wondered if she was having symptoms yet. She pushed the thought aside.

"All he has to do is ask if he wants us to get back together. But maybe there's something to what you say. I'm not going to be mean to him. I still care about him. You don't have to worry about me making a scene."

"For heaven's sake, Lydia, we know you wouldn't do that." Barbara marched back into the house, closing the sliding door behind her.

"You can hang out with me if you like," said Ben. "I can even get you to run the plates of meat in when they're done, so it wouldn't be a sham job."

"That would be nice, Ben." The fragrance of cooking hamburgers wafted in Lydia's direction. "Did Barbara make her signature burgers?"

"You bet! She decided that hot dogs and burgers would be more low key. She didn't want Julio to feel out of place by going too nuts, if you know what I mean." He flipped the burgers again, then looked sheepish. "I didn't mean that to sound like he's low brow. We didn't want to overwhelm him. We thought casual would be best."

Lydia smiled reassuringly. "You did great. He seems very relaxed." The smoky fragrance of burgers wafted past. "I like how Barbara uses the liquid smoke and bacon in hamburgers. They're the best burgers I've ever had."

"Me, too." He plated the burgers and turned the hot dogs again. They were nearly cooked. "Here, you take the burgers in, and I'll follow shortly with the dogs."

When Lydia reached the dining area, she saw that people were sitting at the large rectangular table, spouses or partners opposite each other. Ben and Barbara would be seated at the ends. Lydia placed the plate of burgers in the center and sat in the seat opposite Eric. There was no alternative without making a big deal. Jean looked at her apologetically, and Ian smiled warmly in support.

Lydia turned to her left, murmuring softly, "Emma, would it be convenient if I stopped by your place for a few minutes after the party?"

Shock registered on Emma's face and fear swamped her aura, but only for a few seconds. She recovered and said, "Sure, Lydia. Is everything OK?"

"Absolutely, but there's something I wanted to share with you privately, if you don't mind."

Emma's smile spelled relief. "Of course. We don't have anything planned after this."

Alexander was engaging Julio, who seemed totally at ease. Ben brought in the platter of hot dogs and sat at the head of the table. He clinked his water glass for attention.

"I don't want to be too formal, but I'd like to welcome Julio to our little family. We enjoy doing things together, and we hope that you'll join us often, Julio. We look forward to getting to know you better."

Some hesitant clapping followed, while all eyes looked at Julio. Julio nodded. "I am very grateful for your kindness. Emma has wonderful friends. I will enjoy getting to know all of you." More clapping, and then the conversations started up again, as serving platters were passed around the table.

Lydia sampled some of the salads, then looked up to find Eric's blue eyes drilling through her. His aura was still hard to read, but the silver was stronger and clearer than it had been. So he *had* come out of interest in her, but why?

"I've started a new project of sorts." He tossed the line her way like he was fishing.

"What would that be?"

"You remember the boy I caught in a resident's garage a while back?"

86

"How could I forget?" she answered more scathingly than she intended.

He winced. "The boy's name is Miguel. He's not quite 12. He seemed like a good kid. It was his first slip-up. I don't know why, but maybe because I'd just gone on leave from the Posse, I offered to help him." He paused as if searching for words, or maybe he was gauging her reaction.

"How are you helping him?"

"I got a guest pass and brought him to the Rec Center this week. He likes to run and shoot baskets, and I thought if he had something constructive to do, maybe he wouldn't hang out with guys like Raul."

"Who's Raul?"

"The older kid who talked him into a midnight excursion."

"Did you ever catch Raul?"

"No, didn't try, either. I think he's a goner. But Miguel, maybe he can be saved." As he spoke about Miguel, Eric's energy field transformed. It was nearly as clear and bright as in the past, and whatever blocking he'd been doing was gone. Lydia was speechless. He seemed to take it as a negative reaction and changed the subject. "What have you been doing lately?"

"Well, Jean and Ian and I are going to Denver for that training next week, and we're planning a big psychic fair for May. We hope it will draw in people who might be interested in what we offer."

"I'm sure it will be well-attended." Eric then devoted his attention to his food. Lydia wasn't sure how to interpret what had happened. He was being nice, but not acting like he wanted anything from her. Disappointed, she began to eat, the food like sawdust in her mouth. She spent the rest of the meal talking mostly with Jean, who sat on her right side.

The barbecue was a big success at making Julio feel welcome, and it was nearly 6:30 before the last people left. Eric had escaped soon after dessert. The others trickled home in pairs. Lydia told them not to worry, she'd help Barbara and Ben clean up. A surprisingly short time later, Barbara turned on the loaded dishwasher while Lydia wiped the long counter. Ben had left them alone to talk. He didn't miss much.

"So tell me about Eric."

Lydia continued to scrub the counter as tears welled up in her eyes.

"I wish I knew exactly what was going on. He hasn't been the same with me since the attack. The distance bothered me a lot. I could tell he was holding out on me, but somehow, he was blocking me from reading much, and I don't know what he's hiding. I began to worry he wanted to dump me, but didn't have the guts. The last straw was when I invited him to go to the tapping training with us, he got all huffy about letting me pay for it. I can afford it, and he can't. I got mad that he made an issue of it and walked out on him. He hasn't tried to make up, and neither have I. I feel like it's up to him. Do you think I'm wrong?"

Barbara's brown eyes shone with concern. "I'm sorry, Lydia. I like Eric, and he seemed so good for you. What other man would go to a yoga class?...So that's why he didn't come to class this week?" Barbara shook her head sympathetically. "Being knifed, nearly killed, is a life-changing experience. You said he's struggling with post traumatic stress, but you indicated he was improving. How upset is he about his condition?"

"Very. He doesn't like to feel out of control."

"Who would? I feel sorry for him. But I also feel sorry for you. If there's anything I can do, let me know."

Lydia nodded, her eyes brimming. "Thanks. I appreciate it." She wiped her tears away. "Not trying to change the subject, but there's something I need to talk to you about. Something I've seen in your aura that I think you should know about."

Worry stole into Barbara's eyes. "Something bad?" She self-consciously reached up to her short auburn hair. Lydia found it interesting that Barbara's hand kept going to the very spot that had Lydia worried.

"I don't want you to borrow trouble, but I think it would be wise to do something about it. There's a small blank spot near your left temple. Where your hand is now. That in itself isn't bad, but it means something is out of balance, and if not corrected, I think it could develop into something physical. I don't think it's physical yet."

"What should I do about it?"

"I don't want to sound like I'm selling my services. I wouldn't take money from you, anyway. But I suggest you get a treatment or two or whatever it takes to restore your energy field's integrity. And don't be afraid. It isn't something to worry about yet."

Barbara seemed to calm down, as the green began to seep back into dominance in her energy field. "Of course, I'm happy to pay, Lydia. You don't have to do things for me for free."

"Anyone who was here today doesn't pay. I insist."

Barbara relented graciously. "OK. Thanks. What type of treatment should I do?"

"I can do some work with crystals on it, and if that doesn't clear it up, we can bring Jean and Ian in."

"It's nice to have specialists on call. Shall I make an appointment to come to your office?" She turned to look at the calendar that hung in the kitchen near the phone.

"That might give us some practice. Things have been a little slow."

Barbara laughed. "It won't be that way for long." Then she hesitated. "Now that you mention it, I have been getting headaches lately, and I'm not usually prone to them. Aspirin seems to help, but now I wonder if it's connected to what you are seeing."

"It could be. Don't put off letting me help you. You have my card. Call and make an appointment any time you like. We aren't that busy." She hugged Barbara. "I've decided I really need to talk to Emma about my vision, because now that we are advertising, it's only a matter of time before she finds out, and I don't want her to feel I kept it from her. So wish me luck."

Barbara gave Lydia an encouraging squeeze. "I don't think there will be any problem. Good luck."

Lydia gathered her things and headed next door. Emma let her in and showed her into the living room. Julio wasn't in evidence. "Please have a seat. Can I get you a cup of tea?"

"No, thanks, I won't stay long. I thought this might be a good time to share something about me with you."

Emma sank into the couch next to Lydia, her eyebrows drawn together in question.

"We've known each other a while now, and I'm going to take a chance and tell you something about me that people don't always react well to."

Curiosity was evident in Emma's face, but she said nothing.

"You see, I have this...ability, you might say, this way of seeing more than the average person does when they look at things. Everything has a field of energy around it. People, animals, plants, even objects. I see those fields, and I can tell a lot by looking at them. I can see health problems, emotions, I can even tell when someone is lying. I try *not* to see things, but it's hard not to at times."

Emma's mouth formed a perfect O. "So what do you see about me?" Everyone's first question, if they accepted what Lydia said was true.

"When I first met you, you were very sad and not nearly as healthy as you are now. Your digestion was a problem, I'm guessing."

Emma nodded in affirmation. "Go on."

"I can tell you had serious trauma in your youth, and that you were afraid of men, especially."

"That's true."

"But you have healed a lot lately. You are much healthier, and you are in love. I can see that clearly. I'm so happy for you." Lydia steeled herself. "Not everyone can stand being around me. I lost a husband over it. He couldn't hide anything from me, and he didn't like that. So when I become friends with someone, I tell them, so they can decide if my vision is a problem for them or not."

"Oh, Lydia, I don't mind. I know you won't tell anyone what you see about me, so I'm fine with it. What did you see about Julio?" She stopped, abashed. "Here I am, asking you to tell me about him, when I wouldn't want you telling others about me. Forget I asked." She looked down at her hands, which were clasped in her lap.

"Emma, you don't have anything to worry about with Julio. He loves you."

Emma's eyes shone with joy. She impulsively threw her arms around Lydia and hugged her. That made Lydia's day.

* * *

Ray, 5:25pm

ANOTHER FIFTEEN MINUTES and they'd be home. Ray gripped the steering wheel tightly, trying to ward off the fears that were threatening to swallow him whole. Alan sat in the passenger seat, uncharacteristically quiet, a pensive look on his round, youthful face. Becky played in the back seat, telling her stuffed rabbit all about her new life. The chattering didn't bother him like he thought it might. He hoped Alan didn't mind.

"What did you think of that plane ride, Becky? Was it your first?" Ray asked.

"Of course it was, silly. I'm only ten, and I've never been anywhere."

Ray grinned. She had spirit. "You can call me Grandpa if you like, because that's who I am."

"Maybe. When I get to know you better. Where have you been all my life if you're my Grandpa?"

"Good question. I didn't know you existed. No one told me. If I had known, I would have been there much sooner." He hoped that was the truth.

Alan gave him a sympathetic glance. "How about we eat out for dinner? I think we're all too tired to cook."

"That sounds like a good idea," said Becky primly while posing her rabbit to look at the scenery speeding by.

Ray reached over and patted Alan's leg. "Thanks for all you're doing. It means the world to me," he whispered.

Alan smiled warmly. "What do you like to eat, Becky?" Alan tossed over the seat.

"I eat anything, but I'm partial to Italian food."

She was so precocious with her manners and vocabulary. Ray wondered where that had come from. "We happen to have a good Italian restaurant near home. We'll eat there. Is that OK, Alan?"

Alan's blue eyes twinkled. "Sure. I love that place. Anything that keeps me from having to wash dishes. I'm positively wrung out."

"I wash dishes. I do lots of things now that I'm big."

Ray and Alan exchanged a look. "You can help around the house if you like. In fact, we're going to need your help." Ray hoped that sounded like they were making a family, not hiring a servant.

"Good. I can do almost anything. I can't lift heavy stuff, but I can do a lot."

"Thanks. Once you get settled, we'll see how we can use your talents." Alan flashed him a crooked grin, and Ray suppressed a laugh.

"Becky, we didn't decorate your room, because we want you to tell us what you like. So don't worry about how it looks now. We'll get it all fixed up for you real soon."

"I like the color pink. And I like animals. Can I have a dog?"

Ray bit his lip and looked at Alan for support. Alan chimed in, "We need to wait a while before we talk about pets. But maybe later on you can have one."

Becky accepted that with good grace. Ray looked at Alan and rolled his eyes. That was a near miss. But he suspected the subject was not closed. Just shelved.

Dinner went well. Becky had proven she had perfect table manners throughout the trip. Her Mom had brought her up right. Too bad he'd never gotten to know her. But at least he was taking care of her little girl. That had to count for something.

Becky's eyes were drooping on the way home, but she roused when they pulled into the garage. They put the baggage down inside the door and took Becky to the living room to look at the twilight view of the golf course. Her eyes popped. "This is so beautiful! I love it. Where's my room?"

Ray took her hand, smiling at how small it was and the way she squeezed his. "Your room is this way. Our room is on that end of the house." He pointed to the left.

They walked down the hall and stopped in the doorway. The guest bedroom was furnished with Arizona antiques which gave it a cowboy look. Pleated shades hid the golf course view. Coincidentally, they were a soft rose color. The closet had mirrored doors, and beside it, a door led to the guest bathroom.

Becky shrieked. It was the first loud noise she'd made. "This is perfect. I love it just the way it is. But can I have a pink bedspread?" She ran over and jumped onto the bed, bouncing as if to test it. Her eyes were wide and shining. "You're going to have to get me a desk, but there's room for that. Do I have my very own bathroom?" She hopped off the bed and raced over to the bathroom. Not pink, but sage green. They could get her pink towels and rugs.

"Yes, that's your bathroom. We have our own, and there's a powder room near the kitchen."

"Can I see the rest of the house? Can I see your room?"

Ray looked at Alan, who nodded. They walked back down the hall, Becky running ahead, skipping occasionally. She nosed into the library room, then went farther down the hall to the master suite. When they caught up with her, she had already gone into the room and seemed to be evaluating it. Then she shot over to the patio door and pressed her face to the glass.

Ray came to stand behind her. "You'll be able to see more tomorrow when the sun comes up. It's quite a view. You can even see the mountains beyond the golf course."

She turned around and inspected the room again. "This is really nice. But why do the two of you have only one room? And there's only one bed in it." Ray knew they'd have to answer that question sooner or later. Alan came over and stood by his side, casting a supportive look his way.

"Alan and I are partners, Becky. We live together because we love each other. You're going to have two Grandpas."

She swallowed it like it was no big deal. "Two Grandpas! I'm the luckiest girl in the world!" She threw her arms around Ray. She looked up with bright blue eyes, then adjusted her arms to encompass both of them. Alan gave Ray the most genuine smile he'd seen in ages, ever since this began. He knew it wouldn't always be this easy, but maybe it would be all right.

5
TUESDAY, APRIL 2, 1996

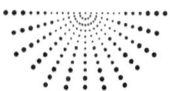

Samantha, 7:00am

*A*s Samantha pulled into a parking space at Temple Landscaping, a whisper of anxiety shivered through her. What if this was a big mistake? Sure, she'd make more money, but how was she going to deal with the attraction she felt for Jack? If only he didn't reciprocate her interest. On Sunday, when she'd brought Beau to his house, the awkwardness was painful. Beau and he seemed to bond instantly, but that only made things worse, as far as she was concerned. She loved Beau, and it meant another connection with Jack. She'd managed to escape without saying or doing anything stupid. She just hoped she could maintain the distance.

She braced herself and walked into Jack's office, only to have Beau rush over, tail wagging his whole body. She leaned down to pet him. "How you doin', big boy? You like living with Jack?"

"Living with me is fantastic. You should try it." Dressed in his trademark black, Jack gazed at her with mischievous, dark eyes.

Samantha tried to continue petting Beau without commenting, but then changed her mind. "I know it's my first day on the job, and I don't want to alienate my new boss, but that's a suggestive comment that doesn't belong in a conversation with an employee. I'd prefer if you didn't tease me that way." She didn't have the nerve to look him in the eye, so she kept petting Beau. She knew she sounded holier-than-thou, and she felt hypocritical pretending she wasn't attracted to him. But if there was any hope of keeping it platonic, she had to set boundaries.

"You're right. Sorry. I didn't mean to be offensive. It slipped out before I could think about it. Welcome to Temple Landscaping. I gave you the tour some time back, but now we need to familiarize you with your duties. Shall we head out?"

She finally looked up into the black of his eyes. He wasn't beautiful, really. But he was devastatingly handsome in a rough way. His chiseled features and prominent nose and cheekbones lent him a Native American vibe, accentuated by his long, shiny black hair, which was tied in a ponytail. *Quit mooning over the man, stupid.* "Before we go, do you mind if I ask how Beau is adjusting to his new life?"

"It's only been two nights, but he's a great dog and seems to love my place. I have a big fenced yard, and he has done really well this morning. I tested him on basic commands yesterday, because I didn't want to take a chance on him running off into traffic. He seems to have no inclination to wander, which is helpful. I think it's going to work out fine. You're always welcome to come visit."

"Thanks. I wanted to report to Mom. She misses him so much, but it will help her to know he's got a good life."

"He and I are going to be best buds, aren't we, Beau?"

The big yellow lab looked at Jack and then barked once.

"I guess that settles it," said Samantha. "I'm glad it's working out. If you have any problems, you need to let me know. I promised Mom he wouldn't end up at the shelter. I'll take him if you change your mind."

"You said Arthur doesn't like dogs."

"That's true, and we don't have a fenced yard. But I'll take him rather than put him in a shelter. I love him, and I promised Mom."

"Don't worry, it's going to be fine." Jack stood up, and Beau mirrored his action. It was charming to see how quickly he'd taken to Jack.

Jack led her to the back lot and pointed at a small red pickup. "That's your vehicle." It was a fairly new, well-kept small pickup truck that had a magnetic sign on the door which said 'Temple Landscaping' with a phone number. "Can you drive a stick?"

Samantha mock-glared at him. "Of course I can. Are you asking that because you think women don't drive manual transmission cars? My first car was a 1965 Beetle with a stick shift."

He flashed his bad boy grin. "OK, OK. You got me. I probably wouldn't have asked a guy. But in my defense, I can't make myself treat you like a guy, since you are *so* obviously not one."

He'd deftly turned the subject around. The fluttering in her stomach was a warning. This was getting way too close to flirting. She better keep it purely professional. "I'll need to get Arthur to drive me to work one day so I can pick it up, since you're letting me take it home."

"That's not necessary. Me and one of the guys will follow you home with it today."

Samantha's stomach tightened. "No, don't do that."

"Why not?"

Was he really that clueless? "Arthur is beginning to wonder why you're being so nice to me. The less he sees you do for me, the better."

Jack frowned. "You haven't done anything wrong, Sam."

Did he mean the diminutive to sound so intimate? No one else called her Sam, not even Arthur. "I know that, but I think he picked up on my feelings and concerns. And that's making him suspicious."

"I'm sorry if it's uncomfortable for you. Is there anything I can do to help?"

"Like I said, the less, the better. Treat me like your least favorite employee."

"I'm not that good an actor." He flashed white teeth in a giant smile. God, he was attractive.

"Just do your best. I'll get Arthur to drive me to work tomorrow. He hasn't got anything planned. But thanks for offering." Samantha went up to the truck, leaned in and saw it was immaculately clean and very low mileage. "This is nice. Thanks a lot. I'm going to enjoy it. And red. I like having something other than white, though they say red takes a beating in the desert sun. I'll have it in the garage, though, so that will help."

Jack handed her the keys. "Well, you're good to go with wheels. Now let's go through and introduce you to the crews and then we'll go back to my office and look at how we assign jobs. It's pretty straightforward, probably a lot like Palo Verde."

The rest of the day was a blur. She met a lot of people, and remembering names was never her strong suit, plus many of the guys didn't speak much English. It was good she had a modicum of Spanish, but to do this job better, she should brush up some more. Everyone was pleasant and welcoming. She found that in spite of trepidation about her ability to deliver what Jack wanted on the job, she was excited to be given so much responsibility and creative freedom.

She saw very little of Jack during the afternoon, which suited her fine. Maybe it wouldn't be so hard to work with him. He had hired her so he could shift his focus, and she was going to operate independently for the most part. He was also eager for her feedback and suggestions, which was a welcome change from Palo Verde.

The commute home that afternoon highlighted the down side of her new job. Before, it was a quick 7-minute drive to get home; now it was 30-40 minutes in heavy traffic. But Jack let her go home early every day and still paid her for 40 hours a week, so she couldn't complain. The money, the freedom and being treated like a valued employee made it worth the effort.

Thinking about money, she'd decided she wanted to put some aside. She needed to bring that up with Arthur. They had so little for emergencies or when she finally retired. She dreaded talking to him about it. It would be hard to hide her annoyance that he'd never provided for her in case he died. Her mother's financial troubles had taught her a lesson, and she was going to take action.

Thinking about Mom caused her to droop. She needed to stop by Desert Breezes on the way home and see how Mom was settling in. Mom would be struggling in the unfamiliar surroundings. She'd forgotten to tell Arthur she was going to see Mom on the way home, but he'd just have to suck it up.

Later that evening, Samantha sat in the living room with Arthur. The TV played low in the background as he sipped a beer and Samantha was working on a glass of white wine.

"So how was your first day?" His interest seemed forced, but at least he was trying.

"It's going to be a great job. I have so much more freedom and power there. I'll basically be doing what Julio used to do at Palo Verde. And finally getting paid for it. Which reminds me, I think it would be wise to take a certain amount of my paycheck and put it aside for the future. We don't have much saved. I don't want to end up like Mom."

Arthur's brown eyes were unreadable. "I know I'm older than you, but I'm in good shape. We have a long time before we have to worry about that sort of thing."

"There are no guarantees. You and I don't even have life insurance. What happened to Mom has made me aware that you need a nest egg or something to fall back on. I'm not saying save all the difference, but put some of it aside, or maybe consider life insurance and use it to pay the premiums. I don't know; I'd feel better if we had a cushion of some kind."

"OK. I'll look into it."

That had gone surprisingly well. She rolled her head in a circle, feeling the aches from having schlepped the furniture and all those boxes up to Mom's new place and suddenly realized how tired she was.

Arthur watched with concern. "Are you sore from the move yesterday?"

"A little bit, but I'll live. You were a big help. Now I can focus on preparing Mom's house for sale. Mary Beth's going to help me with emptying it, and I'll need to spend some evenings and weekends doing that if we want to get it on the market fast, which we need to do." She sighed, overwhelmed by how much work was left.

"Do you want me to help?" He didn't sound sincere, but at least he asked.

"I'll let you know if Mary Beth and I need help. But I was thinking of doing an estate sale to get rid of most of it, after I've seen what's what, so hopefully, there won't be any more moving. You know, there's stuff in the garage I've never laid eyes on. Handmade rag rugs that might have been my Grandma's. Old china. I'll need to check with Mom to see what the history is and what it might be worth before I call in the estate sale folks."

"Hmmm," he said noncommittally. "Well, let me know. I realize you have your hands full with a new job and all this for your mother."

"That's for sure. But I'll get through it." She swallowed some wine and closed her eyes.

"What's the news on Beau? Did you see him today?"

"Yes, he came to work with Jack. He's behaving well and seems quite happy. I think it's going to work out. That's one problem we don't have to resolve."

"Thank heaven for small favors. And your Mom? I'm almost afraid to ask."

Samantha sighed. "You know Mom. Change isn't easy for her. But she has to make the best of it. I'm doing what I can. I think Desert Breezes is a nice place. I hope she can adapt. And I hope she has time to enjoy it before her health collapses completely. I think we got her in there just in time. She isn't moving around well at all. I'm going to have to get her a walker before long, and she isn't going to like that." Feeling grim, Samantha decided to go to bed. "I'm beat. I'm going to hit the sack."

"OK. Sleep well." Arthur continued to drink his beer and fixed his attention on the TV.

* * *

Lydia, 9:10am

LYDIA SCRUTINIZED her reflection in the mirrored closet door. Her hair was still shiny and wavy, but there were circles under her eyes, and she couldn't deny that she had gained weight recently. Ice cream and chocolate were her new substitutes for a lover. Annoyed that her face looked puffy, she grimaced and lectured herself. "Get over him. If he wanted you, he'd have come back. Quit wallowing in self-pity." After she gave up on the pep talk, she drove to the office, where Ian and Jean were waiting to have a business meeting.

As she entered the office, she detected an air of heaviness. When she went into the meeting room, it was apparent from their auras that Ian and Jean had been having a serious talk that was making them sad. *Oh no.*

"What's up? Did someone die?" Maybe she shouldn't kid about that in a retirement community.

Ian didn't respond, leaving it to Jean to say, "We were talking about how little we seem to be making. We get appointments, but nowhere near enough to pay the bills. It's depressing."

"It takes time to build a business. We talked about this two weeks ago. We need to give it time," Lydia said with conviction, but she knew by looking at Jean and Ian that they were less than convinced. "I know we've only had a trickle of business, but we shouldn't borrow trouble. At the class later this week, we're getting certified in a method that works for a lot of problems, and when we get back, we'll advertise the heck out of the Psychic Fair and make it the event of the season for Palm Lakes."

Jean grinned, the worry slipping away. "Oh, Lydia, you are so positive. I wish I could be."

"Me, too," chimed Ian. "I suppose I thought it would take off faster. Do you think this is a bad market for us?"

"That's a good question. Jean and I know that classes sell here. But, I wasn't able to look into profitability. I honestly believe we can sell classes. Whether we can do them for a price or a frequency that generates enough income, I don't know. I think the key is going to be flexibility. We need to find out what people want, and we need to provide it at a good price. I have high hopes for the Psychic Fair. I was thinking rather than charge to attend, which might put people off, maybe we could give them a few tickets when they come in, and the tickets are good for certain things. A mini-reading with Jean, for example. They will be able to sample only a small amount of things for free, but buying additional tickets at a crazy low price will be easy, and that could help offset expenses."

"That might work," allowed Jean, "but I don't have a feel for pricing. What would they feel is a fair price? I get all knotted up when I try to think about it, and I can't dowse, because I'm too invested in the outcome." She sighed, and Ian reached over and put his arm around her shoulders.

Lydia knew she needed to project success, but she couldn't lie. "All we can do is imitate successful events as best we can. I know we don't have all the data, but I still think the Psychic Fair idea is going to be a hit. How we stay visible to them after that, I don't know."

Ian was quietly ruminating. His eyes lit up. "I've got it! We can sign them up for our newsletter. I know we don't have one, but what I mean is we can do a monthly newsletter. I know not all of them will have email, but some do. We were planning on having business cards with our contact details to hand out, and that's good, but to stay in touch, we need to get their permission to write them. We could then send them free information that helps them and maybe occasionally do a discount coupon for something. I can look into free software for doing that."

"Oh, I like that idea. You're a gem, Ian." Jean hugged and kissed him.

Lydia got a lift from their enthusiasm. "Now you're talking. That is a great idea. Other advertising is costly. This would be targeted and very inexpensive. Of course it means more work for you, Ian, because Jean and I are computer illiterate." He waved a hand, brushing off her concern. She could tell he liked having another way to contribute.

"So let's talk about when to have the Fair."

Ian jumped in. "We need time to plan and recover from the tapping course, so I suggest May."

"I agree." Lydia gazed at the Arizona Highways calendar that hung on the wall. "Do you like a weekend for the Fair?"

"Yes," said Jean. "But not Sunday. I think Saturday would be best."

"What Saturday does everyone feel will work best?" Jean and Ian went silent. Jean was obviously dowsing for an answer. Ian seemed to be, also.

A minute later, Jean looked over at Ian. "I get Saturday, May 18th is best by a hair for our goals. What did you get, Ian?"

"The same."

Lydia smiled. "I like it. That gives us enough time to plan it and advertise." She stood up and wrote "Psychic Fair" on the calendar for that date. "Now all we have to do is sort out exactly what we're doing and how we'll advertise."

She sat back down, grateful for something to occupy her mind. This was going to be a challenging event and possibly a turning point in their business. She needed to give it her entire attention, even though Eric was never far from her mind. At least the need to focus on the business dispelled much of the self-pity that was haunting her. They plunged into the details of the event.

* * *

Catherine, 9:30am

WHEN CATHERINE WOKE up with a start, the large red numbers on the clock said 9:30. She'd never slept that late before, although she hadn't been rising with the sun the way she used to. Maybe she was just winding down. She lay there working herself up to getting out of bed. The pain in her joints made it a trial. Wouldn't it be great if she had a bed that could pour her out without dropping her on the floor? Giggling at the picture it made in her mind, she rolled to her side and then scrambled awkwardly out of bed.

Even though she'd been cautious as she rose, a faintness overcame her, and she fell back into a sitting position on the bed. Worse, her head was throbbing, and that nagging pain in her side had gotten more obnoxious. Getting old was no fun at all.

On the next try, she managed to reach a standing position without any weakness, so she trundled into the bathroom and started her morning ritual. She avoided looking in the mirror, as the person who stared back at her bore no resemblance to the woman she remembered being. The reflection would show a short, dumpy, wrinkly old woman with faded blue eyes and hair instead of the vibrant, petite woman she had been at 35. Why did she always think of herself as 35? Another question for which she had no answer.

A strong cup of coffee helped improve her alertness, and she thought about what to make for breakfast. Lately, she hadn't had much of an appetite, not that she was losing weight. And she didn't have the energy to cook. It was lucky Mary Beth brought food and that she could get ready-made meals at Safeway. Back in the day, she loved to cook, but cooking for one was depressing and a lot of work.

Reaching for a banana, she recalled the joke that was making the rounds in Palm Lakes. Whenever someone spoke of doing something in the future, the other person would say, "I can't think that far ahead. I don't even buy green bananas anymore." The first time she'd heard it, she chuckled, but it got old after a few tellings.

The banana ended up being more than she could stomach, so she reluctantly threw the remainder out and poured her pills out of the pillbox. She hated taking pills. But she was regular about it and swallowed them as quickly as possible. *There. Done that for the day. Now what?*

She'd never been an obsessive housekeeper like Mary Beth's mother, but in recent weeks, she'd slacked off even more. Pushing the vacuum around seemed too hard, and she was sick of worrying about dust. She lived in the desert, for God's sake, she ought to learn to live with it. And scrubbing tubs and toilets was pretty much beyond her because of her arthritis. Maybe she ought to hire a housekeeping service, but she didn't want to spend the money. It seemed like something she should do herself. Besides, she didn't like strangers in her space.

She rinsed her coffee mug and dragged herself out to the living room, dropping into the recliner and turning the TV on with the remote. There was nothing to watch, but it made her feel less alone. She glanced at the book on the end table and rejected the idea of reading it. Nothing seemed very attractive lately. The pain in her side rumbled through her again, and she wondered if maybe she should see the doctor. Not so much about the dizziness, but that pain didn't seem right. And she'd always had an appetite in the past. Maybe something was wrong.

She closed her eyes. She felt so tired. Mary Beth was obviously worried about her. That child was so kind. She'd brought such joy to her lonely life. Maybe there was a way she could repay her for her attention and affection. In that moment, she made a decision. She was going to alter her will. It was a simple document, since she had no one to leave things to. She'd go and change the beneficiary to Mary Beth. But how was she going to assure herself that Mary Beth would get her inheritance? Because no one knew that Catherine had over $100,000 in cash secreted in various places in the condo.

Harold had never thought very highly of banks. They'd taken to keeping a nest egg hidden in the house, first in one of the air ducts and later in a wall safe. Here in the condo, she didn't have any good hiding places, so she'd used large jars to stash her cash, and put them at the back of cupboards and cabinets that were chock full of groceries, cans and cleaning goods. No one would ever take a look at her tiny place and think she was rich. She didn't buy nice clothes, didn't have fancy new furniture. She rather liked being surrounded by the things she and Harold had accumulated over the years. It made nice camouflage for her wealth.

So how could she assure herself that Mary Beth would find the cash when she was gone? If she told her about it now, Mary Beth would insist she put it in the bank. And that was not going to happen. Plus, she'd probably argue about Catherine giving it to her. Catherine couldn't contemplate fighting with her over money. But she needed to make sure Mary Beth discovered it. Maybe she could leave a sealed envelope with hints. No. That sounded too much like a treasure hunt. But how could she make sure without tipping her hand too much? She couldn't tell the lawyer about her stash. That would be stupid. Even though James was a nice young man.

Well, it would come to her. She'd have to call a taxi to go to the lawyer. She didn't want Mary Beth to know about it before it was a done deal. And then there was the problem of how to assure Mary Beth got notification when the time came. Mary Beth had no fixed address, so how could she be sure she'd be informed of Catherine's death in a timely fashion? Finally, she settled on giving a copy of the will to Mary Beth along with a sealed envelope containing instructions about the cash, to be opened after her death. That would work.

Her mind made up, Catherine felt much better than she had in days. Yes, she'd call the doctor and make an appointment. And one with the lawyer. The sooner, the better.

* * *

Maddie, 3:30pm

THE KNOCK on the door roused Maddie, who'd been dozing in the recliner. She must have fallen asleep after returning from lunch in the dining room. Slowly dragging herself to her feet, she shuffled towards the door, wondering who it could be. It was too early for Samantha.

Mary Beth stood in the hall, a tentative smile on her face and a casserole dish in her hand.

"Mary Beth! It's good to see you."

The younger woman grinned and stepped inside, pausing to give Maddie a gentle hug.

"What's that in your hand?" Maddie asked.

"What the hell do you think? I made my world-famous lasagna. It's enough for a few meals, so you can cut it up and freeze portions."

"Did you come straight from work?"

"Practically. I had to pick up the lasagna. I made it last night. Show me where you want it."

Maddie pointed to the small refrigerator in her kitchenette. "Put it in there for now. I'll cut it up and freeze it after having it for dinner tonight. I won't have to eat in the dining room. Can you stay for a minute? I can get you a beer or make some coffee."

"I don't need anything to drink, but yes, I can stay. I was so tired after we moved all the stuff in yesterday, I didn't really get a chance to see how it looked. I think it's nice."

Maddie shrugged. How could anyone think this was nice compared to her own home? "I guess it'll do."

Mary Beth spotted the floral arrangement on the small kitchen table. "Who's your admirer?" She leaned over to sniff the flowers, carnations with baby's breath and some ferns. "These smell heavenly."

Maddie harrumphed. "It's a waste of money to send flowers. They just die, and they cost so much. They're from Barbara. We were never close. She shouldn't have done it."

Mary Beth looked at her quizzically. "She can probably afford it, and she only wanted to brighten your day. She knows it's hard to give up your house. How else could she sympathize? I think they're nice."

"Well, I never have liked flowers, not the delivered kind. So often, they bring something that's half dead. I hate seeing people spend that kind of money, and I hate even worse that the flowers they deliver often aren't good. But this is a nice arrangement."

Mary Beth seemed satisfied with her comment. "Samantha coming over today?"

"Yes, she'll help me unpack the few remaining boxes. I'm not sure when she's coming, but she said she'd be here."

Mary Beth wandered over to the sliding glass door that opened onto the tiny balcony with a view of the golf course and the desert and mountains beyond Palm Lakes. "This is a nice view. You were lucky. Many of the rooms look out on the city. Ugh."

"I've already had hummingbirds to the feeder. I sat out early this morning and watched them feed while I had my coffee."

Maddie eased into her recliner, and Mary Beth sat on the couch, her green eyes scanning the room.

"Have you been to the dining room yet?"

"I went for lunch."

"How was it?"

"Oh, so-so. At least I don't have to cook and wash dishes if I don't want to."

Mary Beth grinned. "I know that's a big plus for you. I promise to bring you good food on a regular basis, and I'm sure Samantha will, too, so you won't have to rely on the dining room." Mary Beth brushed a stray strand of wavy dark hair from her face. "When do you think you'll be ready to start up with the jewelry again?"

Maddie felt a rush of warmth. "I was a little tired today, but I'll be ready to get back at it tomorrow. I need Samantha to help me find some of my stuff. We still have to get the shelving for the closet, so that I can find all my materials."

"Then I hope I can come by on Saturday and work with you."

Relief flooded through Maddie. "Yes, of course, you can." She didn't want to admit that she was feeling more lonely here than she ever had at home, in spite of having closer neighbors and help a pressed button away.

Just then there was another knock at the door, and Maddie heard Samantha's voice. "Mom, it's me."

Mary Beth held her hand out to indicate she'd get the door, then shot up and sprinted over to it. Maddie envied her strength and youth. Samantha exclaimed and hugged Mary Beth, and they came back to the living room together.

Samantha looked tired and stressed. Maybe it was because of her first day at the new job and the long commute after moving yesterday. Maddie herself was exhausted, and she hadn't raised a finger. Samantha gave her a hug. "How's it going?"

"OK." She wasn't going to sing the praises of this prison. She missed her home too much.

Mary Beth and Samantha sat together on the couch. They had a nice rapport that pleased Maddie, as if they were sisters. Too bad they wouldn't get to see each other often anymore, now that Samantha had a new job.

Mary Beth looked hard at Samantha. "So how was the first day at the new job?"

"It was tiring, but good. I wanted to tell Mom that Beau was there, and he looked really happy. He minds Jack well, and he's able to be at work with him. Jack says Beau is doing great at home, too. He said he'd bring him by to visit you sometime, if you like."

Maddie hadn't even thought to hope for that. "Will they let me have him in my apartment?"

Samantha nodded. "I checked the rules, and as long as he's up on his shots, he can visit. I don't know when Jack will come. It will have to be a weekend, and I can't promise when. But he seemed sincere, and I told him you'd like that. I said I'd arrange to meet him downstairs and bring him and Beau up, so you don't have to be alone with a stranger."

"I hope he can do it soon. I miss Beau so much." No one could begin to understand how keenly she felt the loss of her dog.

Mary Beth turned to Samantha. "I'm going to be coming to do jewelry on Saturday. Maybe I'll see you if you come over."

Samantha smiled warmly. "That would be nice. I was hoping to pick up the shelving and assemble that on Saturday. I won't be here for too long. There's still a lot to do at Mom's house."

"I can come over and help after your Mom and I finish our jewelry work," said Mary Beth.

The reference to her house plunged Maddie once again into melancholy. A craving for beer overtook her. "Samantha, could you get me a beer? I feel like something cold to drink." She hated being waited on, but the pain was just too much to deal with.

"Sure, Mom." Samantha jumped up. She and Mary Beth were like jack rabbits to Maddie's snail. She used to move that fast; now she could barely walk, and the pain was constant. God, she hated being old.

Samantha quickly poured a Budweiser into a glass, the way Maddie liked it. As she carried it over to Maddie, the foam continued to froth up and a trickle spilled over the rim of the glass and onto the floor. Samantha stepped back and grabbed a paper towel to wipe the glass, and then bent down to mop the floor. "Oh, no, radio beer!"

Maddie wondered what the heck she was talking about. After she mopped up the spill, Samantha grinned at her, almost back to her usual self. "Oh, that's something we said in college. A TV beer has the sweat on the side of the glass, like you see in a commercial. A radio beer has the beer spilling over the top, making a mess. I guess you had to be there." Samantha handed her the now-tamed beer with a twinkle in her eyes.

Maddie took a sip and sighed in pleasure. Now, that was going to help her relax. Then she remembered about Helen. "Helen called today and asked if she could come over. I told her I was a little tired from the move. She said she'll come by later in the week. She knows someone here named Olivia, and she offered to introduce me. Olivia was the previous owner of Helen's dog, Spot. She used to live next door to them. I'm not much of a mixer, but Helen was always so thoughtful, so I said OK. You all moved in to her place now, Mary Beth?"

Mary Beth shook her head. "Almost, but not quite. With helping you move and all, I still have a few things at your place I need to shift over to Helen's casita. But I'm nearly done. I'll return your key to Samantha."

Maddie frowned. It was like Samantha was now the owner of her house. But it didn't pay to complain. Samantha was doing all the work. No one knew how insignificant that made Maddie feel. It was like they put her in this little box and went about dealing with the remains of Maddie's life without consulting her. She suppressed irritation and sipped her beer. She might as well be dead.

* * *

Julio, 3:50pm

JULIO CHECKED the irrigation in their garden plot while Emma pulled weeds. The sun hammered down out of a clear blue sky. The heat never bothered him, but he made sure Emma wore a floppy hat whenever they came to work in the garden, because he was certain her ivory skin would burn easily.

The afternoon sun was slanting golden rays across the community garden plots, illuminating the unique personality of each. Most of the plots were well-tended and had no weeds. Almost all had timers for the irrigation, a necessity in the desert. Theirs had a white picket fence around it, more for decoration than anything else. Rabbits could get over it with ease. The plot next to theirs had a big scarecrow dressed in someone's old clothes. On the other side, a plot had neat stakes with the seed packets skewered on them to identify what had been planted, much the same as he and Emma had done.

He finished his inspection of the irrigation and straightened up, rubbing a kink out of his lower back. On her knees at the end of a row, Emma presented a stimulating image, her loose trousers pulled tight across her backside. He felt himself hardening, a reaction he'd come to accept was going to be the norm. At least for the present. Sometimes he wondered if he had it in him to be with one woman for the rest of his life, but doubts were becoming less frequent.

They had the whole place to themselves. People preferred to come in early morning, when it was cooler, but he had to work, and Emma liked them to do the gardening together. He found it pleasant not having anyone else there. He stalked up behind her, bent down and ran his hand along the curve of her ass with just enough pressure to convey his intentions. She stopped, leaned back and turned around, her amazing blue eyes peering at him sharply from behind sunglasses. "I'm trying to work here."

"I am trying to do something, too," he said meaningfully.

The smile that split her face was filled with promise. "I'm almost done, and then we can go home. I haven't heard about your day. You'll have to tell me."

"I'd rather show you something."

Her eyes narrowed. "I know what you want to show me. I've seen it already today." The teasing was something new, and he liked it.

"I want to show you again."

She rolled her eyes. "Well, if you insist." She reached down and pulled the remaining weeds from that row, then rose to her feet with grace and glided towards the car, pulling off her gloves. He ran to catch up.

Back home--he'd begun to think of it as home--he swept her into his arms the minute they got inside. She pulled back. "I'm all dirty and sweaty."

"So am I."

"I want a shower."

He could work with that. "Only if we shower together."

Her eyes widened as she divined his intentions. "All right."

After the shower, they lay naked on the bed, totally sated. "I think I need another shower."

"Is that a hint?" He leaned towards her and kissed her soundly.

"No, I don't have the energy right now."

He drew lazy circles around her right nipple, watching the shivers race across her skin in response.

"How was your day?"

He didn't stop what he was doing. "The fliers and ad are working. I picked up a new client this morning, Canadians who are leaving at the end of the month. I like working with Canadians. They're easier to please than Americans."

She snorted. "You like me, and I'm not Canadian." She reached over and caressed him. She seemed to revel in her ability to arouse him.

"I don't like you. I love you."

She squeezed him by way of reply, and he almost jumped on her, but she wasn't quite that playful yet, and he didn't want to push it. Instead, he just enjoyed the rhythm of her hand stroking him.

She stopped what she was doing. "It's time you moved in with me. You can quit paying rent on your apartment. It's a waste of money."

"Please do not stop."

"Not until you say you're moving in with me."

He took her hand gently and tried to coax her back to what she'd been doing, but she was stubborn. "We have talked about this before. Are you sure you are ready to let the whole neighborhood know we are a couple?"

"I'm sure." She said it with such conviction, his heart thumped.

"Even so, it is a very big decision."

"I'm ready if you are."

That was the problem. There were so many impediments. The worst fear he had was that he might not be able to sustain how he felt. The more intertwined their lives were, the harder it would be on her if the relationship fell apart.

"I worry about the future." He didn't want to express all his fears, but he didn't want her to think he didn't love her enough.

"We can't control the future. I want to live for now. Will you do it?"

Then she began to stroke him gently again. She never bargained for what she wanted. He'd never known anyone like her. So be it. "I will move in with you."

Then he slowly rolled towards her and wrapped her in his arms.

* * *

Eric, 5:10pm

THE ICE TINKLED MUSICALLY as Eric swirled the liquid in the glass. He didn't put ice in his scotch unless it was a blistering day. But it wasn't only the heat outside that was scorching him. He was royally pissed off at himself for going to Barbara's party. What the hell had he been thinking? He hadn't. He was simply desperate to see Lydia, so when Barbara had called, he jumped at the chance without thinking of the consequences. Being with her had only made him more frustrated with his situation, and he could tell he'd hurt her feelings. As if he hadn't hurt her enough already. What an asshole he was!

He gulped the rest of his drink. Lately, he was knocking back at least three scotches a night. His Dad had been a cop, too, and when he retired, he had descended quickly into surly alcoholism, something that Eric had promised himself he would never do. But quitting the Posse--and he had to admit it, he was done with the Posse--had taken a real toll. Lydia walking out on him was the coup de grace. The only thing keeping him afloat now was the kid.

Today, he'd had his second outing with Miguel, and the boy was so active that it simultaneously lifted and drained him. He'd never been around kids much, and the boy was charming and intelligent. But keeping up with him was a challenge. The only time he went to the Rec Center now was with Miguel, and he had to do what the kid wanted then. He really needed to get back to working out, but he had no energy or motivation.

He picked up the phone and ordered pizza, knowing that if he kept this up much longer, he was going to end up as unfit as other retired cops he knew. Eating, drinking and listening to music that matched his despondency was about all he did anymore.

For some reason, after dark was the hardest time. It was in the evenings that he was most tempted to call Lydia, to ask her to come back to him. He knew exactly what she wanted, and he wanted to give it to her, but unless he could be sure this post traumatic stress was licked, he couldn't take the chance of becoming a burden.

He remembered how awful it was for his Mom, caring for an alcoholic man until he drank himself into a grave. The burden had aged her and turned her bitter. He couldn't do that to Lydia. He knew if he spilled his guts about his worries, Lydia would argue with him. Which was exactly why he'd kept his concerns to himself. He needed to sort out his mental health problem, if that was even possible, before he apologized. So night after night, he held back from calling her.

He was floating in a scotch buzz when the doorbell rang, announcing his pizza had arrived. After gobbling it down without tasting much, he poured himself a third scotch, adding a few more ice cubes. The question kept replaying through his mind, "What can I possibly do to make my life livable?" It seemed like everything that mattered had been taken away from him.

He sat for minutes, and the minutes blended together. The question had become a sort of mantra, the glass in his hand forgotten. Suddenly, he jerked himself back to present time. Looking down, he could see the ice had melted. He'd lost his taste for scotch. Setting the glass aside, he instantly knew what he was going to do. He was going to put together a program for at-risk boys here in Palm Lakes.

It sounded insane, but it felt right. He loved spending time with Miguel. It made him regret not having had kids. A flash of sadness about his ex-girlfriend Sally intruded into his thoughts. He remembered the wonder of feeling the unborn child kick inside her. Even though it was another man's child, he'd been willing to marry her, but she'd rejected him. After it was over, he realized the kid was what he most missed about their relationship. Sally would have been all wrong for him, unlike Lydia, who was perfect. *Don't go there.*

He wasn't religious, but maybe this was God giving him another chance. He was fond of Miguel, and he had to admit it boosted his ego to have the boy looking up to him. This would be a way to make a difference, to help more than one child. Volunteerism was huge in Palm Lakes, and there was no program like that. He could attract people who would be willing to share their time and gifts with kids who might slip between the cracks and go bad. It would be a big project, and he wasn't sure he had all the talents required, but just thinking about it created a rush of enthusiasm, a feeling of being alive again, a sense of purpose. He had to give it a try.

His heart felt full for the first time since Lydia had walked out. He'd need to find people with the right talents to make this work. But if he did, it would be a much bigger contribution than his work with the Posse, and it would occupy his time and keep him from getting derailed by his mental health problems. He picked up the empty pizza box, grabbed his glass and went to to kitchen, where he dumped the remaining scotch, rinsed the glass and then put the trash in the big bin after crushing the box to size. This could work. It had to work.

* * *

Mary Beth, 5:15pm

MARY BETH PULLED into the three-car garage at Helen and Alexander's golf course mansion. As the garage door went down, she grabbed the two bags of groceries she'd picked up on the way back from visiting Maddie. Spot was barking madly on the other side of the door. She stared at the door for a minute before going through, still uncomfortable that the only route to the casita from the garage was through the house and out the front door. It wasn't a long trek, but it felt like such an invasion of their privacy.

Helen sounded off the minute Mary Beth knocked and stepped into the house. "Is that you, Mary Beth?"

"Yes, it's me, Helen." She walked to the kitchen door, reaching down to pet Spot with her free hand on the way. There was no sign of Fido, but he wasn't very sociable. Helen was chopping veggies at the island. "Helen, I have to say I don't feel comfortable having to come through your living space every time I arrive and depart. It just isn't right."

"Oh, nonsense, Mary Beth. It's no trouble at all. You scoot around the corner and out the front door and down the sidewalk to the casita. We have to keep your car off the street."

"You may not mind, but maybe Alexander does."

Helen stopped chopping and looked at her sharply. Her strawberry blonde hair was held back with a cloth headband, and she was casually dressed in yellow capri pants and a sleeveless orange top. She put the knife down and came over to Mary Beth. "Why are you so uncomfortable?"

Mary Beth cast about for an answer. "Well, what if Alexander took it into his head to have you on the dining room table just when I was returning from work? You have a right to do whatever you want in your house."

Helen's laughter was liquid silver. "Oh, Mary Beth, you do have a vivid imagination. I'll make sure I warn Alexander that we can't make love on the dining room table or in the kitchen while you're living here. I think we can manage to restrict our activity to the bedroom. And maybe the bathroom." The twinkle in Helen's eyes said it all. She was one happy lady.

"Go ahead, make me jealous. If you're sure, I'll keep using this route. It just doesn't seem right to me."

"We want you to keep a low profile, so you need to park in the garage. And really, this house is so big, you aren't putting a crimp in our love life. Trust me."

"Don't tease me, or I'll ask for a glass of wine and a full report."

"Alexander won't be home for a while. Come on in after you put your groceries away. We'll have a glass like the old days."

Mary Beth brightened up at the chance to spend time with her old friend. "OK. I'll be back right back."

Minutes later, they clinked glasses and sipped an expensive cabernet sauvignon. "This is way better than what I used to bring to your house. I like living here. It makes me feel rich."

"Me, too," said Helen. "I am really enjoying learning about and trying different wines. Alexander is so knowledgeable--I've learned so much from him."

"Yeah, he can teach me anything he wants to--just kidding. I'm jealous you have such a babe for a husband. But it's so great to see you happy. How's your novel coming?"

Helen frowned. "Slowly. But it's getting there. Sometimes it practically writes itself, and other times I stare and stare, begging the words to come. I think I'm halfway through. I haven't let Alexander read it yet, but I will eventually. I need to work up the courage."

"I'd like to read it when you're through."

Helen smiled warmly. "I'll be sure to give you a copy."

"On another note, I went by Maddie's new place today and took her some lasagna. She likes my cooking, and I thought it might ease her through her transition."

"I spoke with her and arranged to come by later this week. I thought maybe she'd like to meet Olivia. I know she isn't one to socialize, but knowing a few people might take the edge off the newness. Olivia is really down to earth and nice."

"Maddie's so eccentric, it's hard for her to keep friends. She tends to alienate them with her outspoken ways."

Helen paused in thought. "She's pretty direct, but I never minded it. I know she means no harm. Enough about Maddie. Tell me about you. When do we get to meet Ethan, and what's going on with you two?"

"Damn, girl, why does everyone want to ask me that? I wish I knew. Hell if I know. It might be love. But he's older than I am, and that brings all kinds of problems. He's afraid he's too old. And what will his kids think? And then, I haven't told him, but the one time we went to bed--"

"You slept with him?" Helen interjected.

"Just the once."

"Was it nice? You don't have to tell me if you don't want to."

"You're so considerate, Helen. It was better than nice. I'm no expert, and it has been a long dry spell since my divorce, so maybe that colored my perception, but, yes, it was good. My ex, the asshole, was always rushing to the main event. Ethan spent a lot of time on foreplay, and I can really dig that. He's a generous lover."

"You should snap him up."

"The same thought occurred to me. But other thoughts have also occurred to me. Like, even though he's such a generous lover, I noticed the wrinkles on his face when we were in bed, and for some reason they remind me about the age difference, and I wonder if maybe it's a mistake. And then I question my own motives. I am so weary of being shunted from one place to another, never having my own home, wondering about my future, that I have to ask myself if I really care about him, or maybe I'm just tired of being at loose ends and having no financial future. Plus he reminds me so much of my Dad, whom I loved, but it seems a bit weird. Shit, I don't know what to do. Oh, and then the one time he took me to his house, it was plastered with family pictures, and one of his wife was on the bedside table. Doesn't that seem odd? It did to me. Sorry, I'm rambling."

Helen smiled sympathetically. "Look, just take it one day at a time. Sometimes thinking too much is a mistake. Why don't you invite him over for a drink with us tonight after dinner? He might be more comfortable visiting while we're gone if he knows us and knows we welcome him."

"That would be fantastic! I'll call him as soon as I go back to the casita."

They finished their wine and Mary Beth rushed back to phone Ethan.

"Ethan, it's me. I know it's short notice, but Helen and Alexander would like to have a drink with us tonight at their place. Are you free?"

"Sure. What time?"

"Seven. I'll give you directions." She waited while he got something to write with and took down the directions.

"Should I bring anything?"

"No, this is their party, so to speak. I think they want you to feel comfortable visiting me here. They're really nice."

"OK, I'll see you at seven."

They said their goodbyes, and Mary Beth sat on the love seat, contemplating the latest changes in her life. The casita was by far the biggest space she'd inhabited since her divorce, as well as the most luxurious. Hell, it was the nicest place she'd ever lived. The garden tub in the bathroom was jetted. She felt like she was living at a spa. None of the furniture had seen a minute of use. The kitchen was loaded with dishes and cooking implements. She wondered if Helen and Alexander had done that just for her. It was like a model home. She was a little afraid to kick back and relax. And it was so clean. It would have made her mother smile to see how clean it was. No way could she keep it looking like this, no matter how hard she tried. She trusted Helen not to mind. In fact, Helen seemed eager to have her there.

Helen was a true friend. If she hadn't offered her this place, Mary Beth had no idea what she would have done. Probably go rent an apartment she couldn't afford. Palm Lakes felt like home now, and she didn't want to leave, even though she was too young to live here alone. She hoped her affection for Ethan wasn't tied up with her desire to have a legitimate place in Palm Lakes. He was such a good man. He didn't deserve to be taken advantage of.

She went into the bedroom, casting a glance at the boxes still lined up along the wall. Her jewelry stuff was in one of them. She'd need to unpack at least that one before she went to Maddie's on Saturday.

Should she invite Ethan to spend the night? If she did, it meant she was committing to him more. If she didn't, he'd be hurt and wonder if she was toying with him. *Shit. Fuck. Damn.* She wished she had a crystal ball, because the future seemed lost in fog, and she wasn't sure what path to take.

She stripped her clothes off and hopped in the shower, turning the head to the pulse setting to let the water pound the worry away. It was so soothing, she lost track of time. She dried off and dressed in clean clothes. Nothing fancy. Just nice shorts and a halter top. She brushed her thick hair in front of the bedroom mirror, noticing that she'd slimmed down since she'd arrived in Palm Lakes. She'd been afraid quitting smoking would pack on the pounds, but it hadn't worked out that way. She rarely craved a cigarette, and the circles she'd once sported under her eyes were long gone. Her eyes were her best feature in her opinion. A rare shade of light green, almost like a cat's. She smirked at herself, then put on some makeup and jewelry and went to the kitchen for a snack.

She didn't feel like eating a full dinner. Some cheese and crackers would do.

When the clock said it was nearly seven, she went to the big house. She rang the bell and went in without waiting for someone to answer. Alexander strode out of the kitchen. A warm smile graced his face. "Hi, Mary Beth. Ethan isn't here yet. I was just opening the wine. I have a couple bottles I wanted you all to taste."

"Good wine is wasted on me, Alexander, but I won't say no." As she followed him into the kitchen, she saw Helen putting together a tray of nibbles. "Oh my God, you guys are spoiling me. This looks like restaurant quality."

"We love to cook. It's fun for us." Helen looked so at home now. You'd never know that she'd had trouble adjusting to life on the golf course with a husband who looked like a movie star.

The movie star in question walked over to Helen and leaned down to nuzzle her neck. They were perfect for each other, practically an advertisement for a happy retirement. She was suppressing a twinge of envy when the doorbell rang.

"That must be Ethan," she said.

Alexander walked past her to the front door and let Ethan in. Mary Beth was close behind, not wanting him to be too overwhelmed by everything.

"Welcome, Ethan. Come in." Alexander turned to Mary Beth and winked, his emerald eyes alight. Ethan followed him in, looking around awestruck at the beautiful decor and art and giving Alexander the once over. Ethan was dressed in plaid shorts and a white polo shirt. Black socks and sandals completed the outfit. Mary Beth grinned at his sartorial splendor. He was no Alexander--she didn't think she'd ever seen Alexander in shorts, but he'd never wear black dress socks with sandals, she was sure of that. There was something endearing about Ethan's cluelessness.

She wound her arm through Ethan's as they walked into the great room, where the view across the golf course to the mountains beyond was enhanced by a typically spectacular desert sunset. The reds and golds splashed across the sky like a fine painting.

"Wow, this is some view you have," murmured Ethan.

Alexander stood with his arm around Helen, soaking up the beauty. "We love it. Every night it's different. Better than TV. Have a seat."

Ethan and Mary Beth sat on the love seat, and Helen and Alexander took places on the couch. Helen flashed a grin at Ethan. "It's nice to meet you, Ethan. Mary Beth and I have been friends for some time, and I've heard how kind and supportive you've been to her. She's been through a lot in the past year."

Ethan colored in embarrassment. "I haven't done much. We like to hang out, and it grew from there." He threw a pleading look at Mary Beth. She could tell he wasn't sure what to say about their relationship.

"Ethan and I are trying to get to know each other better, to see where things are going with us. We get along really well, but I'm afraid to rush into anything, and so I've asked Ethan if we can take it slow." She turned to him and gave him a reassuring smile. "It will be wonderful to have a private place where we can spend time. I can't thank you enough for letting me stay here, and I promise I won't overstay my welcome. I'm really looking forward to housesitting for you."

"It's turned out perfect for us that you could do it and be so flexible. This way, we don't have to stick to a rigid schedule." Alexander reached over and squeezed Helen's hand. "I can't wait to show Helen France."

Helen smiled shyly, love pouring out her eyes. That's what I want to feel, thought Mary Beth. She wondered if it would ever happen to her.

"Ethan, we want you to visit as often as you like and feel free to spend the night if Mary Beth wishes. Our house is your house."

Ethan looked gratefully at Helen. "It's nice of you to be so hospitable. You have a lovely home. And I second what Mary Beth said. Having somewhere private to visit is great. I haven't wanted to invite her too often to my house. You know how the neighbors can be, and I didn't want to start gossip."

Mary Beth rolled her eyes, but said nothing. She hoped that was the only reason he was reluctant to have her spend time at his house.

After a pleasant visit with Helen and Alexander, which mostly involved amusing stories about Spot and Fido, they walked back to her casita, where she showed him around.

"This is really beautiful, Mary Beth. It's like living in a fancy hotel suite."

"That's what I thought. Makes me feel like I'm on vacation."

"You deserve a break. You've been living in single rooms so long. This is just what you need." He walked over to her and put his arms around her. There was a tentative feel to his actions. Like he was afraid of being rebuffed. It made her feel guilty.

She threw her arms around him and kissed him. "Are you going to spend the night?"

"If you ask, I will."

"I'm asking."

After that, things worked out really well.

6

SATURDAY, APRIL 13, 1996

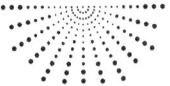

Mary Beth, 11:45am

*M*ary Beth and Samantha sat perusing their menus at a small table in a quiet corner of the Jade Dragon restaurant.

"I think I'll have what I always have," muttered Samantha.

"You don't get tired of Szechuan pork?" Mary Beth grinned at her.

"I'm sure sooner or later, I'll have to try something new, but I love the kick of the spices."

"I'm going to have moo goo gai pan."

"That's not very adventurous." Samantha smiled mischievously.

Mary Beth grimaced. "I'm not really the adventurous sort. In spite of the events of the past year."

Samantha put the menu down and sipped her ice water. "I'm really glad we could get together for lunch. I needed a break."

Mary Beth thought Samantha looked tired, but otherwise was her typical well-put-together self. Her reddish golden hair was in a french braid, and she wore a necklace Maddie must have made. It was a long, double-looped string of carved unakite animals, the marbled green and pinkish stones scattered evenly among smaller clear crystal and gold beads. An unusual piece, it complemented Samantha's coloring perfectly. "You look exhausted, girl."

"Thanks for the compliment."

"Are you glad you took the new job? Is it too much, or are you still recovering from the move and clearing out Maddie's house?"

"Yes. No. And yes. Mom's house is like the Augean stables. I know I'll finish eventually, but she's obstructing me every step of the way, and really, I understand. I can't take a lot of the things she had there. I simply don't have room. And she is dead set against selling it all off. So we're having to compromise and go through lists of what I find. It's hard for her."

"Yeah. I can imagine. She must have felt safe with all her stuff around, and now she's somewhere strange with very few belongings. I know how she feels." She smiled sadly.

Samantha's frown of frustration melted. "I hadn't thought of it that way. You certainly have been through something as bad yourself. It probably helps Mom to know you understand, if she does know. I'm not sure she's aware of much beyond her own circumstances at the moment. She's overwhelmed."

Mary Beth nodded. "I try to bring her food when I come on Saturdays. Today I have lasagna--again. She insists it's her favorite. I figure maybe it will help."

"I bring her homemade soup and bread from my new bread machine. So she isn't having to cook a lot or go to the dining room often. But I don't feel she's happy. Not that she ever was, except maybe when they lived in Moab." Samantha stared off into space for a few seconds.

"Having a senior moment?" Mary Beth quipped as the waitress came to get their order.

Samantha smiled tiredly. After the order was made, she answered. "I've got a lot on my mind. The new job. Getting Mom settled. Clearing her house and selling it. Jack."

"I was waiting for that last one. How's that going?"

"It couldn't be better. I love my new job. I hate the commute, but what can you do about that? And Jack brings Beau to work with him. It's fun to see Beau. Sometimes he lets me take Beau on a job to get him out of the office. And Jack has kept his word. He hasn't done anything unprofessional."

"But?"

Samantha shook out her napkin and placed it in her lap. "Arthur's behaving really weird."

"How's that?"

"He acts suspicious. Even though he was the one who pushed me to take the job, and even though nothing is going on, he looks at me funny. He acts like he wonders if I'm really at Mom's place in the evenings. It's making me jumpy, because there is a strong attraction between me and Jack, but telling Arthur would only make things worse. I don't know..."

"Shit, don't tell him. That really *would* make it worse."

"I try not to say anything particularly nice about Jack. In fact, I avoid talking to Arthur about Jack completely. Maybe that's a mistake. Jack and I have meetings about work, but I really don't see him that much. I'm out in the field overseeing jobs and meeting with clients. I do have a small office where I do my designs, but I honestly don't spend a lot of time with Jack. Which is all to the good."

"Maybe Arthur is feeling bad about all you are having to do. He hasn't helped much at Maddie's, has he? At least he's never there when I am."

"No, it isn't his thing. Well, I don't want to go on about that. Tell me how things are at Palo Verde."

"It's not the same since Julio left. I know he wasn't in the office all the time, but the whole atmosphere has shifted. The brothers are morose and suspicious and even less open to suggestions than ever. I need the job, but maybe I should look for another. I don't have a lot of qualifications. If I were making more money, I could get an apartment and finally start living. I guess I'm going to have to sooner or later. Helen and Alexander leave early in May and will be back no later than sometime in June from their trip, and I have committed to having a concrete plan by then instead of leeching off of someone else."

"I hope it works out for you to stay in Palm Lakes. I'd miss you if you moved."

"Me, too." Mary Beth wished she felt more confident about the future. "Have you heard what's going on with Julio?"

"He started a yard watching and redo business in Palm Lakes and the surrounding area. Helen filled me in. She does yoga with his girlfriend, Emma."

"Do you think he's serious? He was always such a player," Samantha observed skeptically.

"Helen says Emma thinks he is, but Helen also says Emma is very innocent. But she says Emma is really happy and looks great, so at least for now, it must be going well."

"Who would have thought Julio would hook up permanently with an older woman?"

Mary Beth giggled. "He's been hooking up with them for a long time. Just never settled down with one. Maybe he has unresolved Mommy issues. I actually like Julio. I hope it works out for them."

Samantha pointed her chopsticks at Mary Beth. "Speaking of things working out, what's the latest on you and Ethan?"

Mary Beth sighed, staring at the platter of food the server placed in front of her. She waited until they were alone again to answer. "I'm going to do jewelry with your Mom this afternoon, then I am going out to dinner with Ethan. I think something's up. He's nervous."

"Maybe he's going to pop the question."

Mary Beth rolled her eyes. "I hope not yet. I'm still not sure it's a good idea. I sense he's as reluctant to commit as I am. I mean, he'll stay overnight at my place any time I invite him to, but our relationship is so sedate, I wonder if it's a mistake. Or maybe that's the way things should be. Jason the asshole swept me off my feet, basically fucked my brains out, and look how that ended...that came out wrong. I don't mean to imply Ethan isn't good in bed, but my feelings for him don't turn my brain to mush." She took her chopsticks and made a stab at her moo goo gai pan, then gave up and used a fork.

When she finally looked back up, she met Samantha's sympathetic gaze. "We're both going to figure things out...I hope sooner rather than later." Samantha delicately picked a piece of pork using her chopsticks and popped it into her mouth. "Say hi to Mom for me. I'll be at her house today and tomorrow. We're getting closer to the estate sale."

"How about I come help tomorrow?"

"I hate to ask you to spend your day off doing that. But I won't refuse help. It's a gigantic task."

Mary Beth raised her water glass. "Here's to life getting easier for both of us."

Samantha reached for her glass, clinked Mary Beth's and drank. "I'm all for that. Some day, I hope we'll sit here and talk about how totally screwed up life was back in 1996, and how it all turned out great in the end."

Mary Beth wished she could see that end.

* * *

Lydia, 12:35pm

THE MEMBERS OF THE LADIES' yoga lunch group stared at Barbara in sympathy. The noises of the Jade Dragon restaurant seemed to retreat, leaving them in a cocoon of quiet as they digested Barbara's news. Lydia forced herself to speak, in spite of the heaviness of the news.

"This is terrible. How long has it been going on?"

Barbara shook her head, a haggard look on her face. "Amelia has been having health problems for quite some time, but the doctors could never diagnose her. She called me yesterday to say they discovered she has MS."

"Oh, how awful," whispered Helen.

Emma twisted her napkin, speechless and distressed.

Jean looked at Lydia, her bright blue eyes brimming with compassion. Then she turned to Barbara. "Is there anything we can do to help? We'll be glad to do distant healing, if she's open to it."

Barbara's face relaxed in gratitude. "I'm heading out soon for a prolonged visit, so I'll talk to her about it. She's in need of some help with the kids. She's a single mother, and she's not hurting for money, but her condition has deteriorated so much, she can't deal with the kids and run a house."

"Will you have your cell phone with you?" Jean asked.

"Yes, and I'll be able to check email from time to time, too. I'll let you know how it goes." Barbara was sitting next to Lydia, and she turned and whispered, "I know I haven't made that appointment, but as soon as I can, I will."

Lydia patted her hand reassuringly. "Whatever you want to do is fine. You take care of yourself and Amelia."

"I just feel I need to focus on my daughter right now. I don't mean to be dismissing your concerns."

"I know that. Don't worry." But Lydia would worry.

By the time Lydia got home, she felt like falling into bed. Barbara wasn't going to be able to do anything about her own condition until she had helped Amelia to the best of her ability. At least there were several relatives helping, and they were taking shifts at Amelia's home. Barbara said she'd probably be back in a few to several weeks.

The ringing of the phone roused her from her unpleasant thoughts.

"Lyd, it's me."

"Hi, Jean. What's up? Long time no talk."

"I was wondering if you thought there was anything we can do to help Barbara besides doing some distant healing work if Amelia agrees. I feel so powerless. What an awful thing to be going through. I never had children, but it must be terrible to have to watch your child suffer."

"Me, too. I mean, I never had kids, either, so I can only imagine the hell she's going through. But it's more than that. I don't think she'd mind me telling you. I saw something in her aura that bothered me, and I suggested she get some healing, and I told her that she could get you and Ian to work on her in addition to me, and that we wouldn't charge her."

"Oh my God! What's wrong with her?"

"There's a blank spot in the aura near her left temple. Usually that means something is imbalanced in the energy field. Not necessarily that anything is physically wrong. Yet. But I warned her she needs work. I wonder if it's related to the stress of her daughter's condition. In any case, it's not good that she's going to go weeks without treating it. She told me she wanted to focus on her daughter first, and I have to honor that, but I wish she'd given us permission to do healing on her long distance."

"I'll say. But we can't work on people unless we have permission. So I guess we'll have to wait."

The silence stretched out, but Lydia didn't want to hang up yet. "On a totally different subject, I was wondering how you're liking the Botanica products."

"I love them! They're so reasonably priced. And I've ordered several of the essential oils. I'm experimenting with making my own mouthwash and toothpaste. Thanks for introducing me to them."

"Since you like them, I was wondering if you think it might be something we could include in what we offer through our business. Nora has a number of chiropractors under her, and I'd like you to consider if Botanica might be of interest to our clients. I try to be open to adjusting what we offer. Sometimes I'm afraid I'm all over the map."

"Nora's doing pretty well with the business, isn't she?"

"She tells me that she and Luke are going to be fine now, even though his pension fund collapsed. Her Botanica checks are more than paying the bills. She's even talking about paying down the mortgage faster, so they never have to get into this situation again. They love their house on the golf course, and they were afraid they'd have to give it up."

Jean sighed. "That sounds so wonderful! I wish I felt like I were good at selling. I'd love to have a chance to create financial security for us. Ian is adamant about not wanting a typical hourly job, and although I agree with him, I still can't get my head around this business taking off and paying our way. It makes sense to be open to adding Botanica to what we offer. Let's think on it. Surely the natural products go along with our own stand on health and healing. I'll talk to Ian and see what he says, but he's no more into selling than I am."

"I feel much the same way. Nora is an extrovert and has a big extended family and socializes a lot, and she says that is a huge asset when building a Botanica business, although she confessed that she was really nervous about speaking to people at first. Barbara gave her a kick start, doing that party to introduce her. You and I don't have Nora's personality or her sphere of influence, but maybe we could help our clients and add a little to our income."

"We're not exactly great prospects, are we?" asked Jean, laughing.

"No, I guess not, but we have to stay open to whatever will help the business thrive. I've been feeling low, and I don't want to make a decision now. Barbara's announcement has me going in a downward spiral. I'm going to go tap on myself to try and get back into a more positive frame of mind."

"What a great idea! I loved that class. I am so eager to share the tapping with everyone. I've never seen a method work so well. I'm worried for Barbara, too. Let me know if you think of any other way we can help her."

"OK."

Lydia hung up and reclined on the couch, putting her shoeless feet up. She tapped the sequence she'd learned, saying statements to release her fear and worry about Barbara's situation. After a few minutes of tapping, she felt much better. That stuff really worked. If only she were still with Eric. She was sure it could help him, but he was the one who had put the distance between them, and it didn't feel right trying to persuade him to change his mind. She didn't even know what his reasons were, not really. She hadn't given up hope yet, but she couldn't see a way back to him.

* * *

Ray, 1:15pm

"I DON'T KNOW what to do," confessed Ray. He looked at Alan, wishing he'd have the answer.

Alan shrugged his shoulders. He always looked to Ray for leadership, and Ray had to admit, this was really his problem. He was the one who'd brought the child to live with them.

"I'm sorry. I'm at my wit's end. I'm not mean to her, but she won't do what I ask. She acts like some princess. I'm certain she wasn't raised like this. Maybe she's working it. I don't mean to be unsympathetic about all the changes she's been through. I feel like I'm walking on eggshells in my own house--our own house." He slumped onto their bed, defeated. "What worries me most is how this is impacting our relationship." He tried to discern what Alan was feeling, but Alan's face was blank. That only made him more worried. "Say something."

Alan shrugged again, that eloquent way he had of saying it wasn't his problem. Or so it seemed to Ray.

"I was thinking of calling Helen and asking her advice."

Alan's blue eyes widened, then he nodded. "That might be a good idea. Helen has kids and grandkids. Maybe she could help. And she won't say anything to anyone besides Alexander." A smile blossomed on his youthful face, and Ray felt his heart relax. That decided it. "OK, I'll call her right now."

"Do."

"Want to listen in?"

Alan shrugged again, but then said, "Sure, why not?"

Ray went to the phone on the bedside table while Alan went into the library to listen on the extension. He should be able to make the call without any interference from Becky, who was currently watching TV in the living room.

"Helen, I'm glad you're home. It's Ray. I have Alan on the extension. Do you have time to talk?"

"Yes." Helen's voice held a question, so Ray plunged ahead.

"I know this is weird, but I need some child-rearing advice. Becky's been with us going on two weeks, and things aren't going that well. I mean, she's a bright child and basically mannerly and not too demanding, but she isn't minding me. I don't ask her to do much, but she flat refuses to pick up her room or put her dirty clothes in the hamper or help set the table. The other day, she even threw a tantrum and slammed her bedroom door shut. I don't know what to do. It's weird, because the day we came home, she was bragging about how much she could do around the house."

Helen laughed. "I'm sorry, I shouldn't laugh. I know it isn't funny. But I think she's just acting out because of all the change. She's a bright girl, and you told her you were her Grandpa, and grandparents are usually lenient and feed kids candy and take them to the movies. That might be her picture, and she might be resisting having you as a father figure. Which is more what you are. I know, because I spoil my grandchildren every chance I get and laugh up my sleeve when I send them home all wound up. It's kind of mean, but it's fun to be able to pamper them instead of making them toe the line and do homework and chores. But you can't act like a Grandpa. You need to be a parent figure. Which means setting boundaries and teaching her to do things."

Ray felt like whining. "I thought I was. I have asked her to clean her room before bed and make her bed and brush her teeth and set the table for meals. I wasn't harsh about it, but she isn't doing as I asked."

"She's testing you. You said she was smart."

"That she is."

"Children test boundaries to see if they're solid. You'll especially see that at bedtime, if you have an established bedtime."

"You're psychic. Bedtime is one of the biggest hassles we have. She always tries to find ways to stay up later, but if she doesn't go to bed at a decent time, we can't get her up for school in the morning. It's exhausting me completely."

"Don't be hard on yourself. Parenting is difficult. There are books you can read, but really, I think it's about establishing boundaries and rules and doing your best to live the way you expect her to live. Honestly, kindly, productively. You can't see yourself as her friend. You have to be a parent. And that means both you and Alan need to be on the same page. She'll use any crack in the united front to get her way by playing one of you against the other. My kids did that a lot because Lou and I were never on the same page. So you can't ever argue in front of her if you disagree about how to raise her."

Though he was scared at the thought of trying to enforce boundaries, Helen's voice soothed him. He began to feel calmer. "So I'm not a total failure because she's acting this way?"

"No, Ray. She's just a little girl trying to learn where the boundaries are, and if you are strong but loving, she'll settle down. You can't let her win, but you must do it gently. And try to spend quality time with her, like going for walks or to a museum or telling her stories. You guys love to cook. Teach her to cook. She needs positive interaction with you, not just rules. I failed to do that with my kids. It may explain why they don't seem to have much affection for me." Her chagrin seeped through the line.

"So you think time will improve things, and we should just hold fast and keep doing things with her and it will settle down?"

"That's what I think. Try not to foist her off on the TV too much. A little is OK, but right now, she needs people in her life who are committed to anchoring her and caring for her. She may regard you as a way station because she's been passed around so much lately, but I think if you act like parents instead of grandparents, she'll come around. That's what she's waiting for. Someone to claim her and love her."

"Thanks, Helen. The thought of all we have to do is overwhelming. Teacher's conferences. Homework. After school projects. Friends. Buying clothes for her. What happens when she starts to date?"

"Don't think too far ahead. Take one challenge at a time. The future will bring new ones. I used to tell myself when the kids got in school, life would be much easier. I was wrong. Then they had homework and projects and activities that turned me into a chauffeur and tutor. Then I told myself when they became teenagers and they could drive, it would be easier. Then I had to worry about accidents, sex and drugs. I'm not trying to scare you, but you need to know it's a long term commitment. The challenges change, but it never really gets easier. Or it didn't for me."

Ray felt two inches tall. He hadn't thought of most of this. What had he gotten into? He wished he could read Alan's mind at this moment. What if it scared Alan off? He didn't think he could manage on his own. Sighing, he thanked Helen and ended the call, grateful for her promise of assistance and even babysitting if they wanted it.

Alan appeared in the bedroom doorway. His 5 o'clock shadow heightened the impression of weariness his eyes radiated.

Ray patted the bed next to him. Alan came over and sat down heavily. Ray put his hand on Alan's thigh. "So what did you think of Helen's assessment?"

"I think she's a sharp lady. We've been afraid to assert ourselves with Becky. We feel her pain and loss, and instead of giving her something to hold onto, we're trying to buy her affection. We let her get away with too much."

Ray knew he was right, but he had no idea how to put his foot down. He should have asked Helen. "So I think her comment about us presenting a united front was insightful, not that we haven't, but it would be two against one if we stood firm."

Alan snorted. "Two grown men against one little girl. We're such pussies." Then he reached over and put his arms around Ray.

Ray nearly burst into tears. After he pulled himself together, he looked into Alan's eyes. "I don't know what I'd do without you. I'm terrified after hearing what she said. This is a huge commitment. Is it going to be all right with you?" He tried to be open to hearing whatever the truth was, but the thought of losing Alan was horrifying.

Alan drew back and gave him the smile Ray loved so much. "You don't think I'd leave you alone to deal with the little terror, do you? What kind of person do you take me for?" His boyish grin was captivating.

Ray sighed gustily. "I can't thank you enough. I guess we need a game plan so we know what rules we have and how to enforce them. I'm in favor of keeping it simple. Maybe a bedtime, clean her room weekly and help with the meals. I suppose we could offer her an allowance. When she does well, she gets it. If not, she doesn't. And maybe we could teach her how to deal with money when she accumulates it." Ray was warming to the subject now.

"That's the spirit. We aren't going to like correcting her, but we have to learn to, if only for the most basic things. I don't want to crush her spirit, but I don't want to live with a spoiled brat, either."

Ray leaned over and kissed Alan, his hand caressing his cheek. "I love you."

"And I love you. Let's get parenting."

* * *

Christine, 1:45pm

CHRISTINE PUT the finishing touches on her makeup and scrutinized the results in the mirror. Her lips were too thin, she had too many wrinkles and everything was sagging. Shrugging it off, she put her makeup case in the drawer, then put the prescription bottle of her tamoxifen in the cabinet. No one was going to use this bathroom, but no point leaving it out, just in case. She couldn't bear the thought of pity from her sisters because she'd had breast cancer. It was gone, she was almost certain, but she'd be on tamoxifen for a while yet. She'd become adept at pushing her worries deep down so she wouldn't have to face them. It felt like if she could avoid thinking about the cancer, it would really be gone for good.

Jerome was gone for the afternoon. As soon as she'd told him Samantha's induction into CSL was today, he made plans to be gone. She had to admit he was pretty good that way. Samantha was coming a few minutes early, and Christine wanted to make sure the refreshments were all ready, so she hurried into the kitchen and surveyed what she'd already done. Glasses and cups lined up on the counter with plastic plates, cutlery and festive paper napkins. A big pitcher of iced tea sat next to one of lemonade and a bucket with ice. The platter of cookies and cakes came from the Safeway bakery. They were pretty nice for store bought.

The doorbell announced Samantha, and Christine strode to the foyer and opened the door. Samantha always struck her as so young. She'd said she was 42, or was it 43? She didn't look a day over 30. She hoped this was going to work out.

"Come in, Samantha, don't you look lovely!" Samantha wore a Hawaiian print sundress in coral and white and simple, sparkly sandals. Her reddish golden hair was braided in a fancy updo. "Did you do your braid yourself?"

Samantha entered, looking a little tentative. But she smiled at the compliment. "Yes, I did. It's not too hard."

"And that necklace--I bet your Mom made it."

Samantha fingered the red coral necklace. "Yes, I love it, but rarely get to wear it. This gave me a nice excuse to dress up."

Christine wondered why Samantha never got a chance to dress up. Surely Arthur took her places? Brushing the comment aside, she led Samantha into the great room. "We'll do the induction here." Seeing Samantha's fearful look, she said, "Don't worry, it's really simple and you'll be fine. Just remember the responses I told you."

"You're right. I guess I have nerves. I was never in a sorority in college, and I'm not much for joining clubs, like I told you, but I'm looking forward to getting to know you better and being able to spend time doing something other than working and keeping my house and yard." Samantha seemed rather grim for such a pleasant occasion, but Christine knew she'd be OK with CSL. Whether all the sisters would be OK with her remained to be seen.

"I know you haven't met everyone, but you met most of the girls at the presentation you did, and they were simply bowled over by it. There will be some others you haven't met today, but it's already been voted on. You're in. So don't worry. No one expressed any doubts or problems about you as a member of our chapter."

Samantha nodded weakly. Christine had to admit, having a much younger member might lead to a bit of friction; she was pretty, and not everyone was graceful with aging. Samantha had confessed she had no friends who were residents, having hinted that most women didn't seem to want her around their men in a social situation, even if they didn't mind her doing their landscaping. Christine was willing to admit that if Jerome had shown even a spark of interest in Samantha, she might not have campaigned for her to join CSL. But she was willing to risk it. Samantha was a special person, so hard-working, so knowledgeable, so generous. She'd be an asset to CSL.

The doorbell pierced her musings. "I'll get that, Samantha. You relax." A tide of women flowed into the room over the next several minutes, all of them dressed a little bit more formally than usual. The rituals and words Christine had grown to love were said, and Samantha became a sister. The final admonition was never to tell anyone what CSL stood for. The secret meaning was not the publicized one. Cherish, support and love. She loved the reminder that the sisters took care of each other. CSL had given her a sense of belonging she'd found nowhere else.

After the induction, everyone partook of the refreshments, and Samantha appeared more at ease, answering questions posed to her, smiling warmly and even offering advice about people's plantings. Christine was encouraged. By the time the party broke up, Samantha had already offered to drive two of the older ladies to Sedona in the near future, saying she loved getting to see the red rocks and didn't mind the 2-hr drive. Yes, she'd picked well with Samantha. Younger blood was needed to keep things going, and Samantha seemed willing to pitch in.

Maddie, 1:50pm

MADDIE STRUGGLED to slide her swollen feet into the slip-on shoes as she glanced at the clock on the wall. In ten minutes, the bus would be leaving for Wal-Mart and other shopping destinations, and she intended to be on it. She hadn't mentioned her plans to Samantha, because she was sure she would squash them. She'd gotten so overprotective recently, referring to Maddie's crippling osteoporosis and failing memory as if they were reasons for locking her up. Well, she'd have her outing. What Samantha didn't know wouldn't hurt her.

She checked her purse and wallet--she had money and her room key--*take that, Samantha*--and locked up and dragged herself to the elevator. She pushed the button impatiently, and then again when nothing happened after a few seconds. It felt like she was making an escape from prison. She knew it was too early for anyone to come visit. But she still found herself holding her breath and looking over her shoulder like a kid slipping out after curfew. In spite of the anxiety, she felt a little thrill and almost giggled.

She shambled through the busy lobby, not wanting to engage anyone, trying to be invisible. The automatic doors opened for her and heat blasted through. It was like being in an oven. The little white bus with a blue stripe and "Desert Breezes" painted on the side in broad cursive was parked at the curb, motor running, and she could see a couple people already on board through the tinted windows. Excitement filled her as she stepped towards the bus and the door opened. The steps were steeper than she'd like, and she hesitated, uncertain how to mount them, wondering if she even could. She secured her purse on her shoulder, grabbed the bar on the door and stepped on the lowest riser.

"Hold on tight," the driver instructed her. She did. Somehow the steps turned into a platform, and she was transported up to the level the driver was on. She smiled at the cleverness of the device as she stepped onto the floor. The driver, a big Hispanic man with sparking eyes, seemed to enjoy her captivation with the device that had saved her doing the steps. "It's something, isn't it?" he quipped. She nodded wordlessly and made her way back to a seat by the window in an unoccupied row. She watched out the tinted window for the next several minutes while other shoppers arrived. They must be regulars, not having been surprised at the steps the way she was. One of them even clambered up them without the lift.

Maddie continued to look out the window to avoid attracting anyone's attention. She didn't want to have to make small talk. She simply didn't know how. And she was painfully aware that she was not dressed stylishly like the other women who'd gotten on the bus. Her frowsy housedress and slip-on shoes looked more appropriate for lounging around her apartment. But Maddie didn't have any nice clothes, which was one reason for the shopping jaunt.

The bus driver warned them all to hang on, that he was departing, and the adventure began. Maddie felt pretty pathetic regarding a trip to Wal-Mart as an adventure, even a declaration of independence. When had she become so housebound and incapable of doing things? But at least she was doing it.

Many of the passengers debarked at Wal-Mart. Maddie enjoyed using the lift this time, feeling more like a veteran. She hobbled through the blistering heat into the cool of the store, greeted by a senior who was much younger than she. It reminded her that Helen had had a brief stint as a greeter at Wal-Mart before she'd married that handsome rich guy, what's-his-name. The greeter was a portly woman with short, straight gray hair and glasses. "Would you like a scooter, dear?" the woman asked. Maddie wasn't sure what she meant until she followed the woman's pointed finger and saw the motorized vehicles for handicapped shoppers lined up along the wall.

"No, I'm fine, thank you," she replied. She may be old, but she wasn't that crippled yet.

She honestly couldn't remember the last time she'd been to Wal-Mart. It lay before her like a small city. She squinted at the hanging signs, trying to locate the women's wear section, but she wasn't able to read the words until she got right under them. She didn't like to admit to Samantha how bad her eyes had gotten. Well, she wanted an outing, and now she had one. She decided to walk around the place in a circular pattern until she found the women's department.

Rack upon rack of children's wear soon gave way to women's clothing, and Maddie began to browse, looking for some new dresses. She felt like a poor relation when she went to the dining room. The other residents didn't wear threadbare, shapeless old clothes like hers. Mostly, she'd been shopping at Goodwill these past years, picking up used items that suited her, not concerned how they looked. Stanley never took her anywhere, and he did most of the shopping, so what difference did it make if she had a fashionable wardrobe? But at Desert Breezes, she had to get out of her apartment now and then, and she was painfully aware of the contrast between her clothes and those of the other residents. Not one to waste money, she was sure she could find something suitable here.

Thirty exhausting minutes later, her optimism had disappeared. She now remembered why she loathed shopping. The lighting in the dressing rooms was harsh and unflattering. She was forced to look at her bloated and misshapen body and admit that no matter what she wore, she wasn't going to look good, and she hated spending money on not looking good. It was a physical struggle undressing, shrugging into a dress, taking it back off and rehanging it. How many times had she browsed, picked three dresses and tried them all on, only to reject them and start over? She needed a whole new body, not a new wardrobe. Pushing aside the negative thoughts, she decided she needed to lower her standards or go home empty-handed. Not willing to give up, she reframed her search and found three acceptable dresses in short order. Since she was only wearing them in public occasionally, that would do for now.

A sales clerk had seen her struggling with carrying her choices--she'd forgotten to get a cart--and came to her rescue in a very kind way that didn't make Maddie feel like an idiot. By the time she went outside to find the bus, she was so drained she could barely walk. But it had been worth it. She fell asleep briefly on the way back and was grateful for the lift depositing her on the ground without her having to scramble down steps. She couldn't remember the last time she'd had to use steps. Back at her first home, there had been steps, but for years now, everything seemed to be on one level, or there were elevators. Thank heaven.

The lobby was teeming with people coming and going, and Maddie slowly made her way with the tide moving towards the elevator, her bag of purchases dragging on her arm as if it weighed a ton, when she ran into a woman who was standing still, the crowd parting to go around her. Maddie hadn't seen and blundered into her. Fortunately, her speed was so slow, no damage was done.

"I'm sorry," Maddie mumbled as the woman turned to look at her. She was shorter than Maddie, maybe only five feet tall and very thin.

She was one of the few residents Maddie had seen who was dressed like her, in secondhand clothes that were worn and out of style. She had bedroom slippers on her feet and carried a cardboard box that might have been a shoebox with four small stuffed animals in it. One was a horse, another a dog. She couldn't tell what the other two were. The woman's short gray hair framed a wrinkled face devoid of makeup and deep blue eyes with a hundred-mile stare that conveyed vagueness, vacancy or worse.

Finally, the woman's eyes focused on Maddie as if only just noticing her. "Oh." The woman looked down at her box and handled each animal in turn, murmuring to them as if they were real. Apparently assured that no harm had come to them, she nodded vacantly to Maddie and turned away, picking her path slowly across the lobby to a seating area favored by those who liked to get out of their apartments occasionally. She sat on the couch, placing the box gently beside her, and stared out the window.

Shaken by the event, Maddie took the elevator to her place, grateful to finally be able to lay her burdens down. It seemed she'd met one person at this joint who was worse off mentally than she was. It made her grateful for merely being forgetful at times. Too tired to think, she decided she'd unpack later. Right now, she needed a beer. She was parched and weary from the adventure, but it had been fun. Maybe she'd do it again sometime. She didn't want Samantha to know, because she was sure she'd veto it. Or else say she'd take her shopping, which wasn't the same as going on her own. No, she'd have to keep it a secret. That meant she'd have to hide her new clothes and make sure she didn't wear them around Samantha. This was getting too complicated.

* * *

Eric, 3:00pm

ERIC GLANCED at the wall clock in the Rec Center's small meeting room and decided to start the meeting. When he'd advertised about his at-risk children project, he hadn't known what to expect. He was thrilled at the response. Several men and one woman had shown up for the meeting. A good beginning.

138

"Could we get started now?" Eric tried to be heard over the hum of several conversations. Everyone looked up and those who hadn't taken a seat found one.

"I'm trying to test the waters on a project I have in mind. I want to tell you up front, I've never done anything like this before. I'm a retired cop, not a social worker. But a kid got put in my path, and I've been trying to help him by bringing him here to run on the indoor track, shoot hoops, work out, and he really seems to be enjoying it. My goal was to provide him with constructive activities and a role model to help him avoid falling prey to older boys in his neighborhood who quite frankly are criminals."

Heads nodded, so Eric went on, encouraged in spite of his lack of experience. "So I was thinking, wouldn't it be great if we could form a group and help a lot of at-risk kids. It wouldn't have to be only boys, but that would be my emphasis. If we got women involved, they could mentor girls. When I started this, I thought sports-related activities would be enough, but the longer I work with Miguel--that's his name-- the more I see we could do. Everyone has a skill or talent. We could pair up kids who need tutoring with people who like to teach. We could organize group activities, like camping or hiking trips. We could even go to the museum as a group. I haven't thought it out completely, but it seems like something that could have a real impact and would mostly involve us volunteering time and expertise as opposed to money. I wanted to get input from interested parties today to see if it might be feasible to form a group."

He reached for his water bottle and gulped some cold water down, waiting to see what would happen. It shocked him when everyone started to talk at once.

One guy raised his hand and got everyone's attention. He was chunky with thick glasses and merry blue eyes. "I'm Fred. Why don't we go around the table clockwise and see what each person has to say? But may I suggest that we need someone to take notes?"

Eric hadn't thought to bring anything to write on, but the sole woman reached into a canvas bag and pulled out a legal pad and pen. Her mousy brown hair was in a tight bun at the base of her neck. Her glasses rested on her chest, dangling from a jeweled holder around her neck. Her brown eyes flashed with intelligence, and it struck him that she looked like a retired schoolteacher. "My name's Hazel, and I can take notes and then email a copy to anyone who has email."

Luckily, everyone had email, so they started with Fred, the chunky guy with the happy eyes. "I think this is a great idea. I'd love to participate. I have a lot of time on my hands these days, and I love kids. I'm not into sports anymore, but I could tutor a child. I was always good at math. And I belong to the model train club. Some kids really like that. I read a lot. Maybe I could get a bookworm assigned to me, and we could go to the library and check out books and talk about our favorite ones."

Next to Fred, the next person in line, a thin scarecrow of a man decked out in expensive-looking clothes nodded his head. His wrinkled face and frail demeanor made Eric think he was one of the older people in the room, but he spoke energetically. "My name's George, and I used to be a corporate lawyer. My suggestion is if we get enough interest, we could set up a nonprofit. That would allow us to do some fundraising and have other benefits as well. I'm willing to do all the research and paperwork on that, but there would be some fees associated with it, so we'd all have to kick in a little. But it would allow us to bring in funds tax-free and use extra for expenses." There were murmurs of assent and approval.

Eric was next. "I'm Eric Johnson, as you all know. I probably wouldn't tutor anyone. School wasn't my thing, though I did OK. I run, golf, work out on the machines and shoot hoops. So I play sports with Miguel, who loves to run. I'd be happy to participate in camping, visiting museums, etc." He nodded to the man on his left to take his turn.

"My name is Jim, and I'm an accountant. I could do taxes if you set up a nonprofit, and I could be a treasurer of sorts, if you need one, once the money starts coming in." Jim was an earnest-looking fellow with red hair going to gray, and although he was short and not particularly muscular, he seemed fit. "I also play a lot of golf. I could check into what it would take to bring a kid as a guest."

Things were really looking good. Eric could hardly believe it. The next person in line was Hazel. "I used to teach school, and I'd love to offer tutoring for kids. I could also work with girls, if you get any. I can teach them cooking, or...I don't know what, but I'd love to participate. I could be the Secretary of the group if you need one. I have email and don't mind sending out the minutes to everyone."

Looks of relief shot around the room at that offer. A handsome, younger-looking man with a deep tan and flashy blue eyes was next in line. "My name's Martin, and I used to be in marketing and PR. Maybe you could use my expertise in advertising and setting up fundraising events. I play tennis, and I'd be happy to teach a kid to play, or I could let him help me rebuild the antique car I'm working on."

Eric let out a breath he hadn't realized he was holding. "I had no idea what would happen when I put those signs up. We seem to have a lot of expertise at this table, certainly enough to launch the project. How many are in favor of having George look into the nonprofit option?" All hands went up. "George, could you do that? I guess we need to set our next meeting, and we all need to exchange contact information."

Hazel raised her hand. "Everyone write your name, phone number and address on the paper I'm passing around. I'll mail a complete list to all of you later."

"Maybe it would be helpful if in addition to contact details, we each wrote what our skills or interests are?" Martin hadn't bothered to raise his hand, but it was such a good idea, everyone nodded. The paper started making the rounds.

"We need to set up the organization before we advertise to find kids. But it looks like we have everything we need to get going. When shall we meet next, and what shall we discuss, other than the nonprofit option?" Eric searched each face.

Hazel raised her hand. "We could brainstorm about all the activities we could offer, based on our interests and talents. We could talk about possible fundraising events. We could take a vote about creating certain positions within the organization. And perhaps most important, we need to draw up some kind of description and policies for the group and elect officers."

"Plus we have to think of a name," interjected Martin.

Eric was bowled over. "Hazel, did you get all that?"

"Sure, Eric. I'll have it all in the email I send out no later than tomorrow."

"Is a week long enough for everyone to do what they need to do? I'm eager to get this rolling," said Eric. Nods and murmurs of affirmation floated around. "Everyone in favor of meeting next Saturday at the same time, raise your hand." All hands went up.

"Then I guess that's it. We have a project to do. I look forward to seeing you all then."

The meeting broke up and everyone left after congratulating Eric for his good idea. He sat in his chair in the empty room, shaking his head in disbelief. He hated meetings. They were the low point of his former career. He hated paperwork even more. Yet the idea of this nonprofit filled him with excitement. Whatever it took to make it work, he was going to do it. And someone up there was watching out for him, because he had a lawyer, a teacher, an accountant and a marketing guy already. All the chores he'd been dreading would fall to other people. He'd be in charge of background checks. Right up his alley.

* * *

Ethan, 5:20pm

ETHAN WAS SWEATING in spite of the arctic chill of the restaurant's air conditioning. He'd brought Mary Beth back to Casa Linda to propose, but he was terrified what her response would be. Some part of him felt this should be easier and he should be more confident. They'd spent several nights together at her casita, and it seemed to go well, but there was always a miasmic feeling of things unsaid or fears unmentioned.

He fingered the ring box in his pocket as the sweat trickled down between his shoulder blades. Mary Beth was sipping wine, looking around the room they'd been seated in. He'd asked to get the table they'd had the first time they dined here, and she seemed pleased to have returned, as if to an old friend's home. She looked at him and grinned. "This is so great. I never expected to come back again so soon. You're spoiling me." Merriment danced in her pale green eyes.

Throughout the meal, every step of the way, he postponed popping the question. He wanted it to be a happy and memorable night, and he knew it would be without the proposal, and he didn't want to risk spoiling it. Finally, dessert--one piece of carrot cake with two forks-- arrived with coffee, and he knew he couldn't drag it out any longer. It was now or never.

"Mary Beth, I brought you here tonight, because I thought you really liked it, and I wanted it to be a special evening."

She locked onto him expectantly. "Hell, yeah, it's special, but what's the occasion?" She no longer asked him to forgive her cussing. It made him strangely more confident.

He pulled the ring box out of his pocket, getting it stuck on the facing for a few seconds, as she stared at him expectantly. He put the box in the middle of the table. "Oh!" she exclaimed.

"Go ahead, open it." He gave the box a shove closer to Mary Beth, who reached out--not quickly, as if she couldn't wait to open the box, but not as slowly as someone who dreaded saying 'no' would, or at least he hoped.

She drew the box towards her and opened it up. Her eyes widened and she looked up at him. "You shouldn't have done this."

"I want to marry you. I want us to be able to live together like normal people. I want to take care of you. I know I'm a lot older, but I love you."

"Stop with the age crap. I thought we'd gotten past that."

He wasn't sure they'd ever get past it, but he wasn't going to say that out loud. "Will you do the honor of marrying me?"

Her eyes shimmered with unshed tears, and that had to be good, right? Or was she upset? After what seemed an hour, she took the ring out and put it on her left hand, turning it this way and that to catch the light. It looked a little loose.

"We can get it sized if it's too loose. I thought a colored stone for the engagement ring would be different. I wanted something like your eyes. That's a green garnet. The little clear stones are diamonds. I hope you like it."

She nodded, but seemed bereft of words. His stomach began to clench. Then she whispered in awe, "It's beautiful."

Relief flooded him and he felt lighter than air. But then she asked the question he'd been dreading. "Have you told your family about this?"

Sick with worry, he had to be honest. "Not yet. I told them we were dating. I haven't told them I planned to propose. I guess I figured if you rejected me, it would save me embarrassment with them. I'll tell them if you agree to marry me."

Her scowl said he'd done it wrong. "Ethan, I don't know your family, and I know they mean a lot to you, but if you feel afraid to tell them about us, it must be because you know they aren't going to approve. So tell me the truth. Will they approve?"

He felt himself sag. "I don't know. My daughter might be OK with it. I don't think my son will be. I can't be sure. He wasn't very supportive when I told him we were dating, so I assume that means he won't be in favor of a marriage."

Mary Beth's frown struck him in the solar plexus. "I'm not sure this is a good idea, Ethan. I don't want to come between you and your family." At least she didn't take the ring off. Maybe there was hope.

"Look, we don't have to set a date. I'll tell my kids. But what do I tell them? Will you marry me?"

With a look that was more resignation than joy, Mary Beth replied, "Yes. I will marry you."

Feeling totally dissatisfied with the results, Ethan nonetheless counted it as progress. "I still think we shouldn't spend the night at my place, if you don't mind."

"No, I don't mind. And Helen and Alexander will be leaving in a couple weeks. It will be like our own place then." But a shadow of something flitted across her face. He wondered what she was really feeling, but part of him was too afraid to ask, afraid it might be something he wouldn't want to hear.

"Shall we eat this cake?" He picked up a fork and offered her the other one. She gave him a wan smile, and they picked away at the cake until it was gone.

"That was really good carrot cake." The smile didn't reach her eyes.

"Yeah, it was good. Shall we go back to your place and celebrate? I have some champagne in a cooler in my car. I was thinking maybe we could toast the future."

Her green eyes lit up. "Now you're speaking my language. Let's go."

7

SUNDAY, MAY 12, 1996: MOTHER'S DAY

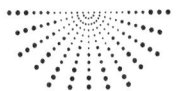

Samantha, 11:00am

*S*amantha stood outside her mother's apartment, a bottle of red wine and plastic grocery bag in one hand, an envelope in the other. Arthur stood behind her holding the ovenproof dish with the homemade cannelloni. She turned and looked at him. "Ready for this?" Arthur scowled at her and nodded. She rapped on the door.

"Come in. It's unlocked," yelled Mom.

Samantha entered and put her items on the small dining table and turned to Arthur, relieving him of the cannelloni, which she put on the stovetop. Then she met Mom in the center of the living room and gave her a hug. Arthur hung back as if unsure what to do, but finally stepped up to Mom. "Happy Mother's Day," he said with little enthusiasm.

Mom frowned at him, then relented. "Thanks." Turning to Samantha, she pointed at the dish. "What's that you brought?"

"I promised to make you homemade Italian, and I found a neat recipe for cannelloni. You put the filled tubes in the pot vertically and pour the sauce over them. All we have to do is cook it. When do you want to eat?"

Mom wandered over to the stove and peered into the pot. "I've never had cannelloni before. It looks really good."

145

Samantha nearly fell over at the compliment. "I think you'll like it. It's just a different version of lasagna, to my way of thinking. And I know that's a favorite of yours. Mary Beth tells me she's been bringing spaghetti sauce and lasagna, and I wanted to make something different."

Mom's smile was reward enough.

"I brought some bread from the bakery. I didn't have time to make any. And a bottle of wine."

Mom went to the table to inspect the bread and wine, then huffed, "I hope you didn't spend a lot on this wine."

Samantha tried not to roll her eyes. "Mom, it's Mother's Day, and so yes, I did splurge a little. Don't worry about it."

"It's after 11 o'clock. We can have a drink now," said Mom. Samantha suppressed a smile as Arthur moved with alacrity to open the bottle and find the wine glasses in the cabinets. He poured a generous measure into each glass, mismatched antiques that each had a story attached to them, and they sat down, Mom on her recliner and Arthur and Samantha on the sofa.

Samantha raised her glass. "To your first Mother's Day at Desert Breezes. May you have many more."

They all clinked glasses and sipped their wine.

"So, Mom, when do you want to eat? It will take a little while to cook. I can do your laundry while we wait."

Mom grimaced. "You don't have to do my laundry all the time."

"I want to. It will save you going up and down in the elevator, carrying heavy things. You know the doctor said not to lift more than two pounds. It's no big deal. But let's decide when to eat."

"Any time is fine," said Mom vaguely. She looked distracted and out of sorts. There was something wrong, but Samantha was loath to ruin the afternoon by quizzing her.

"I'll preheat the oven, then." Samantha got up and turned on the oven after checking that the racks were positioned properly for the large dish she'd brought. She then joined Arthur on the sofa. He sat drinking his wine in silence, his tanned legs crossed. There was something wrong with him, too, but she could guess what that was. He hadn't been right since she started her new job. This wasn't the time to delve into that. Instead, she decided to do the laundry. "I can put the laundry in while the oven is preheating. Is there anything you want to watch on TV today?" Poor Arthur. If only it were football season, he wouldn't have to talk with Mom much.

"No, there's nothing on."

"OK." That meant leaving Arthur to entertain Mom. But he was a big boy. He'd manage. She went into the bedroom and grabbed the laundry basket after pulling towels off the rack in the bathroom, then headed downstairs to the laundry room with a promise she'd return shortly.

Feeling guilty that getting out of that room felt so good, she rode the elevator down to the ground floor and marched to the laundry room. Most of the machines were available, so she picked two and sorted colors for two loads. After putting her money in the machines, she turned to leave the room and noticed a woman had slipped in and was loading a machine in the next row over. Her eyes bugged out when she saw the woman wore nothing but a bra above the waist. Barely able to close her mouth, she tried to recover as the woman looked up and peered at her with lively gray eyes. The bra was barely doing its job restraining her mammoth breasts. Three rolls of fat pooled under the bra, spilling over the top of her slacks. She didn't look demented, but why was she wandering around half dressed?

"Hello," said the mystery flasher with undisguised humor. Was she aware she was nearly half naked?

"Hi," managed Samantha cautiously.

"It's really warm today."

Maybe she thought that was reason enough to dress so briefly. At least she wasn't completely naked.

As the flasher continued to stuff clothes in the washer, Samantha noticed she hadn't sorted them by colors. Clearly, the woman was impaired in some fashion. Samantha fled the laundry room and slipped into the elevator, eager to escape. She wondered if she should report the woman. She wasn't harming anyone, but was she aware of what she was doing?

Shaking her head, she strode down the hall and entered Mom's apartment, returning the basket to the bedroom closet. Then she checked to see if the oven was hot enough. Not yet.

Arthur looked relieved that she had returned, but there didn't seem to be an aura of negativity, so probably they hadn't had a fight. She'd begged him to be on his best behavior today, even though she sympathized with how challenging Mom was for him.

After she took a big gulp of wine, Mom announced, "They removed things from my bathroom cabinet yesterday without my permission."

Samantha couldn't process what that meant. "Who did?"

"That nurse did, the one who works here. She didn't even warn me. She came in while I was out at lunch--wouldn't you know the one time I go to the dining room in ages--and took almost everything from my medicine cabinet. The essential oil you gave me, my Tylenol, everything. They shouldn't be allowed to do that." Mom was simmering with anger now that she'd gotten going.

"Why would they do that?" Samantha wondered if Mom was getting it right.

"When I asked, they said it was something about checking for adverse medical interactions, but I'm not on any prescription drugs, and they still haven't given my things back to me. I think it's wrong they came in while I was gone like that."

Samantha agreed, but needed to be certain she was hearing the whole story. "I'll call them tomorrow and see what they say. Surely, they'll give your stuff back soon."

"They gave some high and mighty excuse about my safety and having to approve any health product I have."

A thought came to Samantha. "So did they take your first aid kit?"

Mom broke into a smile. "I don't think so."

Samantha jumped up and went to the closet. The first aid kit lay on a shelf convenient for Mom's reach. It contained bandaids and over-the-counter medicines that duplicated those that had been removed from the bathroom. So they assumed people only had things in the bathroom cabinet. Good. "It's still here, Mom."

"They aren't as smart as they think they are."

Samantha smiled at the change in attitude. "Maybe you're not as dumb as they think you are."

Mom took it in stride. "No, I'm not. They treat us all like a pack of children. Just because we're a little forgetful at times."

Samantha flashed back to the laundry room. "Some are more forgetful than others. I met another resident in the laundry room. She was only wearing a bra on top."

Mom's eyes widened. "You're kidding!"

"No, cross my heart, no pun intended. I'm serious. She seemed harmless enough, but it freaked me out a little."

Mom had moved on from the violation of her space. She appeared lost in thought for a minute. "I saw a woman downstairs the other day. She was wandering around the place carrying a box with stuffed animals in it. There are some weird people here."

Arthur choked back a laugh. She didn't begrudge him. Mom was eccentric. But at least she kept her clothes on and didn't wander around carrying stuffed animals in a box.

Samantha cautiously changed the subject. "Did Mary Beth tell you the news?"

Mom harrumphed. "Yes, she told me last time she came by. She's engaged to Ethan. She showed me a pretty ring. I still think she's making a mistake. She doesn't seem that enthusiastic about marrying him."

Mary Beth had confided her concerns to Samantha, but she wasn't going to share them with Mom. "Mary Beth has been through a lot this year. And I thought the ring was pretty, too. Not your typical diamond, which I think is boring." She belatedly glanced down at the diamond ring on her left finger. *Oops.* Well, it was true. She was never one for diamonds, and when she'd married Arthur, she hadn't had the nerve to ask for something else. Served her right.

Clueless about Samantha's reaction, Arthur uncharacteristically entered the conversation. "So, Maddie, have you made any new friends?"

Mom regarded him through slitted eyes. "I eat in a lot, because Samantha and Mary Beth bring me so much food. But when I eat in the dining room, I sit with Olivia. She's been nice to me, and she has all her marbles, which is more than I can say for some of the people who live here."

"Olivia used to live next door to Helen and Alexander, right?" Samantha wanted to stay on a topic that didn't incense Mom.

"Yeah, they got their dog from her. Helen introduced us. Olivia tells me that Helen brings Spot over to visit. She could have kept Spot here, because the dog is small, but she said she was getting too old for dog walking, and she could tell Helen loved Spot. Now she gets to visit her without having to feed and walk her." Samantha knew where this was headed, but she couldn't prevent it. "I wish you'd bring Beau by like you said you would. I really miss him."

Samantha's stomach knotted. "I'm sure Jack will bring him by sometime. But I can't make him. I'll try to remind him."

Arthur raised an eyebrow, but said nothing. Any reference to Jack seemed to put his hackles up. Why couldn't Jack have a different name? Jack was a name for a player. Ernesto or Oscar would have been less inflammatory. Arthur had yet to meet Jack, and she hoped to put it off indefinitely, because if he was suspicious now, he'd be rabid if he got a look her tall, dark and handsome boss.

Samantha jumped up and put the meal in the oven and set the timer. "We can eat in about 45 minutes, I think." She collected her way-too-small glass and refilled it. "Either of you want a refill?" After topping up glasses, Samantha relaxed and zoned out as the conversation drifted through safe topics like the weather and sports. It was pleasant to be able to let her guard down.

Then she remembered the gift they'd brought. In all the commotion, it had slipped her mind. She retrieved the envelope from the dining table and handed it to Mom. "Sorry for the sudden change of topic. Happy Mother's Day, Mom."

When Mom opened the card, a slip of paper fell to the floor, which Samantha bent and picked up.

After reading the card, Mom turned her attention to the paper. Her eyes lit up with joy. "Oh, this is wonderful!"

Even Arthur smiled at the reaction. Samantha felt something uncoil within her. "I'll take you to the Bead Store to cash the gift certificate some weekend, if you like."

"This is a big gift certificate. Just what I like."

"Well, I know you don't have cash on hand, and you must be running out of materials by now, so this should help replenish them."

"And then some," said Mom. She handed the certificate to Samantha. "Will you take care of that for me so I don't misplace it?"

"Sure." Surprised that Mom was asking for help, Samantha folded the gift certificate and put it in her pocket, reminding herself not to put it through the wash. *The wash.* "I need to run downstairs and put your clothes in the drier." Samantha shot out the door before anyone could comment.

She counted her blessings when she discovered the laundry room was empty. She transferred clothes as quickly as possible to the industrial size drier, then split as fast as she could to avoid meeting the flasher woman again, who would certainly be back, if she remembered she'd done laundry. She imagined that happened often here, that someone would forget.

When she let herself back into Mom's apartment, she was surprised to see Arthur and Mom in a companionable conversation. Maybe it would turn out to be a good day after all. The smell of Italian food wafted from the oven as she walked past and snagged the wine bottle. She always drank more when they visited Mom. She wondered if it said something about her or about Mom. "Anyone else want a top-up?"

As Samantha refilled glasses, Mom turned to her and smiled a genuine smile, her pale blue eyes shining. "How about a game of Yahtzee before we eat?"

Thrilled to have something neutral to occupy them, Samantha chimed in with a yes. The rest of the visit went smoothly, and Samantha even remembered to get Mom's clothes out of the drier, in spite of having to do dishes after they ate. When they left, she promised she'd call about the invasion of Mom's privacy and the return of her belongings, not that she thought it would do any good. But it made Mom feel better.

Arthur was quiet on the way home, and she hoped he was coming around now that the dreaded visit to the mother-in-law was over. But he'd only been waiting to say his peace. "So, when are you going to bring Beau around to see Maddie?"

Samantha froze. The edge in his voice meant he was looking for trouble. "I don't know when Jack can do it. It's asking a lot for him to use his weekend to visit my Mom. I don't like to push it."

"When do I get to meet the elusive Jack?"

Samantha was stumped. One minute he wanted to meet Jack, the next he was blasé about it. Maybe he was testing her reaction. God, she needed to stop acting guilty. "He wasn't around when you dropped me off at work that day, and what reason would he have for coming out to

Palm Lakes?" She hesitated, knowing she had to say what came next. "If you like, when he brings Beau, I'll introduce you. But you'll have to come to Mom's to do it." She prayed that would put an end to it.

"I'd like to meet the guy who's given you your dream job. And saved Beau. He's going to be your Mom's favorite person."

Oh, dear. This was headed for trouble. "I'll let you know when he sets a date."

Samantha wondered how long she could put Jack off. She was on a tightrope with Mom on one side and Arthur on the other. Arthur wasn't all that intuitive, but if he saw how Jack looked, he'd go ballistic. Dread tied her stomach in knots. She forced herself to look into Arthur's eyes and smile as if nothing were wrong. She hadn't done anything. But she felt she was going to pay, anyway.

* * *

Mary Beth, 3:15pm

MARY BETH SAT across from Catherine, watching her open her Mother's Day card.

"Oh, this is such a lovely card, dear. You didn't have to do this."

"You've been like a mother to me. I appreciate all your support. And love. I'd like to be able to offer you a place to live with me. Maybe someday." Mary Beth sighed.

"Don't feel that way, dear. Things are great right now." Catherine stood the card up on the coffee table and turned to open the slim, square gold box. "I wonder what's in here," she said theatrically.

Mary Beth hooted. "You know."

"I can guess, but I don't know." She took her time opening the box, and when she peeked in, she raised her voice, "Mary Beth, this is exquisite!"

Mary Beth beamed as Catherine pulled the necklace out of the box, letting it fall to its full length. The leopardskin jasper contrasted beautifully with the pale freshwater pearls. Maddie had kept her promise to show Mary Beth how to make the complex necklace, and it had turned out gorgeous.

Catherine held the necklace out to Mary Beth. "Can you put this on for me?"

Mary Beth stood up and did the honors, noting that the length was perfect for Catherine. "There are earrings, too."

Catherine reached for them and replaced the ones she currently had on. "You are too good to me."

"No, I am not good enough. I can never repay you for all you've done for me." She sat beside Catherine on the couch.

Catherine leaned over and gave her a hug.

"So tell me about the wedding plans. Have you picked a date?"

Mary Beth frowned. "Not yet. We've gotten stalled. He told his kids, and it didn't go well with his son." She shrugged as if it didn't hurt her, but it had.

"Is he letting his kids dictate about your relationship?"

"Not as such. But he backpedaled about setting a date. Not that I mind. We're still getting along fine. I'm not sure I'm ready to set a date yet. I can't imagine marrying into a family where I'm disliked before I've even been met."

"Does he still spend the night at your place?"

"Oh, yes. Helen and Alexander left almost ten days ago, and I have the place to myself. It's wonderful. We even had a big meal in their kitchen the other night. Which reminds me. Will you come have dinner with us?"

Catherine laughed. "You know the answer to that."

"I'm sorry I've been so remiss in having you meet him. Things got crazy with the move, and then I got cold feet. It felt like if I introduced you to him, it would be more permanent. And I wasn't sure I was ready for that."

"I won't embarrass you."

"I never thought you would. That would be my Mom's job." She chuckled. "She thought Ethan was too old, and I was sure she was going to get on him about it. But..."

Catherine reached over and patted her hand. "I know you miss your Mom. Today of all days."

"I do. We always made a big deal of Mother's Day." Mary Beth had gone limp.

Catherine gave her a sharp look and struggled to her feet. "I'll be back in a minute."

Mary Beth used the time to give herself a pep talk about not dragging Catherine down with her troubles. When Catherine returned to the room, she was carrying a bulky manila envelope. She sank onto the couch and handed it to Mary Beth unceremoniously. "I want you to have this."

Mary Beth looked at the envelope, but was unable to imagine what it could be. She opened the clip and poured out the contents. A sealed business-size envelope slid out. It had her name on the front and "Only to be opened at the time of my death" and signed by Catherine. The other item was a bulky legal document that Mary Beth recognized was a will. "Is this what I think it is?"

Catherine nodded in affirmation, her double chins wiggling. "That's a copy of my will. Plus a letter to you, but you aren't to open it until I'm gone."

Mary Beth felt tears form in her eyes as she looked down at the document. "I don't like thinking about that."

"Well, you know it's coming. Probably sooner than later, if you believe the doctor."

Mary Beth's jaw fell open, and she searched Catherine's face for answers, but Catherine poker-faced her. "What's wrong?"

"Old age is what. You know I'm not getting any younger, and as I get older, things are falling apart. You've helped me so much, and I appreciate it. I wanted you to know what the terms of my will are. When the time comes, you get everything I have."

Mary Beth didn't know how to respond.

"You know I don't have family. I'm grateful to have you to leave it to. Otherwise, it would just go to some charity. I own this place free and clear. I know it's not much, and you can't legally own it, but you can sell it and that will increase the nest egg you got when you sold your Mom's." Catherine sucked in a deep breath. "I want you to pay special attention to the contents of that letter when I'm gone. I'm not going to talk about it now. But it gives specific instructions about certain belongings I have. Please read it before you take any other action after I'm gone."

154

She could tell by Catherine's demeanor that she wasn't going to get further hints. Overcome by gratitude, she let the tears flow. "I don't know what to say."

"Thank you is plenty," Catherine quipped.

"Thank you for caring about me. You've been a real rock for me this year, and I'll never be able to repay you." She threw her arms around Catherine, enveloping her in a big hug.

Catherine's voice was muffled against her chest. "I want you to have the life you deserve, to feel free and independent. Don't do anything out of fear or worry about money. Come to me if you need money, and I'll help you."

Mary Beth drew back and regarded Catherine. What secrets was this small woman hiding? "Are you a wealthy eccentric?"

"I'm not answering that question. Just remember if you need money, come to me." Catherine's lips were sealed tightly, and Mary Beth knew she wasn't going to get any more out of her today. She wrapped her in a hug again and kissed the top of her blue tresses.

* * *

Ray, 4:00pm

RAY AND ALAN lounged on chaises on the patio. A mister sprayed a fine curtain of chilly water that softened the late afternoon heat, making the view of the golf course fuzzy. Alan was doing a sudoku puzzle, and Ray was reading a book on the history of citrus in Italy.

The sliding glass door moaned, and a small blonde tornado burst onto the patio. "Grandpa Ray! Grandpa Alan! I finished the puzzle. Come and see!" Ray was slow to put his book down, so Becky raced over to Alan, who beamed at her.

"What did you do to your hair?" he asked.

She shrugged one small shoulder. "It came undone."

"My, putting puzzles together must be hard work," Alan observed. Ray grinned at the interaction.

Alan reached over and pulled Becky close to his chaise. "I'll fix it for you."

She fidgeted but didn't complain while he quickly finger-combed her hair after pulling the band off the frazzled braid. He nimbly wove the hair back into a braid and restored the band. "There. That should hold for at least another ten minutes."

Becky grabbed his hand and began to pull. "Come and see what I did."

Alan looked at her fondly. Ray couldn't be happier. He put his book down. "Let's see this puzzle."

They followed Becky to her room, where a puzzle board filled one corner of the floor. On it was a completed map of the United States. "That's very impressive, Becky," said Ray.

Pride shone on her cherubic face, and her bright blue eyes sparkled. "I did good."

"That you did," said Alan. "Can you tell which state is which?" He knew the names of the states were on the backs of the puzzle pieces, which were shaped exactly like each state.

"I know most of them. The ones in the middle are the hardest for me to remember. But I know almost all of them by heart."

Ray stroked the golden hair, noticing that her clothes were getting a little tight. God, she was growing fast. "We're going to need to go clothes shopping for you soon."

She clapped her hands together and jumped up and down. "Oh, goodie."

Alan looked at Ray and smiled. Hair and clothes were things he was expert at, and Ray could tell he was looking forward to the outing.

Ray squatted down and pointed at Texas. "So what's this state, Becky?"

"Texas," she said confidently.

"Very good. How about this one?" He pointed to Alaska.

"That's easy," she said dismissively. "That's Alaska."

"Right you are. You're a smart girl. We can get some other puzzles if you like puzzles."

Becky had already shot off to her desk. "OK, but make them harder next time. I'm going to color now."

Alan and Ray wandered back out to the patio with a detour to the kitchen to make a pitcher of lemonade. "I'll take a glass to Becky," Alan volunteered.

"Thanks. I'll make us a gin and tonic, if you like."

Alan wiped his brow dramatically. "On such a hot day, that sounds heavenly."

Later, back on the patio, Ray didn't reach for his book. Instead, he sipped on his cool drink. "What do you think about how we're doing so far?"

Alan chuckled. "You only ask me every day. My answer is the same. I'm enjoying myself. Surprisingly so." He turned and looked at the sliding glass door as if to check for eavesdroppers. "Becky is fun and smart, and now that we've set some boundaries, she seems to be doing well."

"You're certainly a wizard at doing her hair."

Alan nodded graciously. "Of course I am. No one does hair like I do." They both laughed heartily.

"I'm sure people are noticing her. I don't feel right confining her to the house. The heat will keep her inside most of the time, but she loves to play outside early in the day on weekends. I'm waiting to get a notice from the HOA." Ray ran his hand through his longish gray hair.

"Well, you and I both know it's inevitable. It's a huge violation of the covenants. But having spoken with a lawyer, I'm hopeful we might get them to let us stay. In any case, we'll be together." Alan reached over and took Ray's hand and squeezed it. "We're a family now. I never thought I'd have one. I kind of like it."

"This morning she told me she missed her Momma."

"Yeah, she knows it's Mother's Day. I feel sad for her." Alan sighed.

"If they kick us out, where do you want to move?"

Alan shrugged as if it didn't matter. "I'm not sure I'd stay in the area. This is far and away the best community. I don't want to downsize or settle. I'm afraid I'd begin to resent Becky if we did that."

"We can sell the house and go anywhere you like. I just want us to be together. Like you said. A family." Ray leaned back and picked up his book, watching Alan.

"That suits me. If it comes to it, we'll find somewhere better."

Ray grinned. "I like your attitude."

Alan picked up the sudoku book. "I was thinking we could make dinner together today. Becky is a quick study and likes to do more than set the table. I think she may be a budding chef. Wouldn't that be a hoot?"

Ray smiled. "What are we going to make?"

"I thought keep it simple. She likes Italian. We could make a gourmet spaghetti sauce. Does that suit you?"

"Sure."

Alan flipped through his book to find the game he'd been working on before the interruption. "We probably ought to get started soon. I'd like to simmer the sauce for a while before we eat."

"Any time you say." Ray let the cool mist float over him. There was a great deal of uncertainty regarding the future, but today was nearly perfect.

8
SATURDAY, MAY 18, 1996

Maddie, 10:10am

Once again, Maddie leaned over and unsuccessfully tried to reach her toenails so she could trim them. Her feet were swollen so stiff, the skin looked ready to split. They reminded her of elephant feet, or were they hooves? The weird thing was she didn't feel much in her feet, in spite of how bad they looked. Maybe she was going to have to ask Samantha to cut her toenails. She hated having to ask for help, but her feet looked like something from a horror movie.

Samantha had said there was a beauty salon in the building where they did manicures and pedicures as well as haircuts. She'd always cut her own hair and never had a manicure in her life. She wasn't going to start now, even though it would be a simple solution. Besides, she couldn't afford it.

The struggle to reach her toes had set her heart to palpitating. She was learning to ignore that symptom. It never amounted to much, though it was troubling. It was the joint pain that was the worst. The fentanyl patch the doctor had prescribed this week didn't help much, and all the strain from trying to reach her feet had set off stabs of pain in her joints, especially along her spine.

The fancy red walker Samantha had brought the other day sat parked in the corner of the living room, laughing at the toenail debacle. Damned if she was going to use that, though she had to admit that sometime in the future, she'd be forced to. It was getting too hard to get around on her own. She needed to avoid the devilish thing for as long as possible to prove she wasn't an old cripple.

She waddled gingerly into the bathroom and put away the nail clipper. Looking in the medicine cabinet, she smiled with satisfaction that her belongings had finally been returned to her, along with an apology that they'd entered her apartment without permission. Though the nurse—what was her name? Louise?—hadn't seemed all that sincere. She'd handed Maddie some lame excuse about just doing her job and trying to protect Maddie from drug interactions.

Right. That showed how much they knew. They prescribed fentanyl, and it didn't do a lick of good. Not that she was going to tell them. She was going to quit using it if she continued to have pain for another day or two. She didn't like how the painkiller bound her up more than usual, and if it didn't work, she wouldn't keep taking it.

She'd barely returned to the living room, having detoured to the kitchen area for a top-up of her coffee, when someone knocked on the door. Who could that be? Mary Beth wasn't due for a few hours, and Samantha never came this early. She swayed slowly to the door and pulled it open. Olivia stood in the hallway, a diminutive dumpling with lively brown eyes.

Maddie hesitated a few seconds, not having expected nor desiring company, but Olivia had been kind to her, so she stepped back and welcomed her inside. "Can I get you a cup of coffee?"

Olivia was older than Maddie, more bent over, and a few pounds heavier. "That would be nice, if it isn't too much trouble."

"I have a fresh pot." Maddie made her way to the sink and got a mug out of the cabinet and filled it. "Sugar? Creamer?"

"Both."

"Have a seat on the couch. I'll bring it over." Maddie was worried Olivia might spill it. She didn't look steady enough to carry a full mug of coffee across the room. But who was she criticizing? She could barely do it herself.

Olivia eased herself onto the couch and looked towards the sliding glass door that led to the balcony. "You have a nice view."

Maddie shrugged and set the mug on a coaster on the end table next to Olivia and went back to retrieve her own.

"I like watching the hummingbirds. There are lots of them here. Samantha has to refill both bottles every week."

"You're lucky to have a daughter so close by."

Again, Maddie shrugged. It was nice, but it had its price.

"So where is Samantha today? Will you be seeing her?"

"She's at my house getting it ready to put on the market. The estate sale was last weekend. Now she's getting it cleaned out."

"My, you're lucky. She's a real workhorse. That was fast."

Maddie grunted. "I had to get rid of too much stuff." Tears filled her eyes, but Olivia didn't notice.

"I know what that's like, Maddie. My daughters went through my house in preparation for moving me here, and they made me get rid of nearly everything. The thing that bothered me the most was they told me the majority of what I had wasn't worth donating, let alone selling. They said I should have thrown most of it out years ago." Olivia shook her head, brown eyes filled with sorrow.

"All three of your daughters said that?" Maddie couldn't believe it. Samantha probably thought most of her stuff was junk, but she'd never said it out loud.

"No, just two of them. My eldest appeared shocked. You know how it gets during a move. Tempers flare. Patience wears thin. Susanna is pretty calm, but the other two were eager to get the job done. And my house was big and full of memories. It was so hard to get rid of them. Now we're waiting for it to sell. I guess I'll be glad when it's over. Maybe then I'll be able to stop thinking about it."

They sat in sad, companionable silence, mulling over how unfair life was, and sipped their coffee. Maddie was never one for small talk and wondered what to say next. For some reason, she remembered Samantha talking about the half-naked woman in the laundry room. "Have you heard of a woman who does laundry half naked?"

Olivia giggled. "So you've met her? I've been told her name is Gladys."

"No, Samantha met her on Mother's Day. She was doing laundry for me and ran into this woman who had only a bra on up top. Can you imagine?"

"She must need to have her meds adjusted. Or maybe she's losing it. I'm getting forgetful myself, but I sure hope I don't forget to dress."

Maddie shuddered at the thought. "Something else strange that I saw the other day. When I came back from shopping, there was a short woman in the lobby wandering around with a shoebox of stuffed animals. She looked out of it. Do you know who I mean?"

Olivia nodded her head, compassion in her brown eyes. "I've heard a story about her. It's sad."

Maddie wondered if anyone in this loony bin wasn't sad. "What's her story?"

"Well, I've been told that she was put here pretty much against her will, but she has dementia and couldn't live at home. She had almost no family, none nearby. I heard her son made her sell her house. She had two horses and two dogs, big dogs. So they couldn't come along with her. My Spot could have come here, but no way could I walk her. Helen brings her to visit. Anyway, the animals were quite old. The son decided no one would want them, least of all him, so he had them put down."

Maddie was stunned speechless. Samantha had found a home for Beau and promised he'd never go to the pound. Maybe she'd been luckier than some.

Olivia drank some more coffee. "Apparently she took it so hard, she can't face the fact that they're gone. So she carries around two stuffed horses and two stuffed dogs with her, talking to them as if they are real. She's never seen without them. It's impossible to have a real conversation with her. I tried once. She's just not there anymore. I wonder if her son knows he pushed her over the edge. I don't think he visits often...family can be a real nuisance. I love my kids, but most of the time, they don't seem to have much patience for me and my existence. They're so busy with their jobs and families, I'm like an afterthought. But I'm beginning to like it here. I've made a few friends." She engaged Maddie's eyes and smiled. "Us old folks need to stick together."

Maddie nodded. "Getting old is terrible. It's a lie calling these the Golden Years."

Olivia lifted one plump shoulder dramatically. "What are we going to do? Sometimes I feel like I'm waiting to die. But I'm determined to enjoy some of the amenities here before I do. Tonight is movie night. You want to go with me?"

"What's movie night?" Maddie liked movies.

"They have a big screen in the meeting room on the ground floor, and so it's like going to the movies, almost. The chairs are padded, so it's comfortable."

This sounded like something Maddie could enjoy. "What are they showing?"

"I have no idea, but they have free buttered popcorn. Usually it's an old movie. John Wayne or something."

Maddie's eyes lit up. "I'll go with you."

* * *

Jean, 10:45am

EMMA POPPED her head into the doorway of Jean and Ian's treatment room, the one Jean was using for readings this morning at the Psychic Fair. "You have an appointment for a reading." Her always-quiet voice was laced with concern. Why would she be worried? Then Jean saw why, as Eric Johnson stepped past Emma and sat in the chair for clients.

"I'll leave you to it, then." Emma disappeared. *Coward.*

Jean hadn't a clue what to say. Eric had broken her best friend's heart, and here he sat in front of her.

"So, you haven't been to yoga class in a while." She couldn't resist making him squirm, and at least he had the decency to look guilty.

"I thought it would be uncomfortable for Lydia."

"That's probably true." His hangdog look made her relent. "Well, Eric. You want me to dowse about something for you? My dowsing services haven't been nearly as popular this morning as Ian's tarot readings and Lydia's aura readings." She stared hard at him, six feet of muscle folded awkwardly onto a small office chair. Other than a shadowed look, he seemed well. His clothes were impeccable but casual.

She followed his eyes as he looked down at his sneaker-clad feet. *God, he has big feet.* Finally, he looked straight at her. "I need answers. Lydia explained what dowsing was, but she never showed me how to do it. She said you could get answers to questions your brain can't answer. Is that so?" Hope rang through the words.

"Yes, that's right. What is it you want to know about?"

"Before I say, is what we talk about privileged information, like a doctor or lawyer? I want you to keep the answer in confidence."

Oh, dear, he wanted her to keep something from Lydia. She didn't have much choice. "Yes, I won't tell anyone, not even Ian, if you wish."

"I wish."

"Then what is it you want to know about? We need to come up with a good question."

Eric rubbed his hands on his thighs as if trying to squeeze information out. "I'm not sure how to ask it."

"Give me an idea, some background, what you need to know."

Eric wiped his brow. "I need to know about the future. Can you do that?"

Jean sighed. "Future dowsing is not always that accurate. But I can give it a go."

"I need to know about my health in the future, my mental health. You know I had a lot of problems after Schmidt stabbed me. But the nightmares seem to be gone. However, how can I know they won't come back? And I've had these flashbacks whenever I see blood, which fortunately isn't too often. But they're incapacitating. How can I be sure I won't have a flashback, and instead of being incapacitated, go into aggressive mode and hurt someone?" The strain in his eyes said it all. He wanted Lydia back, but was afraid for her.

Jean's attitude softened. "That's a fair question, and one we can ask. We could go about it a number of ways. We could ask if the nightmares will ever come back. Same for the flashbacks. We could ask if you would ever have an aggressive reaction due to the PTSD. We could make a scale for mental health and define what you'd think is good and what is bad and ask where on the scale you will be after a certain time period."

"Let's do all of that."

"Eric, you know that no method is 100% accurate. I can't promise all the answers will be right. But if we ask a variety of questions, and they all point to the same outcome, that means it's likely to be correct. Will that be enough?"

"Enough for now. Let's do it."

Jean nodded and reached for a pen, scribbling down questions and modifying them. After a few minutes she was ready to dowse.

"The first question I'm going to ask is for how long you will continue to experience occasional nightmares as a result of PTSD." She soft-focused her eyes, emptied her mind and tuned into the question. She saw a time scale and said the milestones out loud, waiting for a blink of her eyes to indicate a 'yes' answer. She went month by month, 1 through 10, without a 'yes' response. So she switched to years. At 1 year, she had no response. Years 2, 3, 4 and 5 gave the same non-answer. No blink at all. She stopped and reworded the question in her head. "Will Eric ever have PTSD-related nightmares in the future?" No blink, which meant 'no.' She didn't want to assume it was correct.

"I'm getting that you won't have nightmares in the future related to the incident with Schmidt."

He sigh gustily and looked down. It appeared his eyes were watering. Wanting to give him cover, she warned him, "Dowsing is not 100%. I could be wanting the answer to be that, but honestly, I felt it was a strong 'no.' Let's look at the other questions. How do you define an aggressive reaction?"

He appeared to be looking inward for an answer. "I'm concerned about a reaction during sleep or on waking or suddenly coming out of a dozing state, something I can't control."

"OK. I can work with that." Jean soft-focused her eyes, emptied her mind and opened it to receive whatever would come. When she asked if he would ever have an aggressive reaction in the future, it felt like she was missing something. So she added the phrase 'partner' to mean sleeping partner, spouse or friend as the recipient of aggression. No blink. A strong 'no.'

"I get the answer is 'no,' you won't have an aggressive reaction like you described as a PTSD response toward any partner you might have in the future."

Eric's shoulders sagged in relief. "How about the flashbacks when I see blood?"

Jean nodded and checked that out, and got that they weren't gone for good. She frowned and came at the question from another direction and got the same answer. She hated to disappoint him. "The flashbacks aren't over. But you know, the tapping therapy we learned could overcome that."

"You think so?"

"It's worth a try. We've seen some really good results on the clients we've had. You know Lydia would be happy to do it for you. But I can, if you prefer not to tell her yet."

His tentative smile encouraged her. If only he'd give it a try, she was certain it would help. "I'll try it. Can you work with me? I can come to your place. I don't want Lydia to know."

Jean scowled at the thought of keeping it from Lydia, but it was the only way she could help her friend. "OK."

"Now can you tell me if I'll be looney in the future and a burden to anyone?"

Jean laughed. "I think we need to define terms. Why don't I use a scale of 0-10, with 8 or more meaning that your mental health is good, very good or excellent, and less than 8 meaning less so, and use the time frame of the next 5 years?"

"You can do that? Wow, that's pretty detailed information."

"Indeed it is." Jean went through her ritual and asked the question, seeing the scale in her mind and saying each number as she went from 0 to 10, pushing away the fear that she might get less than an 8. She had to stay curious and open, or she'd get a wrong answer. When she got to between 8 and 9 and got a blink for 'yes,' she was thrilled. "I got almost a 9. That's a super score!"

"But you're telling me it isn't for certain?"

Jean sagged. "No, it isn't. But the answers are consistent, so I'm willing to bet they are correct. You have turned a corner, and things won't get worse. They'll get better. Especially if you try the tapping for the flashbacks." There, she'd put in a word for Lydia. "Is that why you and Lydia broke up?" She instantly regretted the nosy question.

"Things are complicated enough between us. I can't take a chance on being a lifelong burden to her, or worse yet, a danger to her health. She deserves better than a broken man." His voice had a hard edge. No wonder they'd butted heads. They were both stubborn.

"I think you ought to reconsider your choices, because I believe you are going to be all right." She hesitated to say much more, but couldn't resist putting in a plug for Lydia. "Lydia still loves you, you know. She told me once that she never loved anyone more than she loves you."

Eric's eyes began to fill with tears. "Thanks for the reading. Lydia's lucky to have such a talented, loyal friend."

Jean swept aside the compliment. "I know it's been hard Eric, but get off your ass and get on your knees and beg her to come back to you. You're good for each other. That's all I'm gonna say."

He stood up, nodded and walked to the doorway. "Don't tell her about this. I'll call you next week to set up an appointment."

She shook her head in chagrin. "The sooner the better." Then he was gone. Whatever was she going to do? She stood up and poked her head out of the door, watching Eric stride through the reception room and out the door. She followed slowly into the empty reception area, where Emma sat at the desk, reading a novel from the library. From the cover, it looked like a romance novel. Emma raised her brilliant blue eyes. "What was that about?"

"I had to promise not to tell anyone."

"Do you think Lydia saw him?"

Jean shook her head. "No way. She's been stuck in her office doing readings consistently this morning. She's popular. Unlike me. So she won't know, and we shouldn't say."

Emma bit her bottom lip. "I hate keeping things from my friends."

"Me, too. Plus she'll be able to tell we're holding back." Jean slumped into a chair. She could see out the main door down to the sandwich board at the street, with its colorful balloons and a poster advertising 'Psychic Fair Today'. "It's been slow for me this morning. No one knows what dowsing is. But this afternoon, I'll be busier, I think. People are interested in Reiki. I hope. It's so kind of you to play receptionist so we can each have a private office to work in. It's no good doing things in public."

"It's been my pleasure. Maybe you could explain dowsing to me. Then you could give me a reading, if you don't mind."

Damn. Another hard one, no doubt. Emma was going to ask about Julio. "Sure." Then she began her spiel.

* * *

Lydia, 11:00am

LYDIA SAT behind the small table she was using as a desk and studied the man before her. Bernie hadn't changed much since she'd seen him at Barbara's Christmas party. His mismatched, wrinkled clothes hung on him like he'd slept in them. Balding, overweight and built like a bear, he was nonetheless a gentle soul. It's just that his social skills were so limited, he came across like a pervert.

"So how does this work?" He didn't modulate his voice in the small office, and Lydia cringed at the volume.

"I can see the energy field around your body. It reveals things about you."

Fear flitted across his face briefly. "What do you see?"

She weighed how to say the truth without being negative. The important thing was to give him hope and maybe convince him to get some help. "You carry a lot of grief." He nodded and looked down. "You drink rather more than you should for your health." His shocked stare pinned her. "You are a kind and loving person, but you're lonely. You need to find a partner."

"Yeah, like that's going to happen. No one wants me."

"Why do you feel that way?"

"I try to make friends with women, but they run screaming from me. I guess I should count myself lucky I had one woman who loved me. I don't know how to cope without her." He wrung his hands in his lap. "I've never been any good at socializing."

"Maybe you need to take a new tack."

"How's that?" He looked at her with genuine curiosity.

"Well, do you know what kind of woman interests you?"

He warmed to the question. "I don't know if I can find someone as good as Adele. We had a great marriage. We liked the same things. We never fought. How can I find another Adele?"

"Where did you two meet?"

"I sold insurance, and she was in the office. She was the most efficient person in the whole company. She could probably have run an army. And she didn't mind keeping me on the straight and narrow. I'm lost without her."

Lydia was seeing a side of Bernie she hadn't seen before. She was ashamed at how she'd laughed at his antics. "Have you considered joining a few clubs to see if you could find someone compatible?"

"I don't socialize much. Those parties at Barbara's and the occasional golf game with Ben is about it for me. I can't do small talk, and I need booze to get up my courage to go to a party and talk to strangers. And you're right. I've been drinking more since Adele died."

"I'm going to make a suggestion. Shyness isn't a defect, nor is it a disease. It's OK to be reserved. You just need to find something you enjoy that gets you a little out of your shell. Don't focus on finding a new wife. Focus on learning to live the life you have and be happy. This isn't what Adele would want for you."

Bernie began to smile. "This is more like therapy than a psychic reading." But he didn't seem disappointed.

"Your health needs your full attention, Bernie. And you have some challenges, some big challenges to overcome. But you can do it. If you like, come back later this afternoon and get a healing session with one of us. The flier in the reception area talks about the different modalities we use. That's a good place to start."

"OK, I'll do that. That sounds good." Bernie shot up from his chair in spite of his bulk. His aura was overly yellow from his drinking, muddy from overall bad health and grayed out from grief. His digestion was off, too, but she hadn't wanted to overload him. Maybe he would come for a healing session. She's have to warn Jean and Ian how to help him. Bernie reached his hand out to Lydia, they shook hands and he rolled out of the office like a tank. She sat pondering the mystery that was Bernie as she wiped the sweat from his hand onto her skirt. They'd have to be careful. He seemed like the kind of guy who'd pay for services just to have someone to talk to. They needed clients, but Lydia wasn't certain that was a road she wanted to travel.

After a one-hour break for lunch, during which Jean wasn't looking quite right, but Lydia didn't bother to ask why, they returned for the afternoon healing sessions. Emma had already blocked out several time slots with people who'd come in the morning and were eager to experience Reiki or crystal healing for themselves. Emma took her place behind the desk, looking prim and proper and absolutely beautiful.

"We can't thank you enough for doing this for us, Emma," said Ian.

His accent was having its usual effect. Emma's aura fluttered a little. "I'm having fun learning more about what you do. Jean even did some dowsing for me." Lydia noted that Emma's aura brightened still further with that announcement. Must have been some good news about Julio.

The afternoon sped by, all three of them staying busy giving mini-healing sessions. A few appointments were made for the next week, which was encouraging. By 4pm when they closed the doors, they were exhausted but happy.

"I can stay and help clean up," said Emma, glancing at the refreshments table and napkins and other clutter lying around the office.

"Nonsense, you've done more than enough. We'll buy you and Julio lunch next weekend to say thank you."

Emma's smile transformed her face to even more beautiful. "That would be lovely. I'll talk to you later."

Jean, Ian and Lydia went into cleanup mode and had the place spotless in less than thirty minutes. They compared notes and decided that the event had been a success at introducing them to the community, and now they had to wait and see if it turned into business. Ian was thrilled that they had gathered fifty signatures on their newsletter list and couldn't wait to get started on the newsletter.

As she entered her condo a while later, Lydia let the weariness hit her. It was hard enough being in a crowd of people at a party, but this counseling, reading and healing all day drained her. She felt the pain of the people who came to her, worried about whether she could help them and in general ended up feeling the world was a rough place to live. She needed to smoke a joint to unwind and let it all go. That's when she remembered she didn't have any herb. She'd used it all to make the extract for Eric and had left it at his condo. If she wanted some, she'd have to call him. Tempted as she was, she called her supplier Digger instead.

"Digger, hi, it's me, Lydia."

"Lydia, I'm glad you called. We need to meet."

Lydia was puzzled. "OK. Now? Where?"

"The parking lot of the Rec Center on the golf course side. You know my car. I'll be there in ten."

"OK." Lydia hung up, wondering what the heck was going on. He hadn't even asked her what she wanted. She hoped he'd bring some weed, because it was the only thing that seemed to help her mellow out after intense social exposure like today. She grabbed her purse and headed back to the car. Minutes later, Digger pulled up next to her in the parking lot.

He exited his car and walked over to the passenger side of hers. His graying red hair was pulled back in the pony tail of a man who didn't know how to care for hair, or couldn't be bothered. In spite of the heat, he wore long pants and a long sleeved t-shirt, probably to cover the eczema (or was it psoriasis?) he struggled with. His pale blue eyes telegraphed concern as he slipped into the passenger seat. "Thanks for meeting me."

"I wanted to buy some herb from you. Did you bring any?"

"First things first. I'm going out of business."

"What? What's wrong? You look scared." She hadn't meant it to sound like an accusation, but he was surrounded by the pink haze of fear.

"I *am* scared. You think 'Nam would have been scarier than anything I could experience living in Palm Lakes. But at least in 'Nam, I was loaded for bear and could shoot the enemy, no questions asked. It's more complicated here."

"Whatever are you talking about?"

"A couple young Hispanic guys pounded on my door at 2am a few nights ago. I wouldn't open it, and they said they'd put out the word to the police about my selling drugs if I didn't open up. I had to. They both had guns they were brandishing about. They said I was infringing on their territory, and I had to quit selling or they'd put me down, which I took to mean they would kill me."

Lydia stared at him in horror. "How could they have found out?"

"Exactly. I have a very select clientele, all Palm Lakes residents. I can only think of two possibilities. One is that a client of mine is also a client of theirs, making it look to them like we're in competition, though I can hardly imagine anyone I know dealing with punks like that. The other option is that maybe someone they know saw me at the fast food joint making a deal. We try to keep a low profile, but maybe I got seen there."

"I think the latter is more likely."

"But, Lydia, when I call a meet, it's always when the old farts are there. I do it between meal times and check for anyone who doesn't fit in. Punks like that would stand out. I'm even careful if anyone under 60 is nearby. I think it must be a client of mine, but I have no idea who. That's why I wanted to talk to you. I thought with your X-ray vision, maybe you could help me discover who ratted me out to those punks."

Alarm shot through Lydia. "If I were present when you questioned a person, I could probably tell if they were lying. But it isn't 100%, and do you really want to tell people what's going on? And how would you explain my presence? What about this? Do you have any clients who are new or whom you don't totally trust?"

"I have a couple who fit that description."

"I suppose you could fire them as clients, but what if you're wrong? And how are those guys going to keep tabs on you? How will they know you quit selling?"

"I have no clue. I just know they seemed very determined and threatening, and I don't want to cross them. I think they misunderstood. I don't believe they operate in Palm Lakes. I bet they sell in the surrounding area, and they got the impression I'm selling to their customer base because I was at McD's. However, they wouldn't listen to reason. I had to promise to quit."

"I think maybe you should." Dismay filled Lydia as she realized she had no source for weed. "Damn, I'm out and I needed some herb."

A wan smile bloomed on his face. "Yeah, Lydia, I know you're OK, so I brought the usual amount. But I guess this needs to be the last time. I wasn't doing it as a business. It was more a public service." They made their exchange. Lydia put the baggie in her large purse, which lay on the floor of the passenger side.

"I don't know what I'm going to do in the future. Do you know anyone reliable?"

"I sure don't." He radiated sympathy.

"I wish I could ask Eric what we could do, but we broke up."

Digger raised his eyebrows. "Really? I'm sorry to hear that. You deserve to be happy."

Lydia read a little crush energy in his aura. Digger had always liked her in a shy sort of way. "Thanks, Digger. It might work out. I haven't totally given up."

Digger shook off his lethargy. "I think I'll head out. I've contacted almost all my clients about this. Hope I see you around, Lydia. If things change, I'll let you know." He slid out of the passenger seat and sauntered back to his car.

Lydia put the car in gear and slowly drove home, noting how suddenly things can change. She shouldn't have assumed Digger would always be around. In addition to anxiety about finding a new supplier, she worried about Digger. He wasn't a macho idiot. He'd be OK. Or he should. But what if those hoods returned?

Back in her living room, she unwound with a joint. By the time she finished, she was really mellow and decided to call Eric and ask his opinion. With no second thought as to whether it was a good idea, she dialed his number, only to be handed off to the answering machine. Was he out or was he ignoring her call? Did it really matter? She was being crazy, calling him. She'd promised herself she'd let him make the first move. She hung up rather than leave a message.

* * *

Emma, 2:45pm

THE DOORBELL SURPRISED EMMA. She wasn't expecting company. Julio was in the back yard checking on the irrigation system, so she jumped off the couch, putting her book down on the coffee table. She peered through the peephole and saw a very handsome Hispanic man with a stern look on his face. The family resemblance said he must be one of Julio's brothers. Fear gripped her. She almost ran to get Julio, but then she chided herself for acting so timid. She unlocked the door and swung it open, letting a blast of hot air in.

The heat was almost as scorching as his look. He stood there stiffly in black t-shirt and faded jeans with scuffed cowboy boots, his chin-length, raven black hair hanging shaggily loose, framing his stunning face. His almost-black eyes were icy instead of warm, and his frown warned her he wasn't here to socialize. She took pleasure in noting he wasn't quite as gorgeous as Julio.

"Can I help you?" At least the wrought iron screen door was locked, so there was no way he could force his way in. She found herself fighting the old familiar fear of men as he sized her up in a predatory fashion.

"I'm Sergio. Julio's brother. Is he here?"

"Yes, what shall I tell him?" At least her voice sounded strong. She wasn't going to unlock the door yet, even though it was rude. Keeping him on the other side of it was the only way she could stand up to him.

He registered surprise at her tone; he obviously didn't realize it was all a bluff. Inside she was quaking. He lifted one black eyebrow eloquently. "If he's here, I'd like to talk to him. Now." His imperious attitude marked him as a man who usually got his way.

"I'll get him. Please wait." She knew it was rude not to let him in, but he intimidated her so much that even with Julio in the back yard, she was shaking. She was sure he wouldn't raise a hand to her, but he had a dangerous look in his eyes. She gently closed the door and raced to the back.

Pushing the sliding glass door open, she scanned the yard and saw Julio leaning under a rosemary bush checking the dripper. "Julio, there's someone here to see you."

His head shot up and he stared at her intensely. "Who is it?"

"Your brother Sergio."

Julio stood up, wiped his hands on his jeans and strode across the yard. When he got to the door, he looked at her searchingly. "You look upset. Did he do anything to you?"

Emma shook her head, then reached for him. He put his arms around her. "He looks so mad. I was scared. I didn't even invite him in. I wanted you to be in the room with me. I'm sorry. It's not the way to make a good impression on him."

"To hell with that. What matters to me is you. He has no right to make you scared in your own home." He released her and ate up the floor to the front door, throwing it open. Sergio was still standing in the stifling heat. "What do you want?" Emma came up behind him and waited to hear the answer.

"I wanted to talk with you, but you weren't at your apartment. They said you moved out. Are you living here?"

"Not that it is any of your business, but yes, I am."

Sergio shrugged. "I still want to talk with you. Are you going to invite me in?"

"As long as you treat Emma with respect."

Sergio nodded tightly, and Julio unlocked and opened the screen door. Sergio stepped in, keeping his distance from Emma. She noted he was slightly taller than Julio, and there was no denying they were brothers, their handsome faces stamped from the same mold. She wondered briefly if all his brothers were good-looking. There was a moment of awkwardness, and Emma decided to break it. "Would you like some hot manzanilla tea or iced tea?"

Sergio mumbled, "Iced tea would be nice, thank you." That gave Emma a chance to flee the living room and leave the brothers alone. By the time she returned with a tray of drinks, they were sitting on the couch, regarding one another warily. She hadn't heard what they'd been talking about.

Emma passed out the iced teas and sat on the other side of Julio from Sergio, nestling close to him, drawing strength from his proximity and warmth. She saw Sergio notice the easy intimacy between them. Was he surprised that she had affection for his brother? Did he really think she was taking advantage of him?

Julio put his hand on Emma's thigh, and she knew he did it deliberately. "I am happy here with Emma. We have a garden plot we are working on, and my business is growing." He reached for her hand and squeezed it. "She takes calls for me and makes my appointments, so I can focus on working in the field."

Emma smiled. Julio was trying to convince Sergio she really cared about him, but Sergio looked more skeptical than anything. She hoped Julio wouldn't be disappointed if this visit turned sour.

The silence stretched out between them. Sergio appeared to be searching for words. Finally, his shoulders dropped as he said, "Things aren't the same since you left."

Julio was quick to rebut. "You threw me out. I did not leave by choice."

Sergio looked stung. "We're all regretting what happened, but we're still not happy about your situation. It wouldn't reflect well on Palo Verde. You can't keep secrets for long in Palm Lakes."

"You already made that clear to me when you fired me from the business and banned me from the family. So what are you here for?" snapped Julio. She wasn't concerned they'd get into a fistfight, but it pained her to have Julio go through this again. What *was* Sergio here for?

"We'd like to offer to take business on referral from you. You retain your independence, and it means that only your current clients, who obviously have no issues with you, will be referred to us. We can do so much you can't do. We'd pay a referral fee or commission on each job."

Emma breathed a sigh of relief. That would help Julio expand his business, which he was eager to do.

Julio was smiling now. "I am willing to do that. We need to discuss the amount of commission. I can send you a lot of business." She was proud of Julio's confidence. His client list had grown a lot.

"Come by the office next week. We need to discuss it further." Sergio threw a cold glance Emma's way, but it didn't affect her as much as it had the first time. She suspected he wanted to ban her from going to Palo Verde. Not that she would have wanted to.

Julio squeezed her hand again, then turned to her. "What do you think, Emma?" He always discussed business with her, but she was sure this was more for show than anything else. The offer was a good one, and she was certain he could negotiate a fine commission. But she took the time to reflect, looking for any reasons to say no. She couldn't imagine any. "I think it sounds like just what you need for expanding your business."

His smile cranked to 1000 watts. She didn't know why her answer made him happy. Surely he knew she'd support him.

Julio turned back to Sergio. "I will come in next week and we will discuss terms. But I have one requirement. I will only do it if this means Emma is welcomed into the family."

Sergio's jaw fell open, as if he hadn't anticipated this deal breaker. "I cannot speak for everyone else. I'll let you know when you come by next week, and then you can decide. I am open to it." His scowl belied his words, but Emma was filled with hope. If only Julio's relationship with his family could be mended.

Sergio stood and held out his hand to Julio, who grasped it quickly. Then tentatively, Sergio extended his hand to Emma, almost as if he were afraid she'd refuse. She froze as she thought of having contact with someone who obviously judged her, but forced herself to smile and shake Sergio's hand. Julio led Sergio to the front door and let him out.

When Julio returned, they looked at each other and both let out sighs. "This is exactly what you hoped for," Emma said.

"We will see. It depends on what they say next week. I will not do business with them if they treat you badly." He put his arms around her, and she felt like the most cherished woman on earth.

"I appreciate your support, but I think you ought to consider working with them in any case. They might change their minds about me later once they see it's real between us."

He kissed her forehead. "You are so supportive of me. I am grateful to you. I will not let them disrespect you. But thanks for offering."

She relaxed into his embrace. It felt like things were going to work out after all.

* * *

Samantha, 2:50pm

THE SHORT DRIVE to Desert Breezes would give Samantha enough time to calm down. She hoped. She'd been so afraid Arthur would come along, even though he liked neither Beau nor Mom. Yet in spite of his expressed desire to meet Jack, Arthur hadn't canceled his tennis game to accompany her.

Arthur's snarky remarks and dark looks every time she forgot and mentioned Jack's name were enough to make her act guilty, though she'd done nothing wrong. She'd been immersing herself in work at Temple Landscaping, and she avoided Jack except when they had their weekly meeting in his office, and that was public enough she wasn't worried that she'd do something stupid. He hadn't made a suggestive remark since that first day, but sometimes she caught him looking at her with longing in his eyes.

There was that one time about two weeks ago with the quail chicks. She smiled just thinking about how magical it had been. She'd been leaving an appointment, congratulating herself for the big job she'd landed, thinking about a redesign for the yard that would give the new owners the look and feel they wanted.

As she came up to a stop sign, she saw a flurry of activity in the gutter across the street. A bevy of baby quails, newly hatched little peanut-shaped balls of fluff, were running up and down along the curb, desperate to reach the safety of where their mother sat on top, but they were way too small to make the leap, and Mom was frantic, squawking at them like a deranged football coach.

Samantha pulled over, jumped out of the truck and ran over, grateful there was no traffic, and tried to think how to fix the situation. The curbing was tall and squared off, but at the corner, not far from the ruckus, it sloped gently for wheeled vehicles to gain access to the sidewalk. Glad that she had worn loose shorts with spacious pockets, Samantha went over to the crowd of peanuts and started scooping them up and putting them in her pockets, at the same time herding the few she hadn't caught towards the corner curbing. The agitated mother followed on the sidewalk, and by the time Samantha reached the corner, two of the dozen or so chicks that she hadn't captured scrambled up onto the sidewalk and ran to Mom. Samantha emptied her pockets of the other fluffy darlings, who raced to join their mother. In no time, they disappeared into the bushes. The rescue left her with such a glow that she felt compelled to seek out Jack to tell him about it when she got back to the office.

Seeing his car was in the lot, she went to his office first, but it was empty. She ran him down at the back of the lot, where he was inspecting the irrigation for the newly-delivered boxed trees. As she approached him, he looked up, his dark eyes brightening at the sight of her, and still on a high from her good deed, she almost threw herself into his arms. But she didn't. She told him the story of her daring rescue of the chicks, and he'd chuckled and praised her and even reached over and stroked her bare arm, sending shivers through her body. When she'd finished her tale, she felt awkward, not knowing how to break the spell. His eyes said he was feeling the same way, and once again, she almost fell into his arms. Instead, she mumbled an excuse about having to draw up the new design and retreated to her office, where she stayed until the end of her work day, half hoping he'd come see her and half wishing he wouldn't. He didn't.

She snapped back to present time. Thinking about Jack wasn't a good idea. What she needed was to be neutral and professional. She'd done her best to act nonchalant about Arthur's choice not to accompany her to introduce Jack to Mom, but by the time she'd climbed into her Temple Landscaping truck without him, she'd been shaking. Now as she angled into a parking space at Desert Breezes, she forced herself to take a few deep breaths. She glanced around the lot and confirmed that Jack wasn't here yet. She had time to run up to Mom's.

As she entered Desert Breezes, the transition from baking in the sun to freezing shocked her. She'd never get used to the contrast between outside temperatures in summer and what buildings had the A/C set on. It must be 70 in here, and it was over 100 outside. The lobby was bustling and noisy from a large group of residents in the sunken lounge and people going to the desk to announce their visit and sign in. Samantha got in line, signed in and headed for the elevator. A bent-over elderly gentlemen got on when she did, and as they rode up to the next floor, he gave her a searching look.

"Are you here to see me?" he rasped. He had to be over 80, with wispy white hair and a deeply wrinkled face. He gripped his cane with claw-like hands, leaning on it for support.

She wasn't sure if he was kidding. "No, I'm here to see my Mom."

He sighed in relief. "Good. I didn't know who you were, and I was worried you came to see me." What bothered Samantha was that his statement actually sounded reasonable to her. She smiled at him and wished him a good day as she exited on Mom's floor.

Mom had left the door unlocked for her, and she announced herself as she walked in to find Mom sitting in the recliner wearing a brightly-colored new housedress. It was only then the Samantha recalled she'd been wearing another new dress when they'd visited on Mother's Day.

"Is that a new dress? It's nice." It was good to see Mom caring about her appearance.

"Yes, I got it at Wal-Mart." Mom did a double take the minute it came out. She obviously hadn't meant to tell.

"You went shopping?"

"Yes, they have a bus that goes around. I needed some new things to wear. Everyone here dresses so nicely."

Samantha couldn't argue that, and she was glad Mom had some new clothes, but it scared her to think about Mom on the loose in Wal-Mart. Apparently no harm was done. She smiled to show she wasn't upset. "Jack will be here soon. I just wanted to let you know I'm here, and when he comes, I'll get him signed in and we'll come up."

Mom had the look of a kid on Christmas. "I can't wait to see Beau." *Good. She won't notice anything about Jack.*

"I'm going back down now, OK?"

Mom nodded, and Samantha quickly retraced her path down to the parking lot. Jack had arrived and was parked under a shady tree not far from her truck. He stood beside it, Beau lying in the shade on a loose leash.

"Hi, Jack. Mom's so excited you brought Beau." She leaned over to pet the dog, who gave her a friendly woof. When she straightened up and looked into Jack's eyes, she got a jolt that was nearly electrical. Maybe being outside of work made her more sensitive to his vibes.

He was dressed as usual in black, hair tied in a ponytail. His black jeans had a crease in them, and his cowboy shirt was black with thin white stripes and metal snaps. The cowboy boots were nicer than the work boots he always wore at Temple. When he smiled, the sharp planes of his face accentuated his predatory look, his dark skin contrasting with the white of his perfect teeth. It was as if being freed from the confines of work, he was going to act like she wasn't his employee.

"You look nice." She couldn't think what else to say, picking up on the drastic difference in how he was looking at her. "Mom's waiting. I went up to see her and told her you'd be here soon. Try not to let her offend you. She doesn't have any filters." She was suddenly embarrassed for her mother. What's worse, she remembered how intuitive her Mom was and didn't want Mom to suspect she had feelings for Jack. Tension plucked her nerves. She'd just have to see it through. She led Jack into Desert Breezes, got him and Beau signed in, had to pause for oohs and ahs from a few old ladies and took the elevator up to Mom's floor. On the way, she babbled about the strange old man she'd met on her previous trip up, and Jack laughed, but he didn't take his eyes off her. She hoped he wouldn't look at her like that when they were with Mom, but she didn't know how to approach the subject.

As they walked down the hall, Beau swung his head left and right, taking in the new smells. Before they reached Mom's apartment, he woofed. "Do you think he smells Mom?"

Jack shrugged his shoulders. "Maybe. He's a smart dog."

They went into Mom's apartment and found her standing expectantly, leaning on her recliner for support. Beau tugged on the leash, and Jack bent over to let him free. Beau bounded over to Mom, wagging his whole body, then sat at her feet, his position for getting a treat.

"Oh, I didn't think to have a treat for him," Mom moaned.

Samantha went over to the kitchen area and searched through the cupboards. "How about a cracker? He likes them." She brought the box of Cheez-its over and handed it to Mom.

"He remembers these. We used to share them at night. Didn't we, boy?" By now, Beau could hardly contain himself, his butt hovering two inches off the floor, tail wagging madly.

Mom slipped him a few crackers, and he munched them with relish. Finally, the initial excitement died down, and Samantha introduced Mom to Jack. "Mom, this is Jack Temple, my boss."

Jack reached out to shake Mom's hand. Thank heaven she'd prepped him about Mom's osteoporosis. He had a strong handshake. She watched Mom take in the blazing dark eyes and white teeth, wondering what her impression of him was. No need to worry. She'd tell Samantha later, whether she wanted to know or not.

Mom seemed overwhelmed and stood shaking his hand speechlessly. Jack filled the gap. "I want to thank you for trusting me with Beau. He goes everywhere with me. You trained him beautifully. And although I know he misses you, he seems happy with me. I can bring him back from time to time to visit if you wish."

Mom had dropped Jack's hand by then and nodded with a silly smile on her face, whatever that was about. Knowing that Mom wasn't used to entertaining, Samantha played hostess. "Can I get you a drink, Jack? We have coffee, beer, wine and soda of some type."

Mom dropped heavily into the recliner. "I'll take a Bud."

"I know what you like, Mom," teased Samantha.

"I'll have a beer, too. Just the one, since I'm driving."

Samantha pulled three beers out of the frig and popped the tops. "Who wants a glass?"

"I'll have one," chirped Mom. Samantha already knew her preference.

Jack said, "I'm fine without one. Samantha brought a glass and the can to Mom and set them on the coasters of the small table next to her chair. Then she ferried the remaining two cans over to the couch, handing one to Jack and making sure there were coasters on each end table.

Samantha suddenly realized during the dead air that she hadn't considered what they would talk about. She should have planned. Before she could say anything, Jack addressed Mom. "So Mrs. O'Neill, how do you like it here? It seems pretty nice."

If only she'd thought to coach him about what topics were safe. But the cat was out of the bag now. She turned to her mother, whose watery blue eyes began to flash. "I never wanted to leave my home. I was forced to."

Samantha's jaw dropped. Even though she knew she was taking the bait, she responded, "Now, Mom, no one forced you to. You decided it was time. I was glad you did, but you weren't forced."

"Of course, I was forced. I don't want to be here. I hate it here. You made me leave my home. I miss all my stuff. I was forced to give it away or sell it." Her chin jutted out as if begging Samantha to contradict her.

Mom had become more forgetful since the move, and maybe the move had contributed to it, but this was the most vocal she'd been about not wanting to leave since the day it happened. Samantha felt attacked. She'd spent night after night, weekend after weekend, cleaning up Mom's mess, while squeezing time in to bake and shop for her. Not to mention doing her laundry and trying to solve all her storage problems. The injustice of the remark fired Samantha up, and heedless of whether it was a good idea, she launched a defense. "Mom, you're being unfair. That isn't how it was." Anger was simmering and threatening to boil over. She'd forgotten Jack was even there until he spoke.

"It must have been really hard leaving your home, Mrs. O'Neill. I'm sorry. No one should have to suffer that, and yet so many do these days. But Samantha loves you very much. She's told me all about how hard the move was for you, and how she wished she could make it easier. I shouldn't have brought up the subject. Let's talk about something else."

Samantha felt stymied in her wish to assert her point of view, but she accepted that Jack's mediation was fair. Mom gazed at him with something akin to worship. "You're a good boy, Jack. No one has understood how hard this was on me. Thank you." Mom seemed truly at rest, and Samantha felt awe for how Jack had managed to stop it before it got out of hand.

She couldn't help comparing him to Arthur, who more often than not got into a fight with Mom. Sometimes he stalked away to keep a lid on his anger. Of course it was unfair to compare him to Jack, who had no real connection to Mom and wasn't going to be forced to spend much time with her in the future. Still.

The rest of the visit sped by, with Samantha sharing the story about the baby quails, and Jack looking at her like she was water in the desert. Mom chatted on, apparently oblivious to the looks Jack was giving Samantha. *Thank heaven for small favors.* After clearing up the cans and saying goodbye, Samantha, Beau and Jack walked back to their trucks. She stood while he let Beau into the passenger side. She went to turn and leave, but Jack reached out and grabbed her hand. She stopped, but pulled her hand free. "Jack, someone might see."

"Your Mom seemed to enjoy seeing Beau."

"If you would come back again sometime, it would mean a lot to her." Samantha hated to ask favors, but it really would lift Mom's spirits. "And I wanted to thank you for what you did. It prevented an argument. Sometimes I lose patience with Mom. She doesn't seem to realize how hard I'm working. She only sees what she's lost, and she blames me."

Jack reached towards her, but then pulled his hand back. "I know. I figured if I stepped in but didn't take sides, it would defuse it."

"You were right. I've never seen her settle down so fast. Thank you."

"I did it for you as much as for her." He hitched his index finger into the front pocket of his jeans, which was a very tight fit. "When do you want me to come back?"

"She'd like it if you came every week, but you can't do that. Arthur would really get suspicious if you were willing to make that drive every weekend on your day off. But maybe you could come back in a few weeks?" Samantha knew she was using this as much to see Jack as to let Mom see Beau, but she didn't care.

A smile creased his face. "Sure. Anytime." He hesitated briefly, then walked to the driver's side door. "See you at work." He climbed in and revved the engine and waved to her as he drove away, leaving her feeling he'd taken all the joy in life with him.

* * *

Ray, 4:00pm

RAY HELD Becky in his lap while she sobbed against his shirt. Alan stood in the doorway of Becky's bedroom, a lost look on his face. How could they fix this?

"Becky, honey, I'm so sorry that happened to you." He honestly didn't know how to deal with the tears of a child. Especially when he felt he was to blame for them.

She continued to cry, holding tightly onto him. Then as quickly as it started, it was finished. She looked up into his eyes, her face blotchy and miserable. "Why are people so mean?"

His question exactly. One he'd never been able to answer. Only the truth would do. "Becky, I don't know why people do what they do. I'm really sorry that you got bullied because of me and Alan." His jaw clenched in impotent rage. Even if he complained to the principal, it wasn't likely to help. You couldn't make people be tolerant. "Do you want to go to another school? Maybe we can find one that will work out better." But he didn't really believe what he was saying.

He felt his eyes filling with tears. It had taken a lot of courage for him to come out, and sometimes he or Alan were treated badly, but for the most part, people left them alone. He'd forgotten about the cruelty of children. Maybe it had been a mistake to take Becky on. This wouldn't have happened to her if he'd let her go into foster care. But something deep inside told him that it would have been much worse for her in foster care. Maybe he was just rationalizing, but it felt true.

"No, Grandpa Ray. I don't want to move schools." Her blue eyes shone with defiance and anger. "I want to learn how to fight. They pushed me down and ruined my clothes. I want to be able to fight back."

Surprised at her response, Ray tried to find his way through the maze of emotions and thoughts plaguing him. His eyes locked with Alan's. Alan was grinning, no doubt because of Becky's feistiness. "If you want to learn a martial art, we can get you into a class. But you know, people don't learn martial arts to beat other people up. They learn so they won't have to."

Becky cocked her head at him as if puzzling out the meaning of his words. "I still want to do it."

"Then you shall. Would you like us to contact the principal about what happened?" He felt certain it would do no good, but it was up to Becky.

"No, they'll just get worse if they get punished. I'm going to do like you said and keep ignoring them. I didn't react. I didn't cry. You'd be proud of me. And I didn't say anything or fight, either. I think it helped. They walked away pretty fast."

"That's my girl," Ray said as he patted her head. "Will you promise to tell us if it happens again? I won't do anything without your approval, but we need to know. Is that a deal?"

Becky sniffed and nodded solemnly.

Alan stepped into the room. "Who's up for some ice cream and cookies?"

Becky's eyes lit up. She turned to Ray. "Before dinner?" It was as if the suggestion had chased away the remaining shadows.

"You bet." Ray gently put her on the ground and stood, taking her hand. "Let's see what we can rustle up."

While Becky worked her way through a bowl of mint chocolate chip ice cream and a couple of Oreos, Ray and Alan retreated to their bedroom.

Ray slumped onto the bed. "I knew there would be problems, but this is worse than I expected."

Alan sat next to him and put a hand on his thigh. "We need to teach her how to deal with bullies. It's a good learning experience for anyone."

"But I don't want her beating people up. She's very angry, even though she says she didn't fight back. If it keeps happening, who knows what she'll do. And even if she ignores them, it's going to scar her. Sometimes I wonder if this is a mistake. Not for us. For her." He put his hands over his eyes and sighed.

"Stop talking like that. This kid is the best thing that ever happened to us. And we're raising her to be a compassionate human being who tolerates other ideas and beliefs. Plus, she's a little genius and catches on fast. We'll never have any trouble with her about school work."

Alan was scratching his perpetual 5 o'clock shadow, his blue eyes stern. Ray could hardly believe his ears. It wasn't like Alan to take Ray to task. He never would have expected Alan to argue that Ray had made the right choice. His love for his partner resonated through his body. "You're right. Thank you. I guess I was so thrilled that she took the news about our relationship so well, that I hoped we were over that hurdle. But I was being unrealistic."

"She was a champ about accepting that we love each other and are life partners. But I think she never heard of homosexuality before, and she doesn't care as long as we love her, which we do. She's so innocent. If she'd stayed in that culture a few more years, she would have been programmed to hate us. We're lucky we got her when we did."

"I just hope we're doing right by her. You and I both know the HOA is going to try and oust us from Palm Lakes." Ray couldn't bear to think about the fight that would stir up and how having to move would affect Becky.

"I think we should fight them." Alan raised an eyebrow, waiting for Ray's response.

"I don't know if we can win."

"That's not the point. We should fight. We have to give Becky good example. We don't want her to run from every conflict. We could find a home elsewhere, but what would it say to her? I think she needs to learn to stand up for what she believes." Alan waved his hand. "I don't want her fighting the bullies or goading them, but don't we want her to stand tall and be confident that she deserves fair treatment?"

Becky appeared in the doorway. "Is everything all right?" They'd never be able to hide anything from her.

Ray patted the mattress next to him, and Becky shot over and jumped up and snuggled close to him. "It's OK. We just want to do what's best for you. We're new at this parenting thing."

"I'm so happy to be with you. I love you both. I don't care what other people say. I love you more than anyone else in the world." She leaned in and hugged him. Their little girl was consoling him as if he was the one who'd been bullied. He gave Alan a look. Alan smiled.

9

WEDNESDAY, MAY 29, 1996

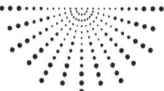

Eric, 2:45pm

*I*t wasn't really quitting time, but Eric saw frustration and boredom on the faces of the other project members. They'd been spinning their wheels for ten minutes trying to choose a name for their project with at-risk children, and he felt it was important not to let the meetings become unproductive. He wasn't the only one who hated wasting time.

He raised his hand to speak. "We've accomplished a lot in the past several weeks. George set up the nonprofit. We've filled the key positions. We've gathered names of 21 people who want to volunteer in the group. The only thing we need now is a name. I think we should stop here. We're not making any progress. All in favor?"

All hands shot into the air. "OK, then I guess we have our jobs. I've got 21 background checks to do. Is next Wednesday at the same time OK for everyone?" He saw no negative responses. "Then we'll meet next week. Try to think up names. Ask your children. Ask your spouse. We'll come up with something."

The meeting broke up as everyone picked up their belongings and headed towards the door. Hazel even gave him a smile before she left.

The schoolmarm attitude had softened when she saw Eric was going to let her do things her way. Why wouldn't he? She was way more into the paperwork than he'd ever be. Thank heaven he only had to do background checks. Paperwork made him shudder, and marketing seemed like voodoo. Yeah, he'd been really lucky.

He was whistling as he entered his condo through the garage door. His project was going to get off the ground. It kept him way more busy than the Posse and filled an empty space he hadn't known he had in his life. But he missed sharing it with Lydia. There hadn't been any nightmares or flashbacks since he'd worked with Jean. Maybe Jean's dowsing was right. Did he dare assume? What if he backslid?

He was so sick of second guessing that he suddenly felt a strong thirst for a scotch. Evenings were the hardest. Sometimes he worked out just to avoid facing the emptiness at home. And to avoid drinking himself into a stupor. At least he had gotten back to working out. But that didn't feel right tonight. He wanted to celebrate.

What the hell! Something snapped inside. He didn't feel complete without Lydia. He stopped debating with himself and strode out of the condo and up the walk to Lydia's place. God, the heat was awful. He should have changed into shorts. When he got there, he stood staring at her door. Maybe she wasn't home. He wasn't sure whether he wanted her to answer or not.

He pressed her doorbell before he could lose his nerve, fidgeting with his loose pocket change. Lydia opened the door, a guarded look on her face. Tongue-tied, he realized he hadn't planned what to say. He just wanted to see her. So badly. She took pity on him. "Come on in, then."

She walked ahead of him to the living room, her hips swaying in the long hippie-style skirt she favored. The peasant blouse was another good look for her. It showed off her cleavage. She wasn't wearing jewelry. Maybe she took it off when she got home. He remembered how it felt to run his hands through the lush dark hair that hung loose to her shoulders. She pointed him to the couch, and he sat, still mute.

She didn't make it easy on him. He was going to have to speak first. "I wasn't sure you'd be home this early."

"We don't keep regular hours. I didn't have any appointments, and Ian and Jean are holding the fort. Would you like a glass of wine?"

Relieved, he nodded his head affirmatively. She sashayed out to the kitchen and returned minutes later with two glasses of chilled white wine. He sipped it, trying to regain some semblance of balance. Just looking at her dark eyes made him want to drown in them. She sank into a chair a good distance away, as if trying to set boundaries. "Why did you quit coming to yoga?"

The question blindsided him. It took him a minute to answer. "You walked out on me. You were angry. I thought it would be awkward."

She pursed her full lips as if gauging his honesty. He knew she was scanning him with her X-ray vision. "You came to the barbecue." *Point taken.* "So why are you here now?"

He heaved a sigh. "I don't know."

"You can do better than that, Eric."

He felt like a kid being reprimanded by Teacher. He didn't like talking about feelings. He didn't know how to say what he felt. But he could tell this was the moment of truth. If he wanted her back, he had to answer. "I guess maybe I was trying to drive you away. I was afraid I was never going to get well. I was worried I'd end up in worse shape, maybe even hurt you unintentionally. I'd been having occasional flashbacks when I saw blood, and I didn't want to tell you about them. But most of all, I couldn't bear becoming a burden to you. I don't bring much to this relationship. You have way more money than I do. You're this sexy, talented psychic any man would want to be with. I thought you could do better. But I know I can't do better than you."

Her eyes widened and her mouth softened as he spoke. She was reading him and he knew she could tell he was being totally straight with her. For the first time in a while. She seemed to reach a decision. "Well, finally."

"Yeah, finally."

"I suppose there are reasons you wouldn't tell me before." Her scrutiny was painful. She wasn't going to let him get away with much.

"I told you I knew guys with PTSD. Some had violent spells at night or on waking. One hit his wife so hard, it knocked her out. I couldn't take a chance on doing that to you." He chugged the last of his wine. "That, and my Dad turned alchie after he retired, not that he had far to go. But it made my Mom's life hell. He should have..."

"That's OK, Eric. I understand. It's hard to think about. But you aren't your Dad. You aren't those other guys. And we were doing so well with the herbal extract, and I was really excited about sharing the tapping. Now that I've used it, I'm sure it can help get rid of any residual emotions you have about the incident. You're going to be fine. And even if you weren't, I'm better off with you than without you." Her eyes were shining with sincerity and love. "I'll get the bottle and we'll have a refill."

He hesitated to tell her he'd been working with Jean, but he needed it all out on the table. "Wait. I have one last thing to say. I did two tapping sessions with Jean after I had her dowse for me at the Psychic Fair. I don't see blood that often, so I can't be sure it worked, but she seems confident. And I'm willing to do the tapping with you if necessary."

Lydia's eyes shone brightly. He'd surprised her in a good way. She seemed to pull herself together, then fetched the bottle from the kitchen, and they spent the next three hours catching up, pausing only for a tasty meal of leftover homemade meatloaf and mashed potatoes with green beans. God, he'd missed her cooking.

He split the last of the second bottle of wine with her and suggested they go into the living room. He still wasn't sure exactly what was going to happen, though she'd reverted to her old self, warm and sexy as hell.

She sank into the couch next to him, and an electric shock went through him when her body pressed against his. He focused on his wine, not wanting to look like a horny teenager, but he could feel the stirrings of desire and knew that soon it would become obvious to her.

Lydia speared him with her dark brown eyes and raised her glass and clinked it with his. "Here's to moving on to the next chapter, whatever that is."

He sipped his wine, pleased with the toast and encouraged that maybe he'd get to spend the night.

She leaned over and planted a kiss on his lips, then opened her mouth and caressed his lips with her tongue. He almost dropped the wineglass. He put one hand around the back of her neck and practically devoured her lips, mouth and tongue. Then he pulled back briefly. "Is there any chance we could take this to the bedroom?"

She reached down and squeezed him meaningfully. Then without a word, she put her glass down and reached for his hand. They walked past the kitchen, and he glanced at the dinner dishes still on the table, but wasn't about to say anything that might cause a detour. As they stepped into her bedroom, he looked around and smiled. "I've never spent the night here. It's beautiful."

She responded with a smile that hinted at a night in heaven. She barely reached his shoulder, but there was something powerful about her in spite of her small stature. He bent down and kissed her thoroughly, then picked her up and carried her to the bed and started undressing her, not caring that the bed wasn't turned down. He was too eager for niceties.

She moaned as he kissed his way down her neck to between her breasts, her hands pulling at his clothes. Her silken skin practically burned his lips, as if their bodies were being welded together, never to be separated. If he had his way, and he was pretty sure he would, neither of them were going to get a minute's sleep tonight.

* * *

Christine, 3:00 pm

THE WINDOWLESS WALLS of the small room where the HOA had its meetings closed in on Christine. The whole session was spinning out of control, and Christine was fighting the urge to yell. She knew it would only make things worse, but people could be such idiots. The chaos that had broken out about the two gay guys having a child living with them had blossomed into complete anarchy, multiple voices ratcheting up in volume to make their points while no one listened. Finally, peeved that the president hadn't asserted himself, Christine took her clipboard and slammed it onto the tabletop. The loud crack got everyone's attention, and silence fell.

Christine felt able to breathe again. The president still sat mute at the head of the table. Fine. She wasn't afraid to speak. "We have to stay focused on the topic at hand. The subject is the violation of the covenant against having children living here full time. These two gentlemen are clearly in violation. This isn't about leaping to judgment about their lifestyle. Our job is to keep Palm Lakes property values high by enforcing the rules."

"How about keeping Palm Lakes property valuable by getting rid of bad elements like those homos?" chirped sour-faced Robin White. "Who'd want to live next door to them, kid or not?" he huffed.

There were a couple murmurs of approval, but no one seconded Robin's comment directly. What was wrong with these idiots? Christine couldn't contain herself. "We are only here to enforce the covenants that all residents agree to keep. This is not a forum for prejudice against people's lifestyle choices, religions or skin color. What's the matter with you? Don't you know there are laws against that sort of discrimination?"

Robin had the good sense to look chastised, but mumbled, "Yeah, but there shouldn't be. This is our chance to get rid of undesirables without worrying about legal repercussions. They agreed to the covenants. They broke them. They should pay."

More murmurs of approval this time. "Of course they have to," agreed Christine. She looked at the president, an elderly man named Joe who clearly felt out of his depth with this. His eyes met hers, and he nodded. "Christine is right. We must enforce the rules, because if we don't, others will break them, and then the sense of community, the spirit of Palm Lakes, will suffer."

"So we send them a notice telling them to get rid of the kid? That seems harsh. Don't you think we ought to call them in to a meeting to explain to us what's going on?"

Marian's reasonable question disturbed Christine. The less you gave people a forum to negotiate, the better. But she could sense the tide was moving in Marian's direction. People always seemed eager to put off hard choices.

Joe raised his hand to get everyone's attention. "All in favor of calling a special meeting to allow the residents to explain what's going on with the child being seen here all the time, raise your hands." An obvious majority of hands shot into the air. Christine thought they were cowards. She kept her hand down, but she wasn't going to win this one. She decided discretion was best, considering she wanted to run for president in the next election. What did it matter? The end result would be the same.

A meeting was scheduled for Monday, June 3rd at 10am, and the session was quickly adjourned.

Christine was even more out of sorts by the time she got home. It was so hard to keep her opinion to herself when she knew she was right, while the majority were off on a tangent. She threw herself into doing laundry. Housework was always good therapy when she had a mad on.

When Jerome came home a while later, he blundered blindly into the unpleasant cloud of toxic thoughts that surrounded Christine. She was transferring a load of clothes from the washer to the drier when he stuck his head into the laundry room. "So, how'd it go today?"

His cheerfulness irritated her. It reminded her of how shallow he was. He never really heard what she said or cared what she thought. "It was shitty."

The jolly look fled from his pale blue eyes. "Oh." Like a trapped animal, he sought an escape. "Sorry. I'll let you get back to what you were doing." He turned to leave.

The fight she'd been suppressing at the HOA meeting blasted out at him. "Why can't you ever show any interest in what matters to me?"

Instead of running away like he usually did, Jerome paused, his back to her. She couldn't see his face. She knew she was being hard on him, but he was acting like such a coward. Why couldn't he be more supportive?

He turned around slowly, an unreadable look on his round face. A quiver of something passed through her. He never engaged her in a fight. At least he never had before. She wasn't sure if she was pleased or not. He'd learned early in their marriage that she could argue him into a corner, and that's why they never fought.

His eyebrows scrunched together as if he were evaluating her challenge. "If you really want to talk about it, I'm willing to listen."

She put her hands on the top of the drier, shocked at his approach. For some unknown reason, tears were threatening. She couldn't let him see that. She forced them back, and then reluctantly responded. "Thanks." It was all she could manage to say. Just spitting out that single word cost her.

"I'll make some tea and we can sit in the living room."

She nodded wordlessly, and he disappeared. She was shaky from the adrenaline that had coursed through her body ever since the meeting. Frustration and anger clattered around inside her, robbing her of good sense. A small part of her knew this was a good development she should encourage, but the larger part of her wanted someone to scream at.

She knew she was hard on Jerome because he let her push him around. She didn't respect him for that. In fact, it was another thing to criticize him for. In rare moments of clarity, she wondered if it were possible for him to do anything to please her.

She trudged out to the kitchen and took the mug he handed her. Once they were settled in the living room, him on the couch and her in a chair a safe distance away, they sipped their tea for a minute. He eyed her as if sizing up how big a fight was brewing. Finally, he broke the silence. "So what happened at the meeting today that has you so upset? Did anyone treat you bad?"

Puzzled at his solicitousness, she waved her hand. "No. Nothing like that. It's just that a particularly difficult situation has come up. A gay couple have a child living with them. Some of the board are itching to use that as an excuse to oust them from Palm Lakes simply because they are gay."

His blue eyes never wavered. "I know how you feel about enforcing the covenants. You've made it clear over and over that you think they should be enforced to the letter. What difference is it to you *why* someone wants to enforce them? The result will be the same, won't it?" His stern tone surprised her. It almost sounded like he was judging her.

"Are you implying I'm as bad as those bigots who want to run them out of town for being homosexual?" She put her mug down. Her hands were shaking with rage. Strangely, he didn't appear disturbed, which was unusual. He was so averse to confrontation as a rule. His implacable stare was a pin in the balloon of her repressed anger. "The president is ineffectual at best. Today he lost control of the meeting and all hell broke loose. I don't care what people think in the privacy of their homes, but they have no right to parade their prejudice at the HOA meeting. I don't want to be part of something like that. I don't understand why they can't just enforce the covenants and leave their petty biases at home."

"Their petty biases are why they want to be on the board in the first place."

That was a direct hit. An angry retort warred with tears at his judgment. "You have no right to act like I'm petty simply because I'm willing to enforce the covenants." She ground her teeth. "Someone has to do it."

"It doesn't have to be you." His quiet reply shocked her. He'd never expressed any opinion about her being on the board. She knew he regarded her as overzealous about the covenants, but never offered more than the occasional sardonic comment about her attitude. What was this about?

The anger had been replaced by curiosity. "What do you mean? Do you object to me being on the HOA?"

"Of course not. I know you need to stay busy. You're a very intelligent person and need something to occupy your brain. But I think this is beneath you. Anyone can enforce the covenants. They're pretty cut and dried. I personally think they are extreme, but you wanted to live here, and I didn't imagine we'd be breaking them. I just think you could find something more challenging and rewarding to do."

The compliment deflated her. She always felt like she needed to prove something to Jerome, because she'd never attended college. Was he being sincere or making fun of the activities she participated in, like CSL and the HOA? What made him think she was intelligent?

Temporarily at a loss for words, she was overcome by the tears she'd been holding back. They trickled down her face as she swiped at them. Her embarrassment threatened to come out as anger towards him. But something stopped her default response. "Don't you think what I do is challenging?"

"No, I don't. Don't get me wrong. I know that CSL is a worthy charity. I know someone has to enforce at least some of the covenants. But neither of those things is much of a challenge for someone of your intelligence." His voice held no humor. She couldn't process what he meant.

"You have to do what you want, but I hope you won't continue on the board. I hope you won't run for president. Retirement should be fun. It should give you a chance to explore new things. You work too hard and don't give yourself enough pleasure. You recovered from cancer, and I think we ought to be grateful for the time we've been given and live our lives differently."

"Differently how?" A flicker of something like hope.

"We could talk about things we might enjoy doing together that are fun. We could travel. We could learn a new language or study something we both find interesting. We don't have to live separate lives now that we're retired. I know you've been through a lot these past few years. I'd like if we could make some changes." Was it longing she heard in his voice? When was the last time he'd spoken to her with any hint of passion or strength of character? She had to admit she liked it.

She brought her mug to her lips to buy time. The peppermint tea was soothing. Her stomach was no longer clenched, and her body had stopped singing with tension. She sighed and put the mug down. Afraid of exposing her deepest fears, she nonetheless was intrigued by his suggestion. But was she hearing him correctly? "I honestly don't know what else to do." It made her feel stark naked to admit that.

"I know. That's why I brought it up. Together we can come up with some great ideas." The smile that cracked his face lit up his eyes. When was the last time he'd looked that happy? She couldn't remember. Before the cancer, for sure.

She found herself smiling tentatively at him, relaxing at the thought of not having to handle everything herself. "OK."

* * *

Julio, 6:20pm

JULIO BREATHED DEEPLY as he stood in the shade of the patio. The slight breeze and the ceiling fan, along with the northern exposure, made it comfortable to be outside. Slipping back into the air conditioned house, he went into the kitchen, where Emma was preparing their post-dinner tea. Putting his arms around her, he nuzzled her neck, and she giggled as she put her shoulders up in defensive posture.

"Be careful. I'm going to spill the tea," she chided him in a voice that sounded less than serious. He could hardly believe how relaxed she'd become with him. Her trust filled him with joy and respect for how she'd overcome her past.

"I am being careful." He kissed her neck and buried his nose in her hair, inhaling the lavender scent of her shampoo. He stepped around her and reached to take his mug from her hand. Crystal blue eyes regarded him with something akin to worship. No one had ever looked at him that way. "It is not too hot. I think it would be more fun to drink our tea outside."

"Great." She followed him out to the patio, where they sat at the small table in chairs with soft padding, sipping their tea in a quiet harmony he was rapidly growing used to. The occasional dog barking or quail calling broke the silence. Having the block wall around the yard gave them privacy, and he really liked that.

"I got a new redesign job today."

Emma perked up. "That's terrific! Congratulations."

He knew she was glad for his success, but he was keenly aware that even now, he couldn't provide for her if they were to marry But he'd made progress. "My brothers have kept their word, and they are doing installation work that I give them for a reasonable price. I am hiring them as subcontractors so I can take care of the finances. It means I have to check behind them, but I am making a good profit."

"How about your yard watching work? I don't suppose you will get many more this summer."

"No, everyone who was going to leave is gone by now. I have about twelve to care for. That is pretty good. The only problem is that some of them are asking about things inside the house. I asked some people I know, and they say it is not good to leave a house for six months and not run any water through the traps, not flush the toilets, things like that. I was also told that it is best to empty refrigerators and turn them off if you are gone that long. I think there is a need for indoor work during the time people are gone, but I do not think they will want to give me their house keys." He tried to maintain a calm look for Emma's sake. No need to let her see his frustration.

Emma's mouth formed an O. "You mean they think you'd steal from them? How could they?" Her brows knit together and she frowned. He loved how protective she was, but he'd put up with this forever, and he couldn't see how she could help.

"These people have expensive homes with very nice things in them, and many of them think Mexicans are thieves, or at least, poor and lacking morality."

"You're an American!" she spit out.

"I know that, but they do not see it that way. I could make more money if I offered house care as well as yard care, but I do not think they will accept me for that. It is a shame not to be able to offer a full service for snow birds. There is so much I could help with. Some of them have golf carts, and the batteries could go dead...Well, I cannot do anything about that." He tried not to brood. He wanted to increase his income so he could ask Emma to marry him. But he saw no easy way to do that.

"I have an idea." Her face lit up as if from an epiphany. "I could work with you. We could go together to the yard watching appointments and you could introduce me as the one who'd do the indoor work, and you could do the outdoor work. I'm sure I can easily do whatever is needed inside, and people might be more inclined to have a woman do the house."

His immediate reaction was to turn her down. How could he impress her with his success if he made her an employee? But then he saw her eagerness. She'd been doing a superb job handling phone calls and appointments. How could she do both? "You are already answering the phone and making appointments. How could you add this? You need to be home for that."

A shadow crossed her face. Then a smile. "We could forward the calls to your mobile phone when we are out of the house. I'd have to carry the appointment book, but that's no problem."

"That seems very complicated." This was not going in the right direction. He wanted to be able to provide for her, not make her work with him. The disappointment in her eyes was like a brick wall.

"Do you mean you would want to go with me making appointments and doing the yard watching during the hottest time of the year? Do you know how little money we get paid for that?"

Her chin jutted out. "I don't care. I would rather be with you doing anything than at home waiting for you to finish work. The times we're together are the happiest for me, no matter what we are doing." Then she flashed him a heated look that clearly was referring to sex. He felt an instant response in his groin. He knew she wasn't consciously manipulating him, but her womanly wiles were definitely improving.

"OK. We can try it. Whenever I have to meet with a potential yard watching client, which won't happen again until next spring, you can come along. And for the accounts we have this summer, I can offer them the additional service for a higher price. We need to make a list of what you would do inside for that money."

She clapped her hands. "I can make a list right now."

"Tomorrow is soon enough. I don't know how many will accept the offer anyway, but it is worth trying."

She leaned over and kissed him on the lips. "Thanks for listening to my ideas and being willing to let me help."

It wasn't the way he wanted it to work out, but what mattered most was how happy and relaxed she was, and that it just kept getting better.

"So what's going on with your brothers about me?"

He hadn't wanted to pursue that. "They are good about the business. I think that this way, they feel whatever you and I do is not harming their reputation, because my clients already have accepted us, if they know about us." He pushed his mug around while he searched for how to say the rest. "They still are not ready to have us over as a couple." There, he'd said it. He hoped she wouldn't be too hurt.

A flash of pain shot through her eyes, and a curtain fell, as if she were hiding her disappointment from him. Then, she raised her head higher and said, "What if we beat them to it?"

What did she mean?

"What if we invite them here? We could do something like Barbara did for us. Have a barbecue or something casual with food and drink, and invite them and their kids over." He could see hope in her eyes.

"What if they said no to our invitation?"

"We won't know until we ask. I won't buy the food until we have a head count. They aren't likely to say yes and then not show up, are they?"

"No, they would not do that." At least he didn't think they would.

She wrung her hands together. "I don't know anything about

entertaining, but I could ask Barbara for advice. We have a grill, and the yard is beautiful, thanks to you. Maybe if they saw us together in our home, they'd be more open to accepting us."

She'd said *our* home. It wasn't the first time she'd said it, but it was the first time it struck him as real. She considered them a couple. And she wasn't afraid to face censure. He'd gone to that barbecue not knowing what would happen. He owed it to her to trust she could be just as courageous with his family.

"OK. I think it is worth a try. It shows we are open to being friendly and socializing. I know what you are hoping. You want to mend fences with my family. You need to understand that might not be possible. But I love you for wanting to try." He reached over and took her hand and squeezed it.

Tears filled her eyes. "It would be so wonderful if you didn't have to give up your family to be with me."

He knew the pain it caused her to see the breach in his family, but he had no regrets. "I have chosen what matters most to me."

Her eyes widened, as they still did every time he declared his love for her.

* * *

Barbara, 7:10pm

BEN PUT a glass of chilled sauvignon blanc in Barbara's hand and sat down next to her, a troubled look in his blue eyes. No doubt he'd noticed how exhausted she was. She stretched her hand to touch his gray hair where it hung on his collar. "You haven't had a haircut in a while."

His boyish grin chased the concern from his eyes. "What do you expect? You haven't been around to keep me on track."

She sipped her wine, trying to ignore the pounding headache she'd been nursing all day in spite of having taken aspirin three times. No need to worry Ben about that, but she was beginning to fret that she should have followed through with Lydia. The pain was exactly where Lydia had seen a problem.

"You're far away, even though you're sitting right here," Ben accused warmly.

"Sorry, I'm just so tired. It's great to be home." She sighed and put the wineglass down. "Amelia isn't getting any better. I don't see how I could have left, except that her ex-mother-in-law stepped up and offered to take over for a couple of weeks. I'm beat."

Ben put his arm around her shoulders and kissed her cheek gently. "All you have to do is sleep, eat and rest until you feel strong again. I don't want to see you doing any housework or shopping. You let me know if something needs to be done."

"Thanks. I'll be feeling fine in a couple days. It's not that I've worked so hard at Amelia's. The kids are sweet. She isn't demanding. I think the worry is wearing me down. The kids are stressing out, and Amelia is scared she's not going to get well. And I wonder what's going to happen if she doesn't. They can't come live here with us. It's against the covenants." She sighed again and reached for her glass, taking a few swallows.

"You obviously can't keep this up forever, even with help. I know you said the doctors weren't giving any prognosis yet, but do you have a feel for things now that you've spent time there?"

Barbara shook her head. "I honestly don't know. I don't want to sound selfish, but I don't like spending so much time away from you."

"I could come with you, but we'd have to bring Jack. Of course, the kids would love that. I could help. We could shut this place down for a while, get someone to keep an eye on it. Isn't Julio doing yard watching? We could hire him."

She knew Ben was thrilled to be retired from the drama of terminal illness and the heartbreak of broken health, so she appreciated his offer. She needed his help. "I don't know if I could face going back without you." Tears started welling up in her eyes. It was time to confess her own problems to him. "I've been having these headaches. I thought it might just be stress."

"That's probably what it is."

"But, a while back Lydia said she saw something wrong with my energy field on the left side of my head. That's where it hurts. She said I should do some work with her, and then all hell broke loose. I think I'm going to call her tonight and make an appointment to see what she says it looks like now, and do whatever she suggests." She reached over and touched his arm. "I know, I know. It sounds so New Age-y. But she has a gift. She doesn't make things up. And she offered to help and won't even let me pay."

Ben gave her a skeptical look. "I love Lydia, too, but don't you think you ought to see a doctor if you're having health problems?"

"I'll make an appointment, if I can get one while I'm still here. But I'm going to do whatever Lydia says. She's very talented and she said if I took care of it soon, it might not manifest as a physical problem. Then I got distracted. Maybe it isn't too late to fix it without a lot of trouble."

Ben gave her a condescending look. *Typical doctor.* "As long as you also make an appointment with a doctor."

"I promise I will. But I'm going to make you eat crow if she can make these headaches go away." She grinned to assure him she was teasing, and he wrapped her in a big hug.

After finishing her wine, Barbara called Lydia and made an appointment for Monday, the 3rd of June. She wanted to try and catch up on her sleep and feel better before Lydia looked at her too hard. No telling what she'd see. It had been grueling being at Amelia's, trying to help her and care for the kids, the house, do the shopping and cleaning. What she needed most was lots of sleep and happy thoughts. But she wondered how she would be able to be happy, knowing the possible future Amelia was facing.

* * *

Catherine, 8:15pm

CATHERINE SIGHED when she saw how late it had gotten. She must have fallen asleep during the show. That happened a lot lately. Reaching for the remote control, she clicked the TV off and pushed herself to a standing position, each joint complaining loudly at the process.

Shuffling towards the small kitchen, she thought again what a great lasagna Mary Beth made. She'd finished the last of it today. Mary Beth obviously thought Catherine had no money, making her so much food. It was true that she almost never went out to eat, and going to a movie was a treat, but that was just habit. She could afford to spend more money on clothes and things. They simply didn't mean that much to her.

As she stood running hot water in the sink to do the dishes, she felt Harold standing next to her. She'd been seeing him lately. It was a pleasure to see her beloved, but she wondered what it meant. He never said anything, just stood there, tall and Ichabod Crane-like, smiling his crooked smile at her, not one day older than 51, his age when he had had a fatal heart attack. It didn't bother her to have him appear. In fact, she'd started conversing with him, in spite of it being one-sided.

"Harold, what are you trying to tell me? Why did you go and leave all those years ago and only come back now?"

No matter how many times she asked, she never got an answer. He continued to smile as if he hadn't heard a word. Kind of like the old days. She'd almost forgotten how tall he was. Too bad she couldn't get him to dry the dishes. The drain was full.

She went to put a mug beside the drain on a tea towel, but her hand lost its grip, and the mug slipped and bounced on the counter, then crashed to the floor and broke into a million pieces.

Damn. She couldn't lean over well enough to clean that mess up. She'd need to get a mop or broom and push it all to the side. Maybe she could ask Mary Beth to clean it up for her.

As she trudged over to the closet, her limbs felt heavy. Harold followed her, silent and watchful. She opened the pantry door and pulled out a broom. As she turned to look back at the broken glass, her left eye wasn't focusing at all. She rubbed it and noticed her face was numb, like she'd had too much novocaine. Then a sharp pain ripped through her head so fast she could barely cry out. It struck her down. The floor came up suddenly, the broom clattering out of her hand. Harold stood next to her feet, unfazed, his warm smile calming her. Her last thought before blackness swallowed her was that she was glad she hadn't landed on broken glass, and she hoped Mary Beth didn't mind cleaning it up for her.

10

MONDAY, JUNE 3, 1996

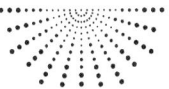

Lydia, 10:30am

ydia led Barbara back to her healing room at the Sixth Sense Consulting office. She'd decorated it in soothing colors, and the pleated window shade blocked most of the light, making the atmosphere relaxed, even sleepy. Mandalas and posters of beautiful landscapes graced the walls, and a massage table dominated one half of the room. In the other half, she had two comfortable chairs with a small table between them, the top covered with crystals she used when doing her healing work and a small boom box for playing soft music.

"I'm so glad you could come, Barbara. I know how busy it's been for you." She pointed to one of the chairs, and they both sat down. "Can I get you something to drink? Water? Tea? Coffee?"

"No, thanks." Barbara was dressed with her usual understated elegance, but lines tugged at the edges of her eyes and mouth, and purplish smudges under her eyes refused to be hidden with concealer.

"If you don't want to talk about it, you don't have to, but I was wondering how things are going with Amelia and the kids." Lydia knew the answer just from looking at her, but she wanted to be polite and show interest.

"Not so good. Her ex-mother-in-law is taking care of things for a little while, but I'm going to need to go back soon. The kids are adjusting, but there's so much to do, and there's no way she can do it herself. Ben and I are wondering what we should do long-term. This back and forth is not enough, but in another way, it's too much." Barbara sighed and knit her hands in her lap. "So I want you to look at me and tell me how this thing is and what I should do about it, in your opinion."

Lydia had already snuck a peek at it, but now she regarded it openly. The spot on the left side of Barbara's head had increased in size and taken on a muddy color. "You're having more symptoms now, aren't you?"

Barbara nodded. "I have a headache most of the time, and aspirin doesn't help. Are you saying that is related to what you are seeing?" Barbara's voice had a slight tremor in it.

Lydia didn't have great news. "You need to have a doctor look at it."

"I've already made an appointment at Ben's insistence. I know I shouldn't have put it off so long. You tried to tell me. But..."

Lydia reached over and took Barbara's hand. "You have a lot going on right now. Don't be hard on yourself. You always put others first, and I know that's a hard habit to overcome. Now you need to take care of yourself. I'd like to recommend a crystal healing session with me. Then we can see how things develop. If it doesn't respond to what I do, I want you to work with Jean and Ian. They have had some miraculous results with clients. I won't say everyone gets a miracle, but we've had our share. Of course, see the doctor, too, but let's hit it from all angles."

The pink was replaced by warmer tones in Barbara's energy field. "Could we do it today?"

Glad that Barbara was on board, Lydia said, "Of course. I planned to do that if it was OK with you."

"Tell me what it involves."

"I'll have you lie on the massage table. I'll put on some soft music. I'll pick some crystals that recommend themselves to me via dowsing, an intuitive method we use. Each crystal has a unique energy frequency, and those frequencies can be used to harmonize and balance the energies in your body. The body has an amazing capacity to heal itself. All I do is kick start that self-healing process.

"You might not feel a thing while I hold the crystals in certain positions over your body. But you might feel something like energy moving through your body. Perhaps you will feel some emotions or see something, like a scene from the past. Just relax. It's OK if you fall asleep. Afterwards, it takes a while for energy to fully transform, so we'll need to wait about three days to see what the results are, but I might get a hint before you go today as to how well we've done. We'll have to see. It takes about 40 minutes for the session. Do you have that much time?"

Barbara smiled weakly, nodded and lay down on the padded massage table while Lydia hovered by her crystals, checking to see which ones would work best for repairing Barbara's aura. She tuned in to the goal of a strong, healthy aura for Barbara and then asked which crystals would help most. Three jumped out at her, so she put them to one side.

As she turned to start the session, her eyes were drawn to the small corner cabinet that held her essential oils and other products from Botanica. Pausing, she opened the cabinet door and scanned the small bottles, again focusing on creating a strong aura and good health for Barbara. She got a big hit on frankincense. No surprise there. It was known since ancient times, when it was valued more than gold for its healing properties.

She snagged the bottle off the shelf and went over to Barbara. "Before I start, would you be open to having me put some frankincense oil on you? It's very powerful for healing many conditions, and it smells nice."

"Sure."

Lydia opened the bottle and poured a few drops onto her fingers. She waved them a few inches from Barbara's nose. "Is this smell OK for you?"

"Ummmmm. It smells delightful."

"Great. I'm going to mix it with almond oil and dab a bit on the side of your head where the aura damage appears." As she gently massaged the oil into Barbara's temple, she could sense Barbara unwinding.

"Is this something that could help?" Barbara's voice was filled with hope.

"Certainly won't hurt. My dowsing indicates it is very helpful for rebuilding your aura."

"Where do I get it?"

"Botanica. You're a member."

"I didn't realize they had essential oils. I'll order a bottle."

Forty minutes later, Lydia finished working with the crystals over Barbara's body and turned off the boom box that had been playing soft New Age music. "Don't sit up too fast. I'm going to bring you some water. Sit up slowly when you feel like it and stay on the table until I get back."

Lydia went to the small refrigerator in the main office and got a bottle of water for Barbara. When she returned to the room, Barbara was sitting on the table looking zoned out. The muddiness was gone from her aura, but there was still a bare patch.

"How does it look?" Barbara asked tremulously.

"Better, but we won't know for certain for a few days. You'll be around for a little while?"

"Yes."

"Then come back no later than the end of the week. I'll give you an appointment. Depending on what I see, we'll go from there. When's your doctor's appointment?"

"You know how that goes. The earliest I could get was about two weeks from now. I only got that much consideration by telling them I have to be leaving town in a few weeks, so they treated it as an urgent case."

"We'll see what we can do before you get your tests. How does your head feel?"

Barbara's eyes defocused as she turned inward. "It doesn't hurt!"

Lydia smiled. "The pain may come back, but I find it encouraging that it's gone. Call me anytime before your next appointment if you have questions or concerns. Will this time on Thursday or Friday work?"

"Either day is fine for me."

"Let's do Thursday."

"Can I please pay you, Lydia?"

"No, I won't take your money. You're family to all of us. We'll do whatever we can to help, and hope that it makes a difference for you."

Barbara sighed in relief. "I'm so glad I came and did this. I feel more confident about the future now."

"Good."

After sliding to her feet, Barbara looked stricken. "I feel bad that I haven't asked you how you were doing. I'm sorry."

Lydia laughed. "My life is getting better all the time. Eric and I are back together. For good, I hope."

A huge smile graced Barbara's face. "That's great news. Will he come back to yoga?"

"I believe he will."

"I'm so glad for you, Lydia. He's a great guy."

"He is indeed, and I'm very lucky."

Barbara slowly trudged to the doorway, picking up her purse from beside the chair. Then she turned and hugged Lydia. The hug was tighter than usual. "I can't thank you enough for all you are doing for me."

"It's my pleasure. Don't forget to get the frankincense and some almond oil. Call me when it arrives and I'll dowse how you can use it to get the best results."

"OK." Barbara left, and Lydia sat in the chair, feeling heavy from the session. She knew she had a tendency to take on other people's stuff, and she better do some clearing or she'd end up sick for sure. She was happy to help Barbara, but more and more often lately, she questioned whether this was something she wanted to do even part-time. It took such a toll on her.

She went to the cabinet, chose two crystals, turned on the music and lay down on the massage table. As she breathed deeply in and out, she focused on releasing anything she had picked up during the session, seeing it leave on the out breath. She sent out energy for a positive outcome for Barbara, but let go of needing to control it. She was scared for her friend, but she needed to trust that all would be well.

Feeling lighter, she visualized her own energy field strengthening, sparkling clean and strong. For a few minutes after that, she focused on breathing. She relaxed so much, she almost fell asleep. When she finally sat up, she felt much better, but she still wasn't convinced that being a professional healer was safe for her.

* * *

Ray, 11:20am

RAY PULLED into the garage and sat in the hot car, pulling himself together. The special session of the HOA had confirmed his worst fears. What if they succeeded in expelling them from Palm Lakes? Shaking off his anxiety, he went into the house to share the news.

Alan was playing with Becky, putting a puzzle together in her room. When Ray stepped into the doorway, both of them looked up, Alan's blue eyes filled with a question, and Becky's filled with excitement. "Grandpa Ray, look at how much we did on the puzzle while you were gone!"

Ray went over and stroked Becky's hair. They had completed huge areas of blue sky and clouds during his absence. "This looks like a really hard puzzle. You are doing a wonderful job." Becky beamed and continued to seek out another matching piece. "Do you mind if I take your other Grandpa away for a grownup meeting?"

Becky shrugged her shoulders, but didn't object. Alan patted her shoulder. "I'll be right back." Then he followed Ray to their bedroom on the other side of the house.

The strain was obvious on Alan's face. "So what happened?"

"About what you'd expect. They don't intend to make an exception for us. I get the distinct impression that there are a few on the board who'd like nothing better than an excuse to rid Palm Lakes of 'our kind,' though no one said as much."

Alan snorted. "They better not. If it even looked like they were discriminating, that would give us legal grounds to fight them."

Ray sighed gustily. "I don't think it would help that much. We signed the covenants when we moved in. It's a contract. We are expected to live by them or suffer the consequences. All I could do was beg for leniency, but they aren't buying it. I could sense sympathy from one woman after I explained the situation, but in the end, the vote was unanimous against us."

Alan slumped onto the bed. "So what can we do? Hire a lawyer? Or just give up and move?"

Frustration burned in Ray. "The one we consulted with wasn't optimistic about our chances. I'm not sure it's worth the investment or the trouble."

They sat side by side in silence, then Alan reached over and took

Ray's hand. "We're going to get through this. I know I said I never wanted kids, but Becky is amazing in spite of the occasional bump in the road. I don't regret our decision."

Tears welled up in Ray's eyes. He squeezed Alan's hand wordlessly.

"You know I'm always saying I'd be happy anywhere as long as I can be with you? Well, maybe we'll get a chance to prove that."

A chuckle bubbled out of Ray. He put his arms around Alan and held him close. "I don't know how I got so lucky, but I'm the happiest guy in the world that I found you." As Ray focused on what was right with his life, a sudden thought occurred to him. "Maybe we don't have to give up after all. We might have more leverage than we know."

Alan sat back and stared. "What are you thinking?"

"Public opinion is a powerful tool." He waited to see if Alan would guess his meaning.

A light dawned in Alan's eyes and a smile split his face. "You wouldn't!"

"Yes, I would. Or at least, I think we need to convince them that we would."

"What about Becky? She's adjusted pretty well. There have been a few negative incidents, but this would make it very public. We don't want to make it hard on her."

"That's the beauty of it. We do it right, we don't have to follow through. We just have to convince them we're willing to."

Alan grinned. "That's perfect. Have they given you a deadline?"

"They made a big show of being charitable and said we had until the end of the month to be in compliance."

"Then I think you should call another special meeting and let them know what's going to happen instead."

Ray finally had something to focus his anger on. "I'm going to arrange that right now."

* * *

Samantha, 2:10pm

SAMANTHA GRIPPED the steering wheel with sweaty hands as she sped down the divided highway towards home. No matter how hard she squeezed, she couldn't stop the shaking in her hands. She felt like she had stepped off a cliff and was falling through the air, headed for a nasty crash. One more thing would be all it would take. Just one thing more, and she'd crack up.

When she didn't calm down, she decided to stop for a cold drink and let the adrenaline bleed out of her system. The burger place ahead on the right would do fine. She pulled into a parking space and went inside and ordered a Dr. Pepper. She put a little ice in the cup and filled it to the brim with soda. She found a table that was out of traffic and sat down.

She fretted about her state of mind as she sipped the syrupy soda, no longer used to such sweetness after drinking nothing but electrolyte-sparked water all the time. She'd lost it big time today, and she didn't even want to consider what the repercussions would be. She'd been so upset, she'd left work early without permission. What was the matter with her? She used to have her life under control. It didn't matter how many things got thrown at her, she managed to handle them. What had changed?

As she drank the soda, she realized she didn't dare show up early at home, or Arthur would have questions. Questions she couldn't answer. Either that, or she'd break down and cry. That would be a dead giveaway.

She brooded as she swished the straw in her drink. How had it come to this? Maybe the smarter question was why did she think she could avoid this outcome? She was aware of her fatal attraction for Jack. Things had been going so well, though.

Maybe it was stress. Even though she had gotten through moving Mom and getting her house on the market, there was still a lot to be done, and Mom was not the most agreeable person to work with. And then there was Arthur. It had never been the same between them after his affair some years back. She pretended she had gone back to loving him, but she didn't have it in her. Something precious had broken, and there was no putting it back together. That's probably why sometimes he was so solicitous, but other times, he was unpleasant. They had almost no sex life and very little in common. They were more like roommates than spouses.

The stress had been piling up ever since Dad died. Maybe she was having a nervous breakdown. What had happened today certainly wasn't typical of how she performed at work.

At first, it had been like every other day she'd worked at Temple Landscaping these past two months. She was very busy and saw little of Jack, which suited her perfectly. Then she'd gone out to the back of the nursery to select a specimen tree for a re-do she had going, and as she'd walked the line of boxes in the stifling heat, she'd examined each palo verde to find the one that had the best shape for the MacArthurs. The trees were well-watered and pruned, unlike the boxed trees at Palo Verde Landscaping. Not for the first time, she thought how wonderful it was to work for a really professional outfit.

In spite of the trees being lovely, she hadn't found one that jumped out at her, and as she turned into the next row, her head looking up into the branches, she literally ran into Jack. It was rare to run into anyone in this section of the nursery, but this was the second time she'd bumped into him here. The first had been the memorable day of the quail chick rescue.

She'd apologized and stepped back from him as he held her shoulders, making sure she wasn't going to fall over. His touch sent waves of electricity through her body. Even when it became obvious she was steady, he didn't remove his hands, and they burned her bare shoulders. She didn't know even now whether he made the first move or she did, but suddenly, she was in his arms kissing him passionately. And she didn't stop with one kiss. After the first positively toe-curling kiss, she came up for air and dove right in again, putting herself at fault. If only she'd pulled away and run.

She did run after the second kiss, the taste of him in her mouth and the impression of his hands all over her body. He stood grimly watching her as she raced back into the office. Without thinking, she'd grabbed her purse and left. It wasn't until she was halfway home that she realized she'd left early without permission.

The Dr. Pepper was gone, though she didn't recall finishing it. She rattled the ice, trying to figure out what to do. She'd broken her promise.

There was no way she could go back, was there? How could she pretend this hadn't happened?

She didn't have a cell phone, and she prayed Jack wouldn't call her at home. Surely, he would not do that. What if he followed her when he discovered she had left? Would he track her all the way to Palm Lakes, and if so, what would he do? Would he confront her at home?

She put her head down on her arms and began to cry. How was she going to fix this? A small part of her mind wondered if it could be fixed. For a while now, she'd been thinking about divorcing Arthur. But the timing was so terrible. Mom was barely getting adjusted to living at Desert Breezes, and if she left Arthur, she'd have to find somewhere outside of Palm Lakes to live. She wasn't old enough to live there on her own, even if she had the money. She had a long commute to work and Mom to care for. And as lackluster as her marriage had been lately, it pained her to think about telling Arthur she wanted a divorce. She didn't think he'd be too surprised. And maybe he'd even buy into the rationalization that the stress of losing her Dad and dealing with Mom was the last straw. But her heart told her he knew something was going on with Jack. He still made snide remarks now and then, but never pressed it. Almost like he was afraid to.

The noises he made said he was threatened by the younger man whom she obviously admired and had so much in common with. He had never gotten along with Mom, and he couldn't change that now. He hadn't really supported her much during Mom's move. It was like they danced around the subject of their broken relationship but never talked about it, because there was nothing to say. Now, with Jack in the picture, the wounded relationship was festering.

Today was perhaps the expiration date on her marriage. She wouldn't have kissed Jack if the marriage was fixable. She knew that. She wasn't the kind to fool around on her husband. She looked at the clock. It was already 2:45. She could head home. Now it wouldn't be so obvious that she'd left early. She could stop by the grocery store and pick up a few items, too. Tonight she needed to go by Mom's. With a heavy heart and a big sigh, she gathered her stuff and climbed back into her truck.

Telling Mom she was getting a divorce would be just as hard as telling Arthur. She didn't know how she could do it. Mom wasn't keen on Arthur, but she had strong views about divorce, and given how she'd put up with Dad all those years, she probably expected Samantha to do the same.

The real problem hit her as she was driving down the road. How was she going to face Jack? She'd been so unprofessional. And then she'd left early without a word. As long as she'd done nothing about the feelings she had for him, it had seemed OK. Today changed everything. It was Humpty Dumpty for sure. There was no doubt in her mind that they'd both be eager for a repeat performance, and she wasn't prepared to cheat on Arthur in spite of everything. And she wasn't sure Jack would understand her reluctance to go through a divorce right now.

She didn't think he'd tell Arthur, but...she felt like a juggler who'd dropped the five balls she was juggling. And they were eggs, not balls. Some part of her just wanted to run away. To escape from the job of caring for Mom. To walk away from Arthur with no penalty. But most of all, to be with Jack.

Jack. She had to call Jack. When she reached Palm Lakes, she went to the Rec Center and used the phone she always called him from. He answered on the first ring.

"It's me."

His voice, instead of sounding angry, was worried. "Why did you run off that way, Sam? Are you OK? Did you go home?"

His concern gave her courage. "I wasn't thinking. I'm sorry. My behavior was unprofessional and inexcusable."

"Quit it, Sam. You and I both knew it was going to happen sooner or later."

She sighed deeply. "Later would have been better."

She could almost hear his smile. "Not for me."

"I'm still sorry. That shouldn't have happened. I won't cheat on Arthur, and things are so difficult now, I don't see how I can ask for a divorce. I've finally faced that that's what is going to happen, but I can't bring myself to do it right now. Mom is having trouble settling in, and I'm a mess from all the things I've been juggling. I need some peace, not another problem."

His sigh spoke volumes. "I'm not going to push you. Are you coming back to work tomorrow?"

"If you want."

"I want."

The double entendre hung between them for a while. She didn't know how she could move forward, but the status quo was intolerable. And she felt that she was hurting Arthur and Jack both. It wasn't only her pain.

"I'm still getting some things done at Mom's house. It's on the market, but the agent wants me to fix a few things to make it more appealing. And I'm eager to sell it fast, so I'm going to offer it for a low price. I expect it to sell quickly. Once that's done, I'll consider extricating myself from this marriage. I have too much on me to do it now. I feel like I'm going to have a nervous breakdown. I can't take any more pressure."

It all sounded like rationalization, even to her, but he bought it. Or let her think he did. "I know it's hard for you right now. I won't push. But I'm not going to apologize for today, and it's going to happen again. If you want to be divorced before then, I suggest you get on with the divorce."

It sounded like a threat, but she knew he didn't mean it that way. "I need to figure out where I'd live. I can't stay in Palm Lakes, and I need to be able to take care of Mom."

"You can live with me. I have a place not far from here. There's plenty of room for you. We can go see your Mom whenever you want. I know she's eccentric, but I think she likes me."

"You're right. She spoke well of you, which is rare for her. Most men don't measure up."

"Then that's settled. When you leave him, you move in here. That should make it easier for you."

A tiny thrill shot through her. The idea of living with Jack hadn't really occurred to her until now. It conjured up images best not thought of, like naked bodies tangled in sheets on a big bed.

She had a long way to go before that was going to happen. "Thanks for the offer. I'll keep it in mind. But I'm serious about needing space to deal with Mom and her stuff. Can you wait for that?"

After the briefest pause, he said, "Yeah. I can wait."

She let out a sigh. "I need to go home. Are you sure you want me to come to work tomorrow? Can we try to act professional? I know it was my fault, but I'm going to do better."

"You did just fine as far as I'm concerned."

"I better go now."

"OK. See you tomorrow."

"Bye." She set the phone down. There were so many unanswered questions. If she left Arthur and moved in with Jack, would she still have a job and get paid? And how could she be sure it would work out? And if it didn't, where would that leave her? No home and no job. It didn't make sense to think about that sort of thing now, but she hadn't made the best choice when she married Arthur, and she didn't want to repeat the error. The two men were so different, but...

She sat there for another minute wondering how things could get much worse. A random thought flashed through her mind. What if Arthur acted like he wanted to have sex with her now? She would only make things more obvious if she turned him down, but she couldn't bear the thought of being intimate with him ever again. The weight of her dilemmas pressed on her, squashing her flat. She had no clue that things were about to get more complicated.

* * *

Mary Beth, 2:15pm

MARY BETH HEARD the garage door go up in the 'big' house, which meant Helen and Alexander had returned from their trip. She rushed into the bathroom, splashed water on her swollen, sore eyes and dried them. One look in the mirror confirmed it was obvious she'd been crying. They'd want to know why.

Ethan had been so solicitous since Saturday, not that he wasn't always that way, but he managed to step in and take some of the weight off her shoulders, the guilt she felt about not having found Catherine sooner, not being able to help her survive. He'd been tender, holding her all night, letting her babble on, cry or just snuggle against him. What a horrible thing for him to have to go through again so soon after her Mom's death. In spite of that, the experience was causing them to bond in a way they never had before. When her Mom died, he'd been there for her, but he kept his distance. This time, he stepped in and did things for her. He didn't complain that she wasn't interested in sex. He took her out to eat and did the dishes after breakfast. He didn't treat her like a cripple, though. He struck the perfect balance of loving support. She wished it hadn't taken Catherine dying of a stroke to make her so sure that marrying Ethan was what she most wanted in life.

She squared her shoulders and left the casita and walked up to the front door of the main house. She let herself in and ran into Alexander as he was putting suitcases down just inside the door to the garage.

"Mary Beth!" His emerald eyes registered her weepy face, but he said nothing. Dressed impeccably as always, he was tanned and looked rested in spite of the long flight.

Helen dragged a small wheeled case in from the garage and came to a stop next to Alexander. Spot yapped around her feet, disturbed that Mary Beth was getting all the attention. Helen reached down and picked up Spot and kissed her. "How's my little girl been? Did you miss me?" Spot replied with a sharp bark.

Finally, Helen turned to Mary Beth, and concern replaced joy. "Is everything all right?"

She'd intended not to cry, but she couldn't help it. Tears began to stream down her face. "I'm sorry. My friend Catherine died."

Helen put Spot down and went to Mary Beth, putting her arm around her, and led her into the living room, a glance to Alexander enough to get him to follow them.

"This is horrible news to return to." Helen sat close to her on the couch, blue-green eyes radiating sympathy.

Helen probably wondered if going through this twice in less than a year would crack her up. It was not unlikely that she would be the one to find Catherine if she died at home, but somehow it hadn't occurred to Mary Beth to worry about that. Finding her mother dead on arriving home for lunch last year was such a terrible experience that she still hurt every time she thought of it.

Mary Beth struggled to tell the story. "I went over on Saturday, like I generally do. I had made her some ravioli. That was her favorite. When she didn't answer, I wasn't worried too much at first. Sometimes she's in the bathroom or has trouble getting up from her chair. I've learned to be patient. But after a few minutes, I began to worry. I didn't have the key she'd given me, so I went around to the back, and that's when I was able to look inside and see her on the kitchen floor. I called the Posse, and they came with the ambulance and broke in without doing too much damage. She'd been gone for a while. The doctor said it was a stroke, and that it was probably instantaneous and not painful. I wish I could be sure. I hope she didn't linger on the floor, suffering and unable to reach the phone to call for help."

Helen held her hand. Mary Beth looked at her gratefully. "I'm sorry. I'm babbling. It was just so awful. Catherine was like a second mother to me, and to find her like that..." Now the tears really began to fall. Alexander stepped over to the small bar and poured a couple fingers of amber liquid in a glass and brought it over to Mary Beth. She chugged it, the flame of the whiskey burning her throat and setting off an explosion of coughs.

Alexander took the empty glass from her. "Would you like another?"

She shook her head and wiped her eyes. "Thanks for listening to me. I'll be OK." But she didn't feel she would.

Maybe her shakiness was evident to them. Helen squeezed her hand. "How about having dinner with us tonight? We aren't doing anything special, but you shouldn't be alone. Or should we call Ethan? He's welcome to come to dinner, too." Helen turned to Alexander, who smiled warmly as if entertaining the day you got home from Europe was normal.

"Yes, why don't you do that," he seconded in his golden radio voice.

Mary Beth's heart was warmed by their thoughtfulness. "I don't want to put you out. You haven't even unpacked." She was embarrassed for being such a drama queen.

Helen let go of her hand and stood up. "Then we'll count on you for dinner at 5:30. Come early if you want, and be sure to invite Ethan." Her voice said it was all settled.

Mary Beth was more grateful than she could say for the kindness. "I know it happened two days ago, but it's burned in my mind. I just need time to get past it. I'm not very good company right now. Poor Ethan, having to do this with me twice in one year. He must think I'm jinxed."

Fido waltzed regally into the living room in his Siamese splendor and jumped up on a chair near Alexander, holding his head up high to make it easier for Alexander to scratch it, which he did absentmindedly. Fido didn't seem to mind the divided attention.

"I appreciate the invitation to dinner, but I'll be OK. Ethan is coming over tonight, and I'd like to veg out. Plus, you need to unpack and settle in and have some privacy."

Helen and Alexander both looked like they wanted to argue, but refrained. Mary Beth stood to leave. "Thanks for the drink. I needed that. Maybe we can get together tomorrow."

"Sure, Mary Beth," said Helen gently. Helen walked her to the door and gave her a parting hug, and Mary Beth returned to the casita. She had monopolized Ethan's time since Saturday, but he hadn't objected. He promised he'd come back for dinner tonight and take her out or they could order in.

She sat on the love seat, her heart aching as it had for the past two days. Helen and Alexander were back. It was time for her to think about moving on. That's when she remember the will. In all the uproar, she'd forgotten that she had a copy of Catherine's will and a letter. She dug the paperwork out of the dresser drawer she'd put them in and sat on the bed staring at them. She still couldn't believe that Catherine was gone forever. Another sob bubbled out of her, but she refused to submit to the pain. She ripped open the sealed envelope that had her name scrawled on it in Catherine's chicken scratch. The letter released a cloud of fragrance as she unfolded it, Catherine's favorite cologne. It was as if she were standing right there.

Dearest Mary Beth,

If you are reading this, then I am gone. (Or else you're a very naughty girl. In which case, put it away until I am.) Please don't mourn for me. I've been falling apart for the past few years, and you gave me extra months of happiness at a time when I thought joy had abandoned me forever. You helped me to forget the aches and pains of a broken old body, and you banished the loneliness of a long-time widow. Your kind gifts of beautiful jewelry and tasty food were like sunshine on a rainy day. Most of all, you gave yourself--your time and your kindness, and that is something I can never hope to repay.

Harold and I were never blessed with children, but if we had been, I would have wished for a daughter like you. And so it makes sense that I have left everything I have to you. It isn't really a lot, but I'm thinking it might be enough to make a difference in your life.

I know you love Ethan, more than you realize, but you have concerns about his children and most of all, about moving in with him just to put a roof over your head, or giving the appearance of that to him and others. I know you, and I know that your integrity is making it hard for you to tell whether what you feel is all love or maybe partly seeing him as an answer to your housing problem. So I'm going to make it a little easier for you to see the truth. You love Ethan, and you two belong together.

My will merely says you get everything. I own the condo free and clear. The title is with my other important papers in a fireproof box in the bedroom closet. You'll want to get that as soon as possible. You can either live there until you marry (I know it violates the covenants, but do it anyway), or you can sell the place. (Of course, if I last longer than I anticipate, you may have moved on with your life, but what I am leaving you can still be of help.)

The most important asset I have is not mentioned in the will, and you will understand why when you see it. I want you to go to my place at your earliest convenience. Go alone. Do not let anyone else have access to the condo until you have done this. Look in three places for large glass jars. One jar is at the back of my closet amongst my shoeboxes. The other is in the corner cabinet in the kitchen behind a lot of canned goods that are stacked high to hide it. The third jar is under the bathroom counter at the very back behind a lot of old stuff that looks like junk.

I haven't gotten the jars out in a while, but I know when I last counted, they had over $100,000 in cash among them. I want you to have that money. You won't have to pay tax on it, and it's enough to give you a fresh start. You don't want to live in Ethan's old house, but you feel unfair telling him that. Both of you deserve a new start for this relationship. Take that cash and the money from the sale of my condo and get a new place to start your marriage. I know you like Palm Lakes, and I hope you stay and think of me in the coming years. I like to think that this parting gift will make your decisions easier and happier, and that you will get the new beginning you so richly deserve.

All my love,
Catherine

PS In the fireproof box you will see the paperwork that is the arrangements for my funeral, which is totally paid for.

SHE PUT THE LETTER DOWN, stunned at the revelation. She'd assumed Catherine was barely making it financially. She wore old clothes and lived in a tiny condo furnished from the 70s. She'd been bringing her food to save her money as much as to pamper her.

$100,000! She had to see if it was real. Of course, it was. But she needed to see it. She got the key Catherine had given her on Mother's Day and drove over to the condo, letting herself in, feeling creeped out at being there alone. The kitchen floor was still strewn with broken glass. She picked up the broom that had fallen to the side and swept the glass into a corner. Then she went to the corner cabinet and emptied it enough to find the large jar Catherine mentioned. It was clear glass, but the inside had a layer of newspaper that prevented Mary Beth from seeing the contents. She gently lifted the jar down to the counter, opened it and peered in. Wads of cash were stuffed in the jar in no particular order. She could see $50 and $100 bills. No smaller denominations.

She put the top back on, in shock at the realization that Catherine was serious. She now had $100,000 in cash in addition to a condo. She could move here right away and then talk to Ethan about their future. One thing was for certain. She wasn't going to live in his old house. They deserved a new place to start their marriage, and she was going to insist. She just needed to figure out how to spring it on him.

She unearthed the other two jars, confirmed their contents and then put them back in their hiding places. She sat in the living room wondering what to do. Someone was going to ask where she got it if she tried to deposit that much money in the bank. Shaking the cobwebs from her head, she decided to worry about that later.

All her problems were not solved yet. She was still too young to live in this condo. Someone would find out and report her. Neither she nor Ethan wanted her in his place, and now that Helen and Alexander were back, she felt she needed to give them space. In the meantime, she was going to move in here and take her chances. It had taken a while for them to discover her before. Maybe it was time to set the date for the wedding and go house hunting.

The phone was still connected, so Mary Beth went to call Ethan and ask him to come over. This changed everything. She'd start by telling him about the condo and feel her way from there.

* * *

Maddie, 6:00pm

MADDIE LAY in the hospital bed, exhausted from the effort of trying to breathe and what seemed like hours of being poked, prodded and answering questions. She'd been short of breath lately, but not like this terrifying shutdown that sent her to the hospital. She'd finally thought to ask for Samantha, and they assured her that her daughter had been notified, so it wouldn't be long before she showed up and started quizzing her about her 'spell.'

She hated being in the hospital, in fact, hated being in the hands of doctors at all. They were a bunch of incompetents, in her opinion. They're the same people who'd told her the pain in her back was all in her head, and years later after a chest X-ray, another doctor asked her when she'd broken her back. Morons. Worse than morons. Making money off of sick people and telling them it's all in their head.

In spite of not wanting Samantha to take charge in her customary manner, Maddie couldn't wait for her to appear. It was scary here, even though the little nurse Dora was very sweet to her. The strange lighting, sounds and smells disturbed her. She longed for the peace of her old home, or even her apartment at Desert Breezes, for that matter. Anything to get out of here.

She struggled to keep breathing even though they had her on oxygen. Her doctor--she wasn't sure how she'd been assigned the man--was a small, dark man named Patel. He had a nice bedside manner, but he pestered her with a lot of irrelevant questions about her diet and lifestyle. Couldn't he see she was having trouble breathing? Finally, he'd ordered some tests and she'd suffered through them.

Samantha flew through the door, her hair pulling out of her normally neat french braid. She ran over to the bed and reached for Maddie's hand. "Mom, what happened?"

So weary she could hardly talk, Maddie replied, "I had trouble breathing."

"Have they done any tests? What did they say?"

Samantha's frenzy was wearing Maddie out. "Yes, but nothing yet."

Her daughter narrowed her green-flecked blue eyes at the coherent answer. Maddie was proud of herself for being so collected in spite of how tired and scared she was.

Samantha slumped into the chair next to the bed. "They told me they'd try to find a doctor to fill me in on your status. I hope he shows up soon." She fiddled with her loosened hair, an uncharacteristically anxious gesture. Perhaps she was worried about Maddie. Or was there something else bothering her? Maddie sensed Samantha was wound really tight tonight, and a part of her felt it might not all be due to her infirmity.

"Is everything OK?" she asked her daughter after a few moments of silence.

Samantha answered too quickly. "Nothing. Nothing at all. I'm just worried about you. It was a shock. I didn't know you'd been having problems." She wasn't saying everything, but Samantha always had kept things to herself. *So be it.*

"It wasn't a problem until today. I thought I was short of breath because I'm old and weak and fat. Turns out there may be more to it. I was scared today, but they got me help fast. I guess you were right about moving to Desert Breezes."

Samantha's mouth opened, but she recovered fast. Truth was, being scared made Maddie really appreciate not being alone in her home. "I hit the panic button on my wall, and they showed up a couple minutes later."

"I'm so glad, Mom." Samantha reached over and held her hand. Her grip was a bit tight, but Maddie didn't complain. It was nice to be cared about.

A woman in a white lab coat stepped into the room and looked at Maddie and Samantha. "Mrs. O'Neill?"

"Yes, I'm Mrs. O'Neill."

The woman had a name tag that said 'Molly Turner, M.D'. She shook hands with Samantha first, who introduced herself, then stood next to Maddie's bed. "Dr. Patel asked me to share the test results we have so far." Her voice betrayed a reluctance to do so. It must be bad news. Maddie had been expecting it.

"We still have some tests to perform. He wants to order a biopsy tomorrow to confirm diagnosis, but the X-rays are pretty clear. You have a growth in your left lung. It's rather large. Too large to remove surgically, especially given your age and condition. If it's metastasized, we can try chemo, but again, at your age, that's not a very pleasant therapy, and the side effects are worse for elderly patients. He won't be able to give you a prognosis until further tests are performed, but this is a life-threatening condition."

Samantha stared at the woman doctor as if not understanding the language.

Maddie wasn't surprised, though. She'd felt something was wrong, something more than the obvious osteoporosis stuff. So this was it. This was what would kill her. She didn't want to die, in spite of not being happy about her life. Regrets began to swamp her and tears ran down her cheeks. The woman doctor fled after mumbling a few platitudes, leaving Samantha sitting dumbly, as if unsure what to do. She was such a fixer. She wouldn't be able to fix this.

Maddie got herself together long enough to bark at Samantha. "Stop looking so grim, Samantha."

Samantha looked up as if seeing her for the first time. She must be in shock. Finally, Samantha found her voice. "We'll wait until all the tests are done. We shouldn't borrow trouble." But it was obvious she already had borrowed rather a lot and was trying to reassure them both. Maddie wasn't buying any of it. This was the end. It was merely a question of how long it would take and how awful it would be.

11

SUNDAY, JUNE 16, 1996: FATHER'S DAY

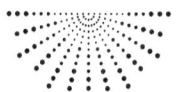

Ray, 9:30am

*R*ay and Alan sat at the dining table, which Becky had set with cloth napkins and even candles, though they weren't lit. She was rattling around the kitchen making them a Father's Day breakfast. Ray looked at Alan, who was grinning widely. "I hope she doesn't burn the house down," Ray said. Alan chuckled. "I'll be happy if she avoids burning the pancakes. What gave her the idea to make pancakes?"

"It must have been my fault. I told her how my Grandma used to make pancakes and pour the mix in the pan in a way that made pictures, like a pig or a witch. She was quite taken with that idea, and I think she's been wanting to try it out ever since. She's using a mix, and she assured me she can add egg and oil and whatever. She pointed out that we've taught her a lot about cooking, and she insisted she do it alone. But she can't reach the stove well, so I brought in the footstool from the garage."

"Becky, you'll ask us if you need help?" Alan yelled.

"I'm doing it myself," she insisted stubbornly.

Ray raised one eyebrow. "As I said."

Alan shrugged. "She'll be OK. We're not that far away." He reached for the Father's Day card that was perched on the table. Ray's heart melted as he watched Alan read it for the tenth time.

The card was one she'd made in school, and it was colorful and included no spelling errors and a large picture of two adult males figures, one little girl with golden hair standing between them holding their hands, and what Ray thought must be a puppy. She hadn't given up on that subject. They were playing a delaying game. Especially not knowing where they were going to be living in a month.

"I did some research on the local papers and the biggest one most people get around here. I found the name of a reporter who does human interest stories and contacted him and asked if he'd be interested in a story like ours. I didn't give too many details, and I didn't give him a name. I just wanted to see if it would fly. He was very interested. So when I go to the meeting tomorrow morning, I can even throw his and the paper's names out there and threaten to give him the story on how they're cruelly turning us and a child out of our homes because of some crummy covenants, and that it looks like a homophobic action to me. They'd be insane to let me give this story to the paper."

Alan didn't look convinced. "What if they call your bluff? If the story gets published, what about the repercussions for Becky?" he whispered.

"It won't come to that." Ray was convinced that the HOA board was so concerned about the reputation of Palm Lakes that they'd do anything to avoid that kind of publicity. But he knew it wasn't 100% guaranteed. "Look, I know there's a chance they'll call my bluff, but my sense is that their number one priority is that Palm Lakes looks good. I'm counting on that. If the story got out, there's no way they could spin it in their favor. The only way for them to win is to bury it."

"Let's hope your gamble pays off. It's a good idea, better than tucking our tails and running. I'm tired of having to put up with the judgment of others. It would be nice to fight back and win for a change."

At that moment, Becky plodded slowly into the dining room, a platter of pancakes balanced in her hands. Her tongue was stuck out as she focused on not tipping the large plate. Ray helped her set it on the table. She put her hands on her hips. "Breakfast is served. You can guess what the pancakes are."

"Did you turn off the burner?" Ray asked.

Becky looked upward as if asking for patience. "Of course, silly." She hopped into her chair and waited for them to serve themselves. Ray put three pancakes on his plate, wondering what he was going to say they looked like. Alan saved him when he started serving himself. "Oh, this one is definitely a cat." Becky leaned over, then smirked. "It's a dog, silly."

"Oh, I knew that. I was just testing you." Alan's blue eyes twinkled as he reached for the syrup and dowsed his pancakes. "Isn't this the best Father's Day breakfast you ever had, Ray?"

Becky rolled her eyes. "It's the only Father's Day breakfast either of you has ever had."

"Well, that, too," said Ray.

They munched on the pancakes, none of which were burned, though a couple were slightly underdone.

* * *

Mary Beth, 12:30pm

MARY BETH SAT on Ethan's patio, a glass of iced tea in her hand. The cool sweat on the glass was comforting in the heat. Though the patio cover kept the sun from beating down on them, the ceiling fan whirred ineffectively to stir the hot, still air. He'd needed to get out of the house after that phone call, and this was the best she could come up with. He obviously wasn't fit for going out in public.

She didn't know how to reassure him. He'd been so supportive of her, she wished she could help him through this, but a loved one threatening you was a different matter from a loved one dying. His son had called to wish Ethan a Happy Father's Day, but the conversation had deteriorated rapidly when Ethan explained that he was definitely going to marry Mary Beth.

She'd only heard one side of the conversation, and Ethan was his usual calm self, but by the end, his voice had risen several notches and acquired a steely edge she'd never heard before. Finally, he told William he wasn't going to talk about it anymore and hung up gently. His son had not called back. Since then, he'd been distracted and vague.

His daughter had called right before William, and Winnie was totally

228

on board with her Dad remarrying if that would make him happy. Unfortunately, it didn't seem to balance out William's negativity.

Ethan was staring off into space, not drinking his iced tea, not saying anything. A frown tugged the corners of his mouth, and his brows were beetled. She didn't feel competent to take the worry off him, but she had to try.

"Ethan, I'm so sorry about William. Maybe he'll come around."

Ethan shook his head, his gray eyes shining with tears. "He won't. He's as stubborn as I ever was. Though I don't think I was ever as unpleasant as he is."

"I don't like being the cause of a rift between you two." She wasn't going to give him up, but she needed to say that much.

He turned to her as if seeing her for the first time in a while. "Don't you dare think like that. You're the best thing to happen to me in years. I won't give you up because my son is throwing a temper tantrum. It's all about money. I guess I'm disappointed that he's waiting for me to die so he can get his hands on his inheritance. He isn't hurting for money. Winnie needs it far more. Which is why I try to help her out. But she's so proud. She wants to make it on her own. Maybe we taught her that, but sometimes I wish she'd accept more help. It's just so strange that he's the one acting this way."

Mary Beth didn't know what to say. She'd never had kids, and she'd been an only child. Everything she knew about family dynamics came from talk shows. "I'm glad Winnie's OK with us. I can't wait to meet her." And she meant it. It would be nice to meet a positive family member.

"Maybe after the wedding. Certainly by Thanksgiving, if you're up for it."

There it was. He still hadn't pressed her to set a date for the wedding, although now she was ready. She'd wanted to see how the problems with William panned out first. She really didn't want to be a bone of contention in his family. He was not a fighter, and she dreaded putting him in a bad situation. Even knowing she was now rich didn't make her feel she was worth that much trouble.

She'd been putting off telling him, not wanting to pressure him in any way, but maybe it was time to let him in on the secret that was bursting to come out. "Wait here a minute." She got up and went to her purse, which was on a table inside, and pulled out Catherine's letter. He was staring at her quizzically when she returned and sat beside him. She handed the letter across to him, not sure how he'd react. "Read this. Catherine left me everything, and it's more than her condo. I didn't tell you until now because I was worried it would just add more pressure. But I want you to know everything, and I also think it might change things for the better."

He held the letter and fixed her with his gray gaze. "Things were so chaotic with you finding her and then the funeral. I should have guessed. Catherine loved you. You were all the family she had." In typical fashion, he didn't chide her for waiting to show him. He opened the letter and scanned it, and an expression of surprise bloomed on his face. He folded it and put it down. "Is this for real?"

She couldn't tell whether he was happy or not. "Yes, it's true. I went to her condo and checked. The money is still there. I don't know what to do with it. It has been safe there for some time, but..."

"You're a rich woman, Mary Beth. You can buy a place of your own." Somehow, he didn't sound happy for her.

"What's wrong?" Why was he looking so dejected?

"You don't need to marry me. You can take care of yourself fine now. You can sell Catherine's condo and buy a lovely house and own it free and clear. With no mortgage payment, you can probably get by with the income from your job. You don't need me." His voice was laced with resignation and despair.

Mary Beth couldn't believe her ears. "Are you breaking up with me?"

Now he looked shocked. "Why would you want to marry an old guy like me when you are independently wealthy?"

"Goddammit, Ethan. First off, I am not independently wealthy. You're right. I could buy a house. So what? Do you think that's why I agreed to marry you? Do you think I'm like William said?" Fury was building within her, and she couldn't help the edge in her voice. How could he think that?

"No, no. I didn't mean it that way. It's just I never could see why a beautiful young woman like you would be interested in me. I knew I could provide for you, and I liked the idea of doing that. It made me feel needed. But now you don't need me. I feel like a liability."

The anger bled out of her instantly. "What do you mean I don't need you? Need isn't only about money and material things. I need you now more than ever. It's you I need, not your fucking money, Ethan. You are all I ever needed. I would marry you even if you didn't have any money." She hadn't realized how true that was until this moment. It felt glorious. This time his eyes held hope. Maybe it was time to ask him to do something. "I want us to start fresh together. I can't live in this house, Ethan. It's too full of Martha. She was a wonderful person, but I can't compete with her. Everywhere I look, I see her picture and her choices for decorating. It's probably one reason I haven't been eager to set a date for the wedding. I had no money, but I didn't want to live in her house. I know that sounds childish, but it's true. Now we can get our own place. I can sell Catherine's and you can sell this one. We can live wherever we choose."

She must have said the right thing. He didn't seem upset. In fact, he drew himself up and straightened his shoulders. "I like that idea."

"I was sure as hell hoping you would, because it's not negotiable, mister." She flashed him a smile.

"Where do you want to live?"

She paused, considering it seriously for the first time in ages. "I'd like to live in Palm Lakes. We both have friends and things we like to do here."

He seemed relieved at her declaration. "I like it here, too. But I'd move away if you wanted."

"This is a joint decision, Ethan. I'm glad we both like it here. What do you say we start looking at homes that are for sale? I know a good realtor."

His smile filled his eyes. "OK. Let's do that. And let's set a date for this wedding."

"Do you have a calendar handy?"

* * *

Eric, 3:15pm

ERIC STEPPED into the bathroom doorway in time to see Lydia frowning at her reflection in the mirror. He found the view arousing. She looked like a goddess of old, all delicious curves. Need pulsed through him. If only Miguel wasn't coming by, he'd drag her back to the bedroom. The annoyed look she threw at him as she tried to cover herself with her hands perplexed him.

"What's the matter? I've seen you naked before."

She looked up at the fluorescent fixture. "Not in this unflattering light, you haven't." She shooed him back so she could partially close the bathroom door and pull her bathrobe off the hook, slipping into it and tying the sash.

"Aw, that isn't fair. I was having a look."

"I don't want you seeing the flab on me. I gained weight while we were apart. Trying to substitute chocolate and ice cream for you was a mistake."

He grinned at her. Was she kidding? "I'm glad you think of me as dessert. And you look great. I don't know what you're talking about."

"I gained eight pounds, and in all the wrong places."

"Nonsense. You're perfect."

"You need an eye exam," she mumbled, but her voice had turned softer.

He reached out and pulled her into an embrace. "Will you quit judging yourself? I like the way you look just fine. Better than fine. I was thinking if we didn't have company coming, I'd drag you back to the bedroom, but they'll be here soon." She peered into his eyes, then looked around him. "So, you can see I'm not kidding." She nodded wordlessly.

He held her close. She was so short, he had to lean down to kiss her neck. "I love you just the way you are. Don't turn into some anorexic scarecrow on me."

Finally, she smiled at him. "I didn't mind being the earth mother type when I was young. I had boobs before all the other girls, and I had to beat the guys off with a stick. But now, gravity seems to be rearranging everything on my body, and the extra weight is eroding my confidence. You really mean what you said?"

How could she ask that? "You're the one with truth vision. You know I mean it."

She shook her head. "I don't understand how. Before me, you dated a 30-year-old with a perfect body."

"Am I ever going to live that down? Sally didn't love me, and I didn't love her. I love you. To me, you look perfect and always will."

She looked at him doubtfully, and he decided she'd just have to figure it out on her own. "Get dressed. They'll be here soon." He kissed her thoroughly and left her to ponder his words.

The doorbell rang minutes later, and Eric answered to see Elizabeth and Miguel dressed in their Sunday best. "Come in."

Miguel was holding a package wrapped in some masculine-looking gift paper. Lydia swept into the living room as their guests sat down. Eric introduced everyone, and Lydia offered refreshments, but they declined.

Miguel glanced at his mother nervously, and she nodded at him. He stood and held the package towards Eric. "I brought you a present to thank you for all you've done for me. It's Father's Day, and that's a good time to say thank you to someone who has been a role model for me." He'd rushed his lines, but must have gotten them letter perfect, because he relaxed into a smile.

Eric was touched by the kindness of the gesture, even though he suspected Elizabeth was behind it. Still, it was good to know she appreciated the time he spent with Miguel. "I enjoy doing things with you, Miguel, and I hope we can continue to do it for a good while." He looked at the package, wondering what it contained. He committed to acting like he loved it, no matter what it was. "Should I open it now?"

Miguel's eyes lit up. "Yes."

The box was narrow and thin. He hoped it wasn't a tie. He'd given up wearing them when he retired. He peeled the paper off carefully, setting it aside as if he'd use it again, even though he wouldn't, just to buy time. Then he cracked the box open. Inside was purple tissue paper with something nestled in it. He pulled back the tissue to reveal a single lottery ticket and a gift certificate for $25 at a local sports store.

"Mom doesn't believe in gambling, but I thought it would be fun to get you a lottery ticket. And if you win, you can share it with me." Miguel's face shone with pleasure.

"I'll be sure to do that. And thanks for the gift certificate. That's a nice store, and I can get some new gear. I really appreciate this." He wasn't sure what to do next, but Miguel beat him to it. He stood up and gave Eric a brief but intense hug. It almost made Eric tear up. Instead, he patted Miguel on the shoulder. "Thanks, son. I like spending time with you, too." He glanced at Elizabeth, who merely smiled.

Lydia repeated the offer of refreshments, but Elizabeth nixed it. "We need to go home. I have to cook a nice dinner for my husband. But thank you anyway." She stood up to prove her intention, and Eric and Lydia trailed them to the front door, where they said their goodbyes.

"That was really nice," Lydia commented after they left.

He could hardly respond. Being given a gift on Father's Day meant more to him than he would have guessed. His eyes met her dark brown ones, and he knew she'd seen his weakness. "It's kind of like having a son without any of the heartache," he joked.

She wasn't buying it. "Eric, you've done such a wonderful thing, not only for Miguel, but for all the kids who will be helped by your organization. I'm so impressed by what you accomplished, and I'm glad you found something you love doing that isn't dangerous." She flashed a grin at him.

"I won't be rejoining the Posse. That's for sure. I like what we've built with Future Leaders, though I confess I think the name is lame." No amount of grumbling had altered the outcome of that vote.

"At least it isn't a name that implies you are helping poor or at risk kids. Even if that is your goal, I think something like Future Leaders is more positive and a sign of what you hope to accomplish, and it may not be sexy, but it will work fine." She encircled him with her arms, pressing her breasts against him, and once again, he thought about taking her back to bed.

He looked down at her upturned face, so full of admiration, and thought once again how lucky he was to have her. "So what's your preference? You said we were going out to eat tonight to celebrate. Do you have any plans before we leave?"

She looked at him like that was an idiot question. Maybe he couldn't read auras, but he knew what she was thinking. "OK, but I get to be on top this time." He picked her up and carried her back to the bedroom. He was tempted to act like she weighed too much as a joke, but even though he had a Y chromosome, he wasn't completely stupid. Instead, he made sure she saw how easy it was for him.

* * *

Emma, 5:15pm

EMMA STEPPED OUTSIDE, where Julio was manning the barbecue and the children were running around the labyrinth, seeing who could complete it the fastest, their squeals and shouts echoing through the neighborhood. She smiled at their antics. Sergio followed her out and went to the larger of two coolers that sat in the shade on the patio. He pulled out two bottles of Corona and extended one to Julio.

"Thanks. That is just what I need. It is very hot today."

Emma had fled the house, hoping to have a moment with Julio alone, but it was nice to see the brothers talking. She decided to return inside after asking about the meat. "How long do you think on the burgers, Julio?"

"Another several minutes. The hot dogs are almost done. I will bring them in soon."

"I can do that," offered Sergio.

"Then I'll go back inside and get everything else ready." Emma slipped inside to start putting out the condiments and salads.

Miguel, Alberto and Ricardo stood in the living room drinking beer and talking shop. God, all but one of the Rodriquez men were gorgeous. She was beginning to think that romance novels weren't total fantasy. She'd never seen such handsome men, and that they were all brothers was amazing. Though, as her eyes fell on Ricardo, she wondered how he felt being a part of such a parade of peacocks. He was the only ordinary one, a bit on the short side and not what you would call handsome. It must be a trial for him. She didn't spend too long feeling sorry for him, because he was the only one that she'd had a negative reaction to. He creeped her out by looking at her like he could see through her clothes. Maybe she was overly sensitive, but she intended to give him a wide berth.

The wives chatted in a separate group, but when they saw Emma head for the kitchen, they joined her en masse. She wished she could remember names. She wanted to make a good impression, but she'd completely forgotten who was who. One was Maria, but beyond that, the names had fled her mind. She gave them her best smile. "I'm going to get out the condiments and finish setting the table. The meat will be coming in soon."

One of the wives, probably the oldest of the bunch, because she had a streak of gray in her raven-black hair and a few wrinkles around her beautiful black eyes, spoke for the rest. "What can we do to help?"

Emma was relieved to have such a mundane interaction. "Well, someone can carry out the mustard and ketchup and other condiments. Let me get the potato salad out." She handed some things to two of the younger wives. "I also have coleslaw and fixings for a tossed salad." She pulled things out of the refrigerator, and more hands reached out to take containers. "I have the salad fixings cut up, but I need to toss them."

The older woman said, "I'll do that if you show me what dish you want it in."

"Great, thanks. Use this bowl. And here are the salad tongs." Emma left her to it and searched the refrigerator for the dressings she'd bought.

In no time, the table was set for a banquet. Julio and Sergio brought in the hamburgers and hot dogs, and there was a brief scuffle as everyone got seated. The children sat at a card table and in scattered places in the living room, because the dining table wasn't big enough. Emma expected there would be quite a mess to clean up after, but it would be worth it if it mended the breach in Julio's family.

Everyone tucked in to the food, and the conversation began to buzz as dishes were passed around the big table. Emma sipped on a glass of wine, then topped up the glasses of the other wine drinkers, all women, noticing the shy smiles on their faces. Relief poured through her. This was going to be a success.

The meal went well, and the kids loved the cake and ice cream for dessert, so excited that the cake was in the shape of a fish. Emma had remembered a cake like that at a birthday party when she was a kid, and it had taken an exceptional effort to figure out how to cut the cake up and turn it into a fish, but she'd managed after a lot of experimenting with pieces of paper instead of cake. She'd gone all out decorating it with gumdrops and other colorful candies. Their reaction made it all worthwhile.

Talk among the men continued to be about work more than anything else. Not even sports seemed to occupy their thoughts as much. It was good to see Julio included seriously in all the discussions. He seemed more at ease than he had been before they arrived.

After dinner, the women piled into the kitchen, pushing Emma aside and telling her they'd clean up--and did they ever. She had to show them where the clean things went, but 'many hands make light work' took on a new meaning for her. It had her longing to be part of a big, warm family. Was it too much to hope that someday they would truly accept her?

What had started out awkwardly ended up warmly, with promises of having Julio and Emma over the next time one of them had a get together. Emma plopped onto the couch after the last person left, filled with satisfaction but exhausted from the effort. "I think it was a success."

"You are understating it. You have brought my family back to me. I will never be able to repay you for that. They love you."

"Well, I don't know that they love me, but it appears they have accepted us. That's what matters. I really like them, Julio. Well, all except Ricardo. What's with him?"

"He is what you might call the black sheep of the family. He is not really interested in the business, but we make sure everyone has a job who needs one. We have given him simple jobs he cannot mess up. He does not really care about the business like the rest of us do."

She didn't want to comment that her impression wasn't about his work ethic, but she decided it had been too nice a day to spoil by asking if his brother was a pervert. She'd just avoid him, and things would be fine.

"The ladies were so helpful. I imagined I would have to work for hours to clean up."

Julio acted offended. "You think I would not have helped?"

"I didn't mean that. I meant that even two of us would have had to work hard to clean up. I can't get over how fast they cleaned everything."

"You are not used to being part of a big family."

"No, this is a new experience for me."

"Cooking, cleaning, everything is done as a group. No one has to do things alone. They are your family now, too."

"Maybe. I'm not sure I've been accepted."

"Trust me. You have. Everything is going to be all right now."

She lay her head on his shoulder and sighed. "I don't think I have ever been this happy. Thank you."

He wrapped his arms around her, held her tight and murmured something in Spanish. She knew what her next project was going to be. She was going to become fluent in Spanish, no matter what it took.

1 2
MONDAY, JULY 1, 1996

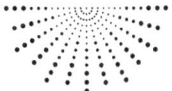

Barbara, 10:25am

*B*arbara practically skipped up the sidewalk to the Sixth Sense Consulting office, bursting with excitement. When she'd phoned to make sure everyone was there, she didn't tell them why she wanted to see them, but Lydia probably guessed she had good news.

The air conditioning in the office was welcome after the blistering July heat. Lydia sat at the reception desk, her eyes filled with question.

"Oh, Lydia, I'm so excited."

"I could tell. You must have some good news."

She rushed over and threw her arms around Lydia as she came out from behind the desk. "Yes, my test results came back clear. They couldn't find anything wrong. Not that I was surprised. Ever since you worked on me, things started getting better. That second session with Jean and Ian did the trick. I haven't had a headache since."

Lydia stared intently at her, and Barbara knew she was evaluating her energy field. "How does it look now?"

"Totally normal." Lydia gave her a wide smile. "Let's tell Ian and Jean."

Jean and Ian were chatting in the back room at the work station. They looked up expectantly as she and Lydia entered the room. Lydia turned to her so she could make the announcement.

"I got the test results this morning. They say nothing is wrong."

Jean broke into a smile and Ian grinned. "That's great news," said Jean. Ian nodded, then added, "We can't take credit for anything."

Barbara felt like taking him to task for being too humble. "I was having headaches and knew something was wrong when I had you guys work on me. I immediately felt better. Lydia said she could see the improvement, and after the session with you two, she said my aura looked good. I only did the tests because Ben insisted, but even he, doctor that he is, admits that what you did must have done the trick."

The awkwardness persisted in silence. "I know there's no scientific proof that what you did healed me, but I believe it did, and I'll be telling everyone I know about your services."

Jean brightened up. "Thanks, Barbara, we can use the referrals. Things are a little slow."

That's when Barbara noticed there were no other clients, and it was Monday, a day that is traditionally busy after a weekend with no access to services. "Maybe it's a summer phenomenon. The snow birds go home for the summer. Here, I would expect winters to be more busy and productive."

"Maybe that's it," conceded Ian, though he didn't look convinced.

"Didn't the Psychic Fair stimulate business?"

Jean looked at Lydia. Ian shrugged his shoulders. Finally, Lydia spoke. "It did for a while, but we've decided that the readings part of our business is never going to be profitable. It isn't the kind of thing most people do very often. And the healing services are apparently still a bit 'out there' for the residents of Palm Lakes. We've had some clients, and some great success stories, but business isn't growing. Maybe people don't want to talk about using such strange methods, even if they work."

Jean was nodding. "She's right. What we do isn't mainstream enough that people are willing to talk about our services except very selectively. We misjudged that we'd get referrals if we did a good job. People seem to be keeping their mouths shut, even repeat clients."

A frown tugged the corner of Ian's mouth down. He didn't add anything, but the atmosphere had turned depressive.

Barbara was so thrilled with her results, she felt an obligation to help them. But she couldn't think how. This wasn't something she could fix by throwing a party and inviting friends. "Gee, I'm sorry to hear this. You guys probably saved my life, and I can't think how to help you. You didn't even charge me. I'm willing to tell anyone who'll listen that they need to come here. And let's face it. Health is a big topic of conversation in Palm Lakes. I promise I'll do my best to refer new clients to you." But she felt it just wasn't enough, and she wasn't sure how much time she'd be spending at home, anyway. "I'm going back to help Amelia soon. We still haven't figured out what the long term solution is to her health problems." Then her eyes lit up. "Could you help Amelia?"

Concerned looks passed between her three friends. It wasn't encouraging.

Ian broke the tense silence. "Amelia has MS?"

"Yes. But we've consulted several specialists, and there seems to be controversy about what the prognosis is. Not everyone has the same experience with the disease. It can be very crippling and debilitating, and it can progress, but it isn't the same for everyone. That's one reason we aren't sure what to do. It isn't life-threatening. But it can ruin the quality of life, and right now she can't do all she needs for herself and the kids." The weight of worry came crashing back on her. "I was just wondering if she might respond to your sessions." She couldn't keep the hope out of her voice and her heart.

Lydia exchanged glances with her colleagues and took the lead. "You know we cannot guarantee any particular results. Even with minor issues, some clients don't see results. On the other hand, sometimes they see great progress or even a cure. It depends on the person. And that is something we can't predict or evaluate with any assurance. We'd be happy to work with Amelia, and we wouldn't charge you, but we can't guarantee results."

Jean and Ian nodded.

"We've been thinking of bringing her here, at least for a little while, to give me a break. It's summer, and the kids aren't in school, so we could give them an extended vacation. She can't stay forever because of the covenants, but I'm willing to push the limit on that in this case. If we bring her here, will you treat her?"

She was surprised when Ian spoke first. "Of course we will. You understand how we work. We'll do our best. It will probably require multiple sessions."

"You know we will," added Jean emphatically. "We'll do everything we can to help."

"I know you will. I appreciate all of you so much." Thinking about Amelia coming to stay with them sparked another thought. "I forgot to tell you. Owen's house sold."

Shocked looks surrounded her.

"Really?" asked Lydia. "I wish Tanya's condo would sell. It might help shift the creepy energy. If it were my place, I'd do a clearing on it. Murder houses tend to be tough sales. Do you think the new owner realizes she's bought the house of a serial killer?"

"I doubt it," said Barbara. "That's the kind of fact that might turn people off. The realtor selling Tanya's place will have to disclose a murder occurred there, but I don't think there's a law about revealing that the former owner was a killer. No violent crime took place on Owen's property. The new owner hasn't moved in, but I heard it's a single woman. She'll be a big improvement over Owen, no matter what she's like."

"That's for sure," said Lydia. "What are you planning to do about telling her about Owen? She'll find out sooner or later."

Barbara shook her head. "I don't know. I don't want to upset her, but you're right. She will find out, and possibly it would be better to tell her up front. I'd like to get to know her a little before springing that on her, but since she's going to be my next door neighbor, I think I owe her the truth."

"That sounds like a good idea," observed Ian. "She might resent you if you don't tell her. She'll surely resent the realtor if she wasn't told. But maybe she was told, and she doesn't care."

Jean and Lydia obviously weren't buying that, and neither was Barbara. "The price was really low, so it's possible, but somehow, I don't think so. Unless they are required to say negative things, most of them won't. It's too much against their vested interest."

"When you get a feel for her, maybe we could invite her to yoga or lunch sometime to welcome her to Palm Lakes."

Barbara fully intended to implement Lydia's suggestion, assuming she was in residence when the time came. "If possible, maybe I can do a little barbecue for selected people. I can't promise, because I don't know exactly what's going to happen in the future."

"We'll help with it if you do a party," said Jean. Lydia and Ian seconded it.

"Well, I better hit the road. I'll let you know about Amelia and the new neighbor as soon as I figure things out."

Everyone hugged Barbara before she left. She went home excited at the prospect of having Amelia get help from her friends.

* * *

Maddie, 1:15pm

MADDIE SAT LISTLESSLY in her recliner, ignoring the blaring TV. The difficulty breathing had progressed from a sometime issue to an everyday one, and she was now getting treatments to assist her. It was annoying having to breathe through the tube thingy that the nurse brought by twice a day for twenty minutes, but she had to admit, it did improve her ability to breathe. For a little while. The creeping loss of lung capacity was frightening, as she knew at some point, they wouldn't be able to help her.

She was aware her time on earth was limited. Stanley had had it a lot easier. He just lay his head down on the desk and that was it. They said he hadn't suffered. Why did a mean old bastard like him rate an easy exit? What had she done to deserve this torment? And it was torment, spending so much time examining her life and feeling regretful.

The other day, she'd found herself nearly having a panic attack when she realized she'd never, ever thrown out condiments, no matter how old they got. She was careful with mayonnaise, because she knew about ptomaine, but she'd never thrown out ketchup or mustard because it was old, and she didn't use them fast.

Then there was the way she kept house. Or didn't. She hadn't told Samantha that she'd gone on strike when Stanley decided they would leave Moab. Moab was the only place she had ever loved, and he took it from her, and she warned him she wouldn't lift a finger to clean house if he made them leave. Maybe he hadn't believed her. Or maybe he didn't care. She couldn't imagine the latter was true. He was obsessive about staying clean, and after the move, he even did the vacuuming from time to time and cleaned the master bathroom. He never laid a finger on her bathroom or bedroom.

Bastard. He never cared what she wanted. And she got no satisfaction from refusing to do housework. She still had to make meals. And it seemed that took up all her time, anyway, so she hadn't won anything.

She stared in the direction of the two-foot-tall statue of St. Martin de Porres that she'd refused to part with, even though it required more space than this place had to offer. She hadn't been to Mass in years, but she was still a Catholic at heart. She'd been raised by the nuns, and she prayed often. She quit going to church when it got all ecumenical. Stanley and she had seen eye to eye on that. But he kept attending Mass anyway, probably to hedge his bets with the Almighty.

Now Maddie was wondering if he'd done the smart thing. Would she be judged because she'd stopped going to church and confession? She had enough things to feel regret about without wondering if she'd be turned out of heaven because of not taking the sacraments.

And should she talk to a priest or make some kind of arrangements for when things got bad? Wouldn't that look like she'd gotten religion at the end and wasn't sincere? What good would it do at that late date?

She'd never been a light-hearted person, at least not since she was a small child, but these past weeks had been filled with more sadness, regret and fear than she'd ever experienced. And that was saying a lot. She almost wished it was over, but she wasn't in a hurry to see what God was going to do with her. She was not feeling very proud of her life right now. She wondered why she never thought about this earlier. She'd just slogged through each day, and it wasn't always easy. But now, looking back, it seemed she must have missed some opportunity for happiness or success, not to mention getting on God's good side.

A knock on the door snapped her out of her sad reverie. It was getting harder to rise from a sitting position, but she didn't want to admit to further infirmities. She was afraid they'd insist she move to the other wing where the Alzheimer's and seriously ill lived. As much as she didn't like this place compared to home, the independent section was far nicer than the other one. She'd have to have a roommate there, and everyone was so bad off. She wanted to stay among the living for as long as possible.

When she finally reached the door, she found Helen waiting patiently with a bottle of wine and a box of chocolates. Helen knew how to lift her spirits. "Come in, Helen. It's good to see you." She turned and let Helen follow her in.

"I brought you a couple little nothings. I know you like wine and chocolate, and you should have some nice ones."

Maddie's spirits lifted as she saw that Helen had remembered her favorite chocolates were Whitman's. "I hope you didn't spend a lot of money on that wine."

Helen ignored her glare. "You know Alexander. He won't spend money on bad wine. So you're stuck with something he'd drink. I guarantee you'll love it. We have plenty of money, so it isn't a problem splurging for wine."

Maddie harrumphed, but didn't argue. The bottles of wine Helen brought tasted good to her, but she couldn't really tell the difference from what she usually bought. Helen put her presents on the counter in the tiny kitchen. "How about I open the chocolates and pour us some wine?"

Maddie normally didn't like people doing for her, but she had to admit, she didn't have the energy or breath to exert herself. "OK. I'll sit down." She slumped into the recliner, stifling a yelp when her spine screamed at her.

"You OK?"

"Yup. Just the bones hurting." Now that Helen had wrestled the bottle open, Maddie was eager to have some wine. "Thanks for coming to visit. I know I'm not great company."

"Nonsense. I love visiting. Is there anything I can do while I'm here that will help you?" She carried two glasses over and went back for the box of chocolates, setting them on the table by Maddie.

"No. I don't need anything. Samantha comes often. She and Mary Beth bring me food." She smiled at that. She loved Mary Beth's cooking. "Samantha even brought Beau to visit this past weekend."

"Did she? That's wonderful! Didn't you say Beau is living with her new boss?"

"Yes, his name's Jack. He's a good-looking boy." Then she looked at Helen. "Nothing like your Alexander." She shocked herself by remembering his name. "But this boy is built. He's tall, dark and handsome, but in a kind of rough way, like a cowboy from the Westerns."

"It's really nice of him to bring Beau to see you. Not everyone would take time out of their weekend for that."

"He seems to be a nice guy. But I don't think he's doing it for me. I think he's doing it for Samantha." Maybe she shouldn't talk about her suspicions. She wasn't much for gossip, but she was certain Jack Temple wasn't driving all the way over here simply out of a sense of compassion for a dying old woman.

Helen cocked her head, her strawberry blonde hair brushing her shoulder. "What do you mean?" She was charmingly naive.

"I'm not sure, but I think he has a thing for Samantha. He looks at her that way, like she was one of these chocolates. She doesn't look at him at all when they're here."

"You think something is going on?" Helen appeared doubtful.

"I'm not sure. I think he likes her as more than an employee. She won't answer my questions about him. She keeps changing the subject." Maddie had never been a gossip, but talking about this distracted her from her own situation. She warmed up to it. "She and Arthur are a bad match, always have been, but she won't admit it. She hates the thought of being a failure at anything. He never liked me. The feeling is mutual. She's always working on something, and he lollygags around playing tennis. She never seems happy. I've given up trying to talk to her about it."

"I like Samantha. She designed the best yard for me when I lived in the condo. She seems really smart and level-headed. I'm sure whatever she does, she'll be OK."

"I think so, too. I don't believe in divorce, not that I hadn't thought about it often with Stanley, but I'd hate to see her go through that." She didn't mention that Samantha was a lapsed Catholic, and that worried her, too. Sometimes she worried about Samantha's soul.

"How's the sale of your house coming?" Helen was obviously ready to change the subject.

"Still not sold. Samantha is doing some things to make it more attractive, and the price is set low, but so far, no one has put in a bid."

"I know you'd like to sell it soon, so I hope the right person comes along quickly."

"Me, too."

Maddie sipped her wine and opened the box of candy and selected one. She savored the flavor as she bit into it. Some things were still wonderful about life. Helen smiled to see her enjoyment.

"You have one, too." She pointed at the box. Helen reached over and took one without looking at the chart that showed what was what. "You're adventurous."

"Not really. I like any kind of chocolate. Is Mary Beth still coming by to do jewelry? I see you have your stuff out. What's your latest project?"

Maddie warmed to her favorite topic. "Given the sentence they've passed on me, I decided to make necklaces for everyone. You can go over and look. I had some nice turquoise and silver, and I think they are going to be lovely. I haven't finished the design, but you can see what it's going to look like."

Helen got up, her wine glass in hand, and perused the materials on the table. Maddie had laid them out roughly how she thought the necklaces would look, but they weren't strung yet. "This is going to be beautiful." She reached out and fingered the turquoise beads. "I love turquoise." She turned shining eyes to Maddie. "Do I get one?"

"Of course you do. You're one of my favorite people."

Helen smiled at the compliment. "I really love wearing your jewelry. I appreciate your sharing your talent." She came back and sat down on the couch.

After more talk about jewelry, Helen finished her wine and said goodbye. Maddie could tell Helen was feeling awkward about Maddie's health situation. Still, she hoped Helen would come by again. She didn't have the nerve to ask her. She knew Helen would do it if she asked, but she wanted it to be Helen's idea.

The room seemed stale after Helen left, and Maddie finished her wine and went to sit at her worktable. There was no telling if she'd be able to finish all of the necklaces or not. At least it gave her something to do besides feeling sorry for herself and worrying about the future. When she was making jewelry, it seemed time stood still and she was filled with peace. She needed to make a necklace and earrings for Helen, Olivia, Mary Beth, Barbara and Samantha at least. And that was going to take time.

Time was one thing she had little of. Money was another. With the house not sold, there was no more money for going to Wal-Mart. Samantha brought her Kentucky Fried Chicken once a week and they played Yahtzee, but she'd made it clear there wasn't money for much else. Damn, but she wished she could have a splurge before she died. When Stanley died, she started thinking maybe with him gone, she could stretch her wings a bit. Guess that wasn't going to happen. She put her magnifying glasses on and set to work on the necklaces. Her worries faded into the background as she focused on improving the design.

* * *

Samantha, 1:30pm

SAMANTHA TAPPED on the door frame of Jack's office. He looked up and broke into a heart-melting smile. "Sam. Come in." He stood up like an old-style gentleman and pointed to the only other chair in his office. She rarely spent time in here since she'd been hired. The room felt like Jack. The framed photos of desert plants and the bookshelf with all the botanical and landscaping references spoke of his love for what he did. She sat down in the chair next to his desk.

"I wanted to thank you for bringing Beau to see Mom. It means the world to her, even though she isn't that expressive. She hates people doing things for her, and it tends to choke her up and that makes her seem unappreciative. But I promise she really did enjoy it. And I think she likes you." That was a weird feeling, but welcome nonetheless.

Jack's dark eyes danced with pleasure. "It was no big deal. She's interesting and eccentric. Plus, I got to spend time with you. Though you seemed pretty nervous."

Samantha shrugged. "I know it sounds weird, but my Mom sees

248

things. She is highly intuitive, and I was afraid she'd see me looking at you and know there was something between us."

"So what?"

"I don't think she'd say anything to Arthur, especially without proof, but she doesn't approve of divorce, and with her health the way it is, I don't like the idea of shocking her. I don't mean she'd miss Arthur. But I'd have to leave Palm Lakes, and even with your generous offer of housing, it would make it hard for me to care for her, not to mention getting the house totally ready for sale." The enormity of all she had to do weighed heavily on her, and she sighed.

"They told your Mom she has months to live, right?"

Samantha flinched at that. "Yes, but I still am having trouble getting my head around it. And it's upset Mom more than she lets on. I don't know how to help her through this. And the last thing she needs is me piling my problems on her. Her health is collapsing. She has no money, and I know she sort of envisioned when the house sold, she'd go a bit wild. For someone of her generation, that is, nothing crazy. She wanted to have some fun now that Dad's gone. And now she never will. It's sad." Samantha looked at her hands and felt the tears filling her eyes.

"If you cry, I'm going to come over there and hold you."

"Don't you dare!"

"I mean it, Sam. I can't stand to see you hurting. How do you think I feel when the only thing I can do to help is bring Beau around?" The dog in question, who was lying partly under the desk, lifted his head and looked at Jack. "It's OK, buddy."

Samantha wanted so much to lean on him. He was strong in every way. Her eyes fell on his workman's hands, big and strong, and for a second she had a vision of them stroking her body. She forced herself back to reality. "I'm sorry about putting you in this situation. I don't want to sound like a cliché, but this is not a good time for me to put myself first. I have to care for Mom." She hated to say it, but if he couldn't deal with it, there was no future for them, because Mom had to come first.

He stared at her with hard, dark eyes. "Have you told anyone about us?"

His question took her by surprise. "Yes. I told my friend Mary Beth everything. She is very supportive of my feelings for you. I have another friend, but we aren't that close, and she's very conventional, so I haven't told her anything other than Arthur and I are living separate lives. I think she can read between the lines, but I'm not telling her more yet."

Jack had a satisfied look on his face. "I'm glad you told your friends about me. It makes me feel more real."

"You're the most real thing in my life, Jack. I'm sorry to always be putting you off, and I promise things won't always be like this. I don't feel any better than you about waiting. I wish I were free to leave Arthur now. I don't look forward to divorcing him, but I can't imagine he's going to care that much. We hardly do anything together anymore. He's always out playing tennis with friends, and I'm working or at Mom's." She fought a reluctance to share more, but felt she needed to. "We haven't had sex in over a year, and before that, it was rare for some years. He had an affair a while back. It ruined everything for me."

One of Jack's eyebrows lifted eloquently. She could see he was processing the information, understanding how she'd fallen for him, though she wasn't ready to say as much out loud. Finally he voiced the worry she'd had frequently for the past weeks. "What if he gets it into his head he wants sex now?"

"I'd have to find an excuse to say no to him. I know it would make him more suspicious, but I can come up with something. I'm tired. I'm having my period. I have a headache. But I don't really expect that to be an issue. I just wanted you to know about that. You're the only one I want." There. She'd said it out loud.

Jack's dark eyes sparkled. "I promise to make it worth the wait once we finally are able to be together."

His words sent chills up her spine and prompted visions of hot, sweaty sex unlike anything she'd ever experienced. "I'll hold you to that promise." God, she hoped she was making the right choice. Her life was going to be very different if she followed through on this. She got up and lingered at the door, hating to leave, but feeling better than she had in ages. "I have a design to finish before I go home. I'll see you tomorrow. Thanks for being so patient with me."

* * *

Emma, 3:45pm

EMMA PACED NERVOUSLY as she waited for Julio to return from work. He'd be home any time now. The last time she'd been this anxious was the day he'd first taken her on a hike. She couldn't believe that was only six months ago. So much had changed. She loved the life they were living, but it wasn't enough anymore. She couldn't explain why, since it was more than she'd ever had. She just knew she wanted more. Maybe reading all those romance novels had given her ideas about happy endings. She smiled at the thought. Julio really was like a hero in one of those stories.

She realized she'd paused in her pacing when she started thinking of Julio. It naturally led to pictures of all he'd taught her about intimacy between lovers. Her heart began to beat faster and her skin heated up at the thought of being able to spend the rest of her life with him.

The door opened and Julio stepped in, removing his straw cowboy hat and wiping his brow. "It is very hot today."

She rushed over and threw herself into his arms, not even minding how hot and sweaty he was. He recovered from his surprise at the extreme greeting. "Did something good happen today?"

She stepped back. "Let me get you a cold drink. Sit down." His look said he recognized she was dodging the question. She went to the kitchen to pour him some iced tea. When she returned, he was sitting on the couch in his accustomed place. She handed him the glass and watched him drain it in one continuous gulp. There was something erotic about watching him glistening with sweat after a hot day's work, his adam's apple bobbing with each swallow of iced tea.

Finally, he put the glass down on a coaster on the coffee table. "So what is the news?"

She drew on all her courage, because she wasn't sure how he'd react to her announcement. "It isn't really news. I've been thinking. Your business is really doing well."

He interrupted her. "You are a big part of my success. You do a lot of the work I cannot do. You also got my brothers to come around."

"Well, I don't think they came around because of me. I think they couldn't face losing you, and I agree with them. I'm glad they saw reason. And now that it's obvious we can have a relationship with them, I think it's time to consider making some changes in our relationship."

For the briefest moment, fear and worry flashed across his beautiful face, but he quickly replaced it with a neutral look.

"I've decided it's time for us to get married." She held her breath, afraid that she'd gone too far. Maybe he'd decided living together was enough. Perhaps he didn't want to be tied down to a woman so much older than he was. Maybe she'd really made a fool of herself assuming he loved her that much. But she had to know.

The dark eyes that had shown so many emotions radiated a new one. Was it wonder? "You told me you weren't going to ask me to marry you, because you'd look like a gold digger. Well, I'm asking you to marry me, even though it makes me look like a cradle robber."

He sputtered in laughter. "Stop it, Emma. Do not put yourself down." He coughed a few times, perhaps to cover his surprise.

Was he going to let her down gently? Her frayed nerves stretched to the breaking point. "Say something, Julio."

He looked at her as if she were his favorite dessert. "If you are sure, then I say yes. But you should not have been the one to propose. I want to marry you, but I did not want to look bad." He stood up, then got down on one knee in front of her and took her hand. "I am sorry you had to ask first. Will you marry me, Emma Lightman, and love me forever as I love you?"

She was glad she was sitting down. Her knees started to shake and she felt lightheaded. "Oh, Julio, you know I will."

He stood and drew her to her feet, taking most of her weight, and pulled her into a warm, sweaty embrace. His kiss held the promise of happily ever after.

* * *

Ray, 4:10pm

THE SOUND of the mail truck intruded on Ray's reading of the newspaper. He was expecting the letter from the HOA about their case any day now.

Stepping into the July furnace, he walked briskly to the mailbox and pulled out the mail. Standing there in the searing heat, he flipped through the envelopes, looking for the HOA return address, and stopped when he saw it.

He could barely wait to open it, but Alan deserved to see it with him. He raced inside and called for Alan. Predictably, Becky showed up first, all excited about what the news was. He patted her blonde head and waited for Alan to make his appearance. As he entered the room, Alan's blue eyes held a question. Ray held out the envelope. "We've heard from the HOA."

Becky pulled on his arm, and Ray let her lead him over to the couch. They sat huddled together while Ray ripped open the envelope and unfolded the letter as if it contained anthrax. Becky seemed unaware of the effect this could have on her life, but Alan was obviously as tense with worry as he was.

When he unfolded it, Ray put on his reading glasses. "It's a short letter." Skipping the salutation, he proceeded to the meat of the letter.

"Here it is:

After a great deal of discussion and debate, the board has decided that even though you are in clear violation of the covenants with regard to having a child living with you, in this case we will make an exception, with the condition that you and your partner will sign a nondisclosure agreement that stipulates you will never discuss this case (in general or the particulars) with anyone, and that you will not break any other covenants in the future. If that condition meets with your approval, please contact the board at the phone number below and set a time for finalizing terms at your earliest convenience.

"Can you believe that? They're acting like nothing happened."

Alan stared at him and then light dawned. "We beat them! We get to stay!"

Becky looked from one to the other. She certainly didn't understand all the specifics, but it was obvious she sensed victory. A huge smile lit her cute face. "Grandpa Alan. Grandpa Ray. We should celebrate."

Ray hugged her. "I know what you have in mind. I'm not sure Chuck E. Cheese is going to do it for all of us. We will celebrate, but it needs to be something we can all enjoy. OK?"

She acted disappointed, but Ray knew she appreciated being treated like a grownup. Alan grinned like an idiot and pulled all of them into a group hug. "What great news."

"You guys are suffocating me," complained Becky a little too dramatically, but Ray leaned back to make sure she was fine. Her mischievous eyes gave her away.

"Alright, you. We'll see about suffocating." And he encircled her, linked arms with Alan and hugged away.

* * *

Christine, 5:30pm

CHRISTINE FINISHED MIXING the homemade chicken salad and plated it on beds of lettuce. Jerome was sitting at the dining table, pouring them each a glass of white wine. She lay the plates down and took her place.

"I like doing a cold meal in this kind of weather," she said.

Jerome nodded and sipped his chilled wine. "I like chicken salad the way you make it."

She knew he'd prefer a thick steak, but she hadn't felt like cooking fancy. "I handed in my resignation to the board today. They didn't try to talk me out of it." She was chagrined that no one had attempted to change her mind. She'd worked so hard. Well, it was done now.

"I think you've made an excellent decision." Jerome sampled his chicken salad. "This is great, as always." He seemed oblivious to her pain.

If it was such a good decision, why did she feel so empty? "This thing with the gay guys was the last straw for me."

Jerome's left eyebrow went up.

"I don't mean I was against the gay guys because they are gay, but that it was a clear-cut case. They should have been told to leave. Instead, the board let them blackmail their way into an exception. It isn't right. If we make one exception, we'll end up making others."

"But you aren't on the board anymore," he reminded her, which raised her ire.

"The whole point of the covenants is to preserve the feel of Palm

Lakes. It won't feel like a retirement community if we allow children to live here."

"But did you really want to make them sell out and move?" Jerome still didn't get it. He was such a softie.

"Yes, they made their choice knowing what the rules are. They should suffer the consequences. But I was the lone voice of reason." Jerome said nothing, but his silence was condemnation. "Why do you judge me for wanting to uphold the covenants?"

"I just think now and then mercy is in order. I disagree with your position, but I'm not judging. I'm thrilled you quit the HOA, regardless of what your reason was."

His calm comments only further ruffled her feathers. But she wasn't going to get into a fight. Instead, she changed the subject. "I was talking to Samantha the other day, and she was talking like she and Arthur aren't getting along, or their marriage is in trouble."

"How's that?" asked Jerome, though she could tell he didn't care what the answer was.

"She said they're living separate lives and have for some time, and she said it with sadness. It sounded to me like she's considering leaving him. And that wouldn't be such a good thing."

Jerome stopped shoving food into his face. He looked surprised. "Why is that?"

"I just sponsored her into my CSL chapter. How would it look if she got divorced so soon after joining? That wouldn't reflect well on me."

"I don't understand what you mean. Surely her private life is her business. Why would your club members care?"

Christine shrugged and dropped the subject. She hoped there wasn't going to be any scandal around Samantha. She'd taken a chance recommending such a young woman. She'd bide her time and say no more to Jerome. It was pointless trying to confide in him.

* * *

Mary Beth, 5:45pm

MARY BETH PUT down the phone. "Boy, Shari sure works long hours. But she has really good news for us." She walked back to the dining table and sat down to her plate of lasagna. It was strange how comfortable she'd grown with Ethan's house once they decided to sell it; she even answered the phone now. Of course it helped that he had Caller ID. She wouldn't answer a call from William, at least, not yet. She still made him come to her condo--Catherine's place--to spend the night. She didn't feel right sleeping or having sex in his marital bed. Maybe she was more old-fashioned than she'd thought.

"I didn't know this, but the home next door to Helen and Alexander is on the market. It took me a minute, but when she said the address, I figured it out. Wouldn't that be cool, to live next door to them? I used to live next door to Helen before she married Alexander, and we were great friends."

"But aren't they planning to move to the Virgin Islands?"

"Yes, but they haven't set a date. They haven't even made a scouting trip yet. She's never been there. Alexander says he loved it, but he'd need to look at it differently if they were considering living there as opposed to vacationing."

"That makes sense," said Ethan. "Do you know anything about the house that's for sale?"

"Well, it isn't the same model as Helen and Alexander's, which is good. We don't want a place that big, do we?"

"I'm open to whatever you want."

She smiled at him, because she knew he meant it. "Well, I don't have family, Ethan. So you need to think how many visits we'll be getting from your family." She hadn't intended to put salt on the wound. "I don't mean to be insensitive. William will probably come around sooner or later, and Winnie has been absolutely charming. She even wants to come to the wedding. So we know she'll bring her kids and visit sometimes, right?"

"If she can afford it. It's easier for me--for us--to visit her. Saves her money. But maybe we could spring for some plane tickets for her and the kids now that we're flush with money."

She liked how he spoke of their finances as joint. He'd sat her down and told her all about his finances when she agreed to wed him. He had more money than she would have guessed. He'd made good investments and saved a lot, and he owned his home. They could afford any house they wanted in Palm Lakes with the proceeds from the sale of two places and the $100K she got from Catherine. It was stunning how big a turnaround this was for her. He'd even told her she could quit her job and just do her jewelry business, and she was seriously considering it.

"To answer your question about the house, the woman who owned it was a widow, and she lived alone. The dog Helen has--Spot--was her dog. She had a fall and she moved into assisted living at Desert Breezes. Helen goes to visit her and takes Spot now and then. But I've never been inside the house. It's big but doesn't have a casita like Helen's."

"How many bedrooms?"

"Three and three bathrooms. Plus a bonus room. We need to go look at it. Are you up for that?"

"Of course. I'm as eager as you are to find the perfect place for us. I never thought about living on the golf course. The views sure are pretty from Helen and Alexander's. I guess ours would be much the same."

"I never expected anything like this. My life fell apart last year. When Jason divorced me for his pregnant girlfriend, I felt so lost. It's funny how I came here as a last resort, nearly out of money and hope. It was such an adjustment learning to live with Mom, but the time together turned out to be precious. We really became closer." It still hurt to think of Mom being gone. "And meeting Helen and learning to make jewelry and starting out on a business. It was so unexpected. And Catherine, she was a huge surprise. But the biggest surprise was you. I know it took me a while, but I came to realize that everything that happened to me, even though it was awful, was to lead me to you. If Jason hadn't left me, I'd still be in a marriage that was a sham. I've gained so much. I even quit smoking."

Ethan gazed at her lovingly with soft gray eyes. "You're the biggest surprise in my life. I thought it was mostly over. I enjoyed working with the old people. Look at me, calling them old. Anyway, I love my family and enjoyed working with The Helpers, but I was lonely. I never thought I'd find love again. You don't expect to find it twice in a lifetime." He reached across the table, and she extended her right hand to his. "You're the best thing to happen to me in ages, and I feel so grateful you love me."

"I can get used to hearing that." She turned her left hand to catch the light sparkling off her ring, willing herself to believe it was all real. It was like living in a fairy tale.

"You better get used to it, because I'll be saying it a lot." He squeezed her hand for emphasis.

* * *

Lydia, 8:15pm

IAN SAT FONDLING his scotch while Jean quizzed Lydia about her decision. "Lyd, are you sure about this?"

Lydia had asked herself that very question hundreds of times in the past couple weeks. "Can you ever be sure? I'm as sure as I can be. I can't keep doing the healing sessions. I love helping people, but even though we aren't getting a lot of clients, I've been doing more work than in the past. And I'm seeing negative reactions. I end up feeling awful, or I have to run to the bathroom with diarrhea--sorry, Ian, too much information-- but it's a consistent pattern, and I believe it means my own health could be harmed if I keep doing this."

Jean's mouth closed on whatever she was going to say. Ian knocked back the rest of his scotch and waded in. "I think you're making the right choice." He put the glass down. Jean turned on him, blue eyes flashing. "What do you mean by that? We need Lydia."

His calm was unruffled. "I'm not arguing that. But if Lydia is having negative reactions after healing sessions, it means she is taking on other people's stuff. If she can't improve her boundaries or figure out how to avoid it, she needs to quit. She'll become a wounded healer otherwise." His compassion was obvious in his hazel eyes.

Jean's feathers settled noticeably. "Well, we don't want Lydia to get sick..."

Lydia held her hands up. "I'll still do readings. That seems to be my more popular service, anyway. You guys can handle all the healing sessions. You are a powerful team together, and I don't think my bowing out will have a negative impact on the bottom line, weak as it is. I'm still keen on doing courses and presentations."

Jean and Ian exchanged one of their trademark silent communications. She could read the worry in Jean's aura; both of them were concerned about the progress of the business. "I'm sorry to dump this on you now. But I don't think it will change anything."

Jean sighed. "That's what I'm worried about. Things need to change. We're getting appointments, but referrals aren't happening often. We've signed up some Botanica shoppers, because environmentally safe cleaning products and essential oils resonate with our clientele. But hardly anyone wants me to do readings or dowsing for them. Ian is doing better than I am, but Lydia, you bring in the most. I think we need to hit the courses angle hard. I don't know why we've let it go this long."

Ian nodded as he listened.

"I agree," Lydia said. "Let's figure out a syllabus and talk about advertising. But not tonight. I'm late for going over to Eric's. If it's OK, I'd like to do this tomorrow."

"Sure, Lydia, we didn't mean to hold you. Just so this isn't the first of many steps back from the business. We need and want you to be a part of it."

Lydia stood up and walked them to her front door. "I love working with you guys and intend to continue doing it. Don't worry." But she knew they would. For her, this was a fun hobby. For them, it was survival. Putting her concerns aside, she went through the house turning off lights and checked that the patio door was locked. Eric was probably wondering what was holding her up.

She made her way through the early evening's darkness, giving Tanya's condo a look as she passed it, wondering how long it would take to sell. The place gave her the creeps. Every time she went by, she had a flashback to seeing Tanya bleeding out on her kitchen floor, Owen shot dead by Eric and Eric struggling to stay conscious after being knifed by Owen. No wonder Eric had trouble overcoming the incident. It was harrowing.

The man who occupied so many of her waking thoughts met her at the door with a glass of wine, no sign of impatience.

"I'm sorry I'm so late. I needed to talk with Jean and Ian until they realized I was still going to work with them, but that I had to give up crystal healing as a profession."

"You sure did me a lot of good with those rocks." His seductive grin warmed her all over. She took the glass of wine from him and followed him to the living room, where they sat side by side on the couch.

"Sixth Sense Consulting is having a hard time getting off the ground. But I am optimistic that we'll find the right formula for it to pay well enough that they can live off it."

Cop's eyes stared at her, parsing her words. He had gotten so good at reading her, she had no advantage anymore. "I think you're wonderful for helping your friends out. They're lucky to have you. So am I, for that matter. I haven't had a flashback or nightmare in ages. I think maybe I'm cured."

His aura was back to its shiny, silvery beauty. And he wasn't hiding anything anymore. "I'm glad I could help. I had selfish motives, of course."

"As long as your selfish motives include wanting to sleep with me, I'm satisfied." The temperature in the room appeared to rise.

"I think it's time we talked seriously about getting married." She must have surprised him, because his eyes widened and his mouth opened slightly. *Come on, Eric, don't make this hard.*

He ran a hand through his short gray-blonde hair, as if in exasperation. "We've gone over this so many times, and I don't want to fight. You know I love you. Why can't we just live together?"

She inspected his aura and saw no defensiveness or anger. That was progress. "For one thing, remember what happened when you were in ICU? I couldn't get in to see you or even find out how you were, because I wasn't considered family. I can't go through that again. Secondly and more important, I don't want to live in two places. It's time we got a home of our own to share." That seemed to floor him. Hadn't he even considered it? "Eric, I want us to really live together, not in two separate condos. And I've decided I want to get away from the murder scene. I don't like having it so close by. I think it would be helpful for us both to move."

"You want to leave Palm Lakes?"

"Of course not. I want us to live in the same house. And I want to be married. We can keep our finances separate if you insist, but that's not how I want it. I'd like us to have a nice house with a two car garage, maybe a hobby room. We don't need something huge, because no one visits us, but big enough so we each have our own space, but together." She could see him envisioning what she was describing. "Wouldn't it be more fun to have a bedroom big enough for a king size bed? And I'd love to have a bigger kitchen. It would make cooking more fun."

"I like to eat your cooking. And the bedroom idea is great." She could tell by the colors of his energy field he was thinking about sex. *Good. Better that than money.*

"I'd also like to participate in your Future Leaders project in some fashion. Do you have a spot for me in your organization?"

His wide smile revealed even teeth. "I'd really like that. Your special gifts could come in handy."

She rolled her eyes. "Don't go telling everyone about me."

"Why not? You're out of the closet now. Aren't you?"

"Yes, but I'd rather not be too obvious about it."

"Either way, your X-ray vision could help me. Not only with the kids, but with other board members. I'm not always good at figuring people out. I've stepped on a few toes already. You can keep me from making a fool of myself."

Lydia gazed at him suspiciously. "I think you're exaggerating, but I'm happy to help. So can we set a date for the wedding and then go house hunting?"

"I guess."

Annoyance began to wrap its hot fingers around Lydia. "I guess? That's the best you can do?"

His boyish grin told her he was pulling her chain. "You're going to pay for that, mister."

He practically growled. "I certainly hope so."

AT LAST: A PREVIEW

Sunday, June 23, 1996

Sophie, 4:00am

She was suffocating under the pressure of tons of earth. She struggled to scream, but no matter how hard she pushed, no sound escaped her mouth. There was no before and no after, just an endless now where she was trapped in powerlessness and confusion. The sheer terror of passing infinity in such a fashion finally propelled her out of the nightmare— that's what it was, though it had seemed so real—into a dark stillness. She gulped air frantically, gasping and choking at the same time.

It took her a few minutes to shed the terror of the dream, it was so vivid. When her heartbeat slowed to normal, her senses informed her that she wasn't buried underground. She was in bed. It was dark, but she could see faint light under a door on the far side of the room. Where was she? Her mind felt numb, her throat dry and scratchy as if she had screamed her head off, though she had no recollection of doing so. The terror crept back as she tried to move her limbs. Her body was unresponsive. Tears dampened her cheeks, but she couldn't raise an arm to wipe them. She could feel her fingers and toes, but they ignored her commands. This was almost as bad as the dream. What was wrong with her?

After a few ragged coughs, she tried to speak the question, but instead of words, all that came out of her mouth was a ragged grunt. That's when she remembered. She was in the assisted living section of Desert Breezes in Palm Lakes Senior Community, where she'd been moved after a stroke. The stroke had robbed her of speech and all but the smallest movement.

She could see from the empty bed next to hers that she didn't have a roommate, and for some reason, that realization fanned the flame of fear into a genuine blaze. Was she just reacting to the residue of the bad dream? Her mind wasn't working clearly. And her memory offered few facts to anchor her.

She couldn't shrug off the feeling of danger. The large red numbers on the bedside clock said 4:03. It would be hours before someone came to get her out of bed, since she couldn't do it herself. Her mind was muddled, but not so much she couldn't have expressed herself, if only she still had a voice. But the stroke had robbed her of that. And her hands were so weak, she couldn't hold a pen and write. She was isolated and powerless. A feeling of despair overwhelmed her.

Why was she so frightened? Then she heard the soft click of the door opening, and it all came rushing back as a shadow filled the backlit doorway. Running was impossible. Screaming was not an option. She wasn't strong enough to throw things or resist. Even if she could call for help, it wouldn't matter. The person charged with caring for her had just entered her room with evil intent. Hot tears flowed down her face. A prayer formed in her mind. "Please help me. Someone, please help me." But no one answered. No one ever answered.

* * *

Tuesday, July 2, 1996

OLIVIA, 9:15AM

Olivia trudged down the carpeted hall after leaving the Desert Breezes dining room. Cooking for one didn't appeal to her, but she did enjoy a good meal. If only the dining room served something resembling fine cuisine. It was passable, but only just.

The rich maroon carpet slid by as she passed decorative alcoves that held shelves with vases of artificial flowers or niches with Native American figurines marking the divisions between apartments. Though the food wasn't anything to brag about, Desert Breezes catered to well-to-do seniors who no longer wanted the burden of a house and property, and it had the decor to prove it. The face it presented was upscale and luxurious; the reality of living here was something else, at least to her. She recalled her daughters oohing and ahhing over how nice it was when they took the tour before she sold her home. Their forced brightness hadn't fooled her then, and occasionally she wished they could be stuck here and see how they liked it, but what was the use of being negative? Deep down, she knew they were doing their best. She just had to cope. Hadn't she recovered from a broken hip, even come out of the disaster more fit and healthy? She wasn't going down without a fight.

As she unlocked her apartment door with the key on the neon pink, springy band around her wrist, she decided a cup of tea was just the thing to soothe her mind. Maddie hadn't been at breakfast again, and she was worried about her. That anxiety added to the weight of having learned that her friend Sophie was in the hospital after suffering another stroke several days ago. Olivia almost felt like she was living in a glorified nursing home. Yes, she needed a cup of tea.

She crossed the tiny tiled foyer and stepped into her kitchenette, which had a half-wall open to the living room that stretched to the sliding glass door and balcony that overlooked the golf course and purple mountains. The apartments on this side of the building had views that were almost as nice as those from her golf course home.

The small dining area opposite the kitchen held a table and four chairs that had occupied the breakfast nook in her previous home. The set was large for the cramped space, but then, all her furniture seemed oversized for this living space, a depressing reminder of how her life had shrunk.

Olivia filled the kettle and put it on to heat, then selected a mug from the cabinet, one that she'd gotten as a present from her youngest daughter years ago. She chose to think of it as a symbol of her daughter's love, though none of her three girls were much in evidence these days. Or so it seemed to her.

A brisk knock on the door shook her out of her moody reverie. She opened the door to Helen Stirling and a young woman. Helen's companion looked to be in her early 40s, with lush dark hair and stunning green eyes. Helen was older by two decades, but was still lithe and youthful, her strawberry blonde hair and smooth skin enough to inspire envy in anyone.

"Come in, Helen, it's nice to see you. How's my Spot doing?"

Helen flashed a warm smile. "She's a little rascal. Always has to be the center of attention. Smart as a whip. They say you shouldn't have a dog that's smarter than you are. I'm afraid I'm in that position." Helen turned and pointed to her companion. "My friend Mary Beth told me she was coming over to see Maddie today, and I wanted to introduce her to you." Helen grinned through the formal introduction. "Olivia, may I present my friend Mary Beth Costello? Mary Beth, this is Olivia Deschamps, who used to live next door to me."

Buzzing with curiosity, Olivia waved them in rather than shaking hands in the doorway. "How about a nice cup of tea?"

Helen grinned. "That would be lovely, if it's not too much trouble. It's already blisteringly hot outside; maybe that's why it seems so nippy in the air conditioning."

Her guests seated themselves on the sofa while Olivia added more water to the kettle and grabbed two additional mugs. She placed a variety of tea bags on a saucer and then loaded the tray with mugs, spoons, a sugar bowl and cream pitcher. The water came to a boil, and she smiled as she poured it into an old teapot that had been in her family for a hundred years.

As she turned around to take the tray into the living room, she nearly bumped into Mary Beth, who reached out. "Here, I'll take that over. It looks heavy."

Olivia nodded in gratitude and sat in a wing chair, glad to let Mary Beth play 'mother.' The younger woman doctored the tea according to each person's preference and passed mugs around.

The twinkle in Helen's eyes hinted a revelation was on the way. "Mary Beth and I are great friends. We met when I bought the condo next door to her mother's before I married Alexander. We used to gossip over a glass or two of wine in the evenings. I was the one who introduced her to Maddie. Maddie's taught her how to make jewelry, and she's selling her pieces at some of the gift shops in the resorts around here. Her work is gorgeous." Mary Beth listened to this with a shy smile, obviously embarrassed at the praise. "She's engaged to a man she met while doing jewelry at Maddie's. Isn't that romantic? Anyway, they're getting married next month and want to buy a house so they can start fresh. And guess whose house they are going to look at?"

Olivia had followed the circuitous path of the story, always one step behind. Then it hit her. She looked hard at Mary Beth. "My old place?"

Mary Beth grinned. "Yes. I stayed at Helen's casita for a couple months while they were in France, and I noticed the houses in the immediate area. I love the view across the golf course, and I was quite spoiled by the luxury. Then after Ethan proposed, we decided we needed a new place to begin our marriage." She paused as if looking for the right words. "He's a widower, you see, and I couldn't bring myself to live in the house he'd shared with his late wife. Maybe I'm being silly, but I want a place that is all ours. It was only after our realtor called and told us about a home she thought we'd like that I realized it was the house next door to Helen's. Can you imagine? I might be able to live next door to Helen again. We have an appointment to check it out this week, and I mentioned it to Helen. That's why she was eager to have me meet you." Enthusiasm fairly sparked off her.

Olivia sighed, remembering. "Well, it's a good old house. It had gotten too big for me, all by myself. My kids wouldn't hear of me staying there after I fell and broke my hip. Helen and her handsome husband were the ones to find me, because Spot—Spot was my dog before she was Helen's—was barking up a storm, because she knew I needed help, lying on the floor like that. So I put it on the market. Can't say I'm happy I did, but I guess it was time." She didn't mean to complain, but it was hard thinking about the contrast between her large golf course home and this cramped apartment.

Mary Beth's eyes shone with compassion. "I sympathize, Olivia. Maddie and I have been friends for a good while now, and she's heartbroken about having to leave her place. In fact, I was staying with her before I stayed at Helen's. It's a long story, but after my Mom died, I had to sell her place, because I'm too young to own it according to the covenants, but I'd made friends and had a job nearby, so I ended up staying here and there with friends in Palm Lakes so I could have time to figure things out. Then Ethan proposed, and I get to stay. I love Palm Lakes."

Olivia wondered how it felt to be the youngest resident of Palm Lakes Senior Community, but then again, everyone looked like a baby to her anymore. Even Helen. She wasn't sure how she felt about Mary Beth buying her house. Helen meant well, but Olivia still hated to be reminded that she'd been forced out of her home. She drank some tea to mask her confusion.

Apparently unaware of Olivia's torment, Helen pressed on in a voice filled with pleasure. "I'm selfishly hoping she and Ethan buy your house. They're wonderful people, and they'll take good care of it. And I'll get to be her neighbor again. She's quit her job at Palo Verde Landscaping in anticipation of her marriage, so I've told her she has to join our yoga group when she becomes an official resident next month." Helen smiled warmly at Mary Beth. If Helen liked Mary Beth, she must be a good person. Since someone was going to buy her house, it might as well be someone Helen liked.

"I hope you like my house, Mary Beth. It would be good to know someone will love it as much as I did. There are a lot of memories there for me." It seemed like all the good things in her life were in the past.

They sipped tea in silence for some minutes. Then a serious look crossed Helen's face. "Mary Beth and I are going to visit Maddie today. It's not her jewelry day, but with Maddie's health so precarious, we both like to visit her as often as we can."

Olivia nodded in agreement. "One thing I hate about living here. They're dropping like flies around me. It was bad enough in the neighborhood, but here, it seems someone dies or gets a death sentence just about every week. Maddie is brave, facing lung cancer with only weeks or months to live. I can't imagine how it feels, slowly losing your ability to breathe. It must be terrifying. And she never smoked a day in her life." She shook her head, still unable to process the incredibility of it. "I just found out that another friend of mine who lives here, Sophie, had a second stroke a few days ago and is back in the hospital. She used to live on this hall, but she had a stroke and they moved her to the assisted living wing. Lost her speech and most of her ability to move. I need to go to the hospital to visit her soon. She's got no one, and she hates hospitals, or so she used to say when she could still talk. She didn't seem to like this place much, either. As much as I gripe, this section is rather nice. But there's something creepy about the assisted living wing." She shuddered to think she might end up there like Sophie. Almost anything would be preferable.

They finished their tea, blanketed by a fog of depression. Helen stood up and began to load the tray. "Would you like to come with us to see Maddie?"

This was a godsend. She knew Maddie needed company, but it wasn't always easy to spend time alone with her now that the cancer was like an elephant in the room. Even without being terminally ill, Maddie was eccentric and sometimes difficult to talk to. But that seemed to be the kind of person Olivia befriended. "Sure, I was going to visit today. I was a little worried when she wasn't at breakfast."

They got up, and Helen carried the tray to the counter in the kitchenette. Then they trooped down the hall to Maddie's apartment and Mary Beth knocked on the door. "It's Mary Beth, Maddie."

"Come in, the door's unlocked," said Maddie in a muffled voice. Olivia was relieved. At least she hadn't died in the night. Horrible that such things were common here.

As they stepped into the apartment, Maddie was struggling to push herself to her feet, body bent and short dirty blonde hair disheveled, like she'd forgotten to brush it this morning. Her pale blue eyes widened to see three people enter her apartment, and a smile cracked her wrinkled face. "Can I get you all some coffee?"

Helen stepped up and gave Maddie a gentle hug, mindful of the pain her osteoporosis caused. "We just had tea at Olivia's on our way here. Nothing else for me."

"Me, neither," said Mary Beth, dropping to the couch and crossing her legs, rubbing her bare thighs. "It's cold in here, especially compared to outside."

Maddie frowned at her. "It's cold anywhere, compared to outside. It's like hell out there."

Olivia sat down next to Mary Beth and chuckled. "Life in the desert. It's hell sometimes."

Helen sat on the chair opposite the couch, and Maddie fell back into her recliner.

"So how do I rate such a crowd of visitors?" asked Maddie.

"I was going to come down today, because I didn't see you at breakfast," explained Olivia.

"I overslept. Been doing that a lot lately."

Helen smiled encouragingly. "You deserve to sleep in. Did you get breakfast?"

Maddie shook her head. "I had a cup of coffee, but I'm not hungry yet. I'll get something later."

"I've quit my job at Palo Verde, and that means I'll be able to come over more often, if you like," said Mary Beth. "We can still do jewelry on Saturdays, but I was hoping you wouldn't mind if I came over more often than that. I promise to bring you some lasagna."

A big smile graced Maddie's worn face. "That would be nice. I love your cooking."

Helen chimed in. "She cooked a great Italian meal after we returned from our trip. I thought Alexander and I were gourmet cooks, but she's amazing."

Mary Beth shrugged her shoulders. "My Mom taught me to cook. She loved making traditional Italian dishes. I guess I got the genes for it."

Olivia listened to the exchange with interest. "I'm jealous. My daughters sometimes bring me food, but mostly I eat in the dining room. I can't make myself cook for just me. The kitchen is so tiny, and all my equipment got given away, and I don't have a dishwasher. It's too much like hard work."

"I agree," said Maddie. "I've lost weight since I moved here. I just don't eat as much."

Olivia saw flashes in the other ladies' eyes that said they wondered if the cancer was the cause of her weight loss. Maybe it was. "I've lost weight since I moved here, too. I still eat junk food, but not nearly as much as I used to. And I just don't feel like cooking. Plus the dining room doesn't have the greatest food."

"You can say that again," grumbled Maddie.

Mary Beth cocked her head to the side and looked at Olivia. "I'll have to bring you some lasagna, if you like Italian food. It's pretty easy to make up a large batch of spaghetti sauce, lasagna or ravioli."

Olivia's mouth began to water in anticipation. "I love Italian food, but I wouldn't want you to trouble yourself."

"I know, but I like to cook. Now that I'm going to have my own place with a spacious kitchen, it will be a pleasure. Besides, I need something to do with my time now that I've become a woman of leisure." Mary Beth's green eyes twinkled.

Gratified more than she could say, Olivia smiled at Mary Beth. "You're an angel. I'd love it, but only if it's no trouble."

That settled, Helen turned to Maddie. "How's Samantha doing? Since Samantha left Palo Verde Landscaping, Mary Beth doesn't see her often, which is sad. They liked working together, and they are of an age." She threw a smile at Mary Beth.

Maddie seemed to consider how to answer. "She may be my only daughter, but she doesn't tell me everything. I know she likes her new job with Jack at his landscaping company. He's fine looking. Tall, dark and handsome like a cowboy. Sometimes I wonder…" It looked like Maddie was deciding whether to say more. "He brings Beau to see me. I miss Beau like you miss Spot, Olivia."

Olivia wondered what Maddie was withholding, but didn't want to press her for more. "Such a shame we had to give up our pets to live here. I could have kept Spot, but without a yard, it would have been a real challenge. And Beau was too big, wasn't he? I haven't met him or this Jack fellow yet, but I'd like to."

"I can have him and Samantha knock on your door next time they visit."

"That would be nice."

The rest of the visit passed quickly, and Olivia returned to her apartment after bidding Helen and Mary Beth goodbye and getting further assurance from Mary Beth that she'd bring her some food. She felt a little guilty allowing someone she barely knew to make food for her, but living here was just so lonely, and Mary Beth's offer had seemed genuine.

Strange, but when she was alone in her house on the golf course, she was less lonely than now. Maybe it was partly because at home, she was surrounded by objects that warmed her heart with pleasant memories. She felt like she was living in a hotel room now, as if one morning, she'd have to check out and leave. Which of course was too close to the truth for comfort.

She went over to the small table where she had the schedule of the mini-bus that ferried residents around town. She could catch the 2:00 bus and visit Sophie in the hospital. She hadn't seen her in a while and felt bad that she hadn't even heard of her second stroke until now. Sophie literally had no one, and Olivia felt obliged to show support.

* * *

STEVEN, 10:00AM

Steven sat on the couch, staring at nothing. It was quiet except for the occasional rumble of the air conditioning unit as it fired up. He could tell it was going to be another scorcher from how often the unit cycled and cringed at the thought of the electric bill. The curtains were closed, cloaking the living room in semidarkness. He preferred the shadows. They kept him from seeing Tanya all around him in the garish decor. His home resembled an upscale bordello, but he had always allowed Tanya to do whatever she wished with the house. Besides, it was easier to give in than to fight; she had no concept of discussion or debate. Probably came from having such a bastard for a father.

He really ought to redecorate so he wouldn't constantly be reminded of Tanya, but the divorce had cost him his meager savings and then some. That's how he justified not making any changes. Maybe he was punishing himself. He'd longed to escape their marriage for years, and when he finally found the strength, look what it led to. Some part of him felt as if he'd killed her himself.

His coffee had gone cold, but he was too listless to get up and refresh it. Why couldn't he break out of this funk? Tanya was his *ex*-wife, and she'd died months ago. For years, she'd done nothing but drink to excess and cut him into little pieces with her sharp tongue. Divorcing her had lifted a weight off his shoulders, but not long after that, Owen Schmidt had killed her.

Steven had been certain she was having an affair with the neighbor down the road, especially after how she'd acted at Barbara's Christmas party, but frankly, he'd been relieved. She'd been focused on someone else, and it had given him a measure of peace. Her affairs always had, which is why he'd never called her on them. And it gave him a chance to divorce her. He'd even begun to nurture thoughts of beginning again. Or at least just having peace and quiet in his life. Was that too much to ask?

The doorbell rang, shattering the silence. He forced himself to rise and shuffled to the door. Barbara Blackstone, wife of his golfing buddy Ben and neighbor a few houses down, greeted him with a kind smile. He let her in, but didn't offer to get her coffee. Everything seemed too hard to do these days, and she was very understanding.

She sat on the couch and he occupied the chair adjacent to it. He didn't make it any easier for her. He knew why she was here, and although some part of him appreciated the compassion, another part of him just wanted to be left alone. She didn't comment on the darkness.

"I came by to see how you're doing and invite you to have dinner with us tonight. Ben is grilling steaks, and I know how you love them. It will do you good to get out of the house."

He sighed. "I know you mean to help, but I'm not fit for company. I haven't even been able to work up to playing golf."

She reached over and gently patted his hand. "I know it's hard, but you need to get out now and then."

"OK, but I don't have much of an appetite." That was an understatement. He'd lost a lot of weight in the past months. He'd never been a jock, but now he was a spindly old guy. "I don't have the energy to cook, either. I know I should eat more." It was the most he was willing to admit.

"Then it's settled. The other thing I wanted to say was that Ben and I are concerned about you. You're our friend. I know it was hard on you about Tanya, and we think maybe you should get some help so that you can get past it."

"I don't want to pay to get shrunk. The divorce took my savings." He felt his mouth twist into a sardonic smile. At least he wasn't paying alimony anymore.

"If not that, how about a group that supports victims and their families? I have a friend who told me about this group that meets once a week at the Rec Center. She said it really helped her. Would you be willing to check it out?"

He hated to be negative, especially when it was so obvious he wasn't functioning well. "Yeah, I guess so."

"Good. When you come over tonight, I'll have the details written down for you. Will you go once and let me know how you like it? I don't want to recommend things if they aren't good, but my friend said it was worthwhile. Have you heard from your children lately?"

He shrugged. "They aren't that close to me. They call maybe once every month or two. It's my fault. I spent all my time working. And Tanya was a rotten mother. Too self-absorbed. Too whatever. Needless to say, she didn't fit in at all with the wives of my colleagues at work. The kids were eager to grow up and leave. I think she embarrassed them. Fact is, she embarrassed me, especially since we retired."

Barbara shook her head. "It must have been hard for her, comparing herself to the privileged wives of attorneys."

He was grateful for a chance to stop wallowing in self-pity. "They didn't dress like her, talk like her, act like her. To them, she was trailer trash, and I suppose they were right. She came from nothing. We both did, really. We shared a dream and the determination to make a better life together, and my becoming a lawyer seemed the best path. She worked hard to put me through law school; we didn't have enough for both of us to go to college, and in any case, she never liked school. Maybe I shouldn't have tried to drag her along with me. Or maybe I should have tried to get her to adapt. Or perhaps I should have insisted we both go to school, because that was what caused the gap between us. She stayed the same; I changed. At the time, it didn't seem so important. We were in love and naive. I wasn't embarrassed about her accent or manner of dress, though maybe I should have been. I only felt embarrassed when she took to the bottle. By then, there was nothing I could do, so I just stayed out of her way as much as possible. Our kids were ashamed of her, because they grew up with advantages, and she seemed like a hillbilly to them, right down to the accent. They never got to know her courage and ambition, the things that had drawn me to her in the first place. She was always stronger than I was, and I admired that. But she'd become an alcoholic by the time they were old enough to notice anything."

Barbara listened, her hands folded in her lap. She was the antithesis of Tanya. Empathetic, understanding, understatedly elegant, quiet. But there was steel in her. That was one thing the two women had in common, he observed silently.

Steven rubbed his face, trying to focus. "I'm rambling. Comes from being alone so much and running all kinds of scenarios through my head. What if I hadn't divorced her? Would she still be dead? Maybe not. But she'd still be an alcoholic. You'd think I'd be celebrating now that I'm rid of her. But somehow I feel responsible. Maybe I should have forced her into rehab before she wrecked the car. She would have hated me even more, but maybe she could have gotten off the booze. There just aren't any answers. I'm sorry I keep boring you with this."

Barbara's eyes narrowed. "You aren't responsible for what happened to Tanya. She chose to drink. She went with Owen. She was an adult. And fiercely independent from what I saw. She didn't want anyone telling her what to do. You know all that, but perhaps joining this group will give you a chance to see that what you are feeling is natural, that it can pass. It's time for you to rejoin the living." Barbara rose, then waved when he stood reflexively. "I'll show myself out. Come over around 4:30. We'll have a drink before dinner, or if you don't feel like alcohol, some iced tea."

He watched her graceful exit and slumped back into the chair. Maybe a hot cup of coffee would be good. He shook himself and stood, then carried his half-full mug of tepid coffee back into the kitchen. He was secretly glad for Barbara's invitations. He wasn't sure how he'd have made it this far if she and Ben hadn't been so persistent about helping him.

* * *

HELEN, 10:45AM

Helen trudged into her husband's office, Spot trailing behind her. Alexander sat at the desk, his back to her, working on his manuscript on the computer. The click of Spot's nails on the tile got his attention, and he turned to look at Helen. She practically melted under his loving emerald gaze.

He rose from his chair and put his arms around her as if she'd been gone for days, not hours. His hands caressed her face and back, then he gave her bottom a squeeze, making her laugh.

"I didn't mean to interrupt your work. I just wanted to let you know I'm back."

He ceased his caresses and looked into her eyes. "How's Maddie? And did Olivia take the news well?"

Helen sighed. "It's so hard to be with Maddie and pretend everything is OK. She is short of breath, weaker, but still feisty. It was easier visiting her with Mary Beth and Olivia. I guess we all feel awkward with death in the room. But I don't want Maddie to feel deserted. Something tells me she needs us, even though she'd never say."

He leaned down and kissed the top of her head. "You're doing a wonderful thing. I know it's hard. But I'm sure she appreciates it. How about a cup of tea or coffee? I need a break. You can tell me all about the visit."

Helen relaxed. Talking with him would help her decompress. "Thanks. Let's do that."

Minutes later, they sat side by side on the couch, her dog at her feet, cups of coffee on the table in front of them. Helen reveled in the warm comfort of Alexander's body close to hers. She couldn't get over how much her life had changed. Was it just last year her abusive husband Lou had died and she'd been thrown into chaos trying to adjust in so many ways? It hardly seemed possible. She reached over and stroked his thigh, then squeezed it. "I am the luckiest woman in the world."

"Of course you are," he teased, then leaned over to kiss her. "Now tell me what's going on at Desert Breezes."

She told herself he was only trying to help her feel better by talking about it, yet his gemstone eyes blazed with sincerity. He was so unlike Lou that it often felt like she was living in a fairy tale. "Olivia was OK with Mary Beth wanting to look at her house, but maybe she was sad, too. I had hoped she would be glad that someone nice was interested, but having to think about it must make her unhappy. Her apartment is lovely, but it's way smaller than her house, and she misses Spot. She's very brave and doesn't complain much." Helen continued to stroke his thigh absentmindedly. "Mary Beth is such a dear. She offered to bring Olivia food when she cooks for Maddie. She has such a generous heart. Olivia perked up at the offer. She says the food isn't very good in the dining room, and she can't bear to cook just for herself." She paused and lay her hand on Alexander's cheek. "I hope we don't end up living somewhere like that. I mean, it looks so nice on the outside, but it sounds dreadful."

"If you don't want to, we won't. I prefer to live on our own if at all possible. We need to stay healthy and fit so we can be independent for the rest of our lives. It's not an easy task."

Helen shook her head. "But it's worth it." Then she resolved to bring up a sore subject. "All the excitement about the weddings, and poor Maddie, and Mary Beth maybe buying the house next door has totally distracted me from what we discovered on our trip to France. But it's creeping back into my mind and plaguing me. It even kept me awake last night. I want answers, but I don't see how I'll ever get them. And now I feel guilty, but I'm not sure it's warranted." She sighed in exasperation. "What do you think we should do?" Alexander gave her a look she'd learned to read. He wasn't going to solve this for her. "I know, I probably will never find out, and I need to just get on with life. But it's hard."

He took her hand and kissed it. "We know more than we did before, but I think you're going to have to be satisfied with what we learned. You'll never get complete closure. It's obvious that the diamonds you found in Lou's safe deposit box were contraband of some kind from the war. People aren't eager to talk about such things, even if they know all the details."

"I don't think the French boy was lying…listen to me calling him a boy. But he was as young as my own kids." He had the look of Lou. The resemblance was so striking, she knew he was Lou's love child. How could Lou have deserted him?

Alexander pulled her back to present time. "We were lucky to track him down. If he hadn't stayed in his mother's old neighborhood, we couldn't have located him. I didn't really expect much, but frankly, we got more than I would have thought, and that only because we traveled to France and sought him out."

"You're right. It must have been so hard on her, a single Mom. Lou was a jerk."

"I'd say that's an understatement. We were lucky the boy heard what he did and was willing to share it with us, especially since all the major players are dead."

Helen heaved a sigh. "I guess so. It's a case of be afraid what you ask for. He was so young when he overheard the argument. Can we be sure he remembered correctly?"

"The details make more sense to us than him, probably, since we found the diamonds and his mother's letters in Lou's safe deposit box."

"He was sure his Mom and uncle were in the Resistance during the war, though they didn't like to talk about it. They were barely adults at the time. I can only imagine what they went through. I keep trying to piece things together, but it's like a puzzle with too many pieces missing. What do you think happened?"

Alexander rolled his eyes. "You've only asked me that same question a hundred times. I'll say what I always say. You know Lou was in France in WWII. Looks like Lou took advantage of the girl. Seems somehow the point of intersection between them was a Nazi officer on the run in the chaos as the war ended. It would appear that although he was captured, he was subsequently released thanks to using the diamonds as a bribe. You can't be sure that Lou then absconded with all the diamonds, but I have to admit that what the boy overheard in the fight between his mother and uncle sounded like an ongoing tirade about Lou's betrayal and seemed to imply more than Lou fathering the boy. I believe Lou always thought about himself first, and he didn't share the diamonds, and he didn't want any further contact. It doesn't look like he ever replied to her letters. That he kept the letters seems to indicate he did have some feelings for her, just not enough to do the right thing. It probably came down to him not wanting to share the diamonds. Yet, he didn't use them, or who knows, maybe he did. We don't know how many there were to begin with."

Helen felt tears come to her eyes. "He left that poor girl on her own, pregnant with his child amid the ruins of a war. And he took the Nazi diamonds that were probably stolen from people who were killed in the Holocaust, and he arranged to let the Nazi go. I feel they're tainted. And if that woman or her brother were still alive, I'd feel we had to share them, but since they were stolen, that seems weird. Of course it's hopeless trying to find the original owners." She sighed in despair.

"We don't know for sure that Lou took all the diamonds, but it does appear that they felt betrayed in more ways than one, based on the ferocity of the argument. What do you feel is the right thing to do? You could give half the diamonds to that young man, but it won't change the past. Who knows if he'd want to have anything to do with them? You told him about Lou, but he seemed uninterested. Maybe he was just hurting. Are you intending to stay in touch with him?"

It was too much for Helen. She'd been so thrilled to find the diamonds, but the pain Lou's past caused was a large price to pay. "I don't feel he wants to ever hear from us again."

"I have to agree with you. I think he wants to forget."

Alexander seemed to find it easy to look at things rationally, but her emotions were all over the place. She felt she ought to do the right thing, but she had no idea what that was. There was no one to give the diamonds back to. "Sometimes I wish I'd never found them. It seemed like a treasure hunt with a fairy tale ending, but it's turned into a depressing muddle. I don't want to profit from Nazi diamonds, but I can't figure out what to do. Sometimes I think we should donate them to charity. I don't know what to do."

"They're yours to dispose of as you choose. I want you to feel good again. I agree that you need to resolve this. It's eating away at you."

His concern warmed her. She knew he wouldn't be upset if she gave the diamonds away, but she needed to hear him say it. "So you really don't care what I do? Even if I give them away?"

"Not a bit. But you need to be aware that our plan to move to the Virgin Islands may become a little more challenging if you do that. We're not hurting for funds, but living there is more expensive than here, and when I said we could move and afford a nice place there, I was counting the diamonds as part of our wealth. But what's important to me is that you feel good and do what feels right to you. We can figure a way to move without the diamonds. It might mean we need to take out a mortgage."

Helen didn't like the idea of debt, so the choice wasn't obvious to her. "I need to think on it some more. Thanks for being so kind about it. Lou would have…"

"Lou was an asshole," he interjected. "You're right that the diamonds are toxic for many reasons. They might be Nazi booty. They were certainly stolen. And Lou kept them hidden all these years. They may be the main reason he never acknowledged or helped his French son. They have a lot of negativity associated with them. Either you should give them to charity or we should convert them to cash and put it in the bank. I know it's kind of counterintuitive, but that way, they aren't a constant reminder of Lou and his transgressions."

"You're right. I'll decide one way or the other soon."

He pulled her into a hug. "Whatever you do is fine with me."

Helen was no closer to knowing what to do, but it felt good to be so loved.

* * *

MARY BETH, 12:05PM

From her vantage point just inside the entrance, Mary Beth spotted Helen and her friends at a table on the far side of the Jade Dragon restaurant. "They're over there, waiting for me. Thanks," she nodded to the woman who seated diners and began to wind her way around tables. She waved to Helen, who beamed at her.

The restaurant was packed, and a dull roar of conversations surrounded her as she picked her way across the bridge over the koi-filled stream that ran through the dining area. The scent of fried foods and Oriental spices made her realize how hungry she was, but as she neared the table where Helen sat, she was strangely overcome with nerves, as if she were going to a job interview. Which was silly. She was usually unafraid of judgment and tended to meet the world head on. But this was her first real social event since Ethan had proposed to her, and it was weird being a legitimate resident of Palm Lakes—well, nearly legitimate—after flying under the radar for so long.

As she approached the table, Helen pointed at the empty chair next to hers, and Mary Beth sat down gratefully and scanned the faces of the other women. On the other side of Helen, a youthful-looking brown-eyed woman with short auburn hair reached across Helen to shake Mary Beth's hand. "Hi, I'm Barbara. Helen used to live next door to me. All of us girls are in yoga class together. We hope you'll join us." She had a firm grip and welcoming eyes, and Mary Beth immediately felt more at home.

To Mary Beth's left, a stunning, quiet woman with sapphire eyes and straight black hair beamed at Mary Beth. "I'm Emma. I bought Helen's old house."

Mary Beth gasped. "You're Julio's..." she paused, struggling to find the right word. "...friend." That hadn't gone well at all. She hadn't meant to blurt out that she realized Emma was Julio's lover she'd heard so much gossip about. "I just quit working at Palo Verde Landscaping. I used to work with Julio. It's so nice to finally meet you." At least she hadn't said, 'I've heard so much about you.' She reached to shake hands, hoping the gesture would put the smile back on Emma's face.

Emma grinned. "I'm getting used to it."

The 'it' could mean anything, but probably referred to people discovering she was living with a Hispanic landscaper 15 years her junior. Of course, it helped that she didn't look a day over 45, if that. No wonder Julio had fallen for her, even to the point of proposing marriage.

The remaining two women, who'd been in a conversation the whole time Mary Beth was putting her foot in her mouth, stopped talking and looked her way. The shorter, earth-mother type with thick, dark hair hanging to her shoulders stood and reached across the table. "I'm Lydia.

I hear you're getting married soon. Emma and I are, too. We thought it would be fun to share our wedding plans."

That sounded good to Mary Beth, who stood up to meet her halfway over the expanse of the table. She wasn't feeling confident about the wedding, because she had no family, and Ethan's son William was dead set against their marriage. She wasn't giving Ethan up, but she worried that the event might resemble a funeral. "I haven't made any plans to speak of, but I'd love to hear what you all are doing."

Lydia's friend reached over to shake hands. "I'm Jean. My husband Ian and I rent Helen's condo, the one she bought after selling her house. I understand she was your next-door neighbor for a while. It's all rather convoluted, when you try to explain it." Jean had blue eyes, short ash blonde hair and a pleasant smile. "Isn't it funny how people are brought together here? If you tried to write a book, no one would believe it."

Mary Beth murmured her agreement. Relieved to have met everyone and trying to remember names, she sat down again as the server arrived to take orders. Everyone was a regular, so it didn't take long. Mary Beth took a sip of ice water, hoping these women would accept her into their little group. It had been so long since she had more than one or two friends.

Barbara took charge of the conversation. "I think it would be great if you engaged ladies shared your wedding plans with us."

Emma paused, looking shy. Mary Beth didn't want to be the first to speak. Lydia laughed. "I'll go first. Eric and I thought August would be good for the wedding. Neither of us have any family to invite. You guys are my main friends. Eric might want to invite someone from the Posse, but basically, we thought we'd do a civil ceremony."

Mary Beth envied her a little, because family didn't guarantee an event would be more fun. She looked at Emma, who was still very withdrawn. Sympathizing with her reticence, Mary Beth charged ahead. "Well, Ethan and I were thinking August as well. I have no one to invite, except Helen, and maybe Maddie, if…" She didn't want to talk about Maddie's cancer and put a damper on everything. "I have almost no one to invite, and Ethan only has his son and daughter and their families. I'm not sure they'll be coming. The only thing we've decided is to marry on a Sunday, to give his kids a chance to travel on Saturday and not use as many vacation days." She wondered if she should express any reservations. What the hell. She'd already told Helen. "Ethan's son is opposed to the marriage, and if he comes, I'm concerned it will be unpleasant, especially since I have no family to balance the situation."

Emma's eyes widened. "I don't have anyone to invite to our wedding either, but Julio has a large family. And they'll all be coming. They're nice to me now, but it will be a bit strange having no one to invite. Other than you ladies." Her hands were clasped in her lap, and she looked down as if considering something. "Julio and I have been thinking about getting married in my back yard. We both love the outdoors so much. But beyond that, we haven't made plans."

Lydia added, "What a great place for a wedding! Your labyrinth has such lovely and peaceful energy, and your yard is beautiful. Eric and I have done so little to our tiny back yards, neither would be suitable." She grimaced.

Emma looked up. "We could have a joint ceremony in my yard." She turned to Mary Beth. "It would be fun to get married the same day."

Jean put her hand on Lydia's arm and grinned. "That would be perfect, wouldn't it, Lyd?"

"If you're serious, I'm in," said Lydia.

Mary Beth had to close her mouth and swallow. Helen had told her she'd be welcomed, but this was a shock.

"Of course, I'm serious," said Emma. "What about you, Mary Beth? Will you make it a triple wedding?"

"I would love to do that. I don't think Ethan would mind me speaking for him."

Barbara clapped her hands together. "It's settled, then. I want to host the wedding breakfast or reception after the ceremony. I'm next door to Emma's, so it will be convenient."

Helen tucked her strawberry blonde hair behind her ear. "Will you be able to do that with Amelia here?"

"Amelia is arriving soon for the rest of the summer, and it will be a bit wild with the grandchildren, but this will be easier to do than my normal August party. Or certainly no more work. I love to entertain, and I would like to be able to contribute something for my friends' special day." She turned to Mary Beth. "You know, Lydia and Jean there, along with Ian, restored my health with their magical healing abilities. Without their help, I'm not sure what would have happened to me."

"We were happy to do what we could," Jean said with a dismissive wave. "You don't owe us anything."

"We'll agree to disagree," said Barbara firmly. "Now all you girls need to do is pick a date."

After a bit of back and forth, the first Sunday in August was chosen, assuming the prospective bridegrooms agreed. Two servers arrived with platters of food, and conversation ceased as everyone dug in. At the end of the meal, they said goodbye after extracting a promise from Mary Beth to join the yoga class. Mary Beth had never done yoga, but if that was how they bonded, she was up for it. After all, she was younger than all of them, so how hard could it be?

After lunch, she pulled into Ethan's garage, glad to escape the heat of the car. The A/C didn't do much even at full blast in July, at least not in the few minutes it took to drive home from the restaurant. The monsoon humidity had her shirt sticking to her back already. The clouds were building into monstrous thunderheads, so it might rain later. Well, they needed it. She dismissed further thought of rain, because so often in the low desert, it didn't materialize.

Ethan sat on the couch with the newspaper, reading glasses perched on the end of his nose. His gray eyes lit up when he saw her. "I missed you. Did you have a nice time?" He knew she'd been concerned about her reception by the other ladies, the age difference being the main issue.

"It went well, just like you predicted." She held her hand up and gave him a sharp look. "No, don't say 'I told you so,' because that would be rubbing it in. They were all as nice as Helen promised, and I have a proposition for you." A wide smile said he was misunderstanding her. "I mean a suggestion the other ladies came up with for our wedding." His leer morphed into a warm grin as she pressed on. "Emma, the one who is living with Julio from Palo Verde, has a really nice yard from the sound of it, and she offered to have an outdoor triple wedding in her back yard. Then Barbara—I think she's the ringleader—offered to do a wedding breakfast afterwards, and she lives right next door." That had surprised Ethan. His jaw was practically on the floor. "What do you think? I was feeling it could soften any negativity from William, because there would be other people present. Oh, and is Sunday, August 4th OK?"

Ethan appeared to be bowled over, but finally found his voice. "That would be perfect for us. I was worried about you not having guests and William being snotty and ruining it. Having all those other people would probably guarantee he'd behave. At least in front of them."

Mary Beth snorted. "That's good enough for me. Let Winnie and her kids stay here, and make William and his family get a motel, if they come. There isn't room for everyone here, and I don't want to be around him too much."

Ethan's smile revealed even, white teeth. "That works for me."

"Before I can quit for the day, I need to go to Catherine's and do some more to get it ready for sale." She grinned at what she had said. "Listen to me—she left her condo to me in her will, and I still think of it as hers. Anyway, I have a few things to do over there. You don't need to come with me. I'll be back later for dinner. Or would you like to eat at my place?"

"Doesn't matter to me, but my kitchen is bigger than yours… Catherine's." He smiled agreeably.

"OK. We'll eat dinner here, but we go back to my place after. I'm going to feel a lot better when we move into the new house."

"You sound sure that we'll get that one next to Helen."

"I'll know when I see it. You loved the views from Helen's place, too, and I know you aren't friends with them, but she has been my best friend since I got here, her and Samantha and Maddie, but Helen most of all. I'd love to live next door to her again."

"Suits me. As long as you like what you see inside. When are we checking it out?"

"Tomorrow, I think. Well, I'll be back soon." She kissed him quickly and headed back out to the car.

As she pulled into the driveway at Catherine's—now her—condo, she spotted Julio across the street at Irene and Henry's place. She walked across the street through the haze of heat and stood patiently next to Julio, who was bent over a sage bush, digging around to find the dripper at its base. When he stood back up and saw her, he jumped in surprise. But then he flashed his 1000 watt smile. He was such a looker, with his long, wavy black hair and dark eyes. "Mary Beth, nice to see you."

He held out his hand to shake hers, a habit she had grown used to while working at Palo Verde Landscaping. It seemed all the Hispanic men were hand shakers. "Where's Emma? We just had lunch a while ago. Are you yard-watching for Irene and Henry?"

"Yes, they are Canadian snow birds, and they will be back later in the fall. Emma works with me on these jobs. She does the inside while I do the outside; she got here a few minutes ago. You can go in the front door if you want to see her."

"I don't want to interrupt what you're doing, but I will go in and thank her again. She told you she invited us all to get married the same day in her back yard?" *Shit.* She should have said 'your' back yard. She wondered if Julio was sensitive about things like that.

Apparently not, because he was still smiling warmly. "Yes, she told me. I think it will be very good. She has no one to invite, and my family is big. This will be much better for her."

"And for me," said Mary Beth. "I'm in the same situation."

"Her friends have been very kind to me. It will be a good day for us all." He pushed the brim of his straw hat back and wiped his forehead.

"I won't keep her long," promised Mary Beth as he went back to work.

Mary Beth found Emma in the bathroom, flushing the toilet and running water in the sink.

"Oh, you scared me!" she gasped when she turned and saw Mary Beth in the doorway.

"Sorry, I saw you were here. I own the condo across the street. This actually used to be my Mom's place. Isn't that a coincidence? In fact, that means Jean and Ian live next door in Helen's old condo, doesn't it? Listen to me babbling on. I wanted to thank you again for your generous offer of having the wedding at your place. It will be such a help to me. I can't tell you how I was dreading it, but now, it will be fun."

Emma surprised her by reaching over and touching her arm. "We all have our private challenges. Marriage is a big step."

"My first ended in divorce, and that's how I landed here. The age difference between me and Ethan has his son angry."

"Yes, that is to be expected. Julio's family were very unpleasant to me at first because I'm so much older than he."

"And it's changed?"

Emma beamed at her. "I finally won them over by ignoring the negativity. I can't promise it would work for you, but don't let yourself be dragged into any fight. Ethan obviously has chosen you, and that's that. Either his son will accommodate or not. At least he doesn't live nearby, right?"

"No, we won't be seeing him more than once a year, if that."

"That should make it easier. In any case, I'm glad we're having a joint ceremony. And it's terrific that Barbara is doing the reception. We're going to pitch in for supplies and all. I need to talk to Lydia, but would you like to contribute?"

"Absolutely."

Emma reached into a pocket and pulled out a business card. "Just call this number, and you'll get me. It's our business number. I'll talk with Lydia and should have a list by sometime tomorrow. Give me a ring and I'll share what we've come up with, and you can offer suggestions. I don't know what Barbara will want to serve, but there are a lot of catering places. We'll have to kind of guess at the budget, but we don't want her to absorb it all."

"Of course. Whatever you decide, I'll chip in."

"That's great," said Emma.

"Well, I'll let you get back to work. When I call, I'll give you my phone number."

Emma nodded. "See you in yoga class. It's the intermediate level that starts in a couple weeks. Let me know if you need help figuring out which one. I forget the exact starting date."

"OK." Mary Beth left the house, noticed Julio was at the side of the house checking the irrigation timer, and swam through the oppressive heat to the condo she couldn't stop calling Catherine's. She imagined her feet were leaving impressions in the asphalt, it was so hot.

Inside, she spent an hour completing the inventory of things to sell in the estate sale. It always made her sad to be here, because the place felt so empty without Catherine's joyful voice. Catherine had been like a mother to her, and it had been such a blow losing her so soon after losing her own mother. And a shock to discover Catherine had left everything to Mary Beth. At least the jars with $100,000 in cash were now safely stashed at Ethan's house. Which reminded her, they needed to funnel that money into a bank account soon. Catherine's bequest had allowed Mary Beth to insist that she and Ethan start their marriage at a new place. The alternative of living in his home had been a sticking point with Mary Beth, because she couldn't bear the thought of stepping into his late wife's shoes. She went back to work filled with gratitude for Catherine's generosity, marveling at the kindness of her new friends.

* * *

MARILYN, 2:30PM

The movers had finished unloading and left an hour ago, and Marilyn had been unpacking boxes ever since. At least they were kind enough to place the furniture where she asked, and she had marked the boxes as to what room they belonged in, so it had gone relatively smoothly.

She paused briefly to get a glass of ice water and gulped it down at the kitchen sink while sweat trickled down her back. She had the air conditioning on, but even set at 85 degrees, it felt horribly hot. The weather report had said it was 114 outside, and in fact, when she stepped inside after being out with the moving truck, it felt heavenly, but after an hour of hauling things out of boxes and putting them in cabinets and drawers, she was overheated and exhausted and tempted to set the thermostat to 70 degrees. She resisted the temptation. It was a dry heat, after all, she consoled herself, snorting at the saying she had already heard at least three times since arriving in Arizona. Maybe they'd get rain this afternoon. The clouds were darkening, but so far, not a drop had fallen.

She put her glass down on the counter, remarking to herself yet again at how unusually clean the house was. It was as if an obsessive house cleaner had lived here, but the realtor had said it was a single guy. Who knew a guy could be so particular? Even the baseboards gleamed. She imagined if she put on a white glove and did a test, it would be spotless at the end. Oh well, it was nice not to have to scrub in order to feel the place was habitable. She thought back to a few crummy apartments from her youth and marveled at how far she'd come.

Tammi had been released from her crate by the sliding glass door once the movers left, and she was lying in a corner of the great room on her dog bed, a quizzical look on her black face with the white stripe down the center. The trek across country from Virginia was a 2400 mile journey, and Marilyn had never been a long-distance driver, and doing it with a 90-pound Akita had its ups and downs. She'd needed to arrive before the moving van, and she'd succeeded, but she was desperately tired from driving so many hours a day. Tammi seemed to have enjoyed all the new sights and sounds, but expressed some uneasiness about what was coming next. Marilyn could relate to that. If only this move would be the solution to her problems.

"Do you need a drink, sweetie?" she asked Tammi, who cocked her head to the side in response. Tammi's food and water dishes lay in the corner of the kitchen on a cute mat with a pawprint pattern. "I'm not really hungry yet, but I got really thirsty." Tammi wagged her curly tail tentatively. The black-and-white pattern of Tammi's fur made her a flashy girl, and her intelligent brown eyes were almost human. Marilyn didn't know what she'd do without her.

"I think I'll quit for today, except to unpack the things we brought in the car. I might even order a pizza. What do think about that?" Tammi knew what the word pizza meant, and she wagged her tail in enthusiastic agreement.

Marilyn brushed her short gray hair back and headed to the master bedroom, which was as spic and span as the rest of the rooms. She wondered what had happened to the previous owner. The price certainly had been right—below market value, in fact, and she liked the neighborhood. All she knew is that he had died and there was a rush to sell his place.

In the bedroom, she emptied her suitcase, putting some clothes in her dresser and hanging a few in the spacious, walk-in closet. It felt good to begin to settle in and mark the place as her own. With two additional bedrooms, she had plenty of space to expand. She wondered if one room should be a guest bedroom and the other, a hobby room. Not that she expected to have any guests. She had no living relatives and few friends, certainly none who were likely to travel this far to see her. She refused to dwell on the sadness that realization stirred up.

She put the empty suitcase into the closet of the guest bedroom, as she felt she wouldn't be needing it soon. She got her pistol out of her purse and put it on the bedside table. It was a Smith and Wesson Ladysmith .38 revolver with Pachmayr grips, and she slept with it under her pillow, at least ever since she left Ted.

She looked out the bedroom window and was reminded that her first order of business was to figure out a fence for the back yard. She couldn't have Tammi running loose, and the dog needed space to exercise. The covenants were terribly strict, so she couldn't have a chain link fence, but surely there would be some affordable type. The buyout package from her job had been generous—in fact, that was what had provided the final impetus for her escape from Ted—so she could probably get the fence installed right away.

Over the next few days, the TV and phone would be hooked up, and she'd be set. She felt a little nervous not having a phone, but it had been impossible to guarantee when she'd arrive, and the phone company couldn't get out today on such late notice. One day wouldn't hurt. She hoped.

She almost couldn't believe she was really here. Was it only two months ago that she'd seen an article in the Sunday paper about the Palm Lakes Senior Community in the Arizona desert? For some reason, it had captivated her, the desert so filled with sunshine and blue skies, the antithesis of Virginia climate most of the year. The green of the golf course and the sparkling lakes surrounded by palm trees spelled paradise to her.

She'd said nothing to Ted at the time. She hadn't been sharing her thoughts with Ted for years, and communication had worsened after her return from the hospital. He wasn't ready to retire, anyway. His life was the police force. She believed it gave him justification for throwing his weight around. Too bad he apparently didn't get enough of that at work.

She'd grown weary of his fits of temper and physical violence. Early in their marriage, he just threw things, but when he saw she wasn't going to walk out on him, he started hitting her. One time, then two times. Never where anyone could see. She had no family and few friends, certainly none she'd talk to about Ted. He was a respected police officer. Who would believe her? He'd said as much a million times.

She'd told him she'd leave him if he ever put her in the hospital. And then, one day, he did. Rehab took a long time, and she could finally drive again, so the Sunday she saw the Palm Lakes article was the day she decided that's where she was going to live. She hadn't told him about the buyout option at her job, which made the purchase of the house via long distance simple, thanks to having kept her finances separate from his. That particular bone of contention saved her; thank heaven she'd held out about it. It was mind-boggling how fast everything had come together.

Why the desert? For sure, being thousands of miles from Ted was attractive, especially considering his reaction to her leaving. One night while he was out with the boys, she had moved out of their home without warning into a small apartment nearby, and she notified him by mail that she was divorcing him. He started stalking her as she prepared for her move, even made threats. Finally, she got a restraining order, but fat lot of good that did. It made her wish she'd simply hit the road and gone to AZ, but she'd wanted to get the divorce in VA and tie up loose ends.

That's when she began to sleep with the pistol under her pillow. She was a crack shot, thanks to a gun course and lots of time at the range, but then, so was Ted. It was a hobby they had both enjoyed when they first knew each other, but at some point, she became convinced he'd end up killing her one day, or her, him, and she didn't want to hang around to see which it would be.

She wasn't getting alimony or any kind of support from Ted. Maybe he wouldn't be able to find her. Perhaps if he abused his police powers, he could trace her. She didn't have the knowhow to get a new identity, and she had to get an Arizona driver's license sooner or later. Maybe if she waited a few months, he wouldn't find her. She'd used her maiden name to buy the house, and Jones was a pretty common name, and she'd never mentioned anything about Arizona to him. She hoped that by removing herself from his life, the whole situation would depressurize, and she could get on with living. She hated to wish he'd find someone else to abuse, but she had to admit she wished his attention would turn elsewhere.

Lingering in Virginia had given her one priceless reward. Tammi, whom she had adopted from an Akita rescue shortly after she left Ted, had turned out to be a wonderful companion, and between Tammi and the gun, she didn't think Ted would be able to sneak up on her.

The ringing of the doorbell and Tammi's single deep bark jerked Marilyn out of her reverie. Who could that be? She cautiously approached the front door and peered through the peephole. A woman with short auburn hair and lively brown eyes stood at the door. Marilyn released the breath she'd been holding. Still, she was slow to unlock the door and left the screen door locked, just in case.

"Hi, I'm Barbara. I live next door." The woman pointed to her left. "I won't keep you for long. I know you must be busy, but I wanted to offer to help you get settled in if I can. I understand you're alone here?"

A little shaken by the personal question, Marilyn hesitated. "Yes, it's just me and Tammi." She pointed at the Akita, who had appeared like a ghost beside her, intently watching the woman for threatening behavior.

"Oh, heavens, what a beautiful dog! We have a Jack Russell. He's kind of hyperactive. Tammi is beautiful and so well-behaved. I won't ask to come in, as I know you are busy unpacking, but how about coming over to our place for dinner tonight? My husband is grilling steaks, and he's good at it. Then you don't have to cook or order pizza and eat alone."

The idea was appealing, as Marilyn was exhausted. "That's awfully nice of you, but I'd hate to leave Tammi here by herself. She's so new to the house."

"If you think she'd get along with Jack, you can bring her."

"I haven't had her that long, but she doesn't seem inclined to make friends with other dogs. I suppose I can crate her. I wouldn't want to leave her for hours, though. She hates being cooped up, and we were in the car for days getting here. I need to get a fence put up."

"I can recommend just the company to do that. Come on over for dinner, and we'll be happy to answer any questions you have about Palm Lakes and make suggestions for any services you want to discover. And of course, the amenities for residents. You're going to love it here."

Barbara's enthusiasm was contagious. "I admit I was thinking of ordering Domino's; it would be nice to get to know more about my new home."

A strange look flitted across Barbara's face. What was that about? But Barbara composed herself so quickly, Marilyn thought she must have imagined it. "We're happy to help you any way we can."

"What time shall I come, and what can I bring?"

"Is 5:00 too early?"

"No. I'm probably going to fall into bed early tonight. It's been a hard week."

"Just bring yourself and your appetite."

"Sounds good. Thanks for the invitation."

Barbara smiled and left, and Marilyn hoped that she'd made the right choice.

* * *

BARBARA, 6:00PM

"Ben, could you pass the salad?" Barbara telegraphed her husband in the silent language learned over years of a happy marriage that things weren't going that well, and she needed his help. She saw him register her concern at how reticent their guests were. Maybe it had been a mistake to invite both Marilyn and Steven without letting them know about the other guest. But everyone was new to Marilyn, and Steven needed to get out of his gloomy house.

Her ploy hadn't succeeded famously, and she was chagrined. Marilyn seemed reluctant to give many details about her life before moving here, and Steven appeared to be absorbed in his own grim musings. The atmosphere was stilted, and she needed to do something to change it.

"Marilyn, your dog is very pretty," ventured Barbara.

A genuine smile illuminated Marilyn's face. "I haven't had her long. She's barely full grown, but weighs 90 pounds. I've taken her to one obedience class, but she clearly needs ongoing education." She snickered to herself.

"Jack could use some training, but we've never gotten around to it," noted Ben.

"Small dogs aren't as dangerous or obnoxious when untrained as big dogs are. Akitas have a reputation, and I don't want to take chances with her. I never let her run off leash, and no matter what it takes, I'm going to have her obedient." She paused and took a forkful of roast potatoes into her mouth and sighed. "These are delicious. You'll have to give me your recipe. I've never had potatoes so crispy on the outside and creamy on the inside."

Barbara was warmed by the compliment. She was proud of her cooking skills. That was one reason she loved to share them. "I'll copy it and bring it over tomorrow."

Jack had parked next to Marilyn's chair, instinctively aware that she was a dog person. Marilyn cast him a glance now and then, and finally asked Barbara, "Is it OK to give him something?"

"We don't feed him at the table. He'd soon take over the entire house if we did. But after we clear the table, you can give him the leftovers if you like. He seems to have bonded with you."

"Dogs and I always get along. Not so much humans." She left that statement hanging in the air, an obvious hint about her past, but Barbara let it slide.

"Marilyn, would you consider joining our little group for yoga? You don't have to have experience. It's just a nice way to socialize."

Marilyn's face lit up, and she said, "That sounds nice. I'd love to. I know there are a lot of clubs here. Do you know of one for dog obedience training?"

"I don't know, but I can find out. I'll give you the Rec Center number in case I come up blank." Barbara was pleased that Marilyn was diving into life in Palm Lakes and surprised that she had acquiesced so easily to the yoga suggestion. Maybe their friendship would grow, giving her a chance to share about Owen's house without looking like a gossip. Marilyn was going to find out sooner or later, and it should be from a friend.

Now she needed to wrestle Steven out of his funky mood. As if he'd telepathically heard her, Ben said, "Steven, it's time you and I went golfing. I've missed that. What do you say to tomorrow? I can easily get us a tee time since it's the height of summer."

A spark of interest stirred in Steven's brown eyes. "Sure, Ben. I've missed it, too." He said no more, but Barbara felt relief that Steven had decided to get into a more normal routine. She needed to remember to give him the referral to the support group before he left. She hated to pressure him, but she knew it would help if he'd go.

Steven had cast a few furtive glances at Marilyn during dinner, but had yet to address her beyond his first 'hello.' Barbara hoped the looks signaled some sort of interest in something outside of his own grief. She had a terrible tendency to matchmake, and when she'd seen Marilyn, she decided maybe it was just what Steven needed to draw him out of his shell. Marilyn was shy, but not depressed. Or didn't seem to be. Only time would tell.

Marilyn appeared to remember something and put her fork down. "You said you could recommend someone to give me an estimate on a fence."

"Oh, yes. You can do two kinds here, or rather three. One is a block wall six feet high. You can see that my other next door neighbor has one of them. You can do a simple wrought iron fence. That is less expensive. Then, there is an intermediate option, which is a low block wall topped by wrought iron, again six feet tall in total. I'll give you Julio's number. He lives next door with Emma. They're engaged to be married. He does excellent work."

Marilyn seemed to take the news in stride, but then she couldn't know that Julio was much younger than Emma and had met her while doing a landscaping job for her. She'd find out eventually, because Emma was part of the yoga group.

"I'm so glad I asked you. You have a wealth of information. I don't think I want a block wall, though it would be very secure. I might just do a plain wrought iron fence."

Relieved at Marilyn's preference, Barbara nodded. "That would be less expensive and it gives a more open feeling to your yard. Not everyone is the same, but some find the walls claustrophobic."

"I think I would," said Marilyn. "One of the things I like most about living here is the big sky. Where I come from, trees block out so much, or buildings. When I stand in my back yard, I can see Four Peaks in the far distance, to the east. It's my only view of the mountains, and I wouldn't want to lose it." She went back to cleaning her plate.

Dessert passed without a hitch, and Marilyn and Steven left at the same time, going in opposite directions down the sidewalk in the still sweltering heat, Steven with a slip of paper on which was written the support group details, and Marilyn with Julio's business card.

"I think that went well," said Barbara.

"Woman, you are always matchmaking." Ben grinned at her, a glint in his blue eyes.

"Well, it worked for Helen, didn't it?"

"Yes, it did. I'm not arguing, just observing."

Barbara grunted and then laughed. "You know me so well. I think we need to shake Steven out of his depression. I don't care if it goes beyond that. I don't know enough about Marilyn to be sure she's right for him anyway. I wish I could find an easy way to tell her about her house. The longer we wait, the more chance there is that someone else will tell her, and I'd hate her to get turned off to Palm Lakes."

Ben snorted. "I don't see how you can tell her in a subtle way that a serial killer owned the house before her and stored trophies of his kills in the master bedroom closet. Or that he killed Steven's wife, or rather, ex-wife."

She sighed. "You're right. There's no easy way, but I'm going to have to find one. And soon."

He pulled her into his arms, and her worries immediately drained away. "It will all work out." His assurances were based on nothing, but as usual, made her feel better.

ABOUT THE AUTHOR

Maggie McPhee is a writer of contemporary 'boomer' women's fiction. The *Autumn In The Desert* series is based on life in a fictitious retirement community in the desert Southwest of the US. She also writes nonfiction under her real name, Maggie Percy.

www.ingramcontent.com/pod-product-compliance
Lightning Source LLC
Chambersburg PA
CBHW070834280626
47161CB00015B/593